EVERY TIME WE BURN

Emma Kavanagh was born in Wales in 1978 and currently lives in South Wales with her husband and two young sons. She trained as a psychologist and, after leaving university, started her own business as a psychology consultant, specialising in human performance in extreme situations. For seven years she provided training and consultation for police forces and NATO and military personnel throughout the UK and Europe.

For more information, tweet Emma @EmmaLK

Also by Emma Kavanagh

The Killer on the Wall
The Missing Hours
Case 48: The Kidnapping of Isaiah Rae (*short story*)
Hidden
The Affair (*short story*)
Falling
To Catch a Killer
The Devil You Know

EVERY TIME WE BURN

Emma Kavanagh

ORION

An Orion Paperback

First published in Great Britain in 2025 as *The Time of the Fire*
by Orion Fiction,
this edition published in 2026 by Orion Fiction,
an imprint of The Orion Publishing Group Ltd.,
Carmelite House, 50 Victoria Embankment
London EC4Y 0DZ

An Hachette UK Company

The authorised representative in the EEA is Hachette Ireland,
8 Castlecourt Centre, Castleknock Road, Castleknock, Dublin 15,
D15 XTP3, Republic of Ireland (email: info@hbgi.ie)

1 3 5 7 9 10 8 6 4 2

Copyright © Emma Kavanagh 2025

The moral right of Emma Kavanagh to be identified as
the author of this work has been asserted in accordance
with the Copyright, Designs and Patents Act of 1988.

All rights reserved. No part of this publication may be
reproduced, stored in a retrieval system, or transmitted
in any form or by any means, electronic, mechanical,
photocopying, recording, or otherwise, without the
prior permission of both the copyright owner and the
above publisher of this book.

All the characters in this book are fictitious, and any resemblance
to actual persons, living or dead, is purely coincidental.
Map and illustrations by Neil Gower.

A CIP catalogue record for this book is
available from the British Library.

ISBN (Mass Market Paperback) 9781 4091 9958 8
ISBN (eBook) 978 1 4091 9959 5
ISBN (Audio) 978 1 4091 9960 1

Typeset by Input Data Services Ltd, Bridgwater, Somerset

Printed in Great Britain by Clays Ltd, Elcograf, S.p.A.

www.orionbooks.co.uk

For the staff and patients at
The South Wales Multiple Sclerosis Therapy Centre

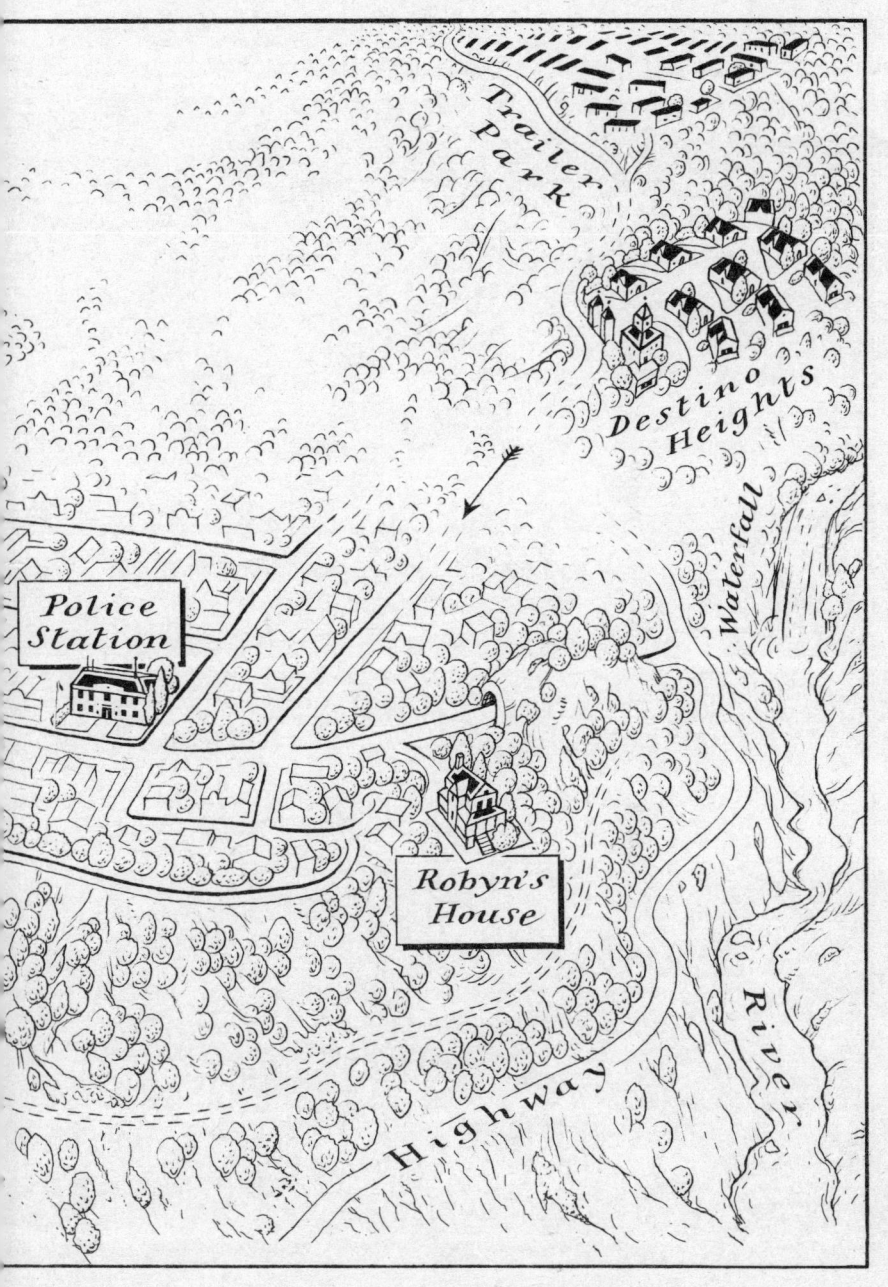

'We shall not cease from exploration and the end of all our exploring will be to arrive where we started and to know the place for the first time.'

– *TS Eliot*

Prologue

Harper Morgan —25th September, 1992, 6.45 p.m.

There is a woman, one who will die this day.

Of course, she cannot know that she has come to the end of her journey – in this world, at least.

She flips on her turn signal, taking the ramp that leads off the Big Sur highway, its steady stream of traffic snaking through the heavy rain up the coast. She follows the road, leaving the crashing waves of the Pacific behind in favour of the distant San Simeon mountains. She does not realise that it is the last time she will see the ocean.

It is a bad night, a hard night to drive: thunder crashing overhead, lightning flashing, weather that comes horizontal against her windshield. The wipers work with a cawing fury, backwards and forwards, backwards and forwards, fighting against the sheeting rain. But it is all for naught, a futile dance of shifting water.

Harper Morgan leans forward, closer to the steering wheel, her fingers gripping, tight enough that her knuckles turn white, lets her thoughts flicker away towards home. Robyn will be in bed by now, her face flushed from her bath, her chubby hands balled into fists, the thumb of the right one rammed into her mouth as her eyelids flicker. Harper hopes that Mack has remembered to turn on the night light. Then comes a rush of rain, thundering hard against the roof, and she grips the wheel harder, forces herself to focus. The road to Destino is snaking, treacherous, following the path of the river down below, the pounding rain turning the timid waters into a raging tumult.

Harper glances down at the folder on the seat beside her. The label on the front of it, the words *Destino Heights* written in looping cursive. The housing development, carved right into the heart of the mountain, has come to haunt her dreams. Luxury mountain homes with the permanent sense of impending doom thrown right on in. She steers the car around a sharp bend, watching as the rain shimmers, slick on the road surface. It will be harder, this. Getting people to concern themselves about the dangers of wildfire is always tougher in the rain. It is as if they have trouble separating this day from that future one, when the air is static and the heat breathless. She glances back at the folder. At least the threat of wildfire is no longer all that she has. This . . . it will change everything.

She is expecting the whole of Destino to show up; the church parking lot full, for once, doors flung open, the glow of it breaking into the dark day. Her thoughts slip ahead, down the waterlogged highway, into the church hall and the gathered people. To the Sandoval family, their lips pursed in irritation. To what she will say.

The rain thunders against the roof.

Harper bites her lip, raises her foot from the accelerator, a concession to the waterlogged road beneath her. Rain coming at her, a blinding cascade. And then a light, a sign flashing by. Destino, 3 miles.

Destino. Home. It is a picture postcard of a place, a stage set of what a California town should be. A kaleidoscope of colours nestled in amongst the trees, ocean breezes that drift from the west meeting the scent of pine from the east. An old town, by California standards at least. A gold rush stomping ground, the first suggestions of home set down in 1853 by gold-dazzled prospectors, convinced that this place would bring them glory and wealth untold. A parcel of flat land tucked behind a hill to one side, mountains to the back of it, lined with twisting streams that flow all the way down to the precipitous gully, becoming a waterfall. Back in the day, those streams had glistened with delicate nuggets of gold.

Destino. Destination. A name that the residents of the town have taken to heart. The end of a long road, a place of homecoming. Few people leave Destino. Those who are born there, they tend to stay, moving from their family homes to smaller places within the same zip code as their parents. And then, once time and life do their inevitable work, they move home. Inhabiting the same place in which they learned to walk, to tie their shoelaces. The residents, they say it is because of Destino's native charms. The realtors, they say it is because of the property market, that those who are born here quickly come to appreciate the value in what they have. Harper herself is an anomaly, a new face amongst the generations of old. This is part of their mistrust, she knows. She hopes that for Robyn it will be different. A Destino child, the daughter of a Destino son. She hopes that Robyn will come to find acceptance here.

Another flash of lightning arcs across the sky. Above the thrum of the engine, Harper's heart beats faster, her body's own sense of portent. It will be fine, she tells herself. She steers along the winding road, steep hills becoming mountains on either side of it. Roads cut off the highway, head up to modest little towns with names like Cherry Grove, and Vine Heights, newly built, suburbs pretending to be something a little more special. Keep going, she tells herself. You are nearly there.

And then she is hydroplaning, the car slick on the pooled highway surface. Harper clutches the wheel tighter, lifting her foot from the accelerator, turning the wheel in the direction of the slide. The folder slips from the seat beside her, spilling financial documents into the footwell. She pumps the brake. For a moment, nothing, and it seems that this is it, her drive ending in a headlong impact into the cliff face. But then, incredibly, the car begins to slow, slow. Stops.

Harper's breaths are coming hard and fast, her fingers trembling against the steering wheel. Oh my God, she mutters. Oh my God. A sense washes over her, of life being saved, disaster being averted. She breathes out, forcing her breath to slow.

Harper leans over, gathering up the papers that have spilled into the footwell. She bounces them on her knee, trying to ignore the dryness in her throat, the pulsing in her temples, slides them neatly into the folder. It's fine, she mutters. Everything is fine.

It is not.

The road becomes thinner ahead, the bends sharper, rocky sides steeper. There are no turnoffs now, no escape from the precipitous highway. The rain thunders, bouncing off the roof of the car.

And then.

What comes next comes fast. A blur of light, the sickening crunch of metal on metal. The car beneath her slipping and sliding on the slick highway. Harper holds on tight to the wheel, and then the car is sliding to the right, and she cannot say whether it is under her pressure or its own.

And then.

Slick highway yields to rough brush, and then there is an incline and the hood is rising and, for the briefest of moments, Harper thinks that this will be it, that the car's skid will grind to a halt amongst the weather roughened brush.

It does not.

And with the forward momentum, comes the knowledge, implacable.

Harper Morgan will die today.

Chapter One

Thirty years later

Robyn Sandoval – 25th September, 6.45 a.m.

There is a woman. She steps carefully onto the wide, wooden front porch, the orange glow from the porch light, tucked up amongst the rafters, all but invisible in the face of the rising sun. Robyn glances back, smiles. Hector hesitates in the doorway, wide pit bull face tilted up towards the light, watching as she moves. Robyn lingers at the top of the steps and waits for the dog to join her, rambling his not insubstantial girth forward. The wooden slats groan beneath his weight, a century's worth of story within the sound.

Robyn raises her chin, the distant smoke catching in her throat. It lingers in the sky, a sheer haze draped across the landscape – a reminder of Seven Hills, thirty miles away, but feeling so much closer. Robyn tightens the leash around her hand and listens for the telltale creak of bedsprings, her mother turning over in bed in the big room above. It is a musical house, this, the type that broadcasts each movement its occupants make. But there is nothing, only the cicadas with their early morning chorus. If you are quiet, you can just about hear the rush of the river from here, the sound wedding itself to the susurration of the trees. It is a relief, that sound, a hypothetical respite from the heat that has already begun to build.

The air is dense, immovable, the sky a bitter blue. It is hotter than it should be, a bubble of heat sitting over California, the walls of it impenetrable, or so it seems to her at least. Today is to be 94°F, the weather channel threatening of worse to come. Robyn lingers, can feel a trail of sweat already snaking its way down between her shoulder blades, and tries to quell the unease that has blossomed in her belly. It is, she tells herself, merely the heat, the pressing down of it creating this feeling of portent.

Or perhaps it is something else. Perhaps it is the certificate, the one that her mother has hung on the wall of the family room, neatly framed in reclaimed wood. Robyn Sandoval has achieved her master's in business. The relief that it is over, bumping right up against the looming spectre of what comes next: the suit that hangs on the door of her wardrobe, her future, just waiting to begin, whether she wants it to or not.

A low grumble of a growl, and she looks down at her feet, at the pit bull, his face contorted into a hopeful grin. She grins right back, reaches down to play with his silk soft ears, then her fingers move to her wrist, setting 'run' on her Fitbit.

'All right, Hector,' she says, softly. 'Let's do it.'

Robyn pushes off from her porch, padding lightly down the front steps and onto the paved driveway. A futs, futs, futs, breaking into the cicada sound, the sprinklers coming to life, swirling water droplets across the neatly trimmed front lawn, the grass defiantly green in spite of the unrelentingly long, dry summer. Along the driveway, a left turn, towards Destino, the house glowing through the surrounding trees.

The big house. That's what they called it. It stands alone on a modest rise, a narrow street that leads off of Main bringing you right to their door, as if the town has built a driveway, just for them. Built by one of the town's mayors, eighty years or more ago, the house had been in a tumbledown state when her parents first bought it. The money pit, her dad had called it, his voice tinged with affection. He had brought the money pit back to life though, had brought in contractors who understood that a house like this, it was not merely a house, rather a piece of history. An echo of Destino itself.

The narrow street comes to an end, a pair of pine trees marking out the corners, and Robyn bursts through them, onto the wide, open thoroughfare of Main Street. She lingers for a moment and looks down towards the highway. The road itself cuts through an arc of rock, its edges smoothed out by an ancient torrent, long dried out. The natural arch has been stretched, widened by man to allow space for a two-lane road that connects the town to the world beyond. The distant sound of the waterfall, softer than it should be.

She lingers. As if there is any real question about which way she will turn. Because it is The Day. Robyn pulls in a heavy sigh, and turns following the road out of town, through the chill of the rock tunnel. She takes it steady. There is no sidewalk here, just a dedicated two-lane road. But the road is quiet, the world still sleeping for the most part. She jogs softly, footsteps bouncing back at her from age carved rock, the sudden cool sending prickles up and down her skin.

Robyn breaks through the tunnel of rock, out into full sunshine, to the place where the highway ends. It is a precipitous conclusion to a painfully winding road, tarmac terminating in a steep cliff face. It is pockmarked with brush, twisted trees that grow out, perpendicular to the cliff itself. A little beyond the highway's edge, a ravine, a stream down below fed by a tumbling waterfall. Modest now, the long drought eking away at its flow until only the slightest trickle remains. But when the snow in the mountains gives way to the fierce California sun, it can be a tumult, cascading down the cliff wall into the steep gully below. That is when the tourists stop, pulling their cars up tight to the town sign, so that they can clamber out, pad through grass, arranging their faces and their phones, perfectly Instagrammable.

It would have been like that on the day that Harper died, when her car lost its grip on the slick surface of the highway, plunging down into the ravine below. An accident that was over in the blink of an eye, the car lost in the depths of the long fall. It wasn't until the next morning that she was found, the car folded in on itself, survival impossible.

Of course, if it hadn't been raining, none of it would have happened. How different would life have been then?

Robyn lingers for a moment, looking up, beyond the waterfall, towards the half-buried shape of Destino Heights. The houses are large there, with wide expanses of glass, the yards well-tended with neatly laid out decks, perfectly buffed grills. A thirty-year-old addition to the town of Destino, that, in spite of all its decades of life, still feels like a newcomer, an unwieldy new appendage. The houses overlook the gully, can hear the waterfall on warm spring evenings.

She sighs, crosses the quiet road, sparing a moment to glance up at the town sign. An oversized affair, painted bright in pinks and blues. DESTINO in large, flowing letters. Then beneath, in slightly smaller script, Journey's End.

Across from the town sign, a simple memorial. A dedication to the dead.

That's the thing with destination. It differs, depending on the turns you take along the way.

Robyn pulls in a deep breath, ducking down, her bare legs cold against the brittle grass. It is subtle, as memorials go. If you didn't know it was there, then there was a fair chance that you would miss it. A simple boulder, looking for all the world as though it had been hewn from the rock face behind. A modest gold plaque, glinting in the sunlight.

Harper Morgan. Wife. Mother. Died September 25th, 1992.

'Hi, Mama,' she murmurs softly.

A breeze sweeps down the cliff face, rustling her hair, and she allows herself a moment to pretend that it is an answer.

Hector settles down beside her, head resting on his paws, dark eyes locked on her.

Robyn imagines the smell of her. Decided long ago, when she was only a little girl, that it would be something sweet, like vanilla or coconut. Imagines soft fingers stroking her cheek. *Everything will be all right.* Robyn's fingertips trace the word. Mother.

Hector lets loose a low yip. Robyn flinches, shakes her head and reaches down, runs her fingers across the soft down of his head. She had been far too young to remember it, only a few days past nine months when the accident happened. Had been just a little shy of a year when she had been placed instead into the arms of Eve and Alex Sandoval, their daughter now, life taking a sharp turn in direction.

Robyn sighs, pushing herself up to standing. Hector looks at her, expectant. 'Come on, then.' She turns, pushes off. She plunges back into the darkness of the rock tunnel, through and beyond into bright light. And it rolls through her head to the rhythm of her feet against tarmac — what if?

As she runs, Hector's paws pad behind her. Back past the big house, her mother's drapes still closed. She pushes harder, the sounds of her footfall rising into a faster rhythm, up onto Main Street, her sneakers hitting the hot, sticky tarmac, the slightest of 'shucks' as they lift off again, the hot air that fills her lungs. There is a brief moment of reprieve as she exhales.

Then she is up into Destino proper. There is just one major thoroughfare — Main Street. It is wide and clean, its sidewalk peppered with bistro tables and boxes of brightly coloured flowers. Its residents spiral off from that street, cabins and houses scattered like so many dandelion seeds around it. There is a bakery and an art gallery, a bar that has stood, in one version or another since gold rush days. There is a store selling wines from just up the coast in Sonoma, cheeses and meats from everywhere else. There is a diner, Elsie's, that has been run by the same family since 1951, that now sells artisan coffees in delicate little cups, the kind of place where you really don't want to mention Starbucks. If you walk up Main Street, weaving your way past kids on scooters and middle-aged women with their reusable to-go cups, the smell of matcha smacking you in the face like a herbal assault, and you come to the end of it, you will find the church. Whitewashed and clapboarded, with a gold-tipped steeple, the church of the holy trinity defending the souls of the town's people. And although attendance has dropped off in recent years, the pastor, a bulbous man by the name of Father Caprese, retains hope that his flock will find their way back to him. He keeps the wooden doors of the church propped open from dawn till dusk, allowing the soft Pacific Ocean breeze to sweep down the pews and bathe the feet of the Lord our God. Sometimes tourists wander on in, tempted by the cool shade inside, a reprieve from the heat, sending Father Caprese's hopes soaring. But he is always disappointed, when they realise that the church has a grand total of six rows of pews, that the glass is resolutely unstained, and that, if they do not move quickly, Father Caprese's mission will extend to include them. Seems that tourists always leave town faster than they arrive.

She runs, thinking of runs she has taken before. In Princeton, then Stanford. Of that thud, thud, thud, sneakers on concrete. Same soundtrack, different scenes. Only, there, on East coast and on West, it had seemed to her that she was Robyn. That the laps of the campus with a steady stride, were just one more part of Robyn, of who she was. Of course, it was different here. Here, in Destino, she was first and foremost, a Sandoval.

To her right, a sound, of a trunk being eased closed, and Robyn slows, peering through the early morning haze towards Buttonwillow Street, its single-storey houses with their carefully manicured lawns, quiet and still. Luis' dark hair is damp, freshly washed, his police T-shirt clinging in patches to his narrow torso, and she looks away quickly, a sense of shrinking into herself.

Hector's breath is heavy against her leg.

She shakes the thoughts away, running with long strides. There is a smell to Destino, of ocean salt and pine, of Elsie's coffee and the vaguest hint of lavender. And, of course, of smoke.

Robyn makes a left at the corner of Destino Vino, across the street, that empty lot. An eyesore, town embarrassment. So much promise there once: an artisan clothing company would bring their production line here, would build a modest factory (although they hadn't used the word factory, likely because it hadn't sounded artisan enough), would set up a boutique up front, would pull people in from up and down the highway. Of course, it hadn't worked. The Sandoval Company had wound up with a defaulted payment, scrabbling to find someone else who wanted to take on an empty patch of land in this economy. Her mom still tutted, every time she passed it, the scar right on the centre of Main Street.

Her feet thump against sidewalk, breaths coming easy, in and out. Wonders if her birth father, Mack, will be awake yet? Up the footpath that runs alongside Elsie's Diner. A shape moves, behind the slats of Elsie's front porch: Mags. A spiral of smoke twists up from between her fingers and Robyn allows a moment to consider – she didn't know Mags smoked.

The footpath arcs upwards, the incline of it pulling at her hamstrings. And Robyn thinks of what is to come, the days ahead. The slick glassed-in offices in San Luis Obispo, the lines of desks, the people who look at her with painted on respect, the kind that is befitting their soon to be CEO. But something else hidden behind it, her own doubt mirrored in their faces. Her? She was to be the CEO? But then, she was the heir apparent, wasn't she? She pushes on, running harder, trying not to think of the days she has spent there, of the motions she has moved through, preparing for the inevitable, the day she will walk in through the front door, will take over the reins that have been waiting for her since the day her dad, Alex Sandoval, died. No. Since long before that. Since the day that she was adopted.

A bird bursts from dense bush, a wild fluttering of wings, and Hector starts, letting out a flurry of barks. Robyn gives a gentle tug on the leash, and Hector looks up at her, sheepish, and then turns to follow, his paws scrabbling against the loose dirt.

The email had come in late last night, long after she had fallen asleep.

Hey sweetheart,
Just wanted to know if you were free tomorrow? You're starting with the Sandoval Co on Monday, right? You wanna get together? Maybe come for breakfast. There's something kind of big I need to talk to you about.
Love you.
Mack

Robyn's breath comes harder now, sweat trailing down between her shoulder blades, between her breasts. Her thighs ache, but she pushes on anyway. Hector, he is just glad to be included. The heat has kept him indoors more than he would have liked lately, the early mornings now the only chance for him to stretch his legs. The breeze whips at Robyn's face, the ache in her thighs clambering upwards, lacing its way around her back and she follows the path as it veers, up behind the diner towards Mack's house. A cottage that has stood there for sixty years and more, that Mack keeps swearing he will do up but he never quite gets around to. Her heart beats a little faster, a feeling of almost-relief. It always seemed to her that Destino looked at her more kindly with Mack beside her.

Her foot loses grip on the gravel beneath. A brief thought

– what if he is leaving? What if that is what he has to tell her? She has only just found him. The thought of losing him again makes her stomach plunge. She thinks of a day, perhaps a week ago, of coming across him unexpectedly. Of Mack sitting on the sofa, leaning over a photograph of Harper, tears streaming down his face. Looking up at her with a start, brushing the tears away with the back of his hand. *I lost my entire family on that day.* And Robyn had sunk into the seat beside him. *You have it back now.* A smile that did not quite reach his eyes.

Today would be a hard day for him. That would be why he had called for her.

Robyn winds her way past the overhanging brush, reaches for the front gate.

Hector gives a low grumble.

'It's OK, buddy. Let's get some French toast, shall we?'

She puts her hip against it, pushes the gate open, allowing the pit bull through before her. Then eases it back into its frame and turns towards the house.

Later, looking back, she will seek the moment. Try to identify that one split second when the world changed. Was it the light? The green-shaded lamp that stands in the kitchen window, its orange light spilling out, vying against the bright light of day. Was it the door? Not locked, but rather just hooked on its catch. Was it the kitchen, bowls crusted with food stacked inside the sink, or the thick, stagnant heat?

'Mack?'

Robyn steps cautiously, into the kitchen, through into the family room. The house is still, seems to be sleeping but for the clenching in her stomach.

Hector gives a soft whine.

'Mack?' Her voice cracks, the voice sounding not like her own. A pile of laundry, stacked on an easy chair. A bottle of Jim Beam open on the coffee table. A fly works its way around the tarnished silver photograph frame, Mack in his younger days, in his CalFire dress uniform, accepting the award of merit. 'Mack?'

She hesitates, lingering at the door to the bedroom. Can hear the distant sound of birds singing. Besides that, silence. Her hands have begun to shake. She pushes open the door. It is still, quiet. Hot enough that her breath catches in her throat, and it feels that she is drowning in the too thick air. It smells of sweat. And something else.

She knows.

Mack lies in the absolute centre of the king-sized bed, on his back. A pillow rests across his face, a trickle of blood has seeped its way down onto the yellow sheet below. His chest, unmoving.

'Mack?' A whisper now, a scream rolled up inside it. There is nothing, only stillness.

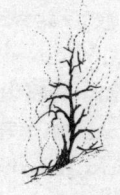

Chapter Two

Mags Reyes – 25th September, 6.45 a.m.

It is not always obvious that this is the moment, the time when the course of your life shifts from one path onto another. But for Mags, that is precisely the way it went. She can date it all back, everything that has followed, to that single moment, that single call. *Your father is sick.*

She thinks of that moment as she steps out onto the front porch of Elsie's Diner, hugging her rapidly cooling coffee to her chest. In the distance, a solitary form, a dog beside it – Robyn, from the big house, and her dog Hector. They run towards her, alongside the empty lot. She watches as they run, long, loping strides, up the path that runs alongside the diner, the incline of it tracing the curve of the mountain. They vanish behind the overgrown brush, the sound of a flurry of wings, the dog letting out a bark. What would it be like, she wonders, to be a Sandoval? Never to have that feeling of racing on an eternal treadmill, constantly fighting to make the finances stack up, never to wonder if the end is just one unpaid bill away?

Mags closes her eyes, and tries to pull in a breath, but the air is thick, the heat of it weighing down on her. She lowers herself, slow, to the wood-slat steps of the front porch and tries not to cry. It's funny, she thinks, how time works. A moment is nothing, there and then gone again. But then there are moments that seem to spill outward, their place in your life becoming unreasonably large, changing everything that follows.

She leans her head back against the wood of the porch, her loose-fit shorts splayed across her thighs, olive skin legs spread out in front of her, her feet bare. Her hair, a chaos of mid-brown curls, is pulled up into a loose bun, and she bounces back against it, the bulk cushioning the blow of the wooden porch behind her. Sweat prickles on her skin. The AC will struggle today, fight to cool the aged diner, will make that deep-throated groan, a death rattle. It will not last much longer, and then . . . there is no money for a new one. Perhaps repair? There would be no reprieve. The long summer months spilling forward into spring, backwards to autumn until it seems that the entire year is consumed with heat. News pundits talk of global warming, of rising sea levels and our impending doom.

She raises her chin, smells the smoke. The fire in Seven Hills has been burning for the best part of a week now, firefighters struggling against the bone-dry land. How long before the inevitable brownouts begin? And then, how do you run a diner? How do you serve customers with no power? She lets it wash over. What, after all, is a little more despair to add to the bubbling pot of ennui?

She listens to the cicadas, the distant whoosh of the river. All else silence.

Had there been a choice? It feels to her now that that was what it was. But back then, in the neat little row house in Walnut Creek, the sound of the passing tram underlining her mother's words, it hadn't felt like a choice at all. Rather an inevitability.

'Your father is sick.'

'I'm on my way.'

Impossible for her to have known then that she had been taking a step, the first on a path that would tilt downhill, making each of the following steps come at her, faster and faster. She had scooped up the children, only six and four then, had loaded the car. Had paused long enough to give Jack the briefest of kisses. 'I'll be back in a couple of weeks.'

How was she to know that she would never return?

She is thirty-six, thirty-seven approaching at the speed of sound. This will be it, she knows, her only opportunity in this day to think these thoughts and to fight back tears. Because soon the phone will ring. Her mother, 'Your children are awake, the sleepover is done. Come and get them.' Gabrielle who is nine and Oscar who is seven. And then the world around her will be in motion and she will move with it, a constant whirl of activity, and she will be thankful for that, because with movement all opportunities for thought and for regret are lost.

'Can we watch a movie tonight?' Oscar had said it, bouncing on the balls of his feet. 'We could make popcorn and watch *Jumanji*.'

'I can't tonight.' She had tried not to look at it, the expression on her son's face. Of disappointment. No surprise, though. 'I have to do the books for the diner. These accounts won't take care of themselves.' Her stomach knots up tight. Because she knows what those books will say. Knows it won't be good. The accountant, a narrow-boned man who looks every inch of what an accountant should be, has been calling her every day for the past week. The knots in her stomach squeeze tighter. It will not be good news. And so, every day she has let the phone ring out, watching the user ID and praying that if she ignores it long enough, then whatever it is will simply go away. Of course, things rarely work that way. And then yesterday, a message. Irritation laced through his voice. 'Mags, you need to call me back. It's serious.'

Mags sets the coffee down on the scuffed porch boards beside her, lights up a cigarette. A small act of defiance. Against whom she isn't sure. Not her children. Perhaps Jack, who hated the smell of smoke. 'I'm allergic,' he would huff. Perhaps her mother. 'Ladies don't smoke.' That look, thick with disapproval, that said that her daughter had managed it, once again, had proven to be the most disappointing of children. Perhaps herself, a direct violation of the being of this Mags, a little of the old Mags, the college Mags, the one who was going to move to San Francisco and practise psychology, the one who smoked weed and wore her hair shaved close to her scalp. The Mags that might have been.

The money was gone. The diner would close. In weeks or months. The future was already written. It was over.

She pulls in another drag, pushes back tears.

It has been a three-hour sleep kind of night, another in a long line of them. Three hours last night, two and a half the night before. Inching her way through the days, her eyes gritty, floors unsteady beneath her. Her mother says it's payback. That she used up her allotment of sleep as a teenager all those years ago, that it was coming back to bite her on the ass now. Mags, she thinks it's the silence. The Destino quiet, loud enough to interrupt her sleep. She misses Walnut Creek. Misses the clack of the tram, the sound of passersby, their voices floating up through her open bedroom window. She misses that feeling of being part of something, of the world consisting of wide-open doors.

It was cancer, her father's doctor had said. The office had been sparse, had smelled of bleach and lavender. Mags had watched as the force from an AC unit pushed at a cobweb that had escaped the cleaner's notice. Where, she had wondered, was the spider that spun it. 'How long do I have?' Her father had asked it like he was asking for the next scheduled bus. The doctor had shaken his head. 'It's hard to say, Kelvin. With treatment, a year, maybe two if you're lucky. Without . . . three months. At the most.'

'Treatment.' Her mother had said, firm. 'He'll have the treatment.'

Her father, glancing at her, brow furrowed, some silent

communication that she managed to miss. 'Bonnie . . .'

'No.' Her mother had said it in that voice that she'd used when Mags had asked to stay out an hour past curfew. 'You are having treatment.'

What would have happened, Mags wondered, if things had played out differently. Had she spent less time pondering the fate of an architect spider, more time concentrating on the words. On the implications. But she hadn't. And her father had folded, helpless in the face of her mother's implacability. 'Treatment, then.'

Mags blows out a slow spiral of smoke, watches it twist upwards. Three years. Three years of chemotherapy that seeped into her father's bones, that folded him up before her. Three years of watching him shrink, smaller and smaller, of watching his hands curl in on themselves, of his gaze become glazed, his voice soft enough that half the time no one would ever know he had spoken.

She closes her eyes. The world felt like a snow globe that has been picked up, shaken vigorously so that nothing makes sense anymore.

It would be better. Things would be better. Once the poison had poisoned the poison. Once the chemo was done, and her father had space to begin a slow recovery. It was just how it was, so her mother said, her chin up, face defiant. Savage treatment for a savage disease. But once it was done . . .

Mags takes another drag of her cigarette. Once it was done. And then? What will happen to her in this distant, promised future? She has done a thorough job of burning bridges behind her.

She blows out a snaking stream of smoke. There must have been other choices, she thinks, other moments beyond that single one. But it seems to her now that there were in fact no choices at all. Rather responsibilities. Her mother, that petite ball of boiling energy, turning inwards, directing the entire force of her attention on her rapidly failing husband, filling her days with him, with his treatment, his medication. It often seems, thinks Mags, that her mother is trying to absorb it, inhale everything about her father in case he is suddenly gone.

And that, of course, left the diner. They had run it alone, Bonnie and Kelvin. Had taken over from Bonnie's mother, once the Parkinson's took hold, Kelvin cooking, the kitchen thick with the smell of bacon and grits, the clanging pots interrupted only by his singing. Her father had had a beautiful singing voice, rich and deep. And Bonnie would watch the front, serving the customers, efficient and scolding in equal measure. Although, she thinks, as the years have passed, those scales have tipped in favour of the scolding.

'We will have to have help,' said her mother, 'especially when the lunchtime rush comes. But then, of course, there isn't enough money, not with the rent on this place being what it is.' Bonnie had shaken her head, lips compressed tight together. 'We will just have to make do.' Had stared at her daughter, challenging. 'You will have to cover.'

But three years on and making do had stopped being enough.

Mags sighs heavily, rubs her eyes. There were her brothers, of course. Nate, down in LA, fighting the good fight on the way to his big break. Directing. Producing. Filling in the gap between anonymity and celebrity with low budget 'erotica', films that sat just on the wrong side of the porn line. 'I would come, I really would, but I'm right on the edge of something here . . .' Mags' wager was that he was right on the edge of chlamydia. And Arthur. A schoolteacher in Salt Lake City. A gentle soul. Which was a polite way of saying that he was absolutely bloody useless, would fold at the first sign of trouble, retreating into the world of VR gaming until the danger had passed.

Which left Mags. She thinks of the phone calls, each one designed to close another door. To the University of San Francisco, asking for a break in her PhD. Yes, she knew she was close. Yes, she knew it was a shame. But it was necessary. Her father was sick, and the diner was in trouble and her mother had her hands full. And there was nobody else. So what choice did she have, really?

Mags lets her gaze drop down to the whitewashed boards of the porch. They are scuffed. Worn. Would need a fresh coat of paint soon.

She focuses on the paint, on the ragged edges of it, as she tries not to think of the other call, but it comes along anyway, just as it always does when she lies down in her bed, and lights go out, and her eyes close. Like it is always there, just waiting for her.

Jack's voice on the other end of the line, painfully pleased to hear from her. The 'We need to talk' and the lengthy silence that comes next as he realises that something is happening here. Then her laying it out, like it is the most obvious thing in the world. That she is not happy, that it feels to her now that her life is a knitted coat that has grown tight over the years, that it pulls across her shoulders and itches her neck, and that she has done all she can in order to make it fit, but perhaps it is time just to accept it. That her body has changed. That the coat has to go.

'But . . . Mags . . . I know things have been tough. You and the kids there, me here. But, honey, it won't always be like this. And . . .'

'I can't, Jack,' she had said. 'It just doesn't feel like this works, anymore. That *we* work.'

Mags runs her bare foot across the rough wood, digging the digit in enough that it begins to hurt. Tells herself that she had had no choice. Had to take off the coat. Trouble was, that had been two years ago. And it turned out that the clothes she wore beneath, that they didn't fit either.

Mags wipes her eyes, takes a sip of lukewarm coffee. Studies the wood.

Maybe she would mix things up a bit. Maybe she would paint it pink. She snorts. Could you imagine?

Because the diner itself has been in Destino so long that it seems it is owned by the town at large, not by her. 'You've moved the lounge chair. Why have you moved the lounge chair? Your grandmother, she would never have moved that lounge chair.' The customers, some of them even called her Elsie. No one caring that Elsie had been dead for the last twenty years. The diner was Elsie's, she ran the diner, ergo . . .

Mags rests her head back against the wood-framed porch. Maybe that was it, why she wasn't sleeping. Maybe it was the creeping loss of identity, as the Elsie-ness of her life worked its way beneath her skin. Really, wasn't she living in Elsie's home, a two-bedroom apartment, ceilings low enough that she was at risk of developing a permanent stoop, right above the coffee shop? Didn't she also have two kids, a boy and a girl, both growing up shorter than they should be because of those goddam ceilings. Mom, she always said there was a reason she had never topped 5'2. Mags tapped off her cigarette, turned her head to look up at the shop, at the apartment above, all still in darkness. It was one of the few mercies. That even if she didn't have sleep, at least she had these few pre-dawn hours in which she could be Mags. Not Elsie, not Bonnie. Just Mags.

She sighs, stubs out the cigarette. And readies herself to live another yesterday. And the day before that. The day before that. She pushes herself up to standing.

And then it happens, something new. A sound breaking the still morning air. A wrenching wail of despair.

Chapter Three

Bonnie Aubrey – 25th September, 6.45 a.m.

There is a sound, the distant barking of a dog. It punctures Bonnie's sleep, mingling with dreams of her grandchildren, of Oscar and Gabrielle pirouetting around her, of Elsie's Diner with Kelvin at the hotplate – and something else that vanishes like a puff of smoke. She lingers there, on the edge of consciousness, reaches for it, but her fingers flail and the not-quite memory slips through them like fog through a grate.

Her eyes open, whether she wants them to or not. A muted light spills in through the gaps that surround the thick drapes. She allows her gaze to focus, to take in the dust motes that dance across the ceiling in the early morning light. And she tries to hang on to it, that feeling that comes only with dreams now, of safety and warmth. Has had little sleep, an hour, maybe two. Her shoulders ache, arms, feels almost like the onset of flu.

If she listens carefully, she can hear it, beyond the swish of the ceiling fan – the sound of her husband's laboured breathing that comes from the room that abuts hers. 'It is better, Bon,' Kelvin had said in that gasping whisper of a voice that he has now. 'You won't be able to sleep with me snoring away.' And she had scowled, had looked at her husband as though he was an errant child, the message, *we're going to be arguing later.* But

Kelvin, he had just ignored her. Did that more of late and she never was sure, was it the chemo, fogging up his brain and his thinking, so that he was no longer really sure quite what was going on? Or was he taking advantage, knowing that she wouldn't fuss too hard. On account of his perilous health.

Her stomach clenches, and, for the briefest of moments it feels like she is falling. As if this path that she has chosen for herself leads her right off a cliff. She clutches on tight to the bedclothes, steadying herself. Tells herself that none of it matters. Not anymore. Only Kelvin. She blinks, forces her vision to clear, the room coalescing before her. The wardrobe. It stands across from the bed, a solid wood mahogany behemoth, passed down from mother to daughter, in a line stretching back for the better part of a century. She stares at it, same as every other morning. At the unrelentingly closed door.

How many times had they argued about that, how many times had she tutted and rolled her eyes? Kelvin never could seem to close that door. Not a dumb man, not by any stretch of the imagination, but always seemed that this one thing remained just beyond him, the closing of a wardrobe door. The irony of it, that now it truly was beyond him. That for Kelvin, raising himself from the queen-sized bed in the spare room was now as impossible as climbing Everest. She lies there now and studies the door that remains unavoidably, irrevocably closed, and a single tear eases its way down her cheek.

She dashes her hand across her face and pushes herself up, resting her back against the headboard. Shakes her head, as though that way she will dislodge the worst of the thoughts. Kelvin, he would be well. Once the treatment was done. It would be well. She is a child, playing hide-and-seek, who hides behind a rake. It would be well. Once this was all done.

Because, if you do not look at it, at death approaching, then somehow it will pass on by.

Bonnie turns on her side, allowing her gaze to fall on the

glowing light of the digital clock. Early enough that she could close her eyes again, could reach out to sleep, the reprieve of the unconscious. But it is too late. The day has already begun, whether she wants it or not.

She shrugs off the light sheet that is making her skin sticky in the early morning heat, and shrugs off the thoughts too, instead returning her mind to Oscar and Gabrielle. They would be awake soon, would crash into the early morning hours with an indecent energy. Oscar has a project due, a diorama of the gold rush. He would need glitter, she thinks. Gold, obviously. Would need cardboard and glue. Gabrielle, she is falling behind in math, or as much math as you do when you are nine anyhow. And if she couldn't do nine-year-old math, what hope was there for the child? Perhaps, she thinks, she should look into getting a tutor. Maggie should have done it, but never had and so here they are. Could you get tutors for nine-year-olds? How expensive would that be? Not too expensive surely? And she could probably stretch to cover it. She thinks then, inevitably, of the bank balance, its paucity of zeroes. Thinks then of the bills that just keep on coming, getting redder and redder. No, she could cover the costs of a tutor. Because if not, what would that say about her, not even able to pay the costs of a tutor, for nine-year-old math for goodness' sakes.

She thinks of Maggie. Of that look she wears now, a semi-permanent frown, little lines of stress that have creased her forehead into an ever-present fold. When did that happen? Had it always been there, but only now was she noticing it? She shakes her head, it will be the divorce, harder on Maggie than she let on. And there were the children. Lovely children, but loud. Exuberant. Was that the word? Too much for Maggie to handle alone. And so Bonnie has to rise from bed, has no choice, because if she doesn't, if she fails to take a shower and style her hair and put on make-up and pants, because if she does not then how will Maggie cope?

Then comes what she has begun to think of as her brain's wake-up call, that spasm of irritation that rolls right in on her as the sleep rolls out. Every morning just the same. Irritation at how expensive the world is; at the diner, just about getting by; at the education system that could let a nine-year-old fall behind at math. At Maggie, pushing and pushing and pushing. *'Mom, we need to talk.'* Irritation about the diner, about the money. At the town beyond her door and the people who once she thought of as friends. But that was a long time ago. Now those friends have disappeared, all merging together into one big homogenous mass of Destino. This used to be such a happy place. Once. Back before life and age had begun to grind her down. And there is another voice, just beyond that, one that always seems to come with Kelvin's turn of phrase. 'Perhaps, Bon, it's not them that's changed. Perhaps it's you.' And she allows herself a moment, to remember the her she was before. With her bake sales and church fundraising and Thursday night choir. With friends scattered every which way throughout the town, up and down the highway, until in the end it seemed that the very road had been built as a connector to her social calendar. Then rolls in more grief, this time not for Kelvin but rather for herself and all that she has lost. And all that she has become.

Bonnie shakes her head, clambers from the bed, allowing the irritation to power her. She shakes out the pillow, more roughly than was strictly necessary. Marches to the window and drives the drapes back, one grandiose sweep. Destino is spread out below, quiet. Waiting. A haze lying over the town.

And then movement catches her eye, a fleeting figure, moving fast. The shape of it and the movement of it identifying her daughter as she runs up the footpath that leads from the diner to the mountain. Towards Mack's.

Chapter Four

Robyn Sandoval – 25th September, 7.00 a.m.

Robyn leans against the door frame of Mack's bedroom, her fingernails digging into the wood, hard enough that they bend, folding back on themselves. Her mouth is open, and somewhere there is the distant memory of a deafening wail. Was that her?

She pulls in a dense breath, exhales a sob.

She releases her grip on the wood, steps forward. She reaches out, hands shaking, lifts the pillow from his face. His eyes are open, a trickle of blood has snaked its way from between his lips. And Robyn feels herself sway, gripping hold of the mattress for support, feels the pillow drop from her fingers to the floor.

The ceiling fan swirls, a wash of hot breath.

'Papa?' Why is she saying that now? What is the point? Because she has kept that word, has cradled it close to her, for the past five years. He has been Mack to her. And each time his name has left her lips, there has been that moment, his face falling, the reaction quickly smothered. 'Papa . . .' she says again, experimental. Has held her cards for too long. No point in playing them now.

Hector gives a soft yip, nudges her leg with his cold nose, and Robyn starts, shakes her head. She has to move. Has to do something. She steps backwards, a feeling like the floor is rising up to meet her, backs from the room, gaze locked on the bed. On her father.

Her heart is thumping, so hard that it feels that it will beat right out of her chest.

Robyn turns, facing into the family room, trying to piece together what she sees. The chaos of it is normal, for Mack at least. Newspapers spread across the coffee table. The print kind, with their edges furled up against a pair of whisky glasses. *Why don't you get your news online like everyone else does?* He had shaken his head, muttered something about kids today. 'You don't get it, you youngsters. It isn't just about the words. It's about the feel of the paper on your fingertips, the print that leaches onto your skin.'

Her fingers reach out, nudge aside a page, the picture on it of a reservoir, its water table down to the base, *Worst drought in a hundred years* the headline. Remembers, fleetingly. when she used to care about such things. Before she had found her father dead.

Hector gives another yip. A nudge. There's something you should be doing. And she looks down at him, blinks. Yes. She needs to call someone. Her head is pulsing, her vision narrowing down to a dark-lined tunnel. She has to call someone. Why hasn't she?

She feels in her pocket for her cell, pulls it out, cradling the phone in her hand. Her body moves her, back out into the entrance hall, through the still-open door onto the front path. Can hear the distant sound of footsteps, coming on fast.

It will be real. Once she pushes the buttons, says the words, this world that has frozen in place will begin to spin again. Only it will spin without him.

Her head pulses, vision murky now.

Hector whines.

Her fingers move. 9–1–1.

She hears herself say it. *'My father is dead.'*

And then her fingers are shaking and her heart is thumping and the world is going dark.

Chapter Five

There is a woman. She feels the rough dirt against her cheek, the unrelenting ground, pockmarked with sharp edged stones. Her skin, it seems, waking before the rest of her. Then comes the weight of warm air, pressing down on top of her, like a comforter pulled up to her chin. She moves her hands, feeling about her, and the comforter is not there. There is light, though, bright enough that it shines through closed eyelids. A stabbing, sickening jolt of pain.

Robyn opens her eyes.

At first, all she can see is brush, dried out tendrils of it inches away from her face, waving in the breeze. She blinks once, twice. Experiments with a palm on the dirt trail, levering herself up. A swell of nausea, her head throbbing with the motion.

Where is she?

Her thoughts kaleidoscope, each one of them more fragmented than the one before. Robyn gives herself a moment, dipping her head, letting the nausea wash over her. She allows her fingers to dig into the dirt beneath them, rough against her skin. She was . . . where had she been? Somewhere else, and there was something . . . it was important. Her stomach clenches. What was it?

Then a thought, of heavy canine weight pressing down on

her. 'Hector?' She looks about, blinking in the bright light. 'Hector?' But there is only silence, the chirping of cicadas.

She breathes in, deep, steadying herself, then turns onto all fours, pushing herself up to standing, a sway as the altitude takes effect. Her vision has begun to widen now, the narrow tunnel gradually stretching outwards. She stands on the mountainside, at the furthest curve of the valley. Looking down, she can see the tip of the church spire down below her, and, beyond that, Destino spread out. She turns in place. How did she get here? The sky blue above, drifting grey clouds. She breathes in, carefully. A smell, one that has been there this whole time, but she only just notices. Of smoke. It winds its way into her nostrils, clambering down her throat.

And then it comes, the crashing realisation. Mack, dead. A pillow pressed down on his face.

It seeps through her, a dreadful heat that spills its way from her forehead, all the way down to her toes. The kind of feeling that disaster brings with it. Her body spasms, a sob working its way up through her chest, forcing its way out.

She needs to go back. She needs to call for help. And then her feet have turned, her body, it seems, moving of its own volition, a build up inside her of . . . not fear, but rather something more focused, more purposeful. Of flight. She stumbles backwards, away from the precipitous drop, body in charge now, mind just along for the ride. Slip-sliding onto the narrow brush-lined trail, struggling to keep her balance as it angles downwards towards the sleeping town below.

She is running. In spite of the world swirling around her, in spite of the dizziness. Her feet slap against the hard-packed dirt beneath them, running shoes struggling to keep a purchase. Only . . . she glances down. Where her electric blue running shoes had once been, now there are pumps, once black, now a murky, washed-out grey. Her heels bounce out of them, toes fighting to cling on.

What . . . ?

A corner up ahead, the trail doubling back on itself. A cypress tree leans out, part crossing the track. Robyn grabs hold of the twisting trunk, clinging to it, her feet sliding on the dry dirt with a heart-sickening drop. She breathes deep, forcing her body to stillness. She looks down.

It is not just the shoes that are different. The washed-out pumps give way to bare legs, a tan two shades darker than had been there an hour ago. Her running shorts have been replaced by denim cut-offs, her vest top with a long sleeve tee.

Robyn inhales, the scent of the cypress riding right alongside the panic. Hands shaking, she tugs at the left sleeve of the tee, pulling it up to her elbow.

Her breath catches in her throat.

Her narrow arms are lined with tattoos, snaking green vines that clamber from her wrist to her elbow.

She stares at her arms. A sob seeps from her, a fresh wave of nausea. It is madness, no other explanation for it. The shock has triggered a psychotic break. Her legs go loose beneath her, a sway threatening to bring her to the ground. She looks up, to Destino below, looking for something, anything to ground her. Follows the line of Main Street down the valley floor, letting her gaze track up the opposite valley wall, towards the cut-out shapes of Destino Heights, bright white against the dark green of trees. Only . . . the development has gone. There are no houses, no neat-cut lawns. Nothing. Just endless forest.

Fear grips her, making her limbs loose beneath her. And then she is running again, mind and body in complete agreement this time. She plunges down the mountainside towards the spread-out town below. As she runs, a thought, her hands flying to the cut-offs that she had not been wearing moments before, searching for her cell. The pockets, however, remained resolutely cell-less. Just a single key on a VW key ring that she does not recognise.

She slides the last couple of feet down the trail, grabbing onto brush to steady herself. She is close now. Not far from home. She glances towards the church, thinking that perhaps Father Caprese . . .

Robyn stops dead.

The church had been white. Moments before, and for the entirety of her existence. She steps closer and runs her hand across the rough surface of the baby-blue wood, expecting . . . what, wet paint? But it is dry and it has begun to fleck, the blue turning purple with weather and with age.

She turns, the church at her rear, facing down Main Street, rivulets of sweat trickling down the nape of her neck. Beyond the church, there is the empty lot, the space that the failing clothing business left behind. And beside that . . . Destino Vino is gone. In its place stands a store, its front lined with the kind of bins you use for flowers, its door arched with a trellis, a heady concoction of vines, of bright purple bougainvillea flowers wrapping their way around. The sign swings in the breeze. Journey's End Flowers.

The ground sways beneath her feet. She ran past it, mere minutes ago. Where has Destino Vino gone? A wave of dizziness sweeps over her, and she blinks, expecting that when her eyes open all will be as it should. But when she opens them, the new store remains. Robyn walks slowly towards the front door. It is dark inside, a chalkboard hanging in the window, the word 'closed' written in a winding script. She raises a hand, lets her fingers run across the soft petals of the flowers, the smell of moss. She takes hold of a petal, pulling it free so that it lies across her palm, the curves of it rippling in the hot breeze.

'What is going on?' she murmurs.

She looks back to the mountain, to the now blue church. Above it, the clouds of smoke, an advance guard of the Seven Hills' fire. They ride their way down the mountainside, slipping on thermals, hanging low over Destino. A shot across the bow.

She folds the petal into the palm of her hand, turning, first to the flower store, then to Main Street beyond. On the corner of Main and Sycamore, the bar stands. Only now it is not Bar 53. Now it has been renamed O'Callaghan's, its frontage painted a deep Irish green, the outside chairs stacked on top of tables.

Robyn walks towards them, reaching out, feeling the cold metal of chair legs beneath her fingers. It is a dream, no other possible explanation for it. A lucid dream, wasn't that what they called it?

Then a smell, something that ran alongside the smoke . . . could you smell in dreams? Then, whether you could or you couldn't, a smell there definitely was. Of cinnamon and coffee.

Elsie's.

Robyn turns, raising her hand to shield her eyes from the early morning sun. And there, right where it had always been, hangs the sign. *Elsie's*. Nausea shifts to relief and she walks. She wants to run but it seems to her that this body is only partially hers to control. The useless pumps flip-flop against the sidewalk. She steps out into the street, not bothering to look left or right, walks slowly along the wide-slung path, up the front steps of the coffee shop. The door is closed, blinds pulled down low. A poster hangs in the window – Destino Wildfire Readiness Programme. But movement then, somewhere within, the sound of footsteps.

She raises her hand, trying not to see the twisting tattooed vines. She bangs the glass of the door, hard enough that it shudders within its frame.

'All right, all right. I'm coming.'

Robyn blows out a slow breath. The dawning realisation that she has a headache, a pulsing, throbbing ache that has wrapped itself around her skull. The footsteps draw closer. The sound of a bolt being drawn, then the door swings inwards.

Bonnie stands in the gloom, an apron tied tight around her waist, her long grey hair tugged into a plait that curls over her shoulder. She looks at her, expectant, holds out a brown paper bag, a to-go cup. 'It's ready. Just like I said.'

Robyn stares at her. Bonnie looks as she has always looked. Small and slender, could be mistaken for a girl, not a woman in her sixties. But there is something different here, in the expression on her face, the way she looks at her. Robyn scans her, looking for it, that slightest of lip curls, that nostril flare of disdain that the Sandoval name always has triggered in the older woman.

Bonnie smiles at her.

'I . . .' It is worse, somehow, this change of expression. Is worse than the blue church and the green bar. Than flowers where wine should be.

Bonnie steps closer, studying her, the smile giving way to an expression of concern. 'What's wrong, sweetie? You OK?'

'Bonnie . . .' There is something she needs to tell her. Something important. But she cannot find it, only left the tail end of a memory, of a disaster underway. 'Bugger,' she mutters, her mouth moving without her consent. 'Bugger, bugger, bugger.'

'Language!'

'Bugger.'

'Hey!'

'Sorry.'

Robyn watches it, as if from afar. Can feel the movement of her lips, but seems like it has little to do with her. She shakes her head, reaches out, clutches the woman's arm. 'Bonnie, I . . . Mack . . .'

Bonnie studies her. 'What? What's wrong with him?' She places her hand over Robyn's own. 'Honey, you don't look so good. You need me to call someone?'

Robyn feels herself pull backwards, feels her fists ball up tight. 'No. No, don't. I . . .'

'Then, you need to get yourself home.' Bonnie's voice has dropped low, soft.

Robyn's feet step backwards. Feels the wooden slats give way to stone path. Her heart thumps, pressure building up in her head. She turns, walking, with long, loping strides, fists balled. A hot breeze sweeps down from the mountain, bringing with it a smell she dimly remembers. Of pine trees and smoke. Her pumps slap against the sidewalk, the pain in her head throbbing. Along Main Street, all the way down towards the rock-chiselled tunnel.

Almost home. Almost home. She rounds the corner, brushing aside the overhanging branches of the birch tree.

But . . .

Her vision tightens up, so that it seems that she sees the world through a pinhole. Her ears fill with the roaring sound of blood rushing through her head.

The house, the one that she left this morning, has gone. In its place, a burned-out husk of a home, little more than four walls, some broken-out windows. A roof that has collapsed in on itself. Robyn walks forward. Knee-length weeds that have broken through the cracked drive brush against her legs. Her breath comes hard, sharp-edged.

Somewhere, at the edge of her senses, the smell of smoke.

And then the world goes dark.

Chapter Six

Robyn Sandoval – 25th September, 7.00 a.m.

It is a feeling of dislocation. Of sliding back into her body. Of having never left. The hot air, pressing down on her so that it feels like she cannot breathe. A canine weight against her leg, soft, a low grumbling.

And then . . .

The wave of dizziness recedes and she looks down at her arms. They are bare, undecorated with tattoos. At her legs, paler now. At the running shoes, electric blue. Hector leans into her, pit-bull fur soft against her skin, is looking up at her, his expression worried. She is sitting on the ground, dried-out grass rough against her legs. Is outside Mack's house once again.

'Robyn?' A face, moving in and out of focus. The faint smell of cigarettes. 'Robyn, are you OK?' A moment, then a tentative hand clasps hers.

She looks down, two hands intertwined.

Up.

'Mags?' She stares at the woman. The sudden awareness that she has grown up alongside her, has known her for all of her life. That she has never really looked at her before. Has she always looked this tired?

'Are you OK?' asks Mags, softly.

For a moment, she cannot find the answer. And then, beyond Mags' shoulder, she sees it. The still-open door. The still-lit lamp.

And it all comes rushing back.

'Mack,' says Robyn, 'he's dead.'

Chapter Seven

Robyn Sandoval – 25th September, 7.20 a.m.

When did they get here? When did Mack's tiny little house go from empty to breathlessly full? Robyn can hear them, voices low, footsteps careful. And, in spite of herself, she strains, listening for her Mack's voice. Unthinkable that she will not hear it again.

'Are you sure you don't want to come on down to the diner?' Mags asks, tentatively. She sits beside her on the wooden deck, legs pulled up to her chest, arms wrapped around them. 'Coffee is on.' She looks to the wide-open door, considers. 'Luis can come find you when he needs you.'

Robyn slowly shakes her head. Her fingers play with the loose threads on her running shorts. A sudden gust of hot wind that winds its way up the mountain, bringing the scent of smoke with it. She raises her hand. She has been crying. When did that start? Hector lies on the floor beside her, head resting on overlarge paws, his gaze fixed on her. He whines softly.

'I'd rather stay,' she murmurs, stroking Hector's snout.

Mags nods slowly.

'You don't have to,' says Robyn, distant. 'You have the kids.' There were children, right? A girl and a boy.

Mags sighs, slowly shaking her head. 'It's fine. They're with my mom.'

Movement then from within the house. Figures crossing from the bedroom to the kitchen. Luis, his hair still shower damp, a ring of wetness on the collar of his uniform. He spares a glance at them, a quick nod. And Robyn allows the memory to roll through her head, again and again. Luis hurrying towards them, taking the footpath with long strides that leave sweat flecked across his brow. Looking from her to Mags, back again, then up to the open door. Is he . . . Robyn shaking her head, no. He is dead. Mack is dead. A moment then, a beat while the words sink in, and then she delivers it, the killer blow. The pillow . . . It was on his face. Someone killed him. The intake of breath from Mags, Luis' face sliding into a hardened neutral, and then the radio raised to his lips and suddenly the world speeds up, sliding beyond her control. Vivienne, the town doctor, sweeping in, her face set, sparing a moment to give Robyn a quick smile, an 'It'll be OK' even though they both know damn well that it will not. Another police officer, one Robyn does not recognise, who trails along behind the doctor.

The young, female officer lingers in the doorway, now, a human dividing line between the living and the dead. She is trying to look casual. It does not work very well. She glances towards them, an accidental eye contact making her start. But then she rallies, forces her face into an effortful smile.

'I can take you home if you like?' the officer says. 'The lieutenant says there's no need for you to stay. He can come talk with you later.'

Robyn opens her mouth, but the words won't come. Or they will, but it seems inevitable that tears will come with them. So she just shuts her mouth again and shakes her head.

The officer nods, although that clearly is not the answer she wants. Falls silent. Now just the whoomp, whoomp of the fan. Then, from Main Street, the sound of an engine, a Porsche approaching, pulling into the space before the diner. Robyn stares at it, the future unrolling with a painful inevitability. The driver's door swinging open, her mother climbing out. She lingers there for a moment, studying the closed-up diner. Then, shaking her head, she turns towards the footpath, walking quickly in kitten heels, her loose-fit blouse swaying in the breeze.

Mags has stiffened, is sitting up taller now, a line of tension running along her jaw.

Hector gives a solitary wag of his tail.

'Robyn.' Eve is not out of breath, in spite of the incline and the early morning heat. She studies her daughter. 'Luis called me.' She reaches down, holds out her hand. 'Come. Let me take you home.'

'Mrs Sandoval . . .' Mags speaks carefully, reluctant, a glance at Robyn. 'I think she would like to stay . . .'

Eve stops, freezing in place. She looks at Mags as if she is seeing her there for the first time, and an expression crosses her face of . . . what? Something cold and hard. Only then the moment passes and it is gone, and Robyn is no longer sure that she did not imagine it.

Eve crouches down before her daughter, takes her hands into her manicured ones. 'My love, there is nothing you can do here. You should come away.' She squeezes her daughter's fingers. 'Come on, Robyn. Let's go home.'

'No.'

'Robyn . . .'

'I'm not leaving, Mom.'

Her mother's expression shifts, a cloud passing across the sun. She nods, stands. 'Fine. I must get back. We have a conference call, and one of us should be there at least.' She studies her daughter. 'You'll be . . . OK?'

Robyn nods.

Eve smiles, lips tight. 'Mags, might I have a word.'

Mags starts, looking between mother and daughter. Reluctantly nods, pushing herself up to standing.

'Robyn,' Eve throws the word over her shoulder, 'don't be too long, OK.'

Robyn nods slowly. Little awareness of what it is she is agreeing to. She watches the two women as they retreat down the mountainside, an uneasy distance between them. Listens for what will be said. But there is nothing, just an increasingly uncomfortable silence. And then Robyn unwinds her legs, pushes herself up to standing. Hector heaves himself to his feet.

'Oh!' The police officer looks startled but more than a little relieved. 'Are you ready to go home?'

'No,' says Robyn, shortly.

The woman is looking at her, expectant, but she sidesteps her, moving around her into her father's house. Hears a soft oh of surprise, the officer falling into step behind her, determined that if she cannot control her, she will at least follow. All is as she left it. The coffee table, the newspaper splayed across the glasses. The bottle of Jim Beam. Can feel Hector's hot breath on her skin, the drapes pulled across the window turning the bright sunlight sepia.

She lingers there allowing herself a moment to pretend. That nothing has changed, that all is as it should be.

'Robyn . . .' Vivienne emerges from the bedroom.

Luis glances up and then is moving behind Vivienne. His arms spread wide like he is going to shepherd Robyn back outside. 'OK. Robyn, do you wanna wait in the—'

Robyn folds her arms, plants her feet. 'No.' Who was she? 'Who would have done this? Who would have hurt him? Everyone loved him.'

Luis and Vivienne share a look, one she is not meant to see. 'What?'

'I need you to have a think,' Luis says carefully, 'anything seem out of place to you? When you got here? Anything strike you as odd?'

'The door,' says Robyn.

'What about the door?'

'It was open. I just figured he'd been out early, forgotten to pull it behind him.'

Luis nods. 'And the light? I noticed the lamp was on in the front window. Did you put that on?'

She shakes her head. 'No. It was on when I arrived.'

Luis' expression does something, and Robyn recoils, staring at him. 'What?'

'You were here pretty early.' He says it lightly, but there is something, just beneath the surface. 'How come?'

Robyn stares at him, the implications of his words settling. A wave of nausea passes over her. 'He asked me to come by for breakfast. He emailed last night. Today is the anniversary of my birth mother's . . . of Harper's death. Mack, he always takes it hard.' She hesitates, a flash of memory, of Mack folded over a photograph of Harper, sunlight catching on the tears that stream down his face. Hard on the heels of the thought, a headache blooms and she raises a hand to her head, forcing herself to concentrate. 'You want to know if it was me. You want to know if *I* killed him.'

'Robyn . . .' Luis holds up his hands, palms out, calming.

The headache is worsening now, has begun to wrap its way around her temples, darkening the edges of her vision. But Robyn reaches into her pocket, pulls out her cell and hands it to the police officer. 'You can check my Fitbit. It tracks my sleep. And it registered my run.' A moment, then, 'I didn't kill him.'

She stares at Luis, her vision a narrow tunnel now, and speaks slowly, clearly. 'I did not kill my father.'

Luis opens his mouth, but she does not hear what it is he will say, because the dizziness, it has already taken her.

The world goes dark.

Chapter Eight

Heat is the first sensation. Dense air blocks up her mouth, her nose. The second sensation is the smell, of musky sweat, stale weed, the faintest soupçon of urine. She opens her eyes. A sensation of having woken into a dream. She blinks, her eyes sticky, shapes moving before vision that has not yet cleared. A rough-knit blanket covers her, its threads catching on her sweat-slicked skin. She does not recognise this ceiling. She lies there, quite still, and focuses on its rectangular shape only a little bit longer than the stretched-out length of her body. Her stomach tightens, twisting in on itself. But she tells herself that it is just that dreamlike state of the newly awakened. Give it a minute and it will all make sense. She strains to listen, the sound of voices in the near distance, ones she does not recognise.

Is it a hospital?

A muted orange light batters its way through thin fabric drapes. They hang stiff in the still air. She turns her head to the left, studying the worn-out fabric, the pattern of twisting yellow flowers. It is stained, yellowed, not by design but rather by age.

Her stomach clenches. If it is a hospital, it is a really crappy one.

She closes her eyes again, takes in a deep breath that catches on the smell. She had been in the house. In Mack's house. There had been Luis and Vivienne and the policewoman whose name she does not know. And her father had been dead . . .

She squeezes her eyes tighter shut. Because that way she will not see the ceiling, cigarette-stained, or the worn-through window treatments scuffed up with God only knows what. She listens to the voices outside, to the rise and fall of them. They are growing closer. Not close enough that she can pick out words, but close enough that the tone of them is clear, the urgency. Perhaps, she tells herself, some accident has come in.

'Yo, Scarlett.'

Dammit.

The door flies open, bringing with it a blast of hot air. Heavy footsteps shake the ground beneath her. It is a voice she doesn't recognise. A name that isn't hers. Or, not anymore at least.

She does not move.

It's a hospital. She has had some kind of seizure.

'Scarlett?'

A mini stroke, perhaps.

Footsteps come closer, the smell of cigarettes overwhelming now, and her treacherous eyes open of their own accord. He leans over her, face pulled into an expression of concern. He is thin; thin enough that the coating of flesh that overlays his skull seems woefully insufficient. There are dark bags beneath his eyes, his chin coated in what is either a failed beard or a failed shave. He studies her and she feels herself recoiling back into the thin pillow.

'Come on. You gotta get up.' His gaze darts around the room. 'Scarlett, I'm not kidding. They say we gotta go.' He has picked up a gym bag now, is stuffing it with clothing that he selects, at random seemingly, from the array that is spread across the floor. He studies the ground for a moment, then turns back to her. 'Serious. They're evacuating the park. Come on. You got to get out of bed.'

He reaches over towards her, skeletal hands gripping onto her wrists. The touch feels extremely real.

Robyn wrenches her arms away from him, forces herself up; a wave of nausea grips her, but she ignores it. She breathes deeply, looks around. It is not a hospital. It is nowhere close to being a hospital.

It is a trailer. She is in a trailer.

The trailer is small, made smaller still by the mounded clothes that lie scattered across the floor, the cups and plates that litter all horizontal surfaces. It smells . . . just bad. A wooden spoon protrudes from the dish filled sink and she grabs at it, waving it in front of her. The world's most useless weapon. The man steps back, looking her up and down.

'The hell you doing, Scarlett? I'm not joking. The cops are here. We gotta *go*.' His gaze darts towards the door, back again. 'Come on. I put your bag in the truck already.'

She steps back, letting the uncertain weight of her rest against the sink and its contents. 'Who are you?' She tries to keep her voice steady, tries not to let the panic show. 'Where am I?'

'Jesus Christ,' he mutters, turning his back on her, shaking his head. He reaches down and drags a backpack from beneath the bed. 'Now is not the time for games, Scar. I am telling you, I do not want to be the one to tell your mother we were the last ones out. She'll skin us alive.' He tugs open a cupboard, scooping shelf loads into the open mouth of the backpack. Spares her a single solitary glance. 'You better get your stuff together.' He throws her a pair of shoes. The same once-were-black pumps she had seen before. Up on the mountain. They land at her feet.

She lowers the spoon, her attention snagging on the smudge-smeared mirror behind the man's head. Her brain screams at her, but she ignores it, stepping closer to her own reflection. Her hair is gone. The shoulder-length waves, the colour of fresh biscuits, vanished. She drops the spoon, raises her hand to her head. It is short now. This hair that is not hers has been cut close to the scalp, is the colour of mahogany, her entire head ringed with a short mop of loose curls. She studies her face. It is thinner than it was before. Before. An hour ago. A moment. Her cheekbones are more prominent, lips thinner. She wears no make-up, the sweat glistens across her skin. She looks down at her arms. At the tattoos.

'Scarlett. For God's sake!' He spins in place, grabbing a box and shoving it into his backpack. 'Shoes!'

She steps into the pumps, feet moving without thought. A throbbing, pulsing pain is building at the back of her skull. 'What is happening to me?' she murmurs.

Whether he had planned to answer or not, he is interrupted by a bang on the door. A fist that is not messing about. 'Let's go, guys!'

The voice. It is familiar to her.

The man throws the backpack over his shoulder, grips hold of the gym bag in one hand, her wrist in the other and drags her towards the door. He hesitates, gives her a look as though he is expecting trouble, then releases her arm, throws open the trailer door.

The heat rolls in.

She recoils, but he doesn't give her the chance to get far. Grabs hold of her wrist again and pulls her out of the trailer, down the short metal steps. The loose-fitting pumps slipping, again. Then she pulls up short, wrenching her arm from his grasp.

I know this place.

The trees surround them, leaning over, brittle and bone dry. The rust speckled trailer stands in a copse, the grass that surrounds it biscuit brown. Beyond the thin wall of trees, movement. Of people hurrying, calling to one another. The slamming of trailer doors, hum of car engines. She turns on the spot. The smell of smoke hangs faint in the air.

The slam of a truck door, and then he is beside her again. 'Would you come? It's a drive to Morro Bay.' He hesitates, then, 'If you still want to, you can leave for Oxnard from there.' He puts his arm around her, steering her towards the truck.

She strains against him, feet fighting for traction on the rough ground. Might as well try to fight the tide.

The sky is blue still, but there is a thin haze of smoke. Her gaze follows the shape of the mountain, the drifting smoke clouds that shroud the summit. She turns to the man, with his shitty Bon Jovi T-shirt and his smell of weed. 'There's no fire. Why are we . . .?'

He hesitates, eyes tracking hers. 'You know the plan. Why are you asking this?'

'Just tell me.' She has his arm now, like the body has taken over, brain just along for the ride.

He stares at her. 'The Destino Wildfire Readiness Programme. Their funded evacuation for high-risk areas. It's precautionary, but we all agreed to it. You know this, Scar, why are you—'

It is a feeling of cold. Of nothing around her fitting the way it is supposed to. Her mind spins and dips, seeking a safe place to land, but there is nothing, only the memory of her father. Dead.

She lets go, steps back, and then turns, and she begins to run.

'Scarlett!'

The loose-fitting pumps flap against the hard-packed soil. She can feel the pull in her calves, the rub from unsuitable shoes. The strain in her chest. Was it from the heat? Or was it because she wasn't used to running? Only, she was used to running, wasn't she?

Just not in this body.

She lets out a sound, a wail-roar hybrid, but it vanishes up into the air. She ducks through the copse of trees, brown grass giving way to rust-flecked trailers. The doors hang open, people rushing down steps, armfuls of belongings thrown into waiting cars. A small boy cries, although no one pays him any mind. A police cruiser stands empty, light silently flashing. She keeps running. Past the cruiser, past the crying child. Past a couple, barely out of their teens, she with an infant against her shoulder, him carrying a TV. They scream at each other. The infant wails.

She runs until it is behind her, until the wraparound trees give way to a propped-open metal gate, the dirt road rutted with tyre tracks. She bursts through onto the open road beyond. Down the hill, running and running and running. Her lungs pull, legs ache. Somewhere in the distance, there is shouting behind her, the dim awareness of a name being called.

She ignores it. It isn't her name, after all.

She runs, not really thinking about where she is running to but her feet know the way nonetheless. She takes a sharp right, running along a narrow footpath onto Brier Lane. Down towards Main Street. She bursts out of the narrow path, onto the open expanse of the thoroughfare. Towards Elsie's Diner. Up the footpath that leads back up the opposite hill.

All that matters is the house ahead.

It does not look like it did when she left it. There is no police car outside. The door does not hang open. There is no smell of death or decay. She turns onto the porch of her father's house, pumps slipping on the gravel, and she bumps up against the recycling box, the empty bottles clinking one against another. A sob escapes from her, but she rights herself and then is at the door. Shut this time, no give in the handle, so she bangs on the wooden face with an open palm. 'MACK! MACK!' Another sob, then, 'Papa?'

The world hangs suspended, waiting. Then the sound of footsteps beyond and the door swings open and he is there, standing, half-dressed in a firefighter's uniform, one boot held loose in his hand. And she tumbles in through the door, is inside his arms, barely listens as he murmurs comfort, uncertainty thick in his voice.

'Hey, what is it? What's wrong?'

'Mack . . .' Her voice breaks, one of those gasping, wrenching sobs that wracks the entirety of your body. 'You were dead! I . . . Oh my God.'

'Hey, it's OK. It was just a dream.' He hugs her tight to him, smelling of body spray and coffee. 'It's OK, Scarlett.'

It is a cold dash of water down her back. She releases her hold, pulls back from him, and then . . .

'I . . .' The dizziness takes hold.

Chapter Nine

Robyn Sandoval – 25th September, 7.20 a.m.

'Robyn?' The voice is distant, comes at her through layers of time. 'Robyn? Are you OK?'

'I . . .' Robyn shakes her head, looks down at her arms. Bare now. She looks about, is back in Mack's house. What the hell is happening?

'Maybe you should sit . . .' A male voice now. She looks up, Luis, his brow creased in concern. 'You look a bit out of it.'

'He was there . . .' Robyn murmurs. 'He was . . .'

Scarlett. The man had called her Scarlett. The name she had been born with. Scarlett Morgan, the name of the other her, before the crash, before The Day.

'Robyn?' Vivienne has stepped closer now, is guiding her towards the open door. 'Let's get you some air. Heather, could you get her a glass of water?'

Heather? Who the hell was Heather?

The policewoman gives a murmur of assent. Heather. Apparently. Robyn allows Vivienne to lead her out into the hot morning air. The sound of a faucet squealing on, of water splashing against glass. Footsteps, and the policewoman – Heather – hands her the glass, gaze darting, like she is afraid to look grief full in the face.

Robyn nods a thanks, takes a sip, because what the hell else is there to do?

Something tickles at the back of her mind, and she looks up, sharp enough to jerk the glass, sending a wave of water slopping over the rim. 'Who was it? Who killed my dad?'

She looks at Vivienne, only now the doctor isn't looking at her, has pulled back, is studying the slip-on loafers that she wears. Robyn thinks of the bottle of Jim Beam. The glasses.

'There were two glasses,' Robyn says, quietly. 'Someone drank with him. Then killed him.'

Luis has followed them outside, lingers awkwardly in the doorway. He grimaces, wipes a hand across his damp brow. 'We don't know anything yet, Rob. We're going to get the crime-scene techs out. Let's just wait and see.'

Bile sweeps up, burning her chest. Prickles of sweat on her forehead. It is not real. None of it is real. She quests about, seeking solid ground on which to stand. Then she thinks of her mother's words. 'I have to go home,' Robyn says, distantly. 'I have a conference call.'

They exchange glances again, and Vivienne makes a soft noise of dissent in the back of her throat. 'Robyn, you've had a terrible shock. Maybe you should cancel . . .'

'No. I have to.' Then, quietly, 'I'm going to be the Sandoval Company CEO.'

There is a lengthy silence then, and Robyn feels her feet move of their own accord. She turns back towards the house, her hand extending, passing the half-empty glass to the police officer. To Heather. She has to go. Because she is a Sandoval. And a Sandoval has responsibilities.

'I'll take you,' says Vivienne. 'Luis, you OK to follow up with her later?'

He nods. 'Get some rest, Robyn.'

Robyn turns, looking down towards the end of Main Street, to where the rock tunnel separates town from highway. She allows her gaze to track its way up the valley wall, up to the houses of Destino Heights, sparkling in the sunlight. 'The fire . . .' she says, distantly. 'Is it coming?'

Vivienne stops, following the path of her gaze. 'You mean the Seven Hills' fire? We're a long way from there. Thirty miles. We don't need to worry.' She tucks her arm through Robyn's. 'Come on. I'm parked down here.'

'You daydream too much . . .' Her dad's voice now. Not Mack's. Her other father. The one of her childhood. The one who had raised her and loved her and given to her. And who had shouted and frowned and scared her so badly that she had wet the bed until she was eleven. *'You never listen, you're never really here. Always off in some world of your own.'*

They are down the path now, past Elsie's. Vivienne's car sits in one of the spaces in front of the diner, nose in. A click of a car door unlocking.

'Robyn? Here you go.' Vivienne's hands guide her into the passenger seat.

'Sometimes I wonder if there is something wrong with that child. Imaginary friends and the stories she comes up with. It's not normal.'

'She's just a child, Alex. She's playing. That's all.'

Vivienne slides into the driver's seat.

'Do your kids . . . do they imagine a lot. I mean, like fantasies, stories . . .' Robyn hears her own voice coming from a great distance away.

Vivienne pulls the driver's door shut behind her, glances across at her. 'Sure. All kids do.'

'They ever . . . I mean, does it ever seem like they lose track, forget where fantasy ends, real life begins?'

'Robyn? What's going on?'

'No, I just . . . I daydream. My dad . . . my other dad . . . he always said that I daydreamed too much. And today . . . I don't know, something has felt off, weird, like I'm slipping, losing track of time, forgetting where I am.'

Becoming someone else.

Vivienne studies her, deep lines riveting her forehead. 'So has this just begun today?'

'Yes.'

'When did it first happen?'

'Just after I found Mack.'

Vivienne considers for long moments, then, 'OK . . . well, I mean, you've had a really nasty shock. To lose your father like that. It can play games with your mind.' She hesitates, choosing her words carefully. 'That said, it does sound rather like a petit mal episode. A form of epilepsy. It's where you lose awareness for a while. We . . . we should get you checked out.'

Robyn nods slowly. Beyond the car windshield, she can see Elsie's. It is dark, closed still. But within she can just make out the faint outline of Mags seated at a table, head in her hands. Thinks of Mags, of her father, Kelvin, fighting off death himself.

Robyn is somewhat of an expert at the losing of fathers. Or should be, at least. Almost six years now since Alex Sandoval's death. And that thought leads inevitably on to the moment when Mack had returned. Was perhaps six months after her adoptive father's passing. Had begun with a knock on the door, voices down the hall as her mother opens the door, an apologetic hello, an 'I thought it was time'. And then it had happened. Not an entire family, not by far, but enough of one that spaces that had been left blank for an eternity began to gain colour and form. He had the same hair as her, that had been her first thought. The same grey eyes, her second.

'Mack was a good man,' Robyn says.

There is a silence then, one that Robyn is only dimly aware of.

Then, 'Y'know,' Vivienne says, conversationally, 'I remember him from when I was a kid. Destino's golden boy. The firefighter, local hero.' She smiles fondly. 'Everyone just adored him.'

'He was so proud of that,' says Robyn, distantly. 'Being a

firefighter. That meant so much to him. Broke his heart when his back gave out, when he had to quit.'

Vivienne opens her mouth, then closes it again. She leans forward, turning the key in the ignition. The car growls to life and the figure beyond Elsie's window sits up straighter, looking towards the sound.

Robyn raises her hand, a thank you. Mags hesitating, then a hand raised in return.

Vivienne backs the car from the space, turning the wheel so that they face down Main Street. It is quiet, still. Too early for tourists.

'I'm sorry,' Robyn says, quietly. 'Your family must be wondering where you are.'

Vivienne glances across at her, voice casual. 'Oh, they're not at home. They've gone on out to Palm Springs. My in-laws have made it fifty years without killing each other, so we're making a party out of it. I'm going to follow along. Once . . .' Her voice peters out, and she shifts her attention back to the road ahead. 'Once I'm ready,' she finishes lightly.

The seatbelt presses against her flesh. A soft huff from the back seat, Hector's head resting on his paws. They drive slowly down Main Street. It looks the same, just as it had done when she had run along it. And yet, it is also entirely different, a Destino rewritten, its golden child lost. Then, inevitably, her mind flits to the memory of another Destino.

But perhaps there was an explanation now. Some kind of sanctioning of her hallucinations.

Epilepsy.

She looks to her arms. Still no tattoos.

'Epilepsy,' she murmurs, quietly.

'What's that?' asks Vivienne.

'Nothing.'

Vivienne nods slowly. Flips the indicator, right, pulling up outside the big house. 'Are you doing OK?'

Robyn nods.

Vivienne hesitates, studying her. Then, 'OK, look, if you're sure you don't need me, I'll drop you off. I have an appointment I need to get to. Up with Bonnie and Kelvin. But I'll be back.' She sighs. 'But if you need anything in the meantime, you call me, yes?' Her words tail away. 'Just . . . you promise me you'll get some rest.'

Robyn's hand moves to the seatbelt, clicks her free. Hears herself say thank you. And then she is out of the car, into the hot still air, is opening the rear door, a thud as Hector hops from the back seat. She moves across the drive, up wooden steps that groan beneath her. The sound of the car, engine purring, pulling away. Robyn pushes open the front door.

The television is on in the den, screen bright with orange flames, yellow-clad firefighters with pickaxes. A helicopter sweeps overhead, releasing its load in a whoosh. The room smells of roses. Sweet, floral. Beneath that, furniture polish. Robyn steps into the den, fingers running along the back of the overstuffed sofas.

'Robyn?' Her mother's voice floats from her office, further down the hall. 'Is that you?'

Her mouth opens to form a yes, but she can't seem to get the word out.

Her gaze hooks on the pile of books stacked neatly on the coffee table. Thick, bound, dense, The Sandoval Company in large print on the front cover. A primer for a budding CEO. Her head throbs, a pulsing pain that wraps its way around her skull.

Footsteps behind her. 'There you are.' Her mother has removed her jacket now, an unwilling concession to the heat. Wears a loose-fit blouse, her blonde, bobbed hair tucked behind one ear. 'Are you . . . OK?'

It is said with the tone of one who is unsure she wants the answer.

Robyn nods.

'Good girl.' She moves towards her daughter, leaning in, cheek pressing on cheek. The smell of lavender. 'It is an awful thing.' She pulls back, studies Robyn. 'But then, I suppose it was always on the cards.'

It takes her a moment, to piece the words together. Then, 'What was?'

Her mother hesitates, takes a step back. 'Well, I just mean . . . with his lifestyle, it always did seem unlikely that he would have a tremendously long life. Of course, no one could have anticipated it happening this way . . .'

It feels to Robyn that her mind has ground to a halt, bogged down in the words. 'What . . .?'

'Oh, darling, you know that Mack was rather fond of a drink,' offers her mother gently.

'OK . . . so he drank whiskey now and again . . .' A thought then, of another version of herself, of pumps that slip from her feet, the rattle of empty bottles in a plastic bin. The label on them, white with a red seal – Jim Beam whiskey. How many of them had there been?

Silence then, of the loaded variety, and her mother's gaze darts anywhere but at her.

'What?' asks Robyn. 'What are you trying to say?'

An exaggerated sigh, a moment, and then her mother fixes Robyn with a look. 'Darling . . . I know you don't want to hear it. I know you don't ever want to hear anything against him. But since he's come back . . . he's gained himself rather a reputation for his drinking.'

'That's not true!'

Eve fixes her with a look, sadness mixed with something else. 'Robyn, I . . . I'm afraid you aren't letting yourself see. You never have wanted to accept the idea that this idealised father of yours was less than perfect. I'm so sorry. But I think it's important you accept the truth, that you don't let yourself get carried away in some kind of fantasy. From what I have heard, he kept Bar 53 in profit.'

Robyn shakes her head, pulling herself up taller. 'It wasn't like that. You're making it sound like . . . like he was an alcoholic. He was *popular*. He had a lot of friends and yes, he would go to the bar with them . . .'

Her mother shakes her head. The sound of distant trilling, a phone ringing. 'I'm saying, before you go mourning the man as a saint, perhaps you should allow yourself to recognise who he actually was. Perhaps it would help.' She reaches out, a quick squeeze of her daughter's arm, then turns on her heel, heading towards the ringing phone. 'You should change. We have the call with the board soon.'

Chapter Ten

Mags Reyes – 25th September, 7.55 a.m.

'Did you hear?' Father Caprese stands in the doorway of the diner, his arm resting heavy on the handle. Breaths come laboured, sweat running along his temples.

Mags raises the coffee pot, eyebrows raised in question, and he waves her away.

'No, none for me. No time.' He shakes his head, mopping at his brow with the back of his hand. 'Awful day. Just awful.'

Mags nods, is not really listening. She grabs a mug from beneath the counter, carefully angles the pot over the top of it. Watches the dark liquid pour out, splashing against the sides of the mug. The television, hung high up on the wall, shows rolling news. A helicopter shot of flames that eat their way through forest.

She is thinking of Eve Sandoval. Of the way she stood, just inside the door, looking about the empty diner, the slightest of curls to her lip. Of the words that seemed to come at Mags, each one slashing at her. Death by a thousand cuts. *'There really is no choice. Difficult economic climate. Sandoval Company really has been very generous . . .'* And the feeling as it settled over her, another increase in rent, this one worse than all of those that had come before. A distant memory of opening her mouth to protest, the words simply refusing to come. The knowledge that these words, they signalled the end for Elsie's Diner.

The coffee splashes, sending a spray of liquid across the countertop, and Mags starts, suddenly aware that Father Caprese is watching her, awaiting a reaction of sorts. 'Yes,' she sets down the pot, 'awful.'

The Father pulls himself up tall, aware that he has an audience now. 'Fifty-eight. Fifty-eight-years-old. It's no age at all, is it? Awful,' he says again. 'Just awful.'

Mags bites her lip, grabs a cloth from beneath the counter, and sweeps it through the spilled coffee more roughly than she should.

'Awful,' she agrees quietly.

Strange, wasn't it, how life worked? How the entirety of her world had come to revolve around her father's desperate fight between life and death. And then death comes, to Mack, to the diner too. Like it has taken a turn, somewhere along the way. Perhaps, she thinks, a butterfly flapped its wings in the Andes.

'Well,' says Father Caprese, 'I should go. Lots to do. Robyn will need someone now, no doubt.'

Mags bites her lip, stifles the groan. As if the poor girl has not suffered enough! 'You take care, Father.' She watches him as he bustles down the long, cobbled path and, for a brief moment, imagines a world in which he trips, landing face first amongst the azaleas. Mags, she thinks, you are not a good Christian.

She spares a moment to hope that Robyn has escaped, has hopped into that expensive car that the Sandovals have, has headed on up the coast, out of town, away from the tender mercies of Father Caprese. But then, the thought of the Sandovals and she is right back to Eve and the diner's imminent demise. Mags sighs, rubs her face. Perhaps money was not sufficient to guarantee happiness after all.

She tosses the cloth into the sink, turns towards the two rough wooden shelves that stand above the counter. Teacups lined up on them, nice and neat in sentinel rows. She nudges the handle of the furthermost one so that it lines up with all the rest. And she feels her stomach knot up into a painful bow. The end is here. Just in a different form to the one she had anticipated.

Then a sound from the rear of the diner, the kitchen door rebounding off the wall.

'Maggie?' Her mother's voice sounds sharp, as if somehow she has already managed to disappoint her. 'Would you help me, please?' She emerges from the kitchen, a box full of pies in her arms. 'Take these. They're heavy.'

It isn't a warning. A 'careful you don't hurt yourself' in not so many words. It is a criticism. A judgement on all Mags has allowed her mother to bear. She takes the damn box, slides it wordlessly on to the counter.

Bonnie huffs, shaking out her hands, and drops her car keys onto the counter with a clatter. 'You heard the news? They said they're warning the communities around Seven Hills to prepare for a potential evacuation.' She pulls her purse from her shoulder, dumping it onto the countertop. 'Advisory, of course. Advice! They can advise all they like. If they think we're going anywhere, they have another think coming.'

Mags shakes her head. 'It won't come to that, Mom,' she says, distantly.

Bonnie moves around the counter, begins straightening already straight chairs. Mags can feel her shoulders rise, tighten. Trouble approaching. Doesn't need to turn to see. It is there in the scrape of chairs against lino, in the thwack, scree of it.

'Where are the kids, Mom? I thought you would have brought them with you.'

'I left them sleeping. Your father is with them.'

Mags looks at her mother. 'Mom . . . Dad shouldn't be looking after them. He's not well enough.'

Her mother waves her hand, lets loose a tut. 'For goodness' sake, Maggie. They'll be perfectly fine.'

Mags places the last cup, an elegant lavender one that she picked up in a flea market in Monterey. Bites her tongue. She considers, then says, softly 'How is Dad today?'

Her mother snorts. 'Oh, you know how that man is. He'll outlive all of us. Tough as old boots.'

Mags' mouth opens. She should tell her. Should say the words. *The Sandovals have increased the rent. There is no money to pay it.* Only she can't get her lips to work, mouth to form the words.

A flash on the television screen then, showing not the fire now but the lands surrounding it. Across the seemingly endless forests, along the mountain ridge, swooping down now to a familiar valley. The highway, the waterfall. The large houses of Destino Heights. Higher up the mountain, sunlight glinting off small trailers half buried in trees. The rolling text at the bottom of the screen – *areas surrounding Seven Hills are warned to prepare for evacuation.*

Bonnie stops, arms folded, studying the screen. 'Evacuation. I ask you! Those people up there in that trailer park. How do they think they're going to pay for that? Some of them, they don't have enough for the gas to get out of town, let alone anything else.' She reaches under the counter, pulls out a cloth and slaps it down onto a tabletop, with a harrumph of displeasure.

The footage has moved on now, sweeping closer in to Destino Heights. It focuses on a driveway, an SUV, its trunk open, a family loading it up.

'Oh, of course,' mutters Bonnie. 'Of course those people are making sure *they're* OK. Up there in their big fancy houses, of course they don't have to worry about how they're going to get out of harm's way. And do you think they're going to spare a second to worry about the rest of us? Of course they aren't. Destino Heights! Shouldn't be called that. Isn't Destino at all, just some rich person subdivision.'

'Mom . . .' Mags doesn't look at her mother, watches the

sweeping camera footage on the television. And she finds herself wondering what is coming. She can feel the disclosure, of their private impending disaster, right there on her tongue. But instead . . . 'Do you think . . . I mean, Dad, with his treatment, it's not going to be easy to move him. If the worst happens, I mean. Do you think we should . . .'

She hears the slap of the cloth onto the tabletop, the harrumph of displeasure. That did it. Mags doesn't turn. As though if she keeps her back to what she has done then she can pretend she hasn't done it. Even at the age of thirty-six, still pretending that she isn't nudging and pushing and barbing, a rebellious teen trying to outdo her mother. It is, she thinks, like the need to pick at a fresh-formed scab. You know you shouldn't. Know that if you do it will hurt and there will be bloodshed, yet somehow the trouble seems worth the pain.

'I'm just saying, Mom,' says Mags, 'the news, they say we need to be ready.'

Silence, the dense, stony type. Then, quietly, Bonnie says, 'You are being cruel. I am not discussing this with you.'

Perhaps, thinks Mags, she should simply let go. Cry. Scream and shout at the impenetrable wall of her mother. Perhaps that would help where all else has failed.

But Bonnie is on the move again, has shoved her chair back, is walking with a wide stride towards the window. She lingers there for a moment, her gaze hooked on the corner of Elm, where mountain gives way to Main. The SUV has made it now, down from Destino Heights. Indicates a left turn, down towards the highway.

'Those people,' Bonnie mutters again. 'Here for the good times. Gone for the bad. Hardly a surprise that the Sandovals would build a subdivision to look down on the rest of us.'

Maggie lowers her head, pulls towards her a cup of all but empty coffee and studies it. Could you drown yourself in two inches of liquid? At this point, it might be worth a try.

'That family . . . they've been a pox on this town.' Bonnie is into it now, has hit her stride, her voice clamouring with boiled-up anger. 'Every year. Every year it comes up. Like clockwork. *Rent raise*. Every damn year. And now this . . . You know they ran Connie's Cupcakes out of business?'

Mags sips the cold coffee. 'Connie's cupcakes tasted like boiled-over vomit.'

Bonnie ignores her, carries right on ranting. 'Logan, he was telling me the other day that if things don't pick up they're going to have to shut up shop. And that Eve Sandoval, she doesn't care. Just rattles along with her fancy clothes and her dyed blonde hair. No thought at all to what she's doing to the rest of us.'

Now. Tell her now.

Only her mouth won't move. Words won't come.

The sound of footsteps in the street beyond. Logan, from Destino Vino, heading up to the store, lingering long enough to give a cheery wave.

Mags waves right back, smile bright, easy. And she tries very hard not to see Logan's gaze, the way it flicks from her onto the empty cafe. Breakfast time. By rights this should be the opening onslaught of their busy time. Only a busy time is something Mags only very dimly remembers. She feels like Sisyphus, pushing away at that damn rock. Every day the same. Wake up, set the tables, put a pot of coffee on, ready the ovens. All for customers who never come. It's the changes, her mother said, people in this town, they like things the way they like them. All this environmentally friendly, vintage nonsense, it's driven customers away. Mags thinks it's Bonnie, with her barely contained rage that's done the driving.

She leans closer to the glass, the heat from it reflecting back on her so that it feels that she is standing beneath a spotlight. She watches Logan, the rear of him still unmistakable with that lengthy walk that looks more like a skip. He holds a phone to his ear, lets loose a tinkle of laughter as someone from somewhere else makes his day that tiny bit better.

Mags shifts her gaze, leaning close to the hot glass, looking up the street towards the church. Workers scurry, so many ants in their fluorescent jackets. They are digging up the street today, cutting a big hole at the intersection of Woodland and Cedar. Some utilities company who have suddenly realised that they haven't caused chaos here for too long. Traffic is going to snarl up, hooked around those orange cones. She turns, looking down the street towards the town sign, back up towards the mountain. Empty. Maybe traffic wouldn't be a worry after all.

Mags closes her eyes, a cold hand on the back of her neck, punching through the unbearable heat of the day. The ceiling fans swirl, achieving little, only the dance of unbreathable air. 'It's quiet out there,' she offers. An olive branch.

'Well.' Her mother picks up a teacup, one of those she had found out at Carmel, with the gold trim, daisy chain pattern lining its base. Bonnie studies it, expression fierce, then sets it back down. 'Of course it's quiet. This heat. Feels like you can't breathe out there. And then with the news and all that hysteria about the fire . . .' She shakes her head. 'Anyway . . . I forgot to tell you, I told the kids they could stay again tonight.'

Mags' stomach clenches, a ringing filling her ears. That was the trouble with this town and this life, it brought few troubles, but those that came were painfully regular and predictable. She breathes deep, once, twice, just as her therapist had told her. 'Mom,' she says, voice carefully calm, 'they have school tomorrow.'

Her mother snorts, wiping her hands on the poppy print apron at her waist. 'Well, it won't hurt them, not this once. Your father wants to spend time with them, Maggie.'

Mags stares down at the mug, torn. Between throwing it on the floor and screaming, or hurling it directly at her mother, cutting out the middleman.

'You need to talk to me about these things,' she says, 'before you suggest them to my children.'

Bonnie looks up at her, straightening her back so she is pulled up to her fullest height of five foot two inches. 'They are my grandchildren, Margaret. And I have already promised them.' Her expression shifts then, a move from fury to charm. 'You have yourself a night off. Watch a movie, go for a drink with that Luis one. He would be thrilled, you just know it. The kids will be fine up the mountain with me.'

She should battle it. On principle she should. Should say no, I am their mother and what I say goes. Only she is tired. Just so damn tired.

'Fine,' Mags sighs, 'take them.'

A police car passes, lights flashing, and Bonnie stops, watching its process down Main Street. And it hits Mags: that she has forgotten, that those short moments with Eve have stripped all else away. She shakes her head. 'Mom . . . I should have said. Mack Morgan, he's dead.'

Chapter Eleven

Robyn Sandoval – 25th September, 8.05 a.m.

She pulls on a pair of loose-fit linen trousers, navy, a single button on the waist. A buttercup yellow blouse, sleeveless. It shows off the arc of her triceps, the lean angles at her clavicle. Yet still she tries not to look at her reflection. It is deliberate, a concentrated focus on the movement of her hands, on the feel of the fabric. Because that focus, it shoos away the thoughts: of Mack, lying dead in his bed, of that other reflection, with short hair and concave cheeks, arms lined with tattoos. Scarlett.

Hector watches her, head resting on paws, head canted to one side.

He knows that something is wrong.

'It's OK, buddy,' she murmurs.

They both know that she is lying.

She has imagined it, more often than she cares to admit. Who she would have been had she remained Scarlett Morgan. Had it never happened, that day and that crash. Has played the story out often enough that it has come to feel like a movie she has seen, time and again.

Perhaps then, she thinks, that is the answer. That the strain of it all, of . . . of what has happened, that it has fractured something in her brain, has catapulted her from this awful reality into a petit mal seizure, populated with a fiction instead.

She pulls in a breath, steps close enough to the mirror that her breath fogs the glass. She stares at the high cheekbones, at the thin lips. A flash now, a sudden vision of her father's features overlaid across her own.

And then it comes, reality hitting home hard.

He is gone.

A tear spills. Grey eyes, just like her father.

It is a little like being a species unto yourself, when you are adopted, when you do not see your own reflection reflected in the faces around you. A painful uniqueness. And then, one day there is a knock on the door and footsteps in the hall and you look up and it is as if the mirror has come to life.

The tears are coming faster now. Robyn pulls out the hairband, lets her hair sway about her face. She brushes it, hard enough that her scalp stings.

There's something kind of big I need to talk to you about.

It is a story left on a cliffhanger. A book with the final pages missing.

It cannot have been a murder. A tragedy, yes. But a cruelty?

Her father, charming and gregarious, sociable and kind. Her father, the hero. Because hadn't she grown up with it, her origin story? Tragic mother, heroic father, CalFire's rising star. And then he comes back and time has passed and life has shifted, age taking hold and his back giving out, until that job of his, it moves just out of reach.

Robyn pulls open her dressing-table drawer. The locket is gold, a narrow chain. A photograph inside of Mack, and a six-week-old version of herself. He had given it to her, back on the day that he returned. 'Something,' he said, 'so that you will know that I never forgot about you.' She fastens it around her neck.

Who would ever want to kill him?

But then, that vicious little whisper in the back of her mind.

You just never let yourself see.

'Robyn?' Her mother's voice filters through the floorboards. Hector lifts his head, curious. 'Are you nearly ready?'

Robyn wipes her tears, the back of her hand slick with them. 'Yes,' she calls. Her voice cracks.

She reaches for the concealer pot. A dust of powder. A slick of lipstick. The reflection morphing now, father's feature's vanishing and giving way to someone new.

Robyn Sandoval. The heir apparent of the Sandoval Company.

Was there ever a question? Ever a conversation about how her life would be?

No. It was a given. An adoption rite. *This is who you are.*

'Well, are you coming? The meeting is in five minutes.'

Robyn steps back from the mirror, bare feet cold on tiled floors. The feel of Hector's weight, nudging against the backs of her legs. Her body moving without her. She walks down the stairs, steps groaning beneath the weight of human and canine combined. The office door stands ajar, laptop open, waiting. Her mother stands, leafing through a thick paper file.

'OK, the board are going to want to have some kind of plan in place for Destino Heights. Fire-wise, that is. So I've spoken to my contact out at county, nudged them in the direction of prioritising the Heights. I mean, who can say how these things go, right? But I've made it clear, as a company we would be appreciative of his help.'

'And the rest of Destino?'

Her mother checks her make-up in a compact. 'What about them?'

'What's going to happen to them? If the fire comes?'

Eve shrugs, tucks the mirror away. 'They're free to do what they want.' She gives her daughter a look. 'It's a case of individual responsibility. They can evacuate whenever they want to.'

'Can they?'

'What do you mean?'

Thinks of the spreadsheets, of profits and loss, of the properties the company owns, up and down Main Street. Of the homes, scattered throughout the town. Of the rents the Sandoval Company charges, that have increased year on year.

'Mom,' says Robyn, quietly, 'people can't afford it. To shut down their businesses, pay for a hotel, for gas, food . . .'

Eve sighs, waves her hand, impatient. 'Honey, I know you're having a rough day, but I'm not doing this with you right now.'

The laptop begins to trill. An incoming call.

'OK,' her mother smooths down her blouse, 'that's them. You want to sit?'

Robyn can feel it, her own traitor body moving to comply. Then, 'No.'

Eve pulls up short, her finger hovering over the answer key. 'What?'

'I can't do this.'

And she turns on her heels and is gone.

Chapter Twelve

Bonnie Aubrey – 25th September, 8.45 a.m.

'The fire is, at this stage, under control. Firefighters say they currently have the blaze contained to the Seven Hills' region. But they have warned that, with winds forecast to increase as the day continues, evacuation orders are becoming more likely by the minute. Residents of Destino, Haven and Fallbrook are advised to check their homes for fire safety. That includes cleaning out gutters of debris and ensuring that all trees and undergrowth are cut well back from the house. They are advised to have a go-bag ready, including important documents and medications, and to stay tuned to the news to chart the progress of the fires and any evacuation notices . . .'

'It doesn't look great, Bon.'

Bonnie can still feel the heat of the early morning on her skin. Sweat clings to her, the cost of the hurry up the mountain. She folds her arms, stares at the screen, the helicopter sweeping across treetops, red flames that clamber up into the sky, reaching for it. And for a moment, she doesn't hear him. Barely talks in more than a whisper now. Not that Kelvin ever was loud. Always seemed to have the volume set to low. Now, though . . . she looks back at him, rolls her eyes theatrically. 'Oh now, you know how people are these days. Always looking for a crisis.'

Kelvin huffs, a version of a laugh. 'Well, if it's crisis they want, it's crisis they're getting.' He angles his head, eyes crinkling. 'Will not be told, will you, Bon?'

She smiles, flaps her hands, turns her head away so that he will not see her cry. She doesn't look at Vivienne, the doctor who seems to be little more than a child to her.

The younger woman makes a show of it, leaning back against the bedroom door, watching the older-than-Moses television that stands propped on the dresser. Making it real clear that she is not looking at Bonnie, that she does not see the tears.

'Well,' Vivienne says, carefully, 'let's hope they keep doing what they're doing. They have good people up there on the fire line.'

Bonnie sniffs. Doesn't really know why, just seems to be an instinct now, like when you go to the doctor's and they tap you on the knee with the little hammer and your leg kicks. Seems to Bonnie that anger is muscle memory these days. 'They best be good people. Not just there so that the whole world looks at them like they're heroes.'

A silence then, dense and heady.

No one looks at her.

It is a thing that happens, this strange fog of invisibility that rolls in, right behind her anger. And Bonnie has a sudden memory of a different version of herself. Of different reactions, smiles and laughter, not at her, but with her. A sense that she had brightened the room by coming into it. Whatever happened to that girl?

'Anyway,' says Vivienne, faux bright, 'you, Mr Aubrey, are all set. You have all your pain meds, yes? And the nurse will be back in the morning anyway, but just for the time being . . .'

Kelvin waves at her, a weary half-smile. 'You run along, Doc. You go have fun with those little girls of yours.'

Vivienne grins. 'Jesse got to have lots of fun on the drive to Palm Springs. The *Encanto* soundtrack on repeat. Now, that's the kind of parental fun I'm OK missing out on.'

Kelvin heaves a coughing laugh, and Bonnie scowls, the wrenching sound of it twisting at her insides.

It was like that.

You didn't see it. Not when you lived it. Did not see the change coming, creeping slow enough that it seemed like it had been there this whole time. You could fool yourself, that it wasn't happening at all.

And then, something happened. Like the doctor coming in, to check on his progress. Making him laugh. Only it's not the laugh you have always known, sounds instead like a seam rupturing, right down in the bowels of the earth. And then you saw it. Like you were riding along behind Vivienne's eyes, taking in the shape of him. A narrow man, always, swimmer's build was what he would say. Scarecrow build, Bonnie would retort. Only now it seemed that all the meat on him had just melted away, that the cancer, or the treatment of the cancer – poison by another name – that the whole of it added together had begun to eat through him. Had started with the meagre portion of fat that had once lined his bones. His cheeks had flattened, turning concave. His jawbone and cheekbones sticking out, sharp enough that it looked as if they would cut through the skin. His hair, once thick and dark, had fallen out, the roots of it battered in an endless cycle of chemo.

'Hush, Kelvin,' Bonnie mutters. 'Stop being silly.' She turns away from the bed, scowls at the television, and tries to ignore the reflection of her husband in the flames. The hair would come back. His body would flesh out, cheeks fill again. Once all was done. Once this was behind them.

'So,' says Vivienne, with that awful faux brightness that people adopt around the dying, 'what is the plan?'

Kelvin leans his head back against the heap of pillows, smiles softly. 'Well, in about an hour, *Judge Judy* is on. I'm gonna watch *Judge Judy*.'

Vivienne smiles wryly. 'I see. Good plan.' She glances up at Bonnie. 'OK, well, I have some paperwork here I need you to sign, so shall we . . .?'

Bonnie nods, turns on her heel and leads the doctor into the family room. She pulls up sharp in front of the windows. The windows are why they bought this house, thirty years ago. Wide eyes that gaze down over Destino, the valley beyond. Bonnie stands, close enough to the glass that she can feel the heat of it sear her skin. Can hear the sound of chatter from the family room downstairs. That high-pitched whine of whatever godawful game the children were playing now, the odd burst of conversation.

'Kids here?' asks Vivienne.

'Their mother wanted some time to herself,' Bonnie says distantly. 'So where's the paperwork then?'

Vivienne sighs, sets her bag down on the sofa. 'Bonnie . . . there's something we need to discuss. With the fire . . . I think it would be wise for us to be prepared. There is talk of evacuation, if the wind changes. If that happens . . . it's going to be far harder to arrange care, to get you both out.'

'I can manage,' says Bonnie, stoutly.

'No,' says Vivienne, firmly. 'You can't. He is very weak. He can no longer stand.'

'I am aware.' Bonnie scowls at her. 'It's me who gets him back and forth from the toilet, who cleans him up when he doesn't make it in time.'

'Yes,' Vivienne sighs. 'It *is* you. And I'm worried that you have so much to deal with here that you're not looking at the bigger picture. Look, there's a hospice, down in Cambria. I've spoken with them. They could take him for a couple of days, just until the threat from this fire has passed. They can have someone up to collect him within the hour. He would be comfortable there. And then, if the worst happens, if the fire comes, you could evacuate without worrying about . . .'

Bonnie does not look at her. Is studying the shape of the valley below, the curves and the dips of it, as familiar to her as her own face in the mirror. This valley, as much a part of the life of her as her children. As her husband. 'No,' she says, distantly.

'Bonnie—'

'Vivienne, we are not leaving.' She snorts. 'Honestly, the whole world has gone mad. Always on the lookout for the next catastrophe, everyone just waiting for the next opportunity to cause panic. That fire is Seven Hills' problem. Not ours.' She turns, fixes Vivienne with a look. 'You youngsters, forever borrowing trouble.'

There is a heavy silence, Vivienne's lips compressed tight. Then, 'It's not about borrowing trouble, Bonnie. It's about being prepared, being aware of which way things could go.'

Bonnie shakes her head, looks away, back to the lip of the mountains that ring Destino. 'You see that ridge? It has protected us, our whole lives. No fire has ever crossed it. You think this is the first time we've had this? You think this is the first time the media has threatened the end of the world? And every time, that ridge protected us.' She can feel it now, the irritation building again. Can feel it seep into her words. 'Kelvin, all he wants is to be in his home. To watch goddam *Judge Judy*. And you want me to ruin that for him?'

Vivienne is quiet for a moment, then says, 'Bonnie. I'm trying to help you.'

A bright, frozen moment. Then a sinking feeling that creeps across her, that memory again of a different Bonnie, the one she used to be. One whose skin didn't prickle with righteous fury, whose words didn't come out sharp and pointed. She purses her lips, then allows herself the slightest of nods.

The closest to an apology she could seem to bring herself these days.

Vivienne moves closer. 'Bonnie,' she says, carefully, 'I'm worried about you.'

Bonnie waves her away. 'I'm fine.'

'Yes,' says Vivienne, slowly, 'I know you're strong. I know that. But I worry, Bonnie. That you aren't letting yourself see the truth of things. That you haven't accepted . . . what's to come.'

There is a cloud now, a wispy tendril creeping over the farthest mountain, hanging above the distant shape of Destino Heights. Can see figures moving along Main Street, Destino beginning to come alive now. Can see the diner, watches as people walk past it, never looking. Wonders when that happened, when the beating heart of the town stilled. Her gaze tracks up, past the diner, towards the little house perched on the mountain.

'I heard,' Bonnie says quietly, 'about Mack Morgan.'

Vivienne sighs. 'Yes.' She steps closer, follows the line of Bonnie's gaze. 'I used to idolise that man when I was a kid. The firefighting. That big fire, the one out in Haven when he saved all those people? Big reason why I wanted to become a doctor. I wanted to help people, just like he did.' She shakes her head slowly. 'I can't believe he's gone.'

The sun has broken through the layer of cloud, is glinting off the gold of the church steeple. 'Those days, they were a long time ago.' Back when the world was brighter, back when she was something other. 'People change.' She turns to look at Vivienne. 'Scary thought, that there's someone out there willing to kill. You know who did it yet?'

Vivienne makes a noncommittal sound. 'Not yet.'

Bonnie nods, looks out towards Destino. 'Terrible thing.'

Chapter Thirteen

Robyn Sandoval – 25th September, 8.50 a.m.

Robyn lets the front door slam behind her, steps out into the hard sun. She raises her hand to her eyes, looks to the ridge. The merest hint of smoke that furls across it, lifted up and carried over by an easy breeze. Her heart thumps. There is a sense of walking away. Not from her mother or the meeting, but rather from a planned out future. But the thoughts of that, the what have I dones? The what will happen nows? They vanish into the early morning heat. Because her father is still dead.

She crosses the front porch, its planks groaning loudly beneath the weight of her sneakers. Down the steps, two, three, and then onto the drive. The breeze sends a shiver through the Indian Paintbrush and their sunset orange petals dance in a wave. She walks steadily and tries to focus, to concentrate on her steps, one after another. Reaches Main Street, takes a right, drops down through the rock tunnel. Traffic is light, the few cars that pass oozing soporifically, as though the heat of the day has slowed them down too. The tunnel is cool, quiet, and then she is through and the sun beats down on her again, glints off a gold plaque.

Harper Morgan. Wife. Mother. Died September 25th, 1992.

The Day. How was it possible that he has gone too? That

The Day had suddenly become THE DAY. Was there some connection? Had Mack died because it was the anniversary of Harper's death? Or was she simply doing that thing that people do, thinking that there are no such things as coincidences when in fact nature throws up coincidences wherever the hell she feels like. Robyn crouches down before the stone, dry grass scratching at her legs. This had always been here, as long as she can remember. Has been the one thing linking this her with that her. A rock with a plaque, a testament to the day on which her world had split in two. She had come here as a child. Her mother had brought her, had picked up a bouquet of lilies from the flower store over in Haven, had picked out her nicest dress and had brought her down here, every September 25th. To remember where you came from. Had never felt real to her, not really. Had simply been a day on which she wore a pretty dress and carried pretty flowers. Destino's child. Because, after all, wasn't that simply who she was? Robyn Sandoval. Born Scarlett Morgan. The girl whose life could be split into two parts.

She reaches out, smooths the tips of her fingers over the plaque. Would it be amended now? she wonders. To add Mack's name beneath?

She hadn't questioned it, not for the longest time. Why death had taken one parent but she had lost two, the entirety of her birth family gone in the blink of an eye. Had simply been the way things were, the shape of her life. There had been cards, Christmas, birthdays. Always signed the same way, *from Mack, your loving Papa*. And then Mack had returned. Had been working, down in LA. Hadn't been able to stand it, remaining in Destino once Harper was gone. 'And I always knew I wasn't enough for you,' he had said, 'not to raise you alone. You deserved better.' And so he had left.

Robyn runs her finger over the ridges of the date. It hadn't been an answer, had it? Not really. *You deserved better. And so I left.*

Her head is beginning to ache, a band of pressure that has wrapped itself tight around her temples, and she gives it the briefest of shakes. Like that will make any difference at all. She pushes herself up to standing, her fingers brushing grass from her legs, and now is moving.

She walks, with long strides. Because it is too much. This and that and all the things that came before. And so she narrows it down, pulls her focus in. On Mack lying dead in his bed. On the blood on the pillow. On two glasses.

He was in Bar 53 last night.

She walks, through the tunnel, cool and then hot again. Onto Main Street. It is so quiet. Robyn glances to her right, along Buttonwillow. There are cars in drives, more than there should have been for this time of day. She slows, gaze drawn by movement on the left-hand side. Two children, little more than toddlers, sit, their legs folded on the dried-out grass. A middle-aged man struggles, angling suitcases into the trunk of an SUV. A vacation, perhaps. Or something else. She raises her nose, sniffs the air. Does the smoke smell stronger now?

Or is it only her imagination, another story to spin.

She thinks of the trailer park, of that other reflection in the mirror. 'Petit mal,' she mutters. 'It is petit mal.' Not madness or a tumble down the rabbit hole. Seizures. Seizures were . . . OK. They were real and made sense and meant that she could tuck the thought of it away, could put it down to the stress of finding her father dead.

Robyn shakes her head, reorients, focusing on her feet again. They carry her along Main Street towards the wide-open doors of Bar 53. Cool, air-conditioned air sweeps out at her, vanishing in the wall of heat.

She hesitates, lingering on the threshold. Then ducks inside. It is cool in here, verging on cold, and Robyn blinks as her eyes adjust to the darkness.

The television plays, rolling out commentary to an empty

bar. 'CalFire is still saying that the fire is currently contained within the Seven Hills' area. But authorities are warning those in the vicinity of Destino, Haven and Fallbrook that they should be prepared for a potential evacuation should the situation change.'

'Son of a—'

'Hey!'

Harry starts, dropping the broom he is holding to the floor with a clatter. 'Jesus. Sorry. Robyn. Hi.' He ducks down, picking up the broom and propping it against the bar. 'Hey. God, I heard. I'm so sorry. Your dad . . . I just . . . I can't believe it.'

Robyn nods. Her head is pulsing. She clears her throat, it comes out as a growl. 'Uh huh. You're open early.'

Harry shakes his head, looks around at the empty bar. 'Yeah . . . I had some wild idea about opening up early, doing breakfasts.' He opens his arms wide. 'Worked out well, don't you think?'

Robyn smiles sadly, nods towards the television. 'The fire is still holding then?'

'Yeah,' Harry sighs, leans back against the bar, folding his arms across his barrel chest. 'Looks like it.' He shakes his head. 'Seriously. I can't afford to evacuate, shut the bar down for God knows how long . . . I'll be lucky if I get to open it back up again.'

Robyn doesn't answer, but glances around the empty bar, back to Harry.

'Yeah, yeah . . . I know . . . damn news is keeping people away. Whole town has been dead for days.' He blanches at his use of the word. 'Sorry. Anyway . . . look, I need to say . . . your father . . . I'm going to miss him. And not just for the cash he put in the till.'

Robyn's lips purse. Harry flushes, waves his hands.

'I didn't mean it like . . .' He sighs. 'They know who did it? Hard to believe something like that could happen in a town like this.'

'Not yet. Do you know of anyone who . . . who had an issue with him?'

Harry shakes his head. 'Nah. Life and soul was Mack. Can't imagine anyone wanting to do this to him.'

Robyn pulls in a breath. 'I need to know, Harry. The truth, I mean. I'm hearing things. People are saying . . . I mean, I know he liked a drink, but . . . I always thought it was just that he was, y'know, being sociable, hanging out with his friends. But now . . . how bad was it?'

The older man looks at her, wary. 'Oh, kid, it—'

'No,' she says, firmly. 'The truth.'

He considers, choosing his words with care. 'He was . . . it was getting pretty intense.' He sighs, leans back against the bar. 'Now, you gotta remember, I've known your dad my whole damn life. We went to high school together, so I've seen how things have played out for him. And, yeah, he's always liked a drink, had a bit of a wild streak to him. He's been getting worse recently, though. Kind of like he'd made it his mission to drink me dry.'

Robyn nods. Is aware now that her heart has begun to beat, louder, louder, seems like it will beat right out of her chest. She shakes her head, fights to concentrate. 'I knew he'd been finding things tough. I thought it was Harper, the fact that the anniversary was approaching. That he was struggling with that . . .' Her head has begun to pound. She rubs her forehead, forcing herself to focus. 'Tell me about last night.'

Harry folds his arms across his chest. 'So he came in, I don't know, maybe around nine. It was pretty quiet. Like I said, this damn news is scaring everyone away. I was pleased to see him. Shifts get pretty long when its just you and the TV. But I guess he wasn't feeling it. Wasn't in the mood to talk. Said he had something weighing on him, that he just wanted to drink and forget about stuff.'

'He didn't say what?'

Harry shakes his head. 'Wouldn't be drawn. In the end, I left him to it.'

'And kept serving him,' Robyn says, quietly.

Harry's expression changes then, shifts. 'Guess you gotta be a business owner trying to keep up with the Sandoval rates to understand.'

It hangs there, sharp in the air between them.

'What about when he left? He walked? I hope . . .' she says softly.

'Well, walk is a strong word,' says Harry. 'He could barely stand. No way was he making it home without help.'

'Who helped him?'

He frowns at her. 'Luis. Luis took him home.' He gives a wan smile. 'I figured if he was OK with anyone, it's gonna be a cop.'

A wave of dizziness washes over her, the pressure at her temples, building, building.

'Robyn? You . . . OK?'

Nausea was coming now, her heart thumping, hard enough that it fills up the world around her.

'Fine.' Her voice comes from far away. 'I'm gonna go get some air.'

And then she is outside and the world is darkening and then, just like that, she is gone.

Chapter 14

There were clear skies on the day that fire broke out in Seven Hills. A vivid blue that stretched across the horizon, not a wisp of cloud. Of course, the people out in Seven Hills, they had gotten used to that by now. That painful blue, unadulterated by white or grey. Had been twelve weeks since the last drop of rain. Twelve long, dry, hot weeks. And what had begun as California gloriousness had descended into something else, something sinister. The residents of this patch of earth, the one that stretches from the Pacific coast towards the Santa Lucia mountains, that reaches from Los Osos in the south, to San Simeon in the north, as one had begun to look to the skies, their gaze pulled by some deep, mammalian instinct. That trouble was coming.

On the day that fire broke out, the blue skies had settled heavy over the land below, the weighty heat, topping a hundred on the thermometer. In Seven Hills, a little town – although perhaps town is stretching the definition of the word – nestled in the foothills of the Santa Lucia range, its residents, they had opened their doors, had looked to the skies, and had felt the faintest stirring of a breeze. For some of them, the breath of air had brought relief. To others, the ones who read the newspapers and who trimmed the trees around their home and who kept a go-bag in the front hall, the breeze had brought something else. Fear.

Funny, isn't it? How the same scene can cut both ways. For some, looking out over the parched, dry lawns, and seeing a place to spread a blanket, yet one more chance to work on a tan. For others, looking out over the parched, dry lawns, seeing fuel.

And it was good fuel. It was the kind of fuel that cried out for fire. The long drought had pulled the moisture from the grass and the trees, making them brittle and crisp. Had drained the moisture from the air itself. And the temperatures, they just kept on climbing. Yesterday one hundred and one. Today one hundred and three. Seemed to some like the whole world was just preparing itself, like what they were seeing was the deep breath before the storm.

In the land above Seven Hills, the dry grass and the parched trees, and the wind that makes them dance and sing, and then . . .

Later, there would be questions, the kind that inevitably follow a disaster. How and who and where and, most of all, why. So many questions, the answers to each of them tumbled up in the next. On this day, though, there was the grass and the trees and the underbrush that had gathered over years and years and years, filling up the forest floor. Because they had been lucky, if luck was the right word for it. There had been no fire here, not for the better part of a hundred years. Oh, there had been the threat of it. Had been smoke hanging in the air, and the heat and the fuel. But these foothills and these towns, they had always remained just on the right side of disaster.

Not today.

It began with a bird. A starling, to be precise, still young enough to be rounded out, its feathers fluffed with grey down. Circling and swooping, sweeping by dried-out leaves with wings extended full. Then it ducked, closing up its wings, descending to a likely perch. Later, the people will wonder, what would have happened had it lingered in the air just a moment longer? How much then would have changed?

That, of course, is all redundant, because the starling descended, claws outstretched, landing on the taut power line that ran right before the line of trees. What happened next was perhaps inevitable. Claws closing around lines, pulling them tight together. Then a spark, an electrical arc that looped out from one to the other, sending thousands of volts through the small bird. His story, then, done. His effects though, were only beginning. He fell, tumbling from the power line to the dried-out land below, landing heavy in amongst the undergrowth.

If you were watching, there would be a moment when that would seem to be the end of it. A sad, bright day. A dead bird.

Then the spark. The flame from the electrocuted feathers catching on the dry brush. A moment when it seems likely that it will gutter and die. Then whoosh.

The fire took hold, eating its way through bone-dry forest and brush, the drought that had come before clearing the way for it. It spread its way across the hillside, lighting up the skies above Seven Hills, fuelled by a wind that blew to the south.

And so it began. The resources deployed, evacuation orders issued. The fire bedding down, settling in for the long haul as it burned. For days and days and days.

But for the people of Destino, all of this might as well be occurring in another world. For Seven Hills was a good distance, thirty miles away as the crow flies. The wind that carried the flame funnelling it towards the south, angling it far enough away that even the most resolute planner begins to question – perhaps then, it would be OK after all . . .

It would not.

Chapter Fifteen

Scarlett Morgan – September 25th, 8.50 a.m.

A tendril of green brushes her cheek. Robyn reaches up, sweeps it away, her fingers lingering on her cheek. Something catches her eye and she lifts her arm. Her stomach clenches. The air, hot, still, light radiating through glass walls of a sunroom she does not recognise. Vines wrap their way around her forearm, clambering to her wrist.

Scarlett.

'Oh God,' she mutters.

Petit mal. Petit mal.

She turns in space, looks down at herself. Same cut-off jean shorts, same once-were-black pumps. She reaches out, runs her fingers across the tattoos, can feel the skin, warm and soft. There is a smell in the air, of bright citrus.

Could you smell things in seizures? Could you feel things in seizures?

'Well,' the voice that comes from her is low and throaty, 'I have clearly lost my mind.'

She closes her eyes, squeezes them tight. Opens them, just a sliver. Nope. Still there.

'Yup. Lost it.'

Her lips are moving and the words come from her, and yet

still it feels as if she is a passenger, along for the ride.

'OK, breathe. Just breathe.'

She inhales, pulling in hot air. Leaves move beneath the pressure of her breath. They hang from carved wooden shelves, draped across wrought-iron struts. Plant upon plant, they climb up to the ceiling, blocking out harsh sunlight. Beside the plants, a basket-weave chair, the seat of it having seen better days, bowed and shaped with years of use. A bag stands open on the floor beside the shelves, a manila folder sticking out of the top. A see-through bag with boxes of medications. A fabric-wrapped first aid kit. A go-bag. Ready to go. A large cardboard box beside it. Printed on it, the words, Destino Wildfire Preparedness Programme.

I don't know this place.

And yet, within that, something about it is familiar.

She pushes aside a dangling ivy, leaning in close to the hot glass. Beyond the windows the soft curve of a hill, the brush and the arc of it ones that she recognises. Can just about see the ridge from here, its proud line of trees. She follows the curve of the ridge. By her reckoning, she is somewhere off the end of Bay Tree Lane. Who does she know here?

She shakes her head, as though that way she will dislodge the craziness of it all. 'I'm not going crazy. I'm not going crazy.' Then, 'I mean, I am talking to myself, and that probably isn't a great sign, but apart from that . . .' Shakes her head again. Like it will be more successful a second time.

It is not.

Then a sound from somewhere deeper within the house. Voices.

She steps closer to the door of the sunroom, can see a family room beyond. It groans with bookcases, overstuffed. A mug of coffee sits, half-drunk, on a coffee table.

'Look, I didn't know what else to do with her. My phone is blowing up. CalFire are calling all the volunteers out to Seven

Hills. Much as I'd love to hang around and deal with . . . whatever this is. I gotta go. People's lives depend on me.'

'Right. Sure.'

'What does that mean?'

Silence, then, 'You can tell yourself you're in it for other people as much as you like. You can kid yourself that you're the hero. But, let's be honest, you haven't traditionally prioritised CalFire. And it's not a great time to start doing it now.'

'Jesus! That was a long time ago.'

'Yeah. It was. Not much has changed, though.'

A pregnant pause then, 'You been talking to Luis?'

'What if I have? What are you worried about?'

'I'm just saying, is all. Don't believe everything he tells you. Whatever. Look. I'm serious. I don't know what to do with that girl anymore. I'm genuinely worried she's losing it. One minute she's hugging me and weeping like she hasn't seen me for the better part of a decade, next she's screaming at me, telling me I'm a shitty father.'

There is a sound then, soft enough to be deniable, a snort.

A loaded silence, then, 'OK, whatever. Only then she's like she doesn't know where she is. Doesn't remember banging my door off its hinges. I'm telling you, that kid's got issues.'

'She's not a kid.' The woman's voice is low, mellifluous. 'She's a grown woman.'

'Fine. She's grown. But seriously, this aggression . . . I mean, we all know what has happened in the past because she couldn't control herself.'

There is a loaded silence. 'I don't think you get to comment on that, Mack, do you?'

'Say what you like about me, but I didn't make her go toe-to-toe with her captain. Whatever she has done to her life, *she* has done. Not me.'

Robyn steps lightly, follows the sound of the voices through the family room, towards the pool of light beyond. The smell of coffee. A tortoiseshell cat sits on the kitchen counter, its tail switching from side to side. Mack stands, his back resting against a narrow refrigerator, legs akimbo, arms folded. An expression on his face that she has not seen before.

Robyn pulls in a breath, can feel the tears prickle at the backs of her eyes. Studies him, the heavy weight on his brow, the way his lip furls. She drinks it in. A story she is telling herself, petit mal. But if this is it, if this is the shape of the seizures, bringing back to her what has been lost, then she does not want to awake.

She steps softly, not wanting to draw attention, to break the moment, this waking dream. It'll be gone soon enough, and when it is gone, her father will be too.

'Mack.' The woman's voice is soft, reproachful. 'I don't know what you want me to tell you. It's been too much for her. All of it. Just too much crazy, too much dysfunction. She's not broken, she's just a bit . . . battered. You are too hard on her.'

'So it's my fault then?'

A sigh. 'You know what? Yes. Yes, Mack, it's your fault. All the chaos. You here. You gone. You here again and gone again. And it's my fault.' The voice gets quieter, barely audible now. 'I should have . . . I don't know . . . I should have done better. I should have paid more attention. I don't know what I should have done. Something. You know she lost this most recent job too? Zeke says she had some kind of disagreement with her manager, something and nothing, and she just walks out. Just tells the manager that Target could go screw itself.'

'For God's sake . . .'

'Well, what do you expect? She learned to run from you. Her entire life, all she has ever seen is you running away when the going gets tough. She does exactly the same thing. You can't get mad at that. She's just doing what she's seen her daddy doing.' A pause, then, 'And she drinks. Because that's what she's seen her daddy do too. She's been offered some job down in Oxnard. Bar manager. Zeke says she's thinking about taking it. But honestly, with the way things have been for her lately . . . feels like there's only one way a job like that is going to end up. Mack . . . we have to do something to help her.'

Robyn's breath catches in her throat, a knowledge of . . . something . . . settling over her. She steps softly, edging towards the kitchen door. The woman wears a loose-fit T-shirt over shorts, dark blonde hair pulled up into a high ponytail. She raises a hand, jewellery free, fingernails unpainted.

A moment of silence.

'We got so much wrong, Mack.'

Robyn steps closer, a board creaking beneath her feet, the sound low but loud enough to break the moment. They turn, startled, the woman's face sliding into neutral. She is older than Robyn has ever seen her before. Her face carries lines, is fuller than in the photos that Mack had kept standing on his bedside table. The eyes though, they are the same.

'Mom?' The word comes out small, tremulous.

Harper Morgan studies her. 'So,' she says, patiently, 'you wanna tell us what's going on?'

Chapter Sixteen

Robyn Sandoval – 25th September, 8.59 a.m.

Robyn is . . . where? She turns in space. Is aware of heat, the faint smell of smoke. She reaches out, touches the wrought-iron of a table, warm to the touch. A car rolls past, just that little too fast, stuffed boxes and linen pressing against the rolled-up windows. She looks up. The sign for Bar 53 swings in a gust of wind that has suddenly swept up.

Bar 53. She looks down at her arms. Bare now.

'I'm going crazy,' she mutters. 'I'm going goddam crazy.'

Robyn pulls out a chair, the legs of it scrape along the ground, lets herself drop into it. Puts her head into her hands.

Reality has frozen now. A memory floating in place. A woman standing before her. A stranger. Then, another look. And this time picking out something new and very, very familiar all at once. Of hair, biscuit-blonde and thick, with that precise same awkward kink that never will do what it is told. Of a face the shape of a heart, a nose with the slightest upturn.

My mother.

My birth mother.

She was a face on a photograph. A character from a story. A scabbed-over wound, never quite healed.

That was her.

That was not her. It is an hallucination, a figment of an overactive imagination. A seizure, brought on by the weighty blow of grief.

And yet . . . she cannot shake it. The tilt of her head, the patient half-smile, the way the lines around her eyes have creased with the years that she has not lived.

A tear spills down her cheek. Not for her father now, but for her mother. No. That was wrong, wasn't it. It was for her, Robyn herself. For the way that reality has crashed back in on her, leaving only cavernous loss behind.

Robyn leans over the table, closes her eyes. Breath coming sharp and shallow. None of it is real. None of it is real. Rather her mind reacting to the horror of what she has seen, rewriting her own history so that the shape of it does not add up to this inevitable conclusion. That they are both gone. That she is once again the last surviving member of her species.

'Robyn?'

She doesn't look up. Not at first. No longer sure if the voice is coming from within or without. Then the weight of a hand on her shoulder and she starts, movement sharp enough to pull at her neck. Mags leans over her, dark hair brushing against Robyn's own.

'Are you . . . OK?' The question is tentative. A look crosses Mags' face then, a wince almost, and she shakes her head, expression apologetic. 'No. Of course you're not OK. How could you be OK? I'm sorry.'

For a moment, Robyn wonders how it is that she knows. Has she somehow looked into her head, seen the madness? Then she remembers. Again.

That in this world, her father is dead.

'Thank you.' She doesn't really know what she is thanking her for. Perhaps for bringing her back into the world.

Mags smiles nervously. 'No thanks required.'

Robyn looks at her, studying her face. The lines in it she

hasn't noticed before, the dark shadows beneath her eyes. The realisation then that the words they have exchanged today are perhaps more than they have shared in the past two years. 'Still,' says Robyn, quietly, 'thank you.'

Mags looks about her, seems to come to some kind of conclusion. 'Do you want to . . . I mean, no problem if you want to, you know, just be left alone . . . but if you want to come to the diner? We could have coffee? If you wanted to . . .'

Robyn struggles to focus. 'Thank you. But I don't want to scare off your customers.'

Mags lets out a bark of a laugh, quickly curtailed. 'There are no customers.' It sits heavy on her face for a moment, but then she shakes her head, refocusing. 'It's like a crypt in there. If you were looking for a place to hide out for a while.'

And then, because her mind has fractured into a thousand different pieces, and because she cannot think of further arguments against, Robyn nods, pushes her chair back, the groaning scrape of metal on wood.

They linger on the sidewalk as another car, this one packed with children and dogs, a golden retriever's nose protruding from the part-open window, glides past.

'Looks like a couple of people have decided to get a jump on evacuating.' Mags looks up the road, towards the church, the roadworks. 'I'm surprised more people aren't doing the same.'

'Are you?' asks Robyn. Only later, when all this is past will the criticism implied within this become clear to her.

But Mags, she doesn't seem to take offence, just shakes her head, gives a sad smile. 'Not really. It's expensive.'

Robyn scuffs toes into the gravel, looks down at her outfit. The pressed slacks, the blouse. The scuffed-up sneakers. *The runaway CEO.* A sudden feeling pressing down on her, of culpability.

'I'm sorry,' she says, quietly.

Mags smiles sadly. 'It's . . .' What was she going to say? It's OK? But it seems that the words will not come and she falls away into silence.

Robyn watches as Mags pushes open the door, the bell fixed above it tinkling cheerfully. It is deserted. Coffee sits brewing on a plate. Cookies circled on a plate on the counter, waiting.

'Please,' says Mags 'take a seat.' She gestures towards the sprawl of unused tables, and reaches across the counter for the coffee pot. 'Cream and sugar is on the table.'

Robyn accepts the mug, heat of it stinging against her palm. 'Thanks. For this.'

Mags slides into the seat beside her. 'I'm so sorry. Mack . . . your dad, he was a good man.'

'Was he?' Robyn startles herself with the question, but finds that she is studying the other woman intensely, as though she will have the answer to it.

Mags glances up at her. 'I . . . I think so . . . Wasn't he?'

Robyn looks down at the dark coffee, swirling the cup so that it swishes up at the sides. 'I was without him for so long. And . . . and when he came back . . . it was so . . . such a relief. That he wanted me. That he wanted to be a father to me. And so, sometimes I think it stops you from seeing, from really understanding who that person is, what they're about. I'm starting to realise that there were sides of him I really didn't know at all.'

Mags nods slowly, sipping from a cup of her own. 'I get that. But I don't know . . . I mean, is that about what comes of being adopted, of reuniting? Or is that true of all of us with our parents? I mean, my mom. She is so different with my brothers than with me. It's like they get to have an entirely different parent.' She shakes her head. 'I just mean, parents . . . when they're with us, they fill that role, don't they, the role of father or of mother. And so, as their children, we don't get to see what the rest of the world sees. For good or for bad.'

'How is your dad?' asks Robyn. Does she care or is she simply trying to make this subject change stick. She cannot really tell.

Mags shakes her head. 'The treatment is hard. It has stripped him bare and he seems so fragile, so weak. Still . . . my mom, she says that he's nearly done now. That soon he'll begin to mend. She takes a sip of coffee. 'It's hard to believe. I can't imagine him going back to the way he used to be.' She sets her mug down, shakes her head. 'Robyn, I'm sorry, we shouldn't be . . .'

'Why not?' Robyn takes a sip of her coffee. Bitter and hot. 'We all have it tough. It's just that toughness looks different for each of us. Besides,' she says with a sad smile, 'the coffee is helping.'

Then there is a tinkle, cheerful and out of place, a sweep of hot air that carries with it the smell of smoke, and they look up. Vivienne carefully closes the door behind her, has pulled her hair up into a high topknot, beads of sweat standing proud on her skin.

'Oh my God, it is *hot* out there.'

Mags forces a smile, pushes her chair back. 'Hey, can I get you a coffee?'

'I'd love a water, if I could? And one of those cookies. I haven't had a chance to eat today.' Vivienne moves towards Robyn, setting a palm on her shoulder, a quick, comforting squeeze. 'Hey. I was looking for you. Do you mind?' She gestures to the chair, pulls it out before waiting for the answer. 'You doing OK?' She studies Robyn as Mags slides a glass of iced water across the table, a plate with two cookies, and settles into a chair beside them. 'Any more of those absences?'

Robyn hesitates, nods. 'A couple. But I'm . . . OK,' she lies.

Vivienne studies her, and for a wild moment it feels as if she can see straight through the lie to the truth. Then she draws in a deep breath. 'Robyn, I just wanted to let you know . . . the medical examiner has been. She found bruising, around

Mack's mouth and his nose. Found traces of flesh beneath his fingernails.' She leans in closer. 'That's a good thing. Whoever did this, he scratched them. If their DNA is in the system, we'll will be able to find them.'

'And if it's not?'

'The crime scene technicians will be here soon. They'll strip Mack's house bare, Robyn, and if there's any evidence there, they'll find it. Robyn?'

Chapter Seventeen

Scarlett Morgan – 25th September, 9.15 a.m.

There is the distant sound of a car engine, a low thrumming, the grumble of tyres against gravel. The honk of a horn and then the engine noise moving further and further away. Then the sound of a door slamming. Footsteps coming closer.

Her heart beats fast in her chest. 'Mom?'

How many times has she said that word across the course of a lifetime? But it feels different now, a new taste to it.

The footsteps draw closer and she turns to face them. Is still in the sunroom. Still surrounded by a forest full of green. A flush rises up her cheeks, her stomach knotting. *I get to see my mommy today.*

Only then the footsteps round the corner, and a voice says 'Scarlett, you just about ready?' And she immediately knows that she is wrong.

He stops before her, brow furrowed. 'Hey. You OK?'

For a brief moment, she can smell the trailer again. That wisp of old food and older linens. But then he steps closer and it vanishes. He – Zeke? – looks different in this place. Perhaps it is something to do with the light, the way it filters through the greenery. Sunken cheeks have given way to sharp cheekbones, a defined jaw. The shadow of stubble now gives contour to his features. He has changed, is wearing a grey T-shirt, blue jeans.

She is surprised to feel a blush rising across her cheeks.

He watches her, and she can see the blush reflected in the way he grins. 'You doing OK there?'

'I'm fine.'

He grins broadly, gives her a mock wink. 'Damn right you are, girl.'

And a laugh comes from her.

Was that me?

He studies her, and for the briefest of moments she wonders if he will see it, will recognise who she really is. 'You feeling a bit better now? I gotta say, you freaked me out earlier.'

She nods, mute.

'I know you're worried about him, Scar.' He shakes his head. 'Like he's fooling anyone. But, he's a grown man. You gotta let him be.' He turns away from her, towards the kitchen. 'We should hit the road. Bonnie and her gang are already halfway to Morro Bay by now. I said we'd meet everyone at the hotel.' Then he hesitates. 'Or are you leaving?'

'What good am I going to do if I stay?' Her mouth moves without her and she finds herself wondering, what is this all about?

He studies her, lips pursed. Then shakes his head. 'Well, your mom said they're gonna need all the help they can get, setting up.' He pulls open the fridge. 'She left us sandwiches for the trip. You wanna soda? Scarlett?'

There is something she needs to remember. Something important. She reaches for the memory of it, only it slips away from her. She raises her arms up in front of her, studying the twisting vine tattoos. There is a rose in there, buried amongst the sharp thorned vines, one that she has not seen before. And now the memory of whatever it was slips, further and further away.

'Scarlett? Coke?'

'Sure.' She is surprised at the sound of the voice, her own but not her own. And, without thought, she is moving, is ducking into the family room that feels familiar and entirely new both at once. It is darker in here. Just the one window to let in the light. Feels like being embraced. She looks about her. There, on a side table, stands a cluster of photographs. Her graduation. Only, it isn't, is it? Because the hair is different and the expression is different. Hers but . . . what? She studies the face, the arch of the eyebrow, the slightest curl of the lip. As if the subject has just got done telling a joke. Her stomach twists and she feels a fleeting sense of envy. To be one of those people who move through crowds with ease, who can laugh and tease, and pull people towards them . . .

Imagine that.

There are more photographs, and she lingers on one of two women. Of her. Her? Arms flung around her mother's waist, Harper's cheek pressed up against hers, her smile wide, hair blonde flecked with white. It arrests her, holds her in place. And her stomach clenches.

A mirror hangs over an old-fashioned tiled fireplace and she steps closer to it, her breath fogging up the glass. Studies the face. It is her own. Isn't it? Slimmer, the cheekbones more pronounced, cheeks a little more concave. But the eyes – they are grey, the same colour they have always been.

She leans in, close enough that her nose touches cold glass.

It is me. I am me.

'Hey.'

She sees his reflection, the shape of him at her shoulder. 'Hey,' she replies.

'You . . . OK?'

She nods, watching the movement of her head in the mirror.

He hesitates. Then, 'Scar . . . I been thinking.'

'Uh oh.'

'Right? And there you were thinking that smell of burning came from Seven Hills. So, I been thinking . . . And, I mean, don't flip out at me here. But I know we said, back when we first met, that we were just gonna be all about living in the moment, just having fun and damn the consequences. And, I mean, it has been, right? It's been fun. Only, I kind of been thinking lately. Maybe it's time to, I don't know, do things a bit differently? Maybe figure out what we want to do next. You know, develop some ambitions beyond that damn trailer and a shitty job stacking shelves in Target. I mean, I know there's this other job, but it isn't exactly the career you dreamed of.' His voice trails away. 'Like I said, just a thought . . .' He turns on his heels, the sound of the refrigerator door opening, of rustling. 'We should get going. I suppose the only thing to be grateful for is that your dad isn't driving out to Morro Bay. Don't fancy the idea of him behind the wheel today. From what I hear, he had one hell of a night – had to be carried home from O'Callaghan's.'

The refrigerator door closes.

There is something here. Something important. She struggles to focus, to pinpoint what about his words has made her heart beat faster.

'Thing is,' says the distant voice, 'I just don't think he gets what thin ice he's on. Guess it's a measure of how desperate CalFire is that he's even allowed to volunteer for them anymore. I suppose they figure six years is enough time for him to have turned his shit around. But even so, if they find out about the drinking . . .'

'What do you mean?'

'Huh?' Zeke reappears in the doorway to the family room.

'Six years? What . . .?'

'You serious?' He steps closer, frowning. 'Seriously, are you. OK? You're freaking me out a little.'

'No, I . . . I'm fine. I just . . .' She raises her hand to her head, 'I have a headache. It's making my brain fog up.'

He studies her, considering, then, 'Babe. Look, your dad can spout that bad back line all he wants. Doesn't negate the fact that he ditched fire camp to go on a four-day bender and got himself fired for it. And that's aside from everything else that happened. And the thing is, he can say he's changed, but if Luis is having to carry him home because he's drained an entire bottle of Jim Beam, it's hardly the shiny new leaf he claims it is.' He shakes his head. 'Look, babe, I don't know what this morning was all about. I'm just saying, I kinda thought we were past the time where you believed all of the shit Mack shovelled in your direction.' He hesitates, looks down. 'I thought . . . I thought we were on solid ground.' Zeke sighs. 'Scar . . . I know trailer park living isn't for everyone. I get that the shit I'm offering ain't exactly the American dream. I'm sorry. I want to do better. I promise, I want to do better. For both of us. Look . . .' He holds out his hand, palm down. 'I've not even had a beer. Not since Sunday.'

'I . . .'

'OK, yeah, fine. So that's mostly because we've been waiting for the trailer to catch fire, but still. I feel like I gotta get credit for that, right?' He takes her hand, folds it tight into his own. 'I'm not your dad, I promise. I'm not Mack. I'm going to do better. I got those school brochures, the ones we were talking about. And I think I can make it work, I really do . . .' He stops, studying her. 'What? What's wrong?'

'I . . .' It tumbles together, thoughts flying faster than she can follow them. Mack was fired from CalFire. There was no sickness. No bad back bringing his career to a premature end. He had lied to her. For years and years. No. He hadn't. He wouldn't. Yes. He had. He would. 'My father – where is he now?'

Zeke frowns. 'When I left he was up at the trailer park. They were cutting in a line, so that the fire can't cross it.'

'I'm sorry.' She pulls her hand free. 'I have to see him.'

And then she is off and is running, a distant shout of 'Scarlett' in her wake. Is out through the front door and down the short run of wooden steps, and along the road, and the stream of cars that line it bumper to bumper, the entire town pouring down towards Main Street. She runs, lungs straining in the heat, calves pulling against the slope of the hill. Is breathing hard. Not exertion only, but also rage that steals her breath, forcing her to pull in the air that is there with great gulping breaths.

A sudden realisation that she has done this before. Here in this body. That it is a giant treadmill where she keeps on, running and running, always towards her father. That he is forever moving, further and further away.

She rounds the corner, looking up to the expanse of mountainside before her. The trailer park, off to the right. No cars coming from there now. All who were there to leave have left.

But then she sees movement, on the curve of the road where they have mounted their defence. Fire trucks with their lights swirling, the deafening thrum of bulldozer engines as they carve their way through brush. Mustard-coloured figures, swinging and hacking, carving into the mountainside, breaking through the foliage so that all that remains is a wide stretch of soil.

Then a figure, standing off to the side, shouting into a radio and there is a flash of recognition.

'DAD!'

She takes off running again.

Mack lowers the radio, scowling. 'What the hell, Scarlett? Why the hell are you still here? You're supposed to have evacuated.'

'Mack.' She moves closer, but he reaches her first, using his body to push her backwards.

'Get the hell out of here, Scarlett. I'm not kidding!' Then he looks over her shoulder, waves an arm. 'Little help?'

Fingers grab hold of her, gentle enough but unrelenting. They spin her around. And there is Luis, face to face with her. His eyes are red-rimmed, sweat runs down his cheeks. 'Scarlett. What are you doing? You're supposed to be helping your mom with the evacuation.'

She opens her mouth, but what she was about to say is lost. For a moment, she thinks that it is fear, only it is different from the fear that she is used to. Hotter. More potent. The feeling builds and builds until it erupts and her body moves entirely without her consent. She throws her arms up, twists violently out of Luis' grasp. 'Get the hell off me!'

Whose words were they?

But there is no time to think, because a look has settled on Luis' face and she knows that trouble is coming.

'I don't want to have to arrest you,' he says, voice quiet but hard-edged.

He steps closer, left hand, palm up in a placating gesture. His right hand is on his gun. And Robyn's brain scrabbles, frantic, trying to get a purchase.

But it seems that this body, it has a mind of its own. And the slender, tattoo-wrapped arms come up and she feels herself shouting 'No!' but no words come out. She is powerless to stop what her body does. The hands, with their nails bitten right down to the quick, they throw themselves forward and then her body arcs forward, leaning into the movement. And she is shoving him, hard enough that he is tumbling backwards.

And the rest of it? That comes in a blur of motion. Somehow she is on the ground, seemingly without having covered the space between. Her face presses down into the burning hot tarmac, arms pulled tight behind her back, cold metal to her wrists, the click of the handcuffs preternaturally loud.

Darkness closes in.

Chapter Eighteen

Robyn Sandoval – 25th September, 9.15 a.m.

'Robyn?'

It comes back to her, a little at a time. The feeling of a warm hand encasing hers, the smell of coffee. Her vision clears, focus pulling to the plate of cookies, uneaten on the table before her. The all but empty diner, Mags and Vivienne looking at her with concern.

'Robyn? Are you OK?'

Vivienne has pushed her chair back, is leaning over her, sliding a glass of water into her hands, her brow furrowed up into tight little knots. 'This is it?' she asks. 'The absences? This is what you were talking about?'

Robyn picks up the water glass, fingers slipping on its wet surface, carefully raising it to her lips. She nods, taking a slow sip of water. The sudden awareness that her hands are trembling.

'It feels like I am . . .' Another me. '. . . far away. Not in my body.'

Vivienne nods, eases into the chair beside her. 'OK . . . I'm going to say it's likely shock from what's happened today. But I don't love this. I'm going to get you booked in for a CT as soon as I can . . . OK?'

Robyn nods, takes another sip.

The television is on. Was it always? A helicopter circles burning forest, a commentator speaking quickly, her tone foreboding.

'And we're getting word that the firefighters tackling the Seven Hills' fire have . . . yes, it seems that the fire is no longer contained. That CalFire has lost control of it. If you look now at our footage from chopper 21, you can see, yes, there's a home right there. The fire is approaching it at speed. Beyond that, and in very real danger now, is the town of Seven Hills to the south of the fire. Oh, this is not at all how CalFire will have wanted this thing to play out . . .'

'Those poor people,' murmurs Mags.

The television footage has switched now, images of traffic lining the highway out of Seven Hills. The helicopter pulls up, the lens widening to encompass miles and miles of forest. There, in the far-off distance, to the west of the fire, a sparkle, the sun glinting off glass embedded in the trees – Destino Heights. 'For those of you in surrounding areas, it might be a good time to really consider your evacuation plans. If CalFire can't re-establish a grip on this thing, it's likely that the evacuation order will be issued for those towns to the south of the fire. Now remember, that's Ridgeway, Hillview and Tupelo. For folks in these towns, although we don't have an evacuation order yet, you're gonna want to start putting your plans in place.'

Vivienne shakes her head. 'This is awful. I'm just hoping the power hangs on. Apparently, they've been having brownouts up in the trailer park all week. If we lose power, it's going to be much harder to keep track of the fire, figure out what we need to do next.'

'Viv,' Robyn interrupts, surprising herself. 'Mack. Did he talk to you about his back?'

'What?' Vivienne looks startled, thrown by the conversational detour.

'He . . . he had to quit CalFire because of his back. You're the town doctor. Did he get treatment for it?'

She hesitates and for a moment it seems as though she will say something. Then she shakes her head. 'No. No, he didn't.'

Robyn stares down at the tabletop before her, tracing her fingernail along the edge. Mack lied to her. There was no troubled back, no forced retirement from ill health. He had lied to her. And Luis? He had carried him home. Here and there. Was that what had happened? Had Luis known, heard perhaps through the emergency services grapevine, that Mack was lying, that he had been fired? Had he confronted him, an argument that got out of hand?

Robyn stands up, fast enough that her head spins. 'I gotta go . . .'

Vivienne reaches up, grabs hold of her hand. 'Rob, look, I know this is a hell of a day. But they're going to figure it out. They're going to find out who did this. But, look . . .' She fixes her with a look. 'I don't love what's happening with you, and I definitely don't want you here when you are having these absences. You need to evacuate. Now. Just in case we get cut off. Go home. Get your mom and get gone . . . OK?'

Robyn nods obediently, her face schooled to stillness. 'I will,' she lies. 'I'm heading there right now.'

She gives a half-hearted smile, slips through the door. That damn bell again with its tone-deaf cheeriness. She walks down the steps, gravel kicking up beneath her feet, scratching at her thighs. And then she is on Main Street and the mountain is there, overhead.

Is the smoke thicker now, or is it her imagination? The newscaster's warnings adding colour where there is none?

Robyn turns and she begins to run. Not towards home. Instead towards the police station. Cars are passing now, a loose stream of them. She walks quickly, past empty stores. The news, the smoke, it's scared people, kept them away. And then, on the next corner, the police station.

It has been painted recently, a cheerful yellow. Is as welcoming as any small town police station is likely to be. But Robyn's heart has begun to beat faster again. She raises her hand, shoves open the door, hard enough that it rebounds from cheery yellow walls, and she starts. A sudden feeling that the wrong her is in charge.

'Hey. Can I help you?'

Robyn stares at her, struggling for recognition. Helen, Heather . . . whatever her name was. She looks older than she did this morning. Her hair has begun to unravel from her tight braid, leaving sweat-slicked strands sticking to her cheek.

'You looking for Luis?' The woman is stuffing paperwork into a filing cabinet. She pauses, blows a strand of hair from her eyes. 'He's still up at the . . . at your dad's house. We haven't been able to get the crime scene techs up there yet, what with . . .' she waves vaguely around her . . . 'all this. He's pushing to get someone to come out in case we get a mandatory evac called. Otherwise, if the house goes . . .' She catches herself, looks at Robyn, guilty. 'Sorry. I meant . . . sorry.'

'What time did Luis come in this morning?' Robyn asks, her words crisp. 'How did he seem to you?'

Helen/Heather rams the file into the cabinet, bending it almost in half under the force of her thrust. She snorts. 'Exhausted. Still is. I told him to go home and get a couple of hours before it all kicked off, but you know how men are.'

Robyn's hands clench up into tight fists. 'He was exhausted . . .?'

'That damn lorry. Out on the highway. You hear about this? Driver decides to go over his driving hours because, of course, he's fine, almost spins out of control on the highway. Jackknifes, misses going over into the ravine by a foot or two. Damn lucky if you ask me. Took them all night to get the road cleared. And thank God they did. You imagine if we had a blocked highway with all this going on?'

Robyn hesitates. 'And . . . Luis, he was there?'

'Yes, he was there. They finally managed to get it moved at about 6.00 a.m. Think he managed to get home to take a shower and then came straight back here. Then, well, I mean, you called about . . . you know . . .'

There is a ringing in Robyn's ears, loud enough that she struggles not to shout above it. 'When?'

'What?'

'When was this? The lorry. What time did it jackknife?'

Helen/Heather is staring at her now, is starting to add two and two, is not getting four. 'Logs said the call came in at 11.15 p.m. Why?'

At 11.15 p.m.

Robyn shakes her head, takes a step back. Her hand goes to her phone in her pocket. Only she doesn't pull it out, doesn't check it because she already knows. The email that her father had sent was timed 11.45 p.m.

'I . . . I just . . .'

'Robyn? Are you . . . OK?'

Chapter Nineteen

Mags Reyes – 25th September, 9.20 a.m.

They stand together in the empty diner, the two women watching the glow of fire from the television.

'I don't like this,' murmurs Mags.

'No,' says Vivienne. She glances across at her. 'I think we need to be ready.' She hesitates, then, 'Will they evacuate? If you ask them too?'

Mags watches the bouncing flames, can feel tears prick at the back of her eyes. 'No,' she hears herself say. 'No, not for me.'

There is a heavy silence, one long enough that Mags glances across at the other woman, trying to read her thoughts in her face. 'What?'

Vivienne purses her lips. 'Mags . . . I need to ask . . . what is your understanding? Of your father's condition, I mean?'

It feels like the other shoe dropping. Like she has waited three years for that question. And before she answers, she knows what will come next.

'That he is struggling. That the treatment is brutal. But that there is hope.' Mags turns to Vivienne. 'It is a lie, isn't it?'

Vivienne considers for long moments. 'I think,' she says, carefully, 'that it would be wise for you to prepare yourself.' She falls silent, then, 'I think it is fair to say that the hope is . . . small.'

'He is dying.' It is not a question.

It hangs in the air between them.

'In truth, Mags, I think the only thing that has kept him going so far is your mother's absolute refusal to accept death as an outcome.' She shakes her head, the faintest of smiles. 'She's a remarkably strong woman. That strength, that unwillingness to admit defeat, it's contagious. Your father seems to have gone along with her, accepting her word as law.' Her smile widens. 'You have to wonder, what she could have done in this world, had she chosen to. Your mother could lead an army. But . . .'

'But she can't stave off death forever,' finishes Mags.

'No,' agrees Vivienne. 'No, she cannot.' She looks across at her. 'I know what a powerhouse of a woman she is. And I know that must be . . . difficult at times. That she can have a tendency to tow the world along behind her. But, I feel that I have to say to you . . . her ability to see what is in front of her, to recognise the world as it is, her willingness to accept a world not to her liking . . . perhaps that's where she's weakest.' She reaches out squeezes Mags' hand. 'Whatever happens here,' she nods towards the television, towards the bright burning flame, 'make your own decisions. For yourself, your children.'

A ping from a cell phone cuts through the silence. Vivienne glances down, frowns. 'It's Jesse. He's freaking out that I'm still here.' She thumbs a quick response. 'OK, I'm going to go get my go-bag, turn off the gas at the house. And then I'm going to head to Palm Springs. I'll try and call your mother one more time, see if I can convince her to reconsider.' She holds up the phone. 'I have my cell. Call me, if anything changes.' She studies her. 'And . . . please remember what I said. What happens next, that's for you to decide. No one else.'

And then she turns on her heel and is gone.

Mags stands in the empty diner, is suddenly aware of her hands shaking. Lets out a breath that emerges as a sob. She moves to the door, reaches out, turns the sign to closed.

The chain of it rattles against the window. She stands, the cold downdraught of the air conditioning raising gooseflesh across her arms.

Her phone buzzes, an incoming text. And she raises it. A text from Jack. *Are you guys OK?*

Another sob. It could not go on like this. This pressure that sits square in the centre of her back, that makes it impossible to pull in a full breath. This sense of always falling, never landing. Once you hit rock bottom, they say, the only way is up. But what if you never did? What if you just kept falling and falling and falling?

Her father is dying.

Would it have made a difference? If she had known? Would she have behaved any differently? She would still have made the choice, would still have come home, have taken on the diner. And perhaps, had she known, she would still have made the choice to leave Jack, to cut the threads that tied them together. Her actions. Her choices. Her consequences to live with. And yet it pricks at her skin, this sense of having lived in a world of her mother's creation. Of looking out at a sky and seeing it is blue and knowing it is blue and being told, no, that is red, and having accepted it, never mind what her own senses told her. Of having spent three years walking on the ceiling after being told it was the floor.

Mags turns her back to the window. The diner is empty. As neat as a pin. But then, of course, it should be. She has cleaned, has wiped down and emptied the dishwasher, has filled up the dishwasher, and lined up the glasses and folded the napkins. All of it merely wadding, a pillow stuffed with not quite enough cotton, so that when the end of the day rolls about, you have made it through, but the pillow is thin and uncomfortable. And yet she has done it. Has made the diner as her mother has deemed it should be.

What the hell am I doing?

She stands there, in that spick-and-span room, feeling a wash of nausea come across her. That all around her, there have been plummeting disasters, death and divorce and fire and financial ruin. And instead of looking at it, instead of dealing with it, with any of it, she has wiped down the bloody countertops.

What happens next, that's for you to decide.

She thinks of the fire footage, of the vast expanse of distance between Destino and Seven Hills, not far off thirty miles. Of course, to a furious wildfire, thirty miles is the blink of an eye. And if the wind changes . . .

Mags begins to move. She crosses the room in long strides, throwing open the door to the stairwell, hurries up the narrow stairs, the boards creaking under her weight. It is quiet. The kids' rooms starkly empty. She throws open the door to the living room. It is hot in here, dust motes hanging in still air. She feels beads of sweat across her forehead. She turns about her, looking for the lockbox. The documents – birth certificates and passports. She pulls open the dresser drawer, pulling out wads of paper, a relief as her fingers touch the cold metal beneath. She pulls it free, stands, her gaze hooking on the dining table. The diorama takes up the surface, white puffed glue hanging on desperately to dried macaroni, purple flecked glitter. They had worked on it for days, her and Gabrielle and Oscar. 'It's important, Mom,' Gabrielle had said. 'The winner of the contest gets a Chuck E. Cheese voucher.' But, inevitably, she had fallen at the last hurdle, at the actual getting the damn thing out of the door and onto the school bus and into the craft show. There had been tears that day, her nine-year-old daughter stomping down off the school bus, face a mask of fury. 'You forgot!' she had said. 'I *told* you it was important, and you forgot. I didn't get to enter anything and Tanya Quinn won and now she gets to go to Chuck E. Cheese.'

She studies the owl, limply glued onto the cardboard tree. It would, she thinks distantly, have perhaps been reasonable for her to argue back. For her to remind her daughter of personal responsibility. To apologise but perhaps also to share out the blame. Only she hadn't. She had stood there on the sidewalk and had felt it crash over her, that inevitable sense of having failed again.

Mags grabs her purse from the back of a chair, feeling around in it for her cell phone. Turns, running quickly back down the stairs, dialling as she goes. She holds the phone pressed tight against her ear, as it rings and rings and rings. And then,

'Hello?' Bonnie sounds hurried, breathless.

'Mom! Oh, thank God. Did you hear?'

'Hear what?'

'They're saying winds have picked up, that they've lost control of the fire.'

A huff, then, 'Oh, that. I heard that. Honestly, these people, nothing but fearmongering.'

A burst of irritation, and Mags closes her eyes, lowering her head into her hands. A sinking sense of expectations being met. This too would not be easy. 'Mom . . .'

'Maggie, this is for Seven Hills to concern themselves with, not us. You worry too much.'

She looks up, gaze drawn by the red glow of the television. Fire marching through a once-was yard. Her stomach knots itself up tight. 'Mom . . . Seriously, why not get dad out now, just out of an abundance of caution. We can manage. Financially, I mean. Vivienne, she can get an ambulance to come out for him. There's that hospice—'

'And us? Where does Vivienne propose we go? She think we're going to sleep in the car?'

'Jesus, Mom! We can put the hotel on the credit card. We'll manage. It's not worth—'

'Maggie, you know how many times we've done this? Evacuating because county got twitchy? Last time we listened, do you know how much it cost us? Better part of a thousand dollars. And that's not taking into account what we lost, with the diner closed.'

'I know, but—'

'Maggie, I am telling you. I have done this before. I have seen this before, too many times to count. And every time they were wrong. And your dad . . . he wants to be here. He wants to be in his home.'

'But, Mom . . .'

Bonnie's voice breaks. 'No, Margaret. I am telling you no. Now, if an evacuation order comes through and you want to go with the kids, then that is your business. They're just helping me makes some pies, though, so you'll have to wait until they're done.' She draws in a breath, then, apparently unable to resist, 'If you feel you have money to waste on a hotel, then you be my guest.'

There is a part of her that has already folded, a part of her yielding beneath the unstoppable force of her mother's will. She looks up at the television, can feel tears pricking at the back of her eyes. Why could nothing be easy? The footage lingers on flames. And for a moment it is unclear what they are consuming. Then the camera zooms out. It is a home. It *was* a home. Vivid flames clambering through wood cladding. In the background a swing set, now nothing but twisted metal.

'No.'

She hears the word come, wonders briefly who said it.

'What?'

'The children. They aren't making pies. I'm coming to get them. We're getting out.'

Silence then, 'Oh, for goodness' sake!'

'Mom. I can't force you to protect yourself. But I can protect my children. I'm on my way.'

She hangs up, the shocked silence reverberating around her. Tucks the phone into her pocket. Has not even released her grip on it when it begins to ring again.

And for a wild moment she thinks that it is her mother, telling her that she has changed her mind, that for once, just this one thing will not lead to war.

She pulls it free, but the name that flicks up is not her mother's but her brother's. She presses receive.

'Nate, hi.'

'Hey, I just saw the news. Are you OK?' The phone line crackles, dipping in and out. 'No evacuation order yet?'

Mags opens her mouth, for a wild moment thinking that she will spill it all, will vent about their mutual mother, about her obstinacies and frustrations. And then she stops. Because she was not their mutual mother, was she? The mother she was for her was so very different to the mother she was for her brother.

'The kids and I are getting ready to go,' she says, limply. 'Mom, she says they're going to wait it out.'

'They are? Well, I mean, I guess, what with Dad . . . he can't be sleeping on some cot in a high school gymnasium. You know how Mom is. I'm sure she's got it all under control . . . OK, well, I'll let you go . . . Oh, shoot . . . I gotta say, real quick, the test came back. It's all clear, so everything is a—' The line cuts, then comes back on again.

Mags hesitates. 'I . . . I'm confused. What test?'

'The test. The genetic thing to make sure we don't all also have the pancreatic cancer gene. Arthur hasn't had his back yet, but fingers crossed. You got yours done, right?'

A tear rolls down her cheeks. Then another. Then another.

When had she last felt it? When had it last seemed to her that she was in control, was driving this train, not just hanging onto the back of it praying that it didn't jump the track? She squeezes her eyes tighter shut, and the tears flood, heavy enough that her breath catches in her throat.

'No,' she says, quietly. 'Not yet.'

'You . . . do . . . Just to . . . safe.'

'Nate?'

But it is too late. The line has gone dead.

She lets her hand drop. And it feels inevitable somehow, the next shoe dropping. It is the conclusion that she has waited to hear, the sure knowledge that she is little but a spare part in this family of hers.

Chapter Twenty

Bonnie Aubrey – 25th September, 9.27 a.m.

'You need to roll the dough. Roll it thinner.' Bonnie takes the pin from her grandson, demonstrates, leaning her weight down onto the recalcitrant dough. 'Show that dough who's boss.'

Destino waits beyond the window, indistinct in the haze from drifting smoke. The children chatter, a steady stream of words, although in truth, Bonnie is not listening. A terrible thing for a grandmother to admit. She is just letting it wash over her, the thrum of the words. The rising and falling rhythm of it. They are here. Bonnie smiles. But it has already happened, even before the smile begins to fade. Her mind moving beyond the sound in the kitchen, to the bedroom beyond.

To Kelvin.

What had she hoped would happen? That the children, the brightness of them, would effect some change, would pull Kelvin from his bed? Would force some kind of miracle? She looks through the open kitchen door to the family room, the easy chair, its cushion all sagged, battered out of shape by the weight of Kelvin's years. And again her breath catches, her stomach lurching with the realisation, the same one again and again. That soon he will be gone.

'Grandma? Grandma? What do I do now?' Oscar waves a

fistful of dough at her and Bonnie shakes her head, batting away the tears that prick her eyes.

'Right then.' She sprinkles flour across the worktop, guiding the children's hands across it. They look to her, eyes round, expectant, and she blinks away the tears. She is needed here. 'We're going to roll it out.'

'Mommy would like this,' offers Gabrielle.

Bonnie smiles, lips tighter than they should be. She turns towards the sink, turning on the tap with her elbow. Doesn't answer. Doesn't want to think about Maggie.

Because the thought of her daughter, it brings with it the memory of her lie.

She washes her hands, brisk enough that flecks of water spray across the sill.

There is music playing, Billie Holiday crooning 'Summertime'. Has deliberately turned off the television. It is all hysteria, media-driven nonsense designed to create fear. She grabs for a towel, rubbing her hands brisk enough that it stings. Smiles at the children, although her attention has moved beyond them, is back in the bedroom, is listening for the sounds of Kelvin's breath. Her own breathing slows, forced downwards as she listens. *Please still be alive.*

'Should we call, Mommy, Grandma? See if she wants to come bake with us?' persists Gabrielle.

Bonnie hooks the towel over the handle of a cabinet, movements brisk. 'Mommy will be here soon. Just as soon as she's ready. Hold on, just a second, my angels.' She cannot bear it anymore, skirts around her grandchildren, and walks with slow, heavy steps to the bedroom.

Is it there? Her breath catches in her throat. She rounds the bedroom door.

He lies in the bed, his eyes open, and for a moment she thinks that it has happened. But then he looks at her, gives a slow smile. 'Hey,' he says quietly. 'Kids doing OK?'

She works to force the breath back into her lungs, to school her face to calm, forcing an expression of barely contained impatience. 'You know how they are. They're getting messy, so they're thrilled.'

'I hear the phone earlier?' His voice is low enough that she struggles to hear him. 'Any news on the fire?'

Bonnie tsks. 'Oh,' she lies, 'it's all the same. Nothing new.' She smiles with a brittle brightness. 'Don't worry. You don't have to go anywhere. You can recline in your bed and relax.'

He smiles, slowly, eyelids struggling to stay open. 'OK, honey, that's good.' His fingers pick at the comforter. 'It is a good bed.'

Bonnie watches him, as his eyes close, his head sinking to the side into soft pillow. Watches as he falls into sleep.

If you lie enough, you can remake the world around you. If you lie enough, you can convince yourself that it is the truth.

She steps back, walking slowly towards the front door. She pulls it open, a wave of heat rolling in on her. There is a tang to the air, a hint of smoke.

Looks down over Destino. And, for just a moment, it comes for her. The truth. And her breath catches in her throat and a sob works its way up through her chest. And her fingers clench, muscles knot. And it seems that she will fold, will collapse right there on the drive.

'Grandma! Oscar threw flour at me!'

It saves her.

She closes her eyes, forces her breath to steady.

Everything will be OK . . .

Bonnie turns, closing the door behind her, walks quickly back into the wave of sound that spreads from her grandchildren. A smile that comes a little easier now.

'Right then, Oscar, pass that fruit. Let's get these pies in the oven.'

Chapter Twenty-One

Scarlett Morgan – 25th September, 9.30 a.m.

The bed is harder now, the room warmer. She blinks. The smell, of stale liquor and sweat. She turns her head, forces her eyes to focus on the room around her, empty but for her. It is small. Sunlight spills in through a window high up on the wall, and dust motes twist in it. She looks up. The window has bars on it.

Damn!

Her head is spinning, but, in truth, she is getting used to that now. She pushes herself up, leaning heavy on her elbow. Forces herself to look down at the arm that supports her, although she already knows what she will see.

The tattoos are there.

Scarlett.

She lets out a breath, forcing it to slow.

Remember . . .

The police station. The policewoman, whatever the hell her name was. That Luis was down on the highway all night. That he might have driven her father home but he could not have killed him.

A thought then. *Oh God. I shoved him.*

And then the sound of footsteps approaching. They echo

hollowly and she forces herself to stand, facing the door. They slow, stop. Then the grind of a key in an old lock and the door swings open.

Luis is framed by the light beyond. He looks worn, still sweat-stained and haggard. Somehow, he looks younger than her. Looking at him now, in this light, at this distance, there are other differences. This Luis carries a little more weight. His cheeks are not as sunken, cheekbones do not protrude as much. He looks softer, although the softness curves into well-built muscles. His hair is shorter, and, in spite of it all, he looks less tired than the Luis she knows. Her gaze tracks down. He also wears a wedding ring.

'So . . .' he says, quietly.

Scarlett's arms move, entirely of their own accord, folding across her body. A protective shield.

'Feeling better?' he asks. 'You took a bit of a turn back there.'

Her lips press firmly together, and for a moment there is a battle, a fight between body and brain. She forces the words out. 'Where am I?'

'Police station. Your boyfriend is waiting for you outside.'

Scarlett considers him 'Have I . . . have I been out of it this whole time?'

Luis hesitates, looks at her oddly. 'You were shooting your mouth off until a few minutes ago. You don't remember that?'

It comes back in bits and pieces, fractured memories of a white-hot fury, of arms flailing wildly, words that shot from her mouth like darts. She nods slowly. 'Yeah . . . it just, I got a bit foggy for a minute.'

'Guess all that attitude can get pretty exhausting,' offers Luis. 'You feeling OK now?'

'I'm fine.' She leans forward on the hard bed, feet flat to the floor as though they are getting ready to run. Although where she would run to is beyond her.

'You know,' says Luis, lightly, 'I don't particularly want to keep you locked up here when we're preparing the town for a wildfire. To be honest, I can think of like a thousand other places I would rather be right now. You think you can keep yourself under control so we can all get out of here?'

A brief, fleeting thought, that she genuinely has no idea whether she can, in fact, keep herself under control or not, but she nods her head anyway. 'I'm mildly insulted you don't want to hang out with me, but sure.'

What??

He considers her for a moment, then the merest hint of a smile. He steps back, nods his head for her to follow, and she falls into step behind him. The hallway is dimmer, lit by a sallow, artificial light, and as she follows she looks about her. A couple of cells that she can see, a couple of offices, their doors propped open, electric fans working overtime to achieve very little. The walls are not yellow now, rather a muted lavender, the paint old enough that it has begun to bubble and flake. She feels it again, that swirling sensation of the world spinning beneath her feet.

Luis stops in front of her, motions her into an office. 'Take a seat for me.'

The windows are bigger here, although still small in the grand scheme of things. They have been flung open wide, a desperate attempt to bring in some air. It hasn't worked. The room is breathless, the heat oppressive. A fan spins on the ceiling, moving dead air from one place to another. It smells of smoke.

'Where is the fire now?' she hears herself asking, words more abrupt than she is used to, that sliver of attitude within them.

Luis glances at her. 'It's still out at Seven Hills. Don't know how long that'll last, though.' He sighs, gestures to a seat. 'Your dad . . . he's worried about you.'

Scarlett sits, tugging at the denim cut-offs that ride up too high on her thigh. The thigh is smaller than the one she is used to seeing, like looking at a denim-wrapped chicken leg. She studies it, distracted for a moment, the oddest sensation of missing thighs she always considered to be chubby. 'Uh huh,' she says, distantly.

Luis hands her a bottle of water. 'You should drink. This heat is a killer.' He pulls a chair out from behind the desk, almost vanishing behind a paper mountain. 'So . . .' he leans back in his chair, his hands scrubbing at his face, then leans forward, 'what's going on with you?'

She shrugs. Because, honestly, where the hell would she begin?

'You been drinking?'

Her fingers clench, pulling themselves into fists. An odd heat builds up, a sudden wild fury, but then, just as quickly, fades away. 'No.' The words come out, unbidden, and Robyn can sense the truth in them.

'So what then? You should have evacuated. Mack said your mom has already left, that you were supposed to follow with Zeke. So why, Scarlett, am I sitting here with you? Why, rather than helping your mom lead the evacuation, did you choose to cause enough of a problem for CalFire that I end up having to intervene?' He shakes his head. 'I mean, I get you aren't their biggest fan, but I feel like I'm having to manage a toddler mid-tantrum.'

'I . . . I don't know.' Well, that was true enough. 'I thought that . . .' What? That you killed my father. You know, the one that was standing next to you, like fifteen minutes ago. She flails. 'I don't know. I just, I guess I lost it.' She hesitates, a word stuck in her throat, then, 'I'm sorry.' She coughs on that, half choking, takes a swig of water.

Luis leans back, nods slowly. 'Look, Scarlett, I know things have been tough for you, past couple of years. But – and I mean this in the nicest possible way – you're a grown-up. Maybe it's time to sort your shit out.'

'Harsh.'

He shrugs. 'True though.' He studies her. 'Look, is there anything . . . do you need help?'

Scarlett opens her mouth. Yes, I need help. I'm losing my mind. I don't know who I am or where I am and inexplicably I seem to be living in the wrong body and somehow this is not my world and I think I'm going mad. The words, however, will not come. She shakes her head. 'I'll be OK,' she says, stoutly.

Then footsteps from the street beyond, the sound of the police station door swinging open behind her, and Luis looks up, angling his gaze out towards the outer foyer. Then he smiles, widely. 'Here comes the cavalry.'

Scarlett's heart stills.

Vivienne looks just as she has always looked. She wears loose-fitting trousers, a narrow strapped top. Her hair is pulled up into a high ponytail, and beads of sweat sparkle on her upper lip.

Suddenly Scarlett feels the urge to cry.

Vivienne's gaze lands on her, their eyes locking, and for a moment relief swells. Only the moment doesn't last. Vivienne nods, a distant smile, then moves past her, touching Luis on the shoulder as she goes. It is an odd touch, fingers reaching almost to his throat. Intimate. Then it is over and Vivienne walks towards the open window, leaning back against the sill.

Scarlett looks, from her, to Luis. Then, finally, to the shelf behind his head. To the baseball, the white of it lost beneath scrawled signatures. To the bobblehead of Colby Allard. To the framed photograph, old enough that it has begun to fade in the sun. Of him and Vivienne together, his arm wrapped tight around her waist. They are young in it, can barely have been out of their teens. She wears white, holds a bouquet limp in her hand.

She doesn't mean to say it, but it comes out anyway. 'You two are married?'

Vivienne glances at Luis, and he raises an eyebrow in return. A moment of silent couple speak. Then he nods. 'Fifteen years.'

Scarlett opens her mouth, closes it again.

'How are you doing?' asks Vivienne quietly.

It takes a moment for the words to work their way through to her. And for a wild moment she wants to cry. Then her shoulder raises in another shrug. 'Fine.'

Vivienne nods, slowly. Then leans in to her husband. 'The trailer park evacuation is just about done. Most everyone is out from there. Starting on Destino proper now. We should go too.'

'They put out a mandatory evacuation?' Robyn hears herself asking.

Vivienne studies her for a moment, frowns. 'No . . . but your mom and Bonnie have the town well-trained. We all know where we're supposed to go.' She shakes her head. 'Wind has picked up though. So . . . better to be safe.'

'OK, Scarlett,' Luis says with a sigh. 'I'm going to let you go.' He pushes back from the desk. 'If you'll take my advice, you'll head on out to Morro Bay.'

Robyn stands, careful. The too thin legs feeling insufficient to support her. She turns on her heel and suddenly is at the door. Then she is outside, the door slamming shut behind her.

The street is the street she has known all her life, the one she has walked a thousand times. Only it is not. The police station no longer sits on the corner of Main and Vine, but has shifted now, is tucked three doors down, in the lot where Destino Vino should be. She steps out onto the sidewalk, her heart thudding. There are flowers in planters set at regular intervals that were not there this morning. A hardware store. A shop selling artisan jewellery.

She can feel panic rising in her. This world is not real. It is some kind of waking dream. She shakes her head, sharply, trying to shake it loose, snap her back to reality. Only it doesn't work and she remains standing on this wrong street, in this wrong town. Then another thought. That in reality, her father is dead. That someone killed him, that she doesn't know who.

Then the smell of smoke penetrates, pulling her back and she turns towards the mountain, to the deep green forest where Destino Heights should be. The smoke hangs there. A whisper of steel-grey cloud, trails of it streaking across the sky as the wind pushes at its back.

'What the hell is going on?' she mutters.

'Buggered if I know,' says a voice, cheerful.

It takes long moments before the words penetrate. She turns. Zeke is wearing a baseball cap. His Bon Jovi T-shirt is ringed with sweat. He grins at her, eyes dancing. 'You done beating up cops now?'

Her body turns from him. 'For now,' she says.

What??? For now???

'So, just out of curiosity, what is your beef with Luis?'

She shakes her head. What answer could she possibly give?

'Cool, cool,' he mutters.

She turns on her heel, heads down Main Street with long, loping strides, Zeke dragged along in her wake.

'Scar . . . where are we going?' Zeke pants, struggling to keep pace with her. 'My truck is parked back there.'

She ignores him, walks faster.

Main Street peters out, stores giving way to houses. She climbs up the modest incline, braces herself, knowing what she will see. The overgrown trees, the deadened wreckage of her home peeking through them. It catches in her chest. How has this come to pass?

She doesn't stop though. Rather, turns her head away from the ruin of her life and picks up her pace.

'Scar?'

She reaches the crest of the hill. Down below she can see the road where it winds its way down through the narrow funnel of rock, right towards the highway. The cars line the road, a steady stream of traffic.

'Damn,' mutters Zeke. 'It's gonna take us forever to get through that.'

She walks quickly, through the rock tunnel, the cars going slow enough that there is little danger. From them at least. She picks her way past, the smell of gas catching in her throat. Idling engines thrum.

She glances back to see Zeke, hurrying to catch her, ducking around wing mirrors.

'The hell are we doing?'

'I need to see something,' she throws over her shoulder, picking up pace.

'What, for God's sake?'

From here, she can hear the water, the sometime deluge now little more than a trickle. Her hands have begun to shake, beads of sweat breaking out across her skin.

'You OK?'

'I don't know,' she mutters. She walks quickly, out into the bright sunlight. The smell of smoke and car exhausts combine, and she coughs.

What is happening? Because this, if it is a madness, then it is of a very specific type. If it is hallucination then it is all-encompassing, has swept through her entire life, rewritten it as something else.

She turns in place. Behind her, on the wide expanse of yellowed grass at the gully's edge, stands the town sign. *Destino.* Precisely where it ever has been and, at the same time, entirely wrong. Yellow calligraphic text has been replaced by baby blue. She stands before it, looking up. Destino. At Journey's End.

'Scarlett, babe. We gotta go. This traffic.'

A statue stands beside the sign, right at the very edge of the gully. It is one she has not seen before. A woman, her hands folded together at the waist, her head lowered. Tendrils of stone hair ring her face. She stands perhaps eight feet tall, bare feet pressed against a block podium. Around the base, a bed of flowers, miraculously still standing in the face of the oppressive heat. She steps closer, hunkers down.

Roses, their scent fragrant and sweet.

It feels like déjà vu. She reaches out, rests her fingers gently on the petal of a dusky pink rose, satin soft. And for a moment she lingers there, unwilling to look up. Because if she does not look up, then it will not be real.

'Scarlett.'

She looks up.

The podium is made of marble. At the centre, a bronze plaque. *Alex and Eve Sandoval. Lost on 25th September, 1992.* And beneath, the words *Never Forgotten*.

Chapter Twenty-Two

Robyn Sandoval – 25th September, 9.32 a.m.

'I said, are you OK?' The policewoman is looking at her, brow furrowed, holds a folder limp in her hands. 'Hey, do you need me to call someone?'

Robyn shakes her head, both a reply and an effort to clear her head. 'I . . .' She has reached out, has set her palm against the wall, and she studies it, cheery yellow beneath the weight of her. 'No,' she says. The texture of the word is different now, familiar. Round-edged and shaped almost as a question. 'Sorry . . . I think it's the heat.'

'Sure.' The policewoman's head is canted to one side. Gesture 135 in the book of sympathetic body language. 'Look, you should get on home.'

Robyn opens her mouth, closes it again, and then turns, leaving a soft 'thank you' in her wake. Steps out into the street. It is Main Street now. The way it is supposed to be. With Destino Vino and Bar 53.

The Destino where Harper died. But that had not happened there, in the other Destino.

In that Destino, on this day, Alex and Eve Sandoval had died instead. And now a feeling, a wave of grief that laps up and over her. Another lost mother.

Petit mal? A hallucination born of stress? Or something other, bigger, stranger? A different version of Destino, a different version of herself?

She turns and begins to walk quickly, the heat pressing down on her, seizing up her chest.

A car swishes past. There is not enough traffic. Where are the people? Why is no one leaving like they were in the other Destino? She knows why though, doesn't she? Because this is *her* Destino. And in her Destino, no one has told them to leave. And the fire, it is far enough away that they can tell themselves they are safe. Even though they sit surrounded by crisp, dry forest. Even though there is one road, a single highway, in and out, an entire town that will pour down onto it, slowing any evacuation to a crawl. But they are not thinking that far ahead, are they? Because there have been no plans, no Destino Wildfire Preparedness Programme. In her Destino, they are not ready for the worst to happen.

She hurries onwards.

It is there, precisely where it is supposed to be. The big house. *Her* house, the place that has contained her life entirely within it. She hurries up the front steps that groan beneath her feet, tumbles in through the front door.

Is solid around her, a structure undeniable.

Hector lets out an excited whine and rushes towards Robyn, snake-thin tail, whipping from side to side.

'Oh, thank God! Robyn, where the hell have you been?' Her mother appears from the den, a bundle of clothes clutched tight in her fingers. 'You need to pack.' She looks older now, the strain beginning to show around her eyes, make-up sinking into the corners.

'Mom.' It comes out as an exhalation, and it feels like she is sinking into the floor. *You are not dead. You didn't die.* 'I—'

'Come on. Come on. We need to hit the road.' Eve turns,

crouching down to shove the clothes into an open suitcase that lies at the foot of the stairs.

For a moment, Robyn wonders if she has missed it. If possible disaster has worked its way right up to inevitable while she was gone. 'What's going . . . have they issued an evacuation?'

'I've got all the paperwork already loaded up in the trunk. You just need to get your clothes.'

'Mom . . .?'

'What? Oh, no. No evacuation. But my contacts on the council say it's only a matter of time. Destino should be fine, only if the wind changes and brings it in this direction, odds are it's going to take out the highway. And then we won't be able to make it to the office.' She pushes down hard on the folded clothing, forcing it into too small a space. 'I thought we could head on up to the apartment in San Francisco. I mean, you're gonna need to be there next week anyway, so rather than risk it . . .'

'Mom . . .' she says again. A new feeling is building in her now. Panic. 'I told you. I can't do this. I can't. I'm sorry.'

Eve studies the suitcase in front of her. Then turns to look at her daughter. 'Can't do what?'

'I can't take over at the Sandoval Company. I can't be the CEO.' She glances down at her arms. The words do not seem to be coming from her and for a moment she expects to see tattooed vines wrapped around her wrists. The arms are bare. It is her. Only her.

Eve doesn't answer for long moments, then pushes herself up to standing. 'Everything is arranged, Robyn,' she says, quietly. 'This is what we have always planned. Since you were little. Remember? Your dad bought you that pink briefcase. And you went around telling everyone to call you Ms Sandoval. Remember?' Her eyes have filled. 'Alex, he was so excited.' She shakes her head, wipes at her eyes with fingertips. 'You're just nervous. That's all. It's cold feet.'

Robyn shakes her head. How to explain it? That she had always assumed. Was raised as a certain person, that it had never occurred to her to question whether that future fitted the shape of her. Her left hand reaches down, strokes her right arm. Suddenly wishing for the vines. For Harper and Zeke and that trailer that smells of decay.

Eve's face has become hard now. 'Is this about Mack? Is that why?' She folds her arms across her chest. 'You're not thinking straight. Once things settle down, you'll feel differently then. We'll talk about this later. Go pack.'

She opens her mouth to argue, but it will be like arguing with the ocean. Her mother has already turned her back on her, is walking with quick strides, her back stiff, irritation rolling from her.

Robyn stands in the empty hall, opens and clenches her hands. She pulls in a deep breath. Walks quickly up the stairs, Hector behind her. The wide polished oak stairs creak beneath her feet. Her heart is beating hard. The landing creaks underfoot, bedroom door ajar ahead, and she steps inside, closing it tight behind her. The ceiling fan spins, pushing heavy air. Her bed is made, comforter folded neatly at its foot. On the closed closet door, her suit hangs, pale aqua, the tags still hanging limp beneath the armpit. Waiting. Robyn stares at it.

It is not just a suit, is it? It is her future, hanging there on the wardrobe door. It is Robyn Sandoval, CEO of the Sandoval Company. It is who she was always going to be.

'I don't want this.' The words slip from her lips, and she clasps a hand over her mouth. A child who has inadvertently cursed.

Then, 'I don't want this!' She says it again, but deliberately this time, lingering on each word.

Her heart beats faster. She pushes herself off from the door and walks towards the suit, picking up the fabric between her fingers.

'I don't want this.' She squeezes the thick fabric between her fingers, balling it up until it has part-vanished inside her clenched fist. Is watching this all unfold as if from a great distance. 'I don't want this,' she says again, words louder now. Harder. Then a downward yank, hard enough that it pulls the jacket from its hanger and the whole thing hangs limp in her hands. 'I don't want this,' she says again, dropping the suit into a ball at her feet.

She stands there, staring at it. A distant knowledge of a corner having been turned here, a choice having been made. But she does not linger. Because her head has cleared now and her future, her immediate future at least, has begun to line up before her.

Robyn pushes herself away from the bedroom door, padding soft on the carpet, running her fingers along her forearms as she goes. She moves towards the mirror, not sure what it is she will find. But it is only her, with sea-salt roughened blonde hair, rounded cheeks. She lingers there for a moment, breath coming again. And she thinks of Scarlett's anger, the internal nuclear detonation of it, always waiting there, ready to blow. And Robyn feels a sense of longing.

Robyn doesn't have a temper. It has been said, often enough over the course of her thirty years, that it has become true. A long fuse that turns into no fuse at all. She stares at herself in the mirror, and probes at it, like probing a tooth for a cavity. Searching for that fledgling spark of inner fire. She looks to her hands, remembering them acting, seemingly of their own accord, fury channelled into her fingers as they shoved Luis. And she thinks of his quiet patience with her, in spite of it. The people, they looked at her differently there, Luis and Vivienne and Bonnie. A familiarity to it, as if they had spent their entire lives watching her grow up and mess up, like they knew what to expect from her, for better or worse. But here, in her Destino? They do not look at her like that. Here they look at her as a Sandoval. Each nod hello, each 'good morning', tainted by this sharp-edged wariness, politeness that has been bought, not earned.

A feeling of nausea washes over her, and she turns from the mirror, hands up to her face.

What have I done? Who have I become?

Who I was expected to be.

She moves towards her desk, pulls out her chair and sinks into it, head in her hands. This morning her world moved in perfect rhythm. Only this morning, each day was a routine, a smooth step following on from the one before. How could it only be this morning that everything changed?

She rubs her hands over her face, palms coming away wet. Forces out a slow, long breath. *Think.* In this life, – in the reality that has existed for her for the past thirty years – Harper Morgan was killed in a car crash, and Mack relinquished her for adoption. And so her future was set, as Robyn Sandoval, daughter of Alex and Eve Sandoval, future CEO of the Sandoval Company.

But this morning, the world slipped out of lockstep, transporting her to a different version of Destino, where Harper Morgan survived, Alex and Eve Sandoval dying in her place. And so she became Scarlett Morgan. With her anger and her drive and the life that had been snatched from Robyn.

She closes her eyes, digs her fists into her eyes. *I don't understand. I don't understand.* Then she forces the thoughts back, opens her eyes and sits up straighter. Because none of it matters, does it, not when you come right down to it? All that matters is the fire and the fact that her father is dead . . .

She pulls her laptop towards her, flips it open and logs into her email. It is there, perfectly where it should be.

Hey sweetheart,
Just wanted to know if you were free tomorrow? You're starting

with the Sandoval Co on Monday, right? You wanna get together? Maybe come for breakfast. There's something kind of big I need to talk to you about.

Love you.
Mack

It's timed 11.45 p.m.

He was alive then. At 11.45 p.m. Which meant that whoever killed him, they killed him after that and before her arrival, a little after 7.00 a.m.

She blows out a breath.

'Robyn.' Her mother's voice is preternaturally calm, as though the words they have just spoken had never been said. 'We have to go. I'm going to start putting the cases in the car. Can you get my laptop from the office?'

Robyn sits there for a moment, an almost Scarlett-like defiance. Strange that there is within her this absence of fear. Perhaps they have cancelled each other out. That the net result of having too much to be afraid of is a total absence of fear. Then she shakes herself, forcing her body to move. Grabs her computer bag, slips the laptop inside and slings it on her shoulder.

'Come on, Hector,' she says softly.

The pit bull pads along behind her, faithfully. Out of the bedroom, down the hall to the office. Her mother's laptop sits on the desk, closed. Then a thought. That, if she is to be the CEO of the Sandoval Company, then she has influence. That perhaps that influence could have use. And that one cannot go through life always doing what is expected.

And so she flips open the computer, logging into the Sandoval Company system. Perhaps some of those profits could be put to a use greater than merely making the comfortable more comfortable. The cost of a bunch of hotel rooms for the people who required evacuation, like up in the trailer park, it would be significant, but surely not more than the company could afford. Robyn pulls up the company finances, moving the mouse quickly through the files.

Expenditure. She clicks on it.

Once she has clicked on it, the name leaps out at her. Because it is one she does not expect to see. Not here.

Mackenzie Morgan.

She tracks the mouse across the line. A two-thousand dollar payment. Once a month, every month, from the Sandoval Company to Mack.

A burst of adrenaline, her heart thudding hard in her chest.

'Robyn! Come on!'

As the world goes dark, the question swirls around her — why the hell was her mother paying Mack?

Chapter Twenty-Three

Scarlett Morgan – 25th September, 9.45 a.m.

She wakes. Her head is resting on hot glass, her body juddering along with the rhythm of the engine. There is no lingering this time, no hanging about in a hypnagogic state. She opens her eyes, blinks in to the early morning sun. She looks down at her arms. The tattoos are there. Scarlett pushes herself upright, straining against the seatbelt, looking about her, at Zeke at the wheel, at the trail of cars before them, twists around to see the trail of cars behind.

'She wakes.' He watches her, then, 'You OK?'

'Uh huh.'

It is the adrenaline. The switch between Robyn and Scarlett comes with the build-up of stress. She drums her fingernails on her knees. How interesting, she thinks.

'You have a good sleep?' Zeke smiles at her.

Her stomach flips. She nods, awkward.

Zeke reaches over, squeezes her hand. Scarlett's fingers slide into the gaps between his, a habit that is not hers. She looks down, dizzy suddenly. Cannot remember the last time she has seen this, her hand (or as near as dammit) entwined in someone else's. How long has it been? There have been men. Relationships, for the want of a better word, scattered here and there.

None of them lasted. She has blamed circumstances, luck. She looks down, watches Zeke's thumb stroking against hers. She has lied to herself. Because each of these fledgling relationships, they had not fallen, but instead had been pushed. It just isn't right. Words she has said how many times to a crestfallen face. The death blow to one more possible future.

'What? What are you thinking?'

Robyn, or Scarlett, rather, shakes her head, forces her attention away from the hand that is wrapped around hers. She nods out to the road ahead, a solid line of cars, brake lights twinkling. 'Guess the evacuation is going well,' she mutters.

They are moving, slow but steady. An SUV ahead of them, the low outline of children in the back, two of them, a dog in between.

'Yup.' Zeke takes a slug from a Dr Pepper can. 'We only got about five miles to Morro Bay. Trouble is, it's five miles of this.' He gestures towards the traffic.

The radio burbles, The Beatles giving way to a newscaster, voice serious. 'Authorities have confirmed that the Seven Hills' fire is now no longer contained and is moving southward towards Seven Hills. An additional evacuation order has been issued for the surrounding towns of Ridgeway, Hillview and Tupelo.'

'Not Destino,' murmurs Scarlett.

'Not Destino,' agrees Zeke, grimly. 'Guess evacuation is an unpopular call. Makes sense they only focus on the towns they absolutely have to. The places the fire is on top of. Trouble is, when fire is on top of you, people panic. Panicking people are not good at evacuating.' He glances across at her, grins. 'How much do I sound like your mom right now?'

'I guess,' she says carefully, 'you can see their point. Not turfing out a whole town without reason.'

'Yeah, but it's not without reason, is it? Seven Hills. It's thirty miles as the crow flies. And that space, it's filled up with forest that's been dried out by the drought. Wildfire speed – you're looking at around fifteen miles an hour. That means, if it shifts, we have about two hours. That's a lot of people to evacuate in not a lot of time. Guess these folks have done the math too – let's be honest, they have had the Wildfire Preparedness Programme lecturing them for years – and so they start to think. That maybe they don't want to wait until smoke has become fire, because maybe then it'll be too late.' He shrugs. 'I mean, don't get me wrong, the fund helps.'

The fund?

'If all these people had to head to a shelter, had to leave their pets behind, else sleep in their car, I'm betting they'd all be making different calculations. Likely they'd wanna wait until they had absolutely no choice, until it was obvious that the fire was coming for them.' He waves at the line of traffic ahead. 'That's what's so genius about what your mom and Bonnie have done. They changed the equation. Setting up the fund, taking a small amount every month from residents, so that when the worst happens they don't have to shell out a ton of money on hotels. They can get out without worrying about that. It's kind of genius.'

'Yes,' she agrees, quietly. 'It is.'

He glances across at her. 'I know what you're thinking.'

'Do you?'

'I get that it's easy to feel invisible. Harper Morgan's daughter, instead of just being Scarlett.'

For an absurd moment, Scarlett feels as if she will laugh. Invisible as Robyn because all anyone can see is the Sandoval name. Invisible here because she can never live up to her parents. Seems that invisibility is her destiny.

She shifts her gaze, watching the dry brush sweep by. Is thinking about money. Of the line in a spreadsheet, month after month. Of two thousand dollars going right from her mother's account into Mack's. Why? It was a lot of money, certainly far too much to be given from the goodness of her heart. Her right index finger trails its way along the snaking vines on her arms. It had seemed to her, since he returned five years ago, that her mother had at best barely tolerated her birth father's presence, their conversations topping out at passing comments on the weather.

The truck hits a divot in the road, and she bumps up in her seat.

'Woah,' mutters Zeke.

She looks across at him, thoughts skipping.

How is any of this possible?

Is it perhaps, some kind of unending dream?

She pinches the twisting vine on her arm, hard enough that it leaves behind a welt. And waits to wake.

'You . . . OK?' asks Zeke again, staring at her.

'Uh huh.' She sighs. It had been worth a shot.

'Scarlett? You been acting kind of weird.' He considers, then adds, 'Even for you.'

'Hey,' she says. 'Where did we meet?'

He gives her a long look. 'You seriously don't remember?'

There are flashes of . . . something. Loud music. Breath that smells of whiskey. The dizzying sense of a floor that will not remain still. She shrugs, attempts a flirtatious look, and Zeke recoils. She clearly needs to practise that one.

'I'm testing you,' she says. 'Go on. Where did we meet?'

'In the Devil's Playground. Templeton. Shittiest damn bar I ever saw. Although you seemed to be enjoying it. I told you you were hot.' He shrugs. 'That was all it took.'

Scarlett nods slowly. 'Feels like a long time ago.'

'Two years, eight months, three weeks and two days,' he says promptly.

That makes her smile. 'Approximately?'

'Yeah. Approximately.'

They inch forward, painfully slow. Scarlett glances around her, surreptitiously. A cell phone sits in the centre console. She glances at it, then up at Zeke. His cell sits in a plastic phone holder suckered to the windscreen. So she takes a chance, picks up the cell, waits for him to ask her what the hell she is doing. But he doesn't, just sits there, staring glumly ahead at the crawling lines of traffic.

She presses her thumb to the ID badge, waits as the swirls fill themselves in. Unlocked. The home screen is blank. Just a template background. She opens the photo app first. A seemingly random mix of attractive landscapes, of sunsets and blue skies, desert and ocean and people. She studies them. Young, all of them, a parade of faces that can't possibly have hit thirty yet. And Scarlett – her – in amongst them, cheek against cheek, eyes with that wide-open dazed look that tells of too many beers, or of something worse. They are happy photos, in bars and on beaches, wide grins and just-ended laughter.

A banner hangs at the top of the screen, and she flicks to it. A calendar alert. *Tomorrow, 4.00 p.m., job interview, Barker's Bar, Oxnard.* She stares at the words, shadows of memory flickering. Of Zeke's voice, high and tense, *'This is stupid.' 'Don't call me stupid!' 'I didn't call you stupid, I called the idea stupid.' 'I have to do something, Zeke. I need a damn job.' 'Yes, but this job?' 'You really think I can't handle myself around all that alcohol?'* An exquisitely long silence. *'Zeke?'*

She glances across at him.

'What?'

'Nothing.'

'Don't go, Scarlett. Don't leave.' 'Why? What's the point in me staying? What's the point in being here, being the screw-up daughter of Harper and Mack?'

A beep from the phone, an alert on the text app, and she presses on it. A text marked Dad. *I don't know what's going on with you. I heard Luis sent you out of town. This CalFire thing is important to me, Scarlett, so please don't do anything else to mess it up.*

She studies it, her insides twisting. Can feel a flush building in her cheeks, heat that rises through her.

'What?' Zeke looks down at her lap, at the phone screen. 'Scar, just ignore him.' He shakes his head, tsking. 'Damn cheek. After everything.'

She shakes her head, closes down the cell phone screen and slides it back into the centre console. Had you asked her what it would be like if she were to wake one day and find that That Day had never happened, that she had the two parents of her birth, that her life had trundled on as it was meant to without the rude interruption of tragedy, she would likely have told you that it would be bliss. That all would be well.

That was the very definition of an origin story, wasn't it? Batman's parents murdered. An accident with gamma radiation that creates a Hulk. It is an interruption, a disaster that shunts your life from one track onto an entirely different one. Was it even an origin story if it was not riddled with loss? The tragic queen in a fairytale. Gentle and good and kind. The king folded in grief, stolen by the thoughts of what could have been. It was tragedy with little room for nuance, the loss a disaster unmitigated. *What could have been* draped in a thick veil of romanticism.

'That guy . . .' Zeke purses his lips, taps his fingers on the steering wheel. 'Look, don't . . . now don't hate me . . .'

'Just say it,' she murmurs, in a voice that isn't entirely her own.

'It feels like, you spent half of your life trying to be one version of your father, the hero version. And then when that went wrong, when all that shit with CalFire happened, you switched lanes and became the villain version.' He glances at her, flushing. 'I don't mean villain. That's too harsh.'

'No, it's not.' Who said that?

'I just mean, the drinking, the craziness. It's like you started embodying that version of him instead. Like you rebelled by becoming the worst version of him.' He shrugs. 'Maybe it's time to just be you.'

The words settle on her and she bites her lip to stop herself from interrupting the flow of them. Because her Mack, in her mind, was not like this. Or, he liked to have fun, enjoyed socialising . . . OK, fine, was a bit of a drinker . . . The thoughts, they come in Robyn's voice, and Scarlett, she finds herself shaking her head. *You're fooling yourself, kid. Your Mack, he was exactly like mine, you just wouldn't let yourself see it.*

Scarlett shakes her head, glances over at Zeke with a half-smile.

'What?' asks Zeke, frowning.

'You're actually pretty smart,' she says.

He grins. 'That's what my university professors said. Right before they said "But we would still like you to leave and never darken our door again."'

'I can never remember what you studied?' she says, casually.

He looks at her, a long look. 'Really? And we've been together how long?'

'Two years, eight months, three weeks and two days,' she says, promptly.

He grins. 'Physics. I studied physics.' He glances at her. 'Yeah,' he sighs, 'it's not a great conversation starter.'

The final chords of 'You Can Call Me Al' drift away, giving way to the opening of 'Wrecking Ball'.

She thinks for a moment, about those spreadsheets. The payments to Mack. 'My dad. He ever ask you for money?'

Zeke hesitates, a change coming over his face.

She sits up taller. 'He has, hasn't he?'

He sighs. 'This is not exactly what I meant by putting Mack behind us.'

'Tell me.'

'Jesus. Fine . . . OK. You remember that time I wrote off my truck out in Tupelo? Remember, I was on my way back from that job hanging sheet rock?'

'Sure.' A flash of a memory. A truck hood folded up, concertina-like.

'You know I called your dad and asked him to come get me?'

'OK...'

He hesitates, then plunges on. 'He offered to keep it between us. If I threw some money his way.'

She doesn't answer, is too caught up in the feeling of sinking.

'I mean, obviously I just laughed it off. Not like I was rolling in cash to just be handing it out left and right.' He catches himself. 'Also, honesty and openness in our relationship too.'

'You're a saint,' she murmurs.

'Bless you.'

'Sod off.' She smiles, fondly.

He grins. Then the sound of distant sirens and Zeke turns, angling his head to look ahead, beyond the line of cars. A fire engine weaves its way along the shoulder, flashing by the all-but-parked cars, sirens blaring. It approaches, louder, louder, deafening, and then it is past and gone, the sounds echoing behind it.

Scarlett turns in her seat, watches it go. Then, attention caught, she rolls the window down, heat rolling right on in, bringing with it smoke, exhaust fumes, the low roar of hundreds of cars crawling. But she looks beyond that, past the traffic and the smog, towards the mountain. Clouds hang over it, dark and foreboding. Not clouds. Smoke.

'That does not look good,' she says, quietly.

'No,' agrees Zeke.

'You think the wind has shifted?'

His silence is heavy suddenly, and she glances back at him. 'I hope not,' he says, carefully.

She turns her face towards the road ahead. The traffic has slowed now, as if driver after driver has been distracted, is looking behind them at the imposing clouds. Her stomach knots up. Heart begins to thump. A sinking feeling that she is lost, that she no longer understands where she comes from, no longer knows who her father is. This man who has a hero side, and a villain. How had she missed it, this dark side of him? Had she been too dazzled by the brightness of the hero, missing entirely the shadows? What did he use to leverage money from Eve? And what were the consequences of that?

Her vision is narrowing now, periphery going black.

Had that money got him killed?

The world shifts to black.

Chapter Twenty-Four

There was a building up. A wall of sound, the animal roar of flame. The fire that had settled itself above the small town of Seven Hills had burned for five days now. Had worked its way slowly through the forests that sat above the town, devouring the fuel left in its path by winter storms. Through the debris of dead trees, the dried-out brush that littered the forest floor.

And, for days, it seemed that man could yet impose mastery on nature. The mustard-clad figures moving about the raging red of the flame, cutting deep trenches to create an enclosure, a wraparound moat for the fire. You shall not pass.

Nature though, she had her own plans.

While the people of the little town below loaded up their most valuable possessions, parsing through the detritus of life and making that most impossible of decisions – what is to be saved, what is to be lost – the world shifted. Perhaps it was a butterfly that flapped its wings in the Amazon. Perhaps a leaf that lost its grip, circling its way to the ground.

Whatever it was, it was enough to bring about a sea change.

There came a sudden whoosh of wind, one that tore its way through the fire, making the flames dance and leap. And, when the wind died, it would become clear to those mustard-yellow figures, that something had changed. That the wind had arced back on itself, blowing now not towards the south and the deep-carved trenches and the huddled town of Seven Hills below. But instead, west.

It began with a single, solitary tree. A pine with a trunk thick enough that you could wrap your arms around it and finger would not meet finger. The tree was parched. Dried out from this year's drought. From the drought of the year before and the year before that.

And so, when the wind whooshed and the embers leapt, when one of them landed in amongst the dried-out needles of the pine tree, it was the work of but a moment for ember to become flame. The tree went up, flames clambering the sides of it, reaching, stretching for its tip. And beyond.

Because the wind was not done yet. Had got a taste for destruction and was determined now to make the most of it.

One tree became two, became three, became four.

And the mustard figures shouted warnings, hurrying towards the flames, axes and shovels at the ready, as though that would do anything at all. Because they had played the game, man vs nature. But in doing so, they had forgotten — sometimes nature cheats.

And so the fire flew, renewed now by this wind at its back. And it began to sweep across the acres and acres of dried-out forest.

And beyond that, Destino.

Chapter Twenty-Five

Robyn Sandoval – 25th September, 9.45am

The transition is easier this time, cleaner than it has been before. A wave of dizziness, one blink, two, and she is at the desk again, the laptop open before her, the spreadsheets laid out. The sound of Hector, his breaths coming in short sharp pants, hot against her leg. Floorboards creaking beneath her, her mother's footsteps, quick and urgent.

Her mother. Eve.

The memories crash back in. Hers. And Scarlett's. Of Zeke's voice.

Robyn shakes her head, focuses on the screen, on the spreadsheets. On that line, two thousand dollars, paid to Mack Morgan each month.

The question inevitable – why was Eve paying Mack?

Robyn chews at her nail. Thinks of the almost-wince triggered in Eve each time Mack's name was mentioned. Funny, isn't it? How they have never discussed it, never gone beyond the briefest of conversations, in all those five years since his return.

'Are you OK with this, Mom?' A smile that did not reach her eyes, a tightness to her jaw that told of the lie. 'I'm fine, darling. Of course I'm fine. It's good that you have a relationship with him. It's good that he's here.'

Robyn leans back in the chair, rubs her hands over her face.

When Mack had said it, had announced his plans to stay, that he had found a little house in Destino, somewhere he could be close, where he could get to know his daughter again, Eve had smiled. Had said, 'Well, if there is anything we can do to help . . .'

Was that it?

Was the two thousand dollars the help?

But she can't shake it, the thought of what Zeke has said. Mack demanding money, the price of secret keeping.

So was there something Mack held over Eve, some secret knowledge, sufficient that she would pay him to keep it hidden. Because if that was true, then . . .

Then what else would she do?

Footsteps in the hall outside, her mother stalking from room to room. Loud huffs.

Robyn scrolls through the expenditure file. The payments go all the way back, right back to Mack's return to Destino.

Robyn leans forward, puts her head in her hands. Mack was dead. Someone had placed a pillow across his face, had held it down. She blows out a slow breath. It was all getting to her, the shock, the strain of it all, building up together, swamping her. Because this, this thing that she is thinking that she cannot even put words to, it is not possible. If for no other reason than, had Eve left, she would have heard. This house is old, mature enough that the bones of it groan beneath the weight of a footstep. And before Eve's door there is a board, one that her father always said they should fix but never did, one that, after his death, her mother had claimed as some kind of memento mori. *'The sound of it, each time I open my door and step out, it reminds me of your father.'* It was a beacon, an alert that her mother was on the move. Unfailing.

As if in agreement, the board groans, footsteps come closer and the office door flies open. 'Robyn.' Her mother has stripped down to a vest top, loose-fit trousers. Her make-up has slipped now, hair begun to work its way free from its bun. 'Robyn, would you come on?' She hesitates, looks from her daughter to the computer. 'What the hell are you doing? We have to—'

'Why were you paying Mack two thousand dollars a month?'

Eve freezes. 'What?'

'The money. Why were you paying my father?'

There is a moment, thoughts flying across her face. Then the shutter comes down. 'I don't know what you're talking about.'

Robyn stares at her, then pivots back towards the computer, stares pointedly at the screen. 'The spreadsheet knows what I'm talking about.'

'A mistake,' Eve says, the words tumbling out. 'Must be some kind of mix-up. Will you come on? I've gotten everything loaded . . .' She turns on her heel, walking with quick strides down the hall.

Robyn pushes her chair back, following along behind her mother. 'Mom!'

'Robyn.' She clatters across the floorboard, back into the master bedroom. The television is on, the screen vivid red with flame. A forest, consumed by fire. 'This is not the time.'

'Are you telling me you've been giving him money from the goodness of your heart? Mom?'

But her mother is not listening, is staring at the television.

The camera has cut away, focuses on a presenter, her expression serious. 'We have breaking news. Reports from the Seven Hills' fire suggest that the wind has now changed direction. Authorities are saying that the fire teams on site have now entirely lost control of . . . Yes, we have confirmation that the fire is now moving away from the town of Seven Hills and those evacuated areas, and is instead heading west, towards Destino. Let me remind you, Destino has not experienced a wildfire in over a hundred years. There is a ridge that runs the length of the valley, that has in the past protected the town down below. That being said, authorities are now advising residents of Destino to evacuate. I repeat, all Destino residents have now been issued an evacuation advisory. If you are in the town of Destino, you are strongly encouraged to begin the process of getting out.'

'Oh God,' Eve breathes. 'We have to go!' She rushes past her, grabbing a framed photograph of Alex from her bedside table. 'We have to go now!' She spins, hurries past Robyn, out of the bedroom.

And time freezes as Robyn watches her mother dart onto the landing, as she watches the dance of her feet, as they sidestep the creaking floorboard.

She stands, frozen in space, listening to her mother as she runs lightly down the stairs, listening for what isn't there. Because no matter what she had thought, her mother could have left the house last night.

And her heart thuds faster and her vision narrows and, right on cue, the darkness sweeps in.

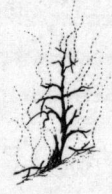

Chapter Twenty-Six

Mags Reyes – 25th September, 9.48 a.m.

Mags has driven this road every day of her adult life. She knows each inch of it. The flat parcel of land that juts out from the side of the road peering over Destino proper. She knows the sycamore tree that was struck by lightning that autumn, just after she turned twelve, the bolt carving the trunk in two, the separate halves pointing in their own directions. She knows the knotted brush that litters the landscape.

Of course, it looks different today.

She can see it in the rear-view mirror, the thunderhead cloud. It hangs back over the highway, up above the waterfall, dark and threatening. It has grown. Since the last time that she looked, it has expanded, filling up the sky from horizon to horizon. The smell of smoke catches in her throat and Mags gags.

She pushes the accelerator further to the floor.

Her stomach has knotted itself up tight, her fingers shaking. And she tries to tell herself that this is normal. Who would not feel such things when a thundercloud of smoke hovers in the rear-view mirror.

But it isn't that, is it?

It is the genetic testing. The one no one bothered to mention.

It was the fact that, for all her pretending, for all her trundling through life and acting as if she was an equal part of the home she was raised in, it was a lie. It was all a lie.

She guides the car around the dog-leg corner, faster than she should. Because that thought, it brings the other lie tumbling back.

The doctors are hopeful. The doctors say that it is just the treatment. The doctors say that your father will recover, that he will be well again.

Her mother had stood before her, her face plastered with that perpetual look of displeasure, and had lied to her. Had recreated her reality into one that suited her.

But then, her mother hadn't been the only one to lie, had she? Mags had told herself that her life was adrift, that her marriage was a failure, that there were no options but to return to Destino, to be entirely who her mother demanded she be.

It comes then, inevitably. The memories of the time before. Of that tiny row house in Walnut Creek, the sound of the trams going past, the neighbours' spaniel barking. Of Gabrielle learning to crawl. Of Oscar, the day he figured out how to pull the skirting boards off the wall with only a butter knife.

Of Jack.

She lets out a sob.

Another memory now, the kitchen in Walnut Creek smelling of garlic and lemon. The phone pressed tight to her ear, her mother complaining about something and nothing. The words spilling, one after the other, after the other. Mags murmuring something that was meant to be soothing, that has a similar effect to gasoline on a fire. Hearing the edge to her mother's voice, the one that said, without saying *you never have been quite what I had hoped you would be.* And feeling tears prick at the back of her eyes and her hands begin to shake, and then a sense of pressure, hands on her shoulders that turn her bodily, her husband's body engulfing her. The phone eased from her fingers,

Jack's voice, calm, soothing, an iron fist in a velvet glove. 'Bon, Mags is gonna have to call you back another time. She's not feeling very well right now.'

'Why is she like this with me? Why can I never seem to please her?'

Jack hugging her tighter. The smell of patchouli. 'Maybe it's because you're a girl. Maybe she pushes you harder because of that.'

'I'll never be enough for her.'

'No. Perhaps not. But that doesn't mean you aren't enough.'

Did she process his words? Did they sink in? Seems like if she had, if she'd truly thought about them, what came next would have played out differently.

Another memory, this one of Jack standing in the street before the diner. A smile on his face that doesn't meet his eyes. He waits patiently as the children clamber in, arguing about something and nothing. Leans in, helps them with their belts and closes the door firmly behind them. Then he turns to her, and she can see his eyes, moist, can see the dark circles, the lines of strain in his forehead.

'Why are you doing this, Mags?' His voice had been quiet enough that for a moment she had considered pleading with him to shout. Anything would be better than these carefully mouthed words, the grief coating them. 'After everything she has done to you? After all she has made you feel? Why are you giving up everything for her?'

And Mags, coward that she was, she had looked away, unwilling suddenly to meet those eyes. 'I have no choice.'

It had felt like that, at the time at least. But if she were asked the question now, she would answer differently. *I did it so that I would finally be enough. I did it so that she could see me doing it, letting go of everything I have ever loved, and then she would know, that she has been wrong about me.*

She lets out a breath, half gasp, half sob, the realisation

settling over her. Of all that she has done wrong. A tear snakes its way out, plunging down her cheek, the cold of it shocking against the heat of the day. So many mistakes. How could one person make so many mistakes?

The road arcs around a wide bend, and Mags steers the car wide, pulling onto the flat stretch of land. The tyres churn at the loose, dry soil, and she pulls the parking brake on hard enough to snap it. A sudden feeling of entrapment and she clicks her belt off, shoves open the driver's door. Is crying proper now.

What have I done? What have I given up?

Destino spread out below her. There is movement now, of cars rearing out of driveways, merging into a line of traffic that snakes its way down Main Street. Mags stares at it, following the shape of the road. Can see the diner from here. The shut-up box with its broken-down front porch, the cladding that hangs from the sides, holding on with a nail and a prayer. And suddenly she hates it. Hates what she has become for it. She looks up at the distant cloud, at the deep black folds. It is closer now. Finger tendrils clambering across Destino Heights, the distant subdivision lost beneath it now. The smoke rakes at her throat.

It is not Mags that chooses the next steps. Rather some long-buried mammalian instinct that triggers her heart to beat faster, her senses to awaken. She turns back to the car, footsteps quick enough that they slip-slide on the loose soil. She leans in, turns the radio on.

'Authorities are saying that all reasonable precautions were taken in the issuance of evacuation orders, but have given no reason for the distinct lack of preparedness we are seeing currently. Experts are warning that the forest in this area is densely packed with brush and debris, and that the failure to implement recommended programmes such as prescribed burns is likely to add considerably to the ferocity of the fire as it hits this stretch of trees.'

Mags lowers herself into the driver's seat. Waiting.

'Again, for those of you just joining us, authorities have warned that they are seeing a change in wind direction. That it is pushing the fire away from the town of Seven Hills – good news for those people – and towards the town of Destino. Authorities have issued an evacuation advisory for this area. They state that there is still a considerable distance between the town and the fire front, and that they remain hopeful they can get the fire under control without further damage to life or property. But for those folks out in Destino, please consider your situation and start putting together an evacuation for you, your family and pets.'

Mags pulls in a deep breath. It tastes of smoke. She pulls the door closed behind her, hand grips the parking brake.

Then a sound, her phone trilling. Jack. She thumbs 'answer' quickly.

'Hey.'

'Hey, did you hear? Are you guys OK?'

'I'm just on my way to get the kids from my mom's. Then we're heading straight out.'

A breath that sounds unsteady, then, 'OK, they're saying there's an evacuation centre in Morro Bay, that they're sending everyone to the high school gymnasium.' The sound of a door slamming. 'I'm just getting into the car now. I'm going to meet you there, OK?'

Mags' breath catches in her throat, and she nods, suddenly not trusting herself to speak. Deep breath. 'Jack, once we get there . . . I think we should talk.' She presses the accelerator hard to the floor, pulling onto the road up the mountain, her wheels spinning.

Chapter Twenty-Seven

Bonnie Aubrey – 25th September, 9.52 a.m.

The television is louder than she would like. Bonnie moves past the children, reaches for the remote control.

'But what does it mean, Grandma?' Gabrielle looks at her, eyes wide. 'What does evacuation advisory mean?'

Bonnie holds her thumb down harder over the volume button, turning it down to a whisper. 'Oh, honey. It just means that people are getting silly. Trying to scare folks, is all.'

Gabrielle studies her and there is a sudden feeling of being seen right through, of having the soul ripped out of her, stretched out on display.

Bonnie sets the control down, harder than she means to. 'You best get your shoes on, Miss. Your mom will be here any minute.'

Doubt flits across her granddaughter's face. 'You and Pop-Pop are coming, though, right, Grandma?'

Bonnie turns her back on the child, schooling her face to stillness. 'Oh, sweet girl, Pop-Pop and I will be just fine. Right here.'

Gabrielle glances at her brother, engrossed in a game on his handheld device, and pushes herself up to standing, walking with measured steps to her grandmother's side. 'Grandma,' she says quietly, 'the news is saying that you should check the perimeter . . .' she pronounces the word carefully, 'of the house. That you should make sure there are no branches or leaves or anything in the gutters.' When did the child turn forty? her granddaughter studies her, seriously. 'Did you do that?'

Bonnie feels irritation rising but forces it into a makeshift smile. 'Oh, sure. That's all done. Don't you worry.'

When were the gutters last cleared? And there was that broken-down old playhouse, little more than a heap of wood now. That should have been cleared away, probably.

Then the irritation fights back, rising up.

No! See? This is what they do. This is what the news turns us into, people afraid to say boo.'

She snorts. 'Lot of fuss and bother about nothing, if you ask me.'

Gabrielle recoils, her expression changing. And, for a moment, a surge of guilt washes over Bonnie. 'Anyway,' she says, forcing cheer into her voice, 'come on. Shoes. Your momma will be mad if you aren't ready.'

Her granddaughter nods slowly, eyes downcast, and moves towards the back door, sneakers scattered like bird seed. And it comes at Bonnie, like the switching on of a light. *Your momma will be mad if you aren't ready.* Sometimes life gives you those moments, the ones of perfect clarity, where you see everything entirely as it is. It lurches up, over her, and for a moment it seems that she will fold up, crushed beneath the weight of it all. *Your momma will be mad if you aren't ready.* I am on your side. But your momma will be mad. Changing a little girl's reality, one sentence at a time.

For a moment, it feels like she can't breathe.

Only then comes the sound of a car on the drive and her shoulder stiffens and her jaw tightens and she readies herself for the perpetual war once more.

The door swings open, and Oscar is rushing past her,

throwing himself into her daughter's arms. 'Did you hear, Mommy, about the fire?'

'I did, sweetie.' Her voice is calm, light. 'Hey, I have some good news for you. Daddy's going to drive up to meet us. He misses you guys so much, he was like, "I'm gonna go ahead and come out to Morro Bay too."'

Oscar lets out a loud cheer. Gabrielle stands up taller, a look of relief flying across her features.

'OK, so let's go. Go grab your bags and then hurry on out to the car, OK? I'm hungry and I reckon we can persuade Daddy to take us for pizza.' Maggie smiles, watches as her children run in the direction of the bedroom.

Then they are gone, and so is the smile.

'Mom, are you packed?'

The initial volley of arrows released.

'No, Maggie. I have already told you. We aren't going anywhere.'

The thud as they hit shields.

'The situation has changed. The fire is now heading in this direction.'

Bonnie turns away from her, shaking her head. 'You young people are such Nervous Nellies.' The clatter of sword on shield, the defiant roar. As if wars can be won by will alone.

Her daughter rounds the counter, is staring at her, arms folded. 'Have you rung for a medical transport?'

She doesn't answer.

'Have you gathered together your paperwork, Dad's medication? Have you made a plan for when the advisory becomes mandatory?'

Bonnie feels it descending. The red mist. Irritation giving way to fury now. At this girl of hers, standing before her, sawing at the very branch on which she stands. 'What is the matter with you?' she snaps. She doesn't mean to. And yet Maggie recoils, and Bonnie realises it really doesn't matter what she meant.

'What is the matter with me?' Maggie's voice sounds different, a barely contained fury. 'What is the matter with *me*?' She glances at the open door, at the distant children clambering into the waiting car. They are far enough away that they will not hear her, but she lowers her voice nonetheless. 'I have spoken to Viv, Mother. I know you've been lying to me.'

A moment then, reality fracturing straight down the middle.

'You told me Dad was doing well. You told me Dad was going to survive this.' Her daughter's voice cracks. 'He is *dying*. And you lied about it.'

Bonnie feels her legs, loose beneath her, reaches out to clutch hold of the countertop.

'Mom, please. I am *begging* you. It is time to stop lying. If not to me, then at least to yourself.' Her daughter steps closer to her, close enough that she can smell the jasmine in her perfume. It is overwhelming. She turns her head away, searching for clean air to breathe.

'Mom . . . you can't . . . you can't keep doing this. You can't keep pretending things are the way you want them to be.'

Bonnie pulls in a breath, or something that is halfway between a breath and a sob, and, for a moment, it seems that the wall will crack, the dam will break.

Then she shakes her head, and the moment has passed.

'You should go say goodbye to your father. We'll still be here when you get back. After you've wasted the precious little money you have.'

Chapter Twenty-Eight

Scarlett Morgan – 25th September, 10.13am

She doesn't know how long she slept, but knows from the texture of her dreams that she has, in fact, slept. Her dreams, they return to her in pieces, memories that are not her own. Of high school hallways. Of heat and flame. Scarlett's dreams. But, overlaying the whole of it, the image of Mack lying dead. She awakens with the jolt of the truck coming to a hard stop, the sudden silence as the engine is switched off.

Scarlett opens her eyes.

The radio is on, the reporter's voice serious. 'We can now confirm that the wind has changed direction, is now blowing towards the west. That means that the fire is now moving away from Seven Hills and has begun to burn across the forest that separates the town from Destino.'

Her breath catches in her throat and she looks to Zeke. His face is tight, eyes worried. Then he sees her looking, rearranges his features.

'It'll be . . . OK,' he says. Is very obviously lying.

She forces herself together, gives him a smile that even she doesn't believe. 'I . . . know.'

He studies her for a moment, on what? 'OK. I'll go get us a

room.' He hesitates. 'I mean, if you're planning on staying . . .?'

Scarlett looks down.

'Well, look, you can decide . . . just let me get the room key and . . .'

'I'll wait here for you,' she says, quietly.

He hesitates then nods and is gone.

She waits, watches his narrow frame vanish inside the low-slung building. Her fingers dance against her knees, leg bouncing, and suddenly she is overwhelmed by it, the need to flee. Scarlett – or is it Robyn? – twitching to return home.

She blows out a breath, gaze caught by movement ahead.

The parking lot is filling up now, a steady stream of cars spilling in from the road. A Chevvy pulls into a parking spot across from them. Scarlett watches it, pulled in by the sensation of being stared at. A woman climbs out from the driver's side, and, for a moment, she doesn't recognise her. Then their eyes meet and recognition hits. It is Mags. Her hair is shorter, worn loose, lightened to the colour of honey. She wears make-up, a loose-fit blouse, looks about a hundred years younger than the last time she saw her. But then, she reminds herself, the last time she saw her was a whole world away. She waits, a sudden yearning for a look of recognition, for Mags to spot something in her that she recognises, some sign that, beneath the skin of Scarlett, some element of Robyn still remains.

Mags looks away, closing the door behind her. An 'I'll be right back' thrown over her shoulder to her mother in the passenger seat, her children who hang precariously through the rear windows. She walks towards Robyn. Towards Scarlett. Her hand raised in a small wave, a wry smile.

And Scarlett finds herself unclipping her seatbelt, opening the car door, clambering out. And then . . . then she is pulled into a hug, and suddenly she can't breathe and tears prickle at the back of her eyes. Mags' cheek is soft against hers. She smells of jasmine. Scarlett's arms grip her, tighter than Robyn had intended to.

'Hey,' murmurs Mags, 'you OK?' She pulls back, studies her. 'You look freaked.'

'I . . .' But it won't work, the words won't come.

'Hey, now.' Mags takes hold of her hands, squeezes them tight. 'We're OK. We're in the best possible place.' She smiles, widely. 'The moms have been preparing for this for years.'

Footsteps break into Scarlett's awareness and she refocuses, beyond Mags' shoulder. She does not recognise the woman who walks towards her. And then, kaleidoscope-like the image shifts, and she remembers an earlier version of herself, of waking up in Scarlett's body, a woman handing her coffee she has not ordered.

Bonnie smiles at her.

It *is* Bonnie. It also is not. It's the smile, it's the way that she moves, the way that her shoulders are slung back, the way that her head is held high. It is a Bonnie she does not know.

'You OK, munchkin?' The woman who is not Bonnie leans in, kisses her light on the cheek. 'What's up?'

She cannot make the words come, but her gaze says it all, locked on the mountains, the smoke filled thunderheads that loom over them. And within it, the slightest suggestion of red. The vanguard giving way to the army proper.

Bonnie follows her gaze, nods solemnly. 'I know. I know,' she says, quietly. 'But look, we are in the best position we can be in, all things considered. The prescribed burns have done what they were meant to. That forest, it has about as little fuel in it as we can achieve, given the drought.'

Mags lets out a laugh, holds out her hands, flexes her fingers. 'I still can't bend my fingers properly after our go at the undergrowth.'

A flash of Scarlett memory: the heavy scent of pine, sweat that pours off her skin, the weight of a shovel in her hands, the sound of voices that bounce from the canopy above – enough of them that it seemed as though all of Destino had entered the forest, intent on clearing it of debris. Of fuel.

'You just have to hang onto the fact that we've done everything we can. We've given Destino it's best chance.' She shakes her head. 'Can't stop fire. Fire is a fact of life. We can take the fury out of it, though, and that's what we've done.'

Bonnie turns, studies her; for a wild moment it seems that she will notice, will recognise the Robyn in the Scarlett. Then, 'I know this is hard for you. You're used to being up there. To dealing with this stuff yourself. To be stuck here with us must be tough.' She shakes her head. 'Look, you get settled and we'll go find your mom. I'm willing to bet she's got enough jobs waiting to keep all of our minds occupied.'

Mags smiles. 'I should go get us checked-in.' She turns back towards her car. 'Come on, you little reprobates. Let's go.'

The children tumble out of the car. The boy – Oscar? – walks slowly, head down, his attention focused on the games console in his fingers. The girl runs, long, loping strides, her head constantly turning back towards the mountains, the looming fire. She pulls up sharp beside them, her hand waving back in the direction they have come. 'You see it? That's bad, right? Oh, it's so bad.'

Bonnie glances at Scarlett, a wry smile. 'Oh, it'll be fine. Fire is just nature's way of having a good clear-out. Think of it as a forest spring clean.'

The girl nods, face serious. Then her gaze shifts, locks on Scarlett. 'You know,' she says conversationally, 'when I grow up, I'm gonna be a firefighter. Just like you were.'

Chapter Twenty-Nine

Scarlett Morgan – 25th September, 10:35 a.m.

The room is cold. Shockingly so after the sweltering heat of the day, air conditioning turned up to arctic heights. Two queen-sized beds, comforters tucked tight around them. Clean. Basic. Scarlett stands there, in the doorway, the door open at her back, the distant glow of the burning fire. She should close it, block out the hot air, the lingering smoke. Only she can't. Because it feels suddenly like that door is *the* door, that shutting it will shut out Robyn, the other Destino. The one where they are not ready.

Zeke moves behind her, closes the door.

'I just saw your mom,' he says brightly. 'She's a couple of rooms down. Number 221. Says you should go see her once you're settled.' He dumps the keys on the dresser. 'I'm going to take a shower.'

She nods, tight. Not trusting herself to speak. Waits as he closes the bathroom door behind him, listens to the squeal of the shower, the thrum of water.

She moves then, into the room, leans against the dresser, a mirror hung on the wall behind it, studies the face looking back at her. The rough pixie cut, the colour of mud. The concave cheeks, cheekbones that stand painfully proud. The dark circles beneath the eyes. She stares at her, the woman in the mirror.

I'm gonna be a firefighter. Just like you were.

She holds her hands up in front of her. As if they will hold some telltale sign of this history she knew nothing about. Forces herself to focus, searching for memories. The feel of weight, digging hard into her shoulders. The mask that cuts into her cheeks, the axe as it swings up, over her head. And something else, fear. Enough that it is blinding. And then, hard on its heels, anger.

She stares at Scarlett in the mirror.

Scarlett stares back, implacable.

It is Destino. And yet it is not her Destino. A thousand small changes. And one big one. Harper Morgan did not died. The Sandovals died in her place.

She thinks of the changes. Of the town sign, nothing like the one that her father's family had erected. Was that the one destroyed in the crash? She thinks of Main Street. She has been raised with it, the family lore that tells of how the Sandovals had built the town, or the bits of it that counted, at any rate. Some great-great-great uncle had laid the stones for Main Street, forming the first building – the bar that would go onto become Bar 53. Then he extended, building a second, a third, rents bringing in enough money to restore the big house. The name Sandoval coming to mean something, even if lately all that something was skyrocketing rents. Then her grandfather. He had commissioned the church, a block of ranch houses, just off Main Street. And then her father. His marker had been laid by Destino Heights, the large double-fronted houses buried within the trees.

The shower squeals off.

It all came back to that one day, that one moment, when a car went off the highway.

She moves from the mirror towards the window. Looks out towards the mountains, the red glow of fire. There is, of course, another difference. Beyond Robyn or Scarlett, beyond

Harper or the Sandovals. That her Destino is not ready.

She feels a sudden burst of fear. Everything she knows is there, in that version of her town. And the fire is coming.

She has to go back.

Scarlett closes her eyes, thinks of the looming fire. Her heart rate increases. She thinks of the fire eating through the home in which she was raised. Her head begins to ache. Thinks of the people, trapped by a wall of flame. Thinks of Mack. No one there to discover the truth without her.

She waits for the darkness.

It does not come.

She opens her eyes, lets out a sob. *I have to go back, I have to go back.*

Wake up! She digs her fingernails, Scarlett's fingernails, into the flesh of her upper arm, pressing in hard enough that jolts of pain shoot up to her spine. Wake up! Tears billow up and over. *Please, wake up.* She lets out a sob. *I want to go home. Please, I want to go home.* Her skin is electric now, panic building. *Wake up wake up wake up!*

Nothing.

She looks around the room, her gaze landing on the keys on the dresser. And she moves towards them, grasping them tight. She grips the key in her fist and, in one swift movement, rams it hard into the flesh of her right thigh. A spasm of pain, sharp enough that she cries out, the tears flowing properly now.

'Jesus!' Suddenly Zeke is there. 'What the hell is wrong with you?' The bathroom door hangs open, steam billowing out, a patch of bright white light in the dark room. He looks younger now, a towel slung around his waist, and she works hard not to notice the arc of tight muscles that vanish down beneath the towel.

The key stands proud, wedged into the pale flesh of her thigh.

'Don't —'

Ignoring him, she wrenches it back out again, blood bubbling from the fresh wound.

'Shit!' Zeke shouts. 'What the hell are you doing?' He leans past her, pulling a balled-up shirt from the floor beside the bed, pressing it against her leg. His breath coming hard. 'Here. Press this . . . no, don't move it, just wait. Jesus, Scarlett.' He looks up at her, horror-struck. 'What the hell were you thinking?'

She opens her mouth, closes it again. The tears drying up now under the pressure of his gaze.

'Come.' He loops his arm about her shoulder, guides her to the bed. He smells of soap. 'Sit. Scar . . . you're really starting to freak me out. What the hell is going on?'

Scarlett stares up at him. And then, she says it.

'Zeke.' She watches Scarlett's lips move at her command. 'Do you think this world is all there is?'

He looks at her, blank.

'I mean,' she says, choosing her words carefully, 'do you think there could be others. Other worlds? Where things worked out differently. Like, I mean, where we made different choices.'

He studies her for long enough that she wonders if he suspects her of a stroke. 'You're talking about the many-worlds theory,' he says finally.

She stares at him. 'OK . . .'

'So what has that got to do with you?'

Scarlett waves her hand. 'It's . . . I can't explain, but could you just . . . what's the many-worlds theory?'

Zeke considers, then shakes his head. 'This day is *weird*. OK, so, the many-worlds theory . . . it's really interesting and just . . . super-insane,' he says, planting himself on the bed, pulling the towel around him. 'So, there's this classic experiment in physics, called the double-slit experiment . . . OK, there's this long-standing debate in science, about whether light is made up of particles or waves. Now, in order to figure this out, scientists, they aim a beam of light at a plate with two slits in it. You ask your average member of the public, what are we going to see and odds are they are going to say "Well, Zeke, you're going to see two strips of light, roughly the same shape and position as the slits." Right?'

'OK . . . does this . . .'

'Shh, wait. I promise I have a point. Instead, what we see is an interference pattern – basically this pattern of light and dark lines – forms on the screen behind it. What that tells us is that the light is behaving as a wave.' He waves his hands. '*But* – and this is where shit gets crazy – scientists then tried going right back to basics. Instead of aiming a light through the slits, they shoot a single photon through.'

Scarlett raises her hand.

'Yes?'

'What's a photon?'

Zeke grins. 'It's an elementary particle. Essentially, the smallest possible particle that makes up light.'

'Thank you.'

'You're welcome.' He puts his hands on his hips. ' OK, so they shoot a single photon through the slit. What do you think happens?'

'Um . . .'

'The photon still forms an interference pattern.' He makes a mind-blown gesture.

'Should I be taking notes?'

'If you feel it will help you in the exam,' Zeke replies, primly.

She grins, in spite of herself, can't help notice the gleam of sweat that traces his clavicle.

Zeke says, brightly, 'So, what they realised is that, in some ways it behaves like wave, in other ways, like particle.'

Robyn blinks at him. 'What . . .'

'Wait,' he says, waving impatiently, 'I'm getting there. OK, so based on this experiment, we realised that things are not what we thought they would be. We thought light would behave as a wave or a particle. Turns out, it's both. So, this entire field sprang up, trying to explain why this would happen. I mean, how can something be two different things at the same time? One of the ways of explaining this was the many-worlds interpretation.' He studies her. 'You still with me.'

'Yeah, just . . . Quick question . . . how the hell do you know all this?'

He grins, sheepish. 'I told you. I was a physics major. Had big plans on being the next Neil deGrasse Tyson. That was before . . . well, just before.' He drifts off for a moment, losing focus. Then he shakes his head. 'So, many-worlds theory, it postulates that there are as many worlds as there are branches of a tree. That each world starts, essentially, when a decision is made. Different choices lead to different worlds.'

'So . . .' She struggles to concentrate, thrown by these words coming from Zeke's mouth. 'OK, so, if something were to happen, say an accident . . .'

Zeke wriggles, the towel riding uncomfortably low. 'I love this shit! OK, so theory suggests that something like an accident could lead to a branching-off point. Go left, you create one future. Go right, you create another.'

'So, the worlds, they would look the same apart from—'

'Yeah, so apart from the accident. Or, its consequences.'

She studies him.

'What?'

'Nothing . . .'

Zeke grins, ruefully. 'You're trying to figure it out, aren't you? How I got from that to this?' He looks down. 'We never did talk about it, did we? In all this time. I gotta tell you, I always appreciated that. How you never asked what the hell went wrong with me.'

She shakes her head, making a show of looking down at her

leg, the blood beginning to dry out now. 'I don't think there's anything wrong with you.' Her voice is quiet.

Zeke snorts. 'Yeah, right.' He shifts, pulling the towel tighter around him. 'All right. It's the apocalypse. So let's do this.' He sits up straighter, sighs heavily. 'I had this idea of being a scientist. A somebody.' He plays with the nap of the towel. 'Turns out it wasn't as easy as I thought it would be, being away from home, getting my head around it all.'

'What happened?' she asks softly.

He shrugs. 'I got depressed.' He says it matter-of-factly. 'Pretty bad. Couldn't get out of bed. Should have talked to someone really, done something. My parents were great. They just . . . I didn't want to worry them.' He raises his arm, turning it over so she can see the insides of his wrist. The track marks. 'So I tried self-medicating.' He laughs without any discernible humour. 'Turns out it's not particularly helpful. Well, that's not entirely true. It's really helpful if what you're shooting for is not giving a shit. Really helpful. Right up until it's not.' He rubs his cheek, stubble rough against his palm. 'It all fell apart. Obviously.' He raises his arms wide, indicating the room around them. 'And so, here we are.'

She studies him and feels the sudden urge to hug him. 'I'm sorry.'

'Life, isn't it? Which just leaves one question.'

'Yes?'

'Why are we talking about quantum physics?'

For one wild and wonderful moment, she considers telling him, spilling it all out so that she is not alone in this.

'Scarlett?' He is waiting, patient, head tilted to one side like a golden retriever. A remarkably chiselled golden retriever.

She shakes her head, those arms of Scarlett pushing her up from the dresser, legs moving her towards the door. 'I need a minute.'

And then she is outside into air that is heavy with smoke,

dense heat. She closes the door behind her, and steps onto the narrow sidewalk that rings the motel. The parking lot is full now, setting sun bouncing from the cars. She watches as a family van searches for a space, creeping along the rows. The windows are open, a German Shepherd and a small girl hanging out of the rear. She catches a glimpse of the car's inside, rammed tight with belongings. The car doubles back, slowly passing by, and she squints into the sunlight, at the driver. It is a woman, perhaps a decade older than her. She is crying.

Scarlett shakes her head, looks back up towards the mountains. The fire wide and wicked, a black thundercloud of smoke hanging over it. Inevitable.

And then comes the headache, the sense of her heart beating faster. And she lets it go, does not fight it or force it, just lets it go.

Darkness closes in.

Chapter Thirty

Robyn Sandoval – 25th September, 10.35 a.m.

'Robyn?'

The transition is like stepping through a door. From one world into the next. Robyn snaps to, steps back. Eve standing there, on the landing, a bag slung over her shoulder, is staring at her, expression concern and fury all mixed up together. 'Robyn, we have to go. Come on. Get your stuff.'

'Was it you?'

'What?'

'Mack. Was it you?'

Eve recoils, stares at her. 'What are you talking about?'

'Did you hurt my father?'

'What?' The colour drains from her mother's face. 'I . . . Robyn, how can you ask me that? How could you think—'

'Why were you giving him money?'

Eve sets the bag down on the floor, reaches out a hand to her. Robyn recoils.

'Robyn, this is . . .' Eve sucks in a breath. 'OK, look, I know this has been a really tough day for you. But you're not thinking straight. This. The whole thing about being CEO. It's just . . . it's shock. Let's go, get to San Francisco and then—'

'It isn't shock.'

'Robyn—'

'I can't do it, Mom. I'm not who you want me to be.'

'No, my darling, but you will be. You're just scared, because it feels so big. But once you're in it, you'll take to it like a duck to water. I promise you will. You were born for this.'

Robyn looks down, voice low. 'But I wasn't, was I, Mom?'

Eve stares at her, her eyes filling.

'But more important than that, Mom, I don't *want* to. It's not who I want to be. And the truth of it is, I've never considered it, whether it was really for me or not. Whether I actually wanted the life that's being planned for me. Not until now.'

Eve dashes her hand across her eyes. 'That's what I said to you. It's shock, Mack's death. It's made you doubt what you know. You just . . . you can't make big decisions today, Robyn, you just can't.'

Robyn doesn't answer, because the truth of it, that Mack's death was only a part of a greater, more insane whole, is more than she can even begin to explain.

'I'm sorry, Mom,' she says, quietly.

Then Eve's expression changes, her nostrils flaring, lips pursing. 'Do you have any idea how ungrateful you sound? Do you have any idea how many people would kill to be in your position?' The colour has drained from her, her eyes narrowing.

She looks, in short, like a different version of the mother Robyn has always known. And suddenly the kaleidoscope shifts and she sees it, the Eve she has only heard of: hard, cold. This would be what Connie would have seen, that day she came to the door, begging for more time to pay her rent. 'Connie's Cupcakes is all I have.' And Eve Sandoval, hard as stone. 'No.'

Another image then. Of that same stone Eve, pressing a pillow onto Mack's face.

Robyn feels her legs go limp beneath her.

'Robyn.' The expression has shifted again now, hard yielding to soft. 'I . . . look, we'll talk about this. I promise we'll talk about this. Only not now. The roads are going to be a nightmare. The fire is coming. We have to *go*.'

'You're right,' Robyn says quietly. 'I do have to go. Take Hector, evacuate without me.'

She turns on her heels, runs downstairs, stopping to pull on a pair of heavy boots. Too hot for the day, but they'll provide some protection from the fire. The sudden realisation that this thought is not hers, but rather Scarlett's. She shakes her head, pulls open the front door, can hear her mother calling her name. She lets the door slam shut behind her. Can smell it now. It fills the air, lining her throat, her nostrils. Robyn starts to run.

The fire is coming now. She can see the distant glow of red, a line that cuts across the mountain. In front of it, the distinct shape of Destino Heights, the lights of fire trucks on the wide-open lots, protecting the big houses.

Robyn turns away from the smoke clouds, left onto Main Street. There are cars, more now than there were, entire lives stuffed inside five doors. And yet, everywhere she looks there are people. They stand on the sidewalk, knotted together, their heads close, gazes locked on the sky. On the distant crimson glow.

And she stops.

Because you can see it here, what the loss of Harper has meant.

Can see the uncertainty, heads turning, seeking someone to tell them what to do.

Robyn is dimly aware of the sound of traffic, of the chattering, of her own mouth opening. The voice that comes out is Scarlett's.

'If you can get out, you should go now!' she shouts.

For a second it seems that no one has heard her. Then heads begin to turn in her direction. Faith, from The Artist's Way, a sweater pulled tight across her shoulders in spite of the heat, moves closer. She has been crying. 'Do you really think so? I mean, we don't really know. Not really. It could turn away. The wind could change direction. It did before. And surely the ridge . . .'

Robyn reaches out, clutches the narrow woman's hand. 'By the time we know for sure, it will be too late.'

Faith studies Robyn, and then her expression changes. She nods, once, turns on her heel and hurries towards the clustered group of Destino-ites. Robyn hears the words, 'We have to go. Now.'

Robyn watches them split, hurrying off in various directions. She turns then, looking towards the diner, Mack's house perched precariously above it. Was it possible? That her mother, the woman who had held her hand and changed her diapers, could have done this terrible thing?

There is a sudden vision of a future. One in which the fire comes and Mack's house is gone. One in which she never knows whether her worst imaginings are after all true, and her mother is a murderer.

She turns on her heel, walking quickly. She will go into Mack's house, will photograph it, everything that she can. Gather up the items that have been left behind, waiting for crime scene technicians that will not come. Because if she doesn't, if she doesn't get there, there will be no answers. It will be over and done with. No one will ever be able to tell her who killed her father.

She darts across the road. Passing Bar 53, its windows dark.

Another honk, traffic snarling up around the road works outside of the church. The sound of shouting.

She will take the trail up past the diner, will retrace her steps from this morning, will cut across the footpath— A thought. Of Zeke's fingers entwined within hers.

She stops in her tracks, looks back towards the mountains, the distant red glow. Her gaze tracks down, following the curve of the mountain towards the rock tunnel entrance to town. Up, to the waterfall, Destino Heights. And there, just above it, buried in trees, the trailer park.

Robyn's stomach twists. Did they know?

The message had come out on the television. But the power, the brownouts up in the trailer park. What if they didn't know?

She turns on the spot, looks down towards the police station, crawling with activity. No. They would have . . . someone would have . . . Wouldn't they?

She should go. This wasn't her responsibility. Mack's death. Finding the answers. That was her responsibility. Only her feet won't move, are glued in place. Memories flooding in, not hers but Scarlett's. Of the trailer park, the smell of stale beer, the sound of children shrieking, of thin metal doors slamming.

'Dammit!'

She takes off running, not towards the mountain now, but rather, back along Main Street, towards the police station, darting through the lined-up cars, choking on the engine fumes. Then the distant view, a figure emerging from the station, one she knows.

'Luis!'

He looks towards her, following the sound of her voice.

She hurries towards him. Wants to say – what? Sorry I thought you were a murderer? Sorry for mildly assaulting you in another world?

'The trailer park.'

'What?'

'This fire. If it does cross the ridge, it will be on top of them. They'll have no time to get out. Luis, they may not know. If their power was off, if they didn't have televisions . . . The people there, they're sitting ducks.'

Luis studies her for a moment. 'The evacuation protocol. It calls for them to get out immediately. At the first advisory.'

'Great,' says Robyn. 'Do they know that?'

His face pales then, the truth of her words dawning. 'I gotta find someone to go up there.'

'Let me go,' Robyn says. 'Let me warn them.'

He hesitates, studies her for a second then gives a nod. 'Go.' He pulls a key out from his pocket. 'Take my car. Get those people evacuated. We've already put the word out in Destino Heights, so the traffic is going to be bad. Use the sirens if you need to.'

Robyn doesn't stop to discuss, grabs the keys and takes off at a run, past the gathered crowd. Luis' car is parked outside the police station and she clambers in, jamming the key into the ignition, swinging it into a tight turn, forcing her way through the backed up traffic of Main Street. She angles the car into the empty northbound lane, then putting her foot down, dives around the line of cars, cutting through and taking a hard left onto Vine.

She is driving too fast, houses flashing by, petering out, lawns getting wider, neighbours farther away, until finally there are none left, only a sentinel line of trees. They overhang the road, a tunnel of green. She spares a moment to glance up at the brown tinge of them. They will go up fast. She grits her teeth, tightens her grip on the wheel. The road wraps its way around to the left and she follows the curve.

Large signs shout of Destino Heights, California's most exclusive development. The subdivision itself is hidden by the trees that overhang the road. Then a break, and she can see beyond, to the glassed-in, black wood-clad boxes. Up ahead, a Mercedes emerges from the entryway, takes a hard left, swinging out wide enough that she has to swerve. She watches in the rear-view mirror as it speeds down the mountain.

The trailer park is further up the mountain road, the sign for it buried in the overhanging trees. She turns the wheel hard, tyres spinning on the loose soil. Within the trailers, figures move beyond windows. People going about their days. After all, haven't they spent their entire lives listening to the story of how Destino has never burned? Small wonder, then, that they consider themselves safe. She spares a moment to pity them, the chaos she is about to bring. Then she lays her hand flat on the horn. The sound of it breaks through the quiet park. A pregnant pause; she leans harder on the horn. Then a rush of sound, doors opening.

Robyn pushes open the car door, clambers out, and deep breath, bellows, 'Evacuate! Evacuate! Fire is coming.'

There is silence, hanging disbelief. Then movement. A flurry of activity.

'How long?' a young woman with a child on her hip calls out.

'Not long,' Robyn shouts out in return. 'You have to go now.'

Word is spreading. She can see it in the sequence of opening trailer doors.

Robyn slams the car door, begins to walk the park, trailer to trailer. She is concentrating, checking that each trailer contains movement, the inevitable activity of evacuation. And so she doesn't notice it right away, just where she is standing.

And from somewhere beyond a narrow tunnel of trees, the sound of a door opening, of footsteps on creaking metal steps.

'Hey,' says a voice, 'what's going on? Are we evacuating?'

Robyn freezes. Another one of those moments where suddenly it is not clear which world she is in.

'Zeke?'

The figure emerges from the gloom of the trees, looking the same as he had the last time she had seen him, but also totally different.

He squints at her. 'Do I know you?'

Chapter Thirty-One

Scarlett Morgan – 25th September, 10.37 a.m.

'Scarlett? You . . . OK?'

Scarlett shakes her head, reaches out to grip hold of his narrow arm. Doesn't remember the darkness coming. Seemed that she blinked and was someone else. 'My mom . . .'

In this moment, she is in between worlds, in between mothers. Is not entirely sure which one it is she means.

Zeke frowns. 'Your mom? She's over in the conference room, setting up.'

Scarlett looks at him, is suddenly aware of the vice grip she has on his arm, releases it with a start. 'My . . .'

'You OK?' Zeke leans in closer, studies her, frowning. 'You look a bit . . . out of it.'

She glances around herself, at the packed-full parking lot. The air presses down on her, sea salt stains her lips, smoke catching at her throat. A bedroom door swings open, a burst of sound flooding from inside. The sound of a child crying. And then back at Zeke, watching her, his face heavy with concern. What is it about him? Why does it make her feel safe, to see him worrying about her?

'I . . . I should go see my mom,' she says. Then, 'You'll be . . . OK?'

Zeke hesitates, seems taken aback by the question. Then he smiles, the kind of smile that changes his features, lighting them up. 'I'll be OK. You go on ahead.'

She smiles right back, the movement awkward, alien, and steps off the walkway onto the hot tarmac of the parking lot. The sky is bright blue, pockmarked with thick, smoke-filled clouds. Robyn walks more quickly than she should, the heat of the morning pocking her skin with beads of sweat.

I'm going to see my mommy.

It is a flash of childlike thought that makes her stomach tangle up on itself, and for a second she wonders if she is about to cry. Then, inevitably, comes the thought of the other mother, her narrow arms pressing down on a pillow, moulded to Mack's face beneath. Of his body struggling in its instinctive fight for air, but still she pushes and pushes and pushes until he gives up the fight.

No!

Scarlett shakes her head, shoves the image away.

Tries to tell herself that she knows Eve, deep down, knows that she is not capable of this. But then an insidious little thought – you knew Mack too. And in both worlds he has failed to live up to your expectations of him. Then another thought, of the email.

There's something kind of big I need to talk to you about.

Perhaps it was the money. Perhaps he had been about to confess it, to explain his actions and whatever hold he had over Eve. What could there ever have been, sufficient that she would have parted with so much money for so long?

She reaches out, tugs open the lobby door. A reassuring bing-bong, a burst of air-conditioned air. There is a line at the front desk, an elderly couple at the front, arguing with the clerk about their room allocation. A woman stands behind them, a toddler on her hip, silent tears drifting down her cheeks.

A television is mounted on the wall, a low burbling, red flickering of the mountains above Destino. Some people in the line stare at it, as though they just can't pull their eyes away. Others stand with their backs to it, the sound of their deliberate inattention deafening.

She eases past them, towards the open doors of the conference room. It is a wide-open space, little clue as to what is coming for it, the walls lined with trestle tables, loaded with boxes yet to be unpacked. Harper, she is alone. Is buried elbow-deep in a cardboard box, focus intent on what is inside.

And so she has a moment or two to linger there, to study her. Her hair is pulled back into a loose braid, strands of it flopping down into her eyes. Is darker than hers, coarser. How often has she imagined this moment? How often has she considered what it would be? To stand before the mother of her early life, to see her own own features reflected in another face. In her imagining, it would be like looking into a mirror. It wasn't. Life is rarely that simple. Instead, it was like seeing an optical illusion, stranger one moment, then a flash of something, and features that she hasn't seen before pop out. Cheekbones that are the same and jawline that is the same and the figure that is the same. And then it is gone again and she is a stranger once more.

Harper looks up, attention drawn by the weight of Scarlett's gaze on her. 'Hey.' She frowns. 'You OK?'

Scarlett opens her mouth, but cannot find the words. She nods.

'You hear the wind changed?' asks Harper.

She nods again. 'I heard.'

Harper pulls blankets out of the box. Separates them and begins to fold them neatly. 'It'll be OK. It'll be OK.' She looks up, gives her daughter a wry smile. 'Have I convinced you yet?'

'Totally,' Scarlett says. 'I'm completely chill now.'

Harper's smile widens. 'We're ready. We've put a lot of energy into making Destino defensible.' She gestures to the boxes. 'Kind of feels like we've been preparing for this moment for the past thirty years, doesn't it?'

'You say "we",' says Scarlett carefully, 'but it was you.'

I have seen the world without you in it. And in that world none of this has come to pass.

Harper shrugs. 'Yeah, well, I may have decided to drive the crazy train, but everyone else jumped on board.'

Scarlett steps close to the table. Stands beside her mother. A thrill runs through her, and for a wild moment it feels like she will cry. But then she reaches out a shaking hand, pulls a blanket towards her and begins to fold. Forces herself to breathe. 'I thought you'd be busier in here. Evacuation craziness . . .'

'There is no craziness. I mean, I don't intend to toot my own horn, but everyone knows where they're meant to be, what they have to do. It'll get busier later, once people have gotten into their rooms, settled down . . . once the reality of what's happening hits them.' Harper looks up, grins. 'Then we'll be plenty busy.'

Scarlett cradles the blanket close to her. 'Mom . . .' It tastes different, here, in this world. 'Can I ask you something?'

'Go for it.'

'What made you want to do this? How did you know this is what you should be doing?'

Her mother studies her, then turns, scoops up a pile of blankets, carrying them to the waiting trestle table. 'You never know. Not really. I'm just fumbling around in the dark like everyone else.'

'But all this . . . without you, Destino would have none of it.'

Harper studies her. 'Sweets, I'm nothing special. I'm just a mom who got a bee in her bonnet. Guess the only difference between me and the people who didn't do it is I ignored that little voice – you know, the one that tells you it's not your place, that problems like this are for people higher up the food chain.' She grins. 'That, and the whole Destino Heights thing filled me up with so much righteous fury that I stopped giving a flying fart about what anyone else thought.'

'Destino Heights?' Cold water pours down Scarlett's neck.

'Destino Heights. I thought I told you this story?'

She shakes her head, no, her fingernails digging into the soft down of the blanket.

'Huh . . . OK, so, this company,' says Harper, 'they put this proposal in – God, must be thirty years ago. They wanted to build a subdivision of big, big houses up in the forest. They're saying they're gonna cut a swathe right through the forest, right up over the waterfall, put a bunch of mansions up there.' She shakes her head. 'It's just, the damn arrogance of it, y'know. This wealthy family, this company . . . I mean, the Sandovals, they had been buying up Destino for years.'

The name hangs in the air, bright between them.

'They owned pretty much every property up and down Main Street, half of the houses in Destino. Which, I mean, whatever, but you could see the way the wind was blowing. They'd started to gradually ratchet up the rents, people, they were starting to struggle to stay in their homes. And, you know, it just incensed me. That they already had the town, and now they're gonna take the forest too. Build mini-mansions that the people of Destino would never be able to afford. It would put strain on local utilities, on schools, roads. And it would be dangerous. Homes right there in the forest, one road in, one road out. When the wildfires come – and let's face it, it's California, wildfires are gonna come – those houses up there, they would be death traps.' Harper leans down, drags a box towards her, rips the sealing tape off the top. 'So I went after the proposal. I dug deep, chased down every angle of the damn thing.' She starts pulling toiletry kits out of the box, shrugs. 'I could write a thesis on "Destino Heights And Why It Is Bad". And it looked like I was winning. The report comes out, yes, Destino Heights would be a bad move, yada, yada. So, we thought we were safe. Then, just like that, the council reverses itself and Destino Heights is passed. They're making plans to start building, so we plan this big town meeting, one last chance before the work begins. And I was optimistic that I could turn the tide. Turns out, I didn't need to.'

'Because of the crash,' says Scarlett, quietly.

'Because of the crash,' agrees Harper, solemnly.

'You were there that night.' It is not a question.

Harper turns her back on her, busying her hands arranging the toiletries on the table. 'I was. Not the kind of thing you forget.' She looks at her daughter. 'Awful night. Just awful. And of course, all I'm thinking about is getting to that damn meeting, dealing a death blow to Destino Heights. But the weather, God . . . The highway, the roads were just a damn mess. Everyone was heading towards the church hall to argue it out. They must have been behind me, not that I saw them. It was all I could do to keep my attention on the road ahead.' She shakes her head. 'I always wondered what happened. Why I made it through, they didn't. I remember coming into Destino, and I mean, I don't know what happened, whether I was dazzled by the headlights coming towards me, but my tyres just went out from underneath me. Hydroplaned right up to Main Street. I was so lucky, so lucky it wasn't me.'

Prickles run over Scarlett's skin and she breathes out a slow breath. 'So, the Destino Heights proposal . . . that died with the Sandovals?'

'Pretty much. The company, well, it didn't last too long after the accident. And I guess, without the Sandovals there just wasn't the appetite for it.'

There is the sound of voices in the lobby beyond the wide-open doors, high-pitched and lyrical, drawing closer.

'I guess Destino Heights just wasn't meant to be,' murmurs Harper. 'Which worked out pretty well for Averill, anyway.'

'Wait, who . . . ?'

A trio of children tumble in through the door, their parents towed behind them, and Harper smiles widely. 'Hi, guys. How are you? OK, so what are you missing? What can we help you with?'

They flow around Scarlett, splitting apart, coming back together. Words tumbling out, one on top of the other. And then the darkness comes.

Chapter Thirty-Two

They are ready, the people of Destino. Or so they think anyway. Have taken the preparations laid out by the county. Or . . . at least, some of them have. These people, they have go-bags and water and documents to hand. True, some of those go-bags were packed years before, their contents long out of date. Or they were packed in haste, a collection of half-useless belongings, grabbed in the final moments. The residents, they know their evacuation routes. Or, they are pretty sure they do. After all, haven't they lived here for decades, know this town like the back of their hand? And, sure, the evacuation routes are narrow, and the exodus, when it comes, will be large. And the roadworks on Main Street block off the road in front of the church, creating a narrow funnel of escape.

But they will be fine. They have gassed up their cars – or did they gas up their cars? Was it something that was on the to-do list that simply slipped off the end of it into the other detritus of life? They have readied their lots, have removed combustible materials from the surrounds of their homes. Apart from the shed, because the shed is useful and what harm would it really do, having a shed anyway? And those trees whose branches reach out, scratching at the windows in the winter storms . . . Because they are trees, and you weren't supposed to, were you? Eco-friendly and all that stuff? And besides, who moves to Destino if they don't like trees? So, of course they kept the trees.

No, they have undoubtedly done all that they can do.

The fire flares across the mountainside, a sudden burst of life that sweeps through the waiting trees.

And down below, the residents who have come out into their front yards, who stand beside their loaded-up cars, because they are good citizens and sensible and because they listen when the county says that they should get out, they gasp, a collective intake of breath.

And as one, they think, this is it. It's time to go.

But then the fire, because it can be contrary like that, it dips down, vanishing back beneath the ridge. And now it is simply cumulous clouds of smoke again, an eerie red glow that lights the sky.

And the residents, they exhale, look to one another, exchange embarrassed grins. That was close! And they tell themselves that they were right to wait. Because little Martha at number 9, Vineland, she never can sleep in a hotel, and they've only just gotten her sleeping through the night, so of course they shouldn't go. Not if they don't have to. And Rory at 345 Oakland, he can't find that damn cat. Never does come when he calls. Be better off without it, and he would never get a cat again. But he will leave. He will. Just as soon as he finds the cat. And the Simmons at 93 Bay Tree. They flat can't afford it. Dan, he lost his job a couple of months ago and they're burning through his severance faster than that fire is burning through shrub. Hotels, they are expensive when you are two adults and three kids and a golden retriever and a hamster named Chunky. So it would have to be the shelter, the one that they have set up in some sports hall in Morro Bay. Only a shelter . . . Remember what they said, about the Superdome in New Orleans, about what happened there in Katrina? That was a shelter, and the thought of it . . . . no, they would be better off just riding it out at home.

Besides, they tell themselves, Destino doesn't burn. The ridge, it always protects us.

And the fire, it appreciates all that they have to say on the matter. But when all is said and done, it is a fire.

And it is going to do what the hell it wants to do.

Chapter Thirty-Three

Mags Reyes – 25th September, 10.45 a.m.

The car moves down the mountain fast. Mags' fingers cling tight to the steering wheel, brush whipping by them as they follow the curves of the road. She glances across at Gabrielle in the passenger seat, Oscar in the rear-view mirror. Their gazes are fixed forward, faces drawn.

'Hey,' she says, quietly, 'it's OK, guys.'

The children nod in synchrony, do not answer. She pushes the accelerator closer to the floor.

It feels like an escape. Like she has burrowed her way out from underneath a life sentence and now is running, faster and faster and faster. They whip past the parcel of land that overlooks Destino. The clouds are closer now, have clambered their way across the outer valley wall, tendrils of smoke reaching out to the waterfall, the trailer park. To Destino Heights. And then the road curves and they are gone again.

It is freedom ahead. It is reparation and recovery.

Mags' chest heaves and she cannot tell if it is relief or terror. There will be no more lies. There will be only truth. And the truth of it is that she has been terribly, horribly, catastrophically wrong. They fly past the two-trunked tree, so fast that the lightning scar vanishes. Perhaps she can makes amends. But that feels too much, like flying and falling all at once, and so she shakes her head.

'Daddy will be on his way to Morro Bay now. I wonder if he'll make it before us.' Is met with resounding silence. 'That would be nice, wouldn't it?'

The road arching back on itself, Destino splayed out below, the sight of it forcing her foot up from the pedal. The clouds loom now, have risen up on their haunches, bunched-up thunderheads. And at their base a deep crimson glow of fire.

'Oh my God!' Gabrielle has leaned forward, the seatbelt tight across her torso, one hand braced on the dash. 'Oh my God, Mommy!'

'It's OK, sweetie.' The resolution for unremitting truth has vanished. 'We're going to be just fine. It's just the glow that we're seeing, that's all. It's not the fire itself. We still have plenty of time to get out.'

A hand, then, from the back seat, grips hold of her elbow. 'What about Grandma and Pop-Pop?'

Mags shakes her head, does not answer.

The road tilts, steeper and steeper, and then spits them out alongside the church, smack bang into the traffic that snakes its way around the roadworks. Mags angles the car out, forcing her way between a Prius and a Taurus. Does not see her daughter's hand move towards the radio until it is too late.

'And it is just ripping through that forest. It's now about ten miles from Destino, so its crossed a lot of ground quickly. Absolutely unreal, the speed of this fire. We haven't seen anything like this since the Camp fire. Of course, there's gonna be a lot of build up there. These forests, they haven't had a fire in decades and what that's going to mean is that there has been no clearing of dead brush, fallen trees, things like that. All of that is going to be there, just waiting. And to a fire like this, that's just fuel.'

Mags' hand moves towards the radio. Gabrielle smacks it away. 'No, Mom. I want to hear.'

'Now what about prescribed fires,' says a different voice. 'We've heard a lot about these lately. But of course, in this particular area, the opposition has been particularly vocal in their resistance.'

'Well, of course, what you have to understand,' says the first voice, 'is that part of Destino itself is actually built into the forest. So, we have this area known as Destino Heights, and, I mean, you can understand their concern about prescribed fires being set when this is where they live. You know, there are issues with keeping control of any fire, how do you guarantee it doesn't get out of hand, things like that. And there are also concerns about what it does to the aesthetic of the area. Now don't forget, Destino is popular with tourists, for no small part because of its location, the look of the forests, and so there are gonna be knock-on effects if that look is ruined and the tourists stop coming. We're talking a significant potential impact on the local economy . . . Of course, on days like today, you gotta wonder whether they regret their stance.'

Oscar lets out a small squeak and burrows back further into his seat. Mags pulls up tight to the Prius, moving her daughter's hand gently aside. 'I think that's enough for now, Gabs.'

She turns the dial, flipping through channel after channel until she finds music, the chords weaving themselves in through the rough tread of the road. 'Country ain't never been pretty . . .' Mags sings it loud, slapping the wheel in time to the song. 'Come on, Gabs.' She glances across at the passenger seat, grin wide, tacked on. 'You have special dispensation to say shit.'

Her daughter nods, mute. Silent tears track down her cheeks. Mags reaches across, squeezes her daughter's hand. 'How about you, buddy? You wanna sing with me?' She looks in the rear-view mirror. Her son has curled himself into the back seat, his cheek pressed up against the rear. He doesn't answer.

'Mommy,' says Gabrielle. When had she last called her Mommy? 'What is going to happen to Grandma and Pop-Pop?'

The Prius rolls forward, a sudden break in the traffic, and Mags eases the car forward. And she tries to ignore the question, but she never was going to be able to, was she? Not if she was honest with herself. And hadn't she just said it, that the truth was what mattered? Because no ambulance would reach them now, not with traffic backed up like this. Even if her mother would call one, which she wouldn't. And so their survival, it all hung on that dark cloud up ahead, on the streak of red within it. It all depended on luck. A flip of the coin, a gust of wind, this way or that.

Mags pulls her cell phone from the centre console, punches in her mother's number. The phone rings, rings. 'Hello, we cannot take your call . . .' Mags leans closer to the steering wheel, her fingers digging in so tight it seems that they will snap. 'Son of a bitch,' she mutters.

'Mom?' Gabrielle is staring at her now.

'Nothing, sweetie. They're going to be fine.'

The traffic inches forward, past the roadworks, onto Main Street proper. And then, up ahead, a solution of sorts. Mags grimaces, pulls the wheel over hard, yanking the car out of traffic and into the bay in front of Bar 53.

'Mommy?'

'It's fine, guys. Just one second.' Mags takes off running towards the parked car, the figure that stands at the open trunk. 'Viv!'

The doctor turns, searching for the source of her name, confusion flying across her face. 'Mags! What the hell are you . . . I thought you'd left.'

Mags nods, struggling for breath. 'I am. I was. Look, are you going? Are you heading out?'

'I'm just leaving. Jesse and the kids are meeting me in Morro

Bay.' Vivienne pushes the button to close the trunk. 'Why? What do you need?'

Mags glances back at the car, her children sitting up straight, watching her. 'My parents. They're still up there. My mom never rang for the ambulance.'

Vivienne's face drops. 'Shit. I thought . . . oh my God, Mags. . . . OK, I'm heading up there and I'll load them into my car —'

'No,' says Mags. 'You have Jesse and the kids. Look, Jack, he's coming. He's on his way to Morro Bay now. Will you take them, Gabrielle and Oscar? Can you get them to their dad? He's going to meet us at the shelter.'

'Mags,' says Vivienne, warningly.

'No, it's OK.' Mags rubs her face. When did she cry? 'I'm not going because I feel I have to, or because I'm trying to prove something. I'm going because it's who I am.'

Vivienne stares at her. 'OK . . .'

Mags waves her hands. 'Whatever, look, it doesn't matter. I just . . . *I* am making this decision. For me. For my family. But I need to know the kids are safe, so can you . . .?'

'I'll look after them.' Vivienne reaches out, squeezes her hand. 'Mags, you should be aware . . . Your dad. I don't know if he . . .'

'I know.'

Chapter Thirty-Four

Bonnie Aubrey – 25th September, 10.51 a.m.

Bonnie sips at her hot tea. The room is dark, drapes drawn on the bright sky beyond. Sounds float up to her from the town. The honk of horns, purr of traffic. Another sound, this one further away, the groaning growl of helicopters circling. She sits in the recliner that once was Kelvin's, back in the days when he could get up from bed, could march his way down here to the family room, plopping himself down in it. She rests her head back, closes her eyes, drinking in the smell of his cologne. It has seeped its way into the fabric, so that it seems that no matter who sits in this chair, Kelvin is always right alongside them.

But there is that other smell, the one that hangs in the air. Smoke.

Bonnie sips at her tea and tries to feel it, the fear that surely is there somewhere. She quests, a tongue probing a filling. But there is nothing, only a stultifying numbness. Grief, then? Surely there would be grief. For Kelvin, for the diner, for the life she had known and the life she should have known. But that is not there either.

She waves the cup, one of those bone china ditsy monstrosities that Maggie was so proud of, the movement reckless, tea spilling up and over the rim, splashing down onto the bare skin of her arm. It is hot enough that she flinches.

Bonnie nods, satisfied. Not fear or grief. But it is something.

She sets the cup down with a clink on its matching saucer. Wipes her arm on her sweater and stands awkwardly. She steps, one foot before another, the floorboards creaking beneath her. They were a symphony of sleepless nights, an infant resting against her shoulder. She hesitates in the doorway to the family room. A powerful memory. Of her daughter, mere months old, a tiny wisp of a thing, fever heat radiating from her, enough that it made Bonnie sweat. Of the movement of it, bouncing up and down and up and down, the boards beneath her feet singing in time, Bonnie's tears mingling with her daughter's. Of the prayer she had made: 'Let her make it through this, Lord, and I will be the best mother I can possibly be.' The fever had broken before dawn. God keeping his part of the bargain, Bonnie letting hers go.

She walks slowly along the hall.

Kelvin's door stands ajar. Dust motes dance in the air. He lies, his head resting soft against the propped-up pillows, face lined with tension.

Bonnie lingers in the doorway, watching her husband. Images flit before her. Of the day they met, a bowling alley in Cambria that smelled of beer and feet. Of their wedding day in his parents' backyard, beneath a draped pergola, the smell of honeysuckle and freshly mown grass. She lingers in the doorway and she thinks about choices, of doors that she has opened, others she has kept shut. And she remembers who she used to be, back then. Seems to her now that they are different people, that her and this.

There is a shift in his breathing, and Bonnie's own breath catches in response. She steps closer, the floorboard creaking beneath her. Kelvin opens his eyes, blinking.

'Bonnie?'

'Hello.'

He stares at her, struggling to focus. 'What is it? What's wrong?' His voice is little more than a whisper. He always could sense trouble, no matter how much she tried to hide. 'Is it the fire?'

Bonnie forces a smile, shakes her head. 'No, my love. The fire is right where it was. There is no need for us to worry. You close your eyes, go on back to sleep.'

He studies her, for long enough that she thinks he can see it, right through the lie to the ugly truth beneath. But then his eyelids begin to sag and his breathing softens until it is barely there at all.

Chapter Thirty-Five

Robyn Sandoval – 25th September, 10.55 a.m.

'You're here.' She hears the words, the realisation that the worlds have switched, that she is Robyn again. She stares at Zeke, this long, lean figure that, until now, might as well have only existed in dreams. Around them, perpetual motion, doors opening and slamming, shouting. But none of it is registering with her, because instead she is thinking of his fingers laced into hers. She shakes her head, forcing herself to concentrate.

He looks good, this version of Zeke. Is carrying a bit more weight to him, a bit more colour in his cheeks. His shoulders have more heft to them, biceps well defined. A flush builds in her cheeks.

'I'm here,' Zeke agrees affably. He eyes her, expression doubtful. 'I . . . I'm really sorry but my memory . . .' Then another look, something akin to panic. 'Oh God, did we, did I . . . ? Hey, I'm sorry but you gotta know, I was a mess back then, and I don't remember a lot of—'

'Zeke.'

'Yes.'

'It's fine. We haven't slept together.' Although, technically, that wasn't true, but best not to muddy the waters any further.

He exhales, shoulders sinking. 'Oh, thank God. Not . . . I

mean, not that I wouldn't because I totally would, because . . . Damn!'

Heat rushes from her toes to her scalp, her skin tingling.

Zeke looks away, working hard to focus anywhere but on her. It is only then, as he is looking around, apparently seeking an escape route from this conversational cul-de-sac, that he notices the chaos that surrounds them. 'What's going on?'

Robyn glances behind her. Each trailer door stands open. Each car and truck waits patiently, as worldly belongings and protesting children and frightened pets are thrown inside. In a trailer immediately behind them, an elderly woman limps across the dried grass, carrying a small white dog. Robyn opens her mouth, ready to call out, 'You have to help the people who don't have transport. You have to work together to get everyone out.' But she doesn't need to. The woman climbs into a neighbour's van, tucking the dog neatly in beside her.

She looks about to see the scene playing out across the park. Streams of people converging on waiting vehicles, shoehorning themselves in.

'We're evacuating,' she says, briefly. 'The fire is coming.'

'Damn,' Zeke says again. 'OK, I gotta get my stuff.'

Robyn spares a moment to scan the park again. Satisfied, she says, 'Good. I'll come with you.'

Zeke stares at her. 'Uhhh . . . OK.' He clearly thinks she is insane. And, let's be honest, in terms of options to explain what was going on right now, that one was right up there. But still he lingers, showing her the way, allowing her to go ahead of him.

The trailer looks the same, there or thereabouts. On the outside, at least. Inside, it is different. It smells clean. The counters are wiped, the bed is made, a long line of books stand propped against a window. *Something Deeply Hidden*, and *A Brief History Of Time* and *The Elegant Universe*, all of them well read, cracked spines and dog-eared corners. She stands to one side, lets him squeeze in past her, pull an empty backpack from the wardrobe, and begin setting clothes inside.

'So,' he says as he works, 'I'm confused. Which, hey, isn't that unusual, but still . . . how do you think you know me?'

Robyn lets out a snort of laughter. 'I wouldn't even know where to begin.'

Zeke flips open another cupboard, this one stacked with binders, dense with paper. He removes them, slower now, reverential almost, and, for Robyn, a coin drops.

'You went back to college,' she says quietly, almost to herself.

Zeke hesitates, looks down at the schoolwork, back at her. 'Was it AA? Was that where I met you?'

She shakes her head, gives a small smile, a sudden feeling as if she is going to cry.

'Yeah,' says Zeke, slowly, 'I transferred to Northridge to finish up my undergrad.' He drags another mountain of paperwork from the back of the cupboard, stacking it on the table. 'Working on my master's in San Luis Obispo.'

'Oh . . .'

Robyn looks around the trailer, and Zeke laughs. 'Right? Trailer-park master's. Sounds like a game show.'

'No, I—'

He waves it off with a grin. 'Don't sweat it. I like living here. It's cheap. Means I don't have to work another job alongside studying.' His grin widens. 'Let's say, I've figured out that overdoing it doesn't work out too well for me. I've learned to manage my expectations of myself.'

'That's good . . .'

He glances at her, a look that lasts longer than it should, and her face flushes again. Dear God. Something else too, a feeling of suddenly feeling settled. Like you get when you come home after a difficult day, when you pull the door shut behind you. That feeling of being cocooned and safe. Perhaps this is why she is here. Perhaps altruism only goes so far, concern for the residents of the trailer park is just a cover. Perhaps she is here for him.

Robyn shakes her head, struggling to concentrate.

'So,' he pulls open a drawer, begins to fish out chargers, electrics, 'you a cop?'

Robyn hesitates. 'No . . .'

'So how come you're doing this? Why are you calling the evacuation?' He pauses, peers out the window. 'With a cop car . . . did you steal that?'

Robyn laughs, despite herself. 'The evacuation is starting. It's pretty crazy down there. Not enough people and too much to do. So, I volunteered.'

He is studying her, and it seems that her tongue has become unwieldy. She shakes her head. 'I guess I had a bad feeling. They say the fire is moving faster than they had expected. And if it comes to us, this park will be hit first. I wanted to make sure you all got out.'

And I wanted to know if you were real.

'Well, that's pretty cool of you. And how do we know each other again?' He grins. 'Whatever it is,' says Zeke cheerfully, 'you can say it. I'm pretty sure nothing you can say can shock me at this point in my life.' He studies her. 'You're not my long-lost sister or something?'

Oh God, I hope not!

What???

She shrugs, the movement strangely conscious. 'I don't know. Maybe it was in Bar 53?' She takes a deep breath, stomach sinking ever so slightly. 'OK, so, you are good to get out, right? Because I . . . there's somewhere I need to be.'

He zips up the holdall. 'Hot date?'

'Not exactly.'

She could stop now. She could back off, walk away. This man does not need the crazy that is her day. She is getting a headache. But, apparently her mouth has already decided on a course of action while her brain was still debating.

Zeke throws the bag over his shoulder, waits.

'My dad.' Oh God, she was saying it. 'He was murdered this morning.'

Zeke's face falls. 'Oh my God. I'm so sorry. How . . .?'

'I don't know. I don't know who did it or why.' She hesitates, then tumbles on regardless. 'And the best bit is, if the fire does come, if Destino burns, I'm never going to know. Because everything is in that house and the crime techs haven't been able to get to it because—'

'Of the fire,' says Zeke.

'Right.' She blows out a sigh. 'So, whatever, it's fine. I'm going there. I'm going to go and, y'know, just see if I can save any evidence. So that way I'll know . . .'

If my mother killed him.

Zeke stands, holdall held limp in his hands, staring at her. 'OK, I was wrong. Apparently it is still possible to shock me.' He steps closer to her. 'I'm so sorry. Are you . . . OK?'

Robyn suddenly cannot form words, seems that she has spent them all. She turns from him, looks over her shoulder, out of the trailer window, can just about make out the park beyond, the traffic moving now, cars lining up, one by one waiting to escape. 'We should go,' she says, quietly.

He stares at her for long moments, then sighs. 'Agreed.' He shakes his head, pushing himself up to standing, grabs the backpack and weights the folders in his arms. 'I gotta say, you have had one hell of a day.' He steps aside, letting her lead the way. 'Let's get out of here.' Then he stops, colour draining from his face. 'Oh, crap.'

Robyn follows his gaze through the window to the park outside, the evacuation, and a sudden thought crashes in, of a piece missing from this particular jigsaw. 'Wait, where's your truck?'

'Yeah,' says Zeke slowly, 'it's in the shop. Goddam starter fuse.'

'So how are you going to evacuate?'

'Um . . .'

Robyn digs into her pocket, pulls out Luis' car keys. 'I can get you to Main Street. You can get a ride out from there.'

She hurries past him, footsteps reverberating on the metal steps. The smoke is heavier now, has draped itself across the trailer park. On the horizon, a red glow. Robyn's heart begins to beat harder. She looks back at Zeke, waves him towards the patrol car.

'You should get in.'

'*I* should get in? Where the hell are you going?'

She shakes her head. 'You wouldn't believe me if I told you.'

Darkness falls.

Chapter Thirty-Six

Scarlett Morgan – 25th September, 11.05 a.m.

There is the sound of a baby crying. A raw, primal scream. Her eyes flicker open. The baby looks at her. It has been strapped into a car seat, and it is raging, its face red, arms flapping in a blind fury. Its mother stands beside it, a sweat-slicked toddler on her hip, the small sneakers of yet another child protruding from beneath the plastic chair.

'Up!' says the mother, making no effort to bury her own fury.

'No!' The shriek comes from somewhere beneath the row of plastic chairs.

The baby screams louder.

She is lying, her cheek pressed against hot plastic. She blinks, raising an arm. Tattoos. Of course.

Scarlett pushes herself up.

The woman with the toddler spares a moment to glare at her and she glares right back, until the mother looks away, distracted by the disembodied sneakers that kick her shins.

Where the hell am I?

She turns. There is a thrum of sound, voices echoing off the high ceiling, the burr of engines, the smell of gasoline.

A voice crackles from a tannoy. 'Bus to Fresno will be leaving in five minutes from stand B.'

She groans. Mutters, 'Dammit, Scarlett. What the hell have you done?'

The baby has stopped screaming, is staring at her, eyes squinting above puffed-up cheeks. The sneakers keep kicking.

There is a backpack beside her, crushed from the weight of her head resting upon it. She paws at it, feeling the soft touch of clothing. There isn't much – a couple of T-shirts, a pair of jeans. She pulls open the front pocket. There it is. The bus ticket. One way to Oxnard.

The bar manager job. Scarlett's stomach turns over.

The baby studies her. Must have found something to entertain it, face splitting into a wide grin.

Scarlett looks away, half turning her body away from the child's frank stare.

She studies the ticket, looks up at the signage. Oxnard. Stand E. Departures in twenty minutes. She shakes her head, stands up, dodging past the mother, who holds on to the sneakered foot in a wild attempt to drag it out.

She throws the backpack over her shoulder, marches towards the ladies room.

The baby begins to cry again.

The bathroom is quiet, the smell of urine overlain with a pungent lavender, chemical and hard. She throws the backpack onto the counter, rests her hands on the sink and stares at Scarlett in the mirror.

'Dammit!'

The memories coming back, of the intervening time. Of that rising sense of pressure, with Zeke there and Harper there, Bonnie and Mags, and all of Destino so it seems. And then her, Scarlett, the child who never did seem to quite be who she was supposed to be. Remembers unpacking the boxes and stacking cans and cans and towels and then . . . A bump of the table, an inadvertent nudge with her hip, had sent the heap of towels sprawling. Her mother's soft 'oh' of surprise. Only it hadn't felt like surprise, had it? Not then. Had felt like an inevitability, the criticism implied.

Scarlett runs her fingers through her hair. Memories now of that sinking sense of despair, of never being good enough, not even to stack towels. And then of turning, of walking out, her mother's soft 'Scarlett' trailing behind her.

She clutches the sink and stares into the mirror. What else? What else brought her to a bus station on her way to a job surrounded by alcohol? Then the image comes, the television that hangs up high on the conference room wall. The glow of red from the flames. The sound of shouts, the dull roar, fire language. A reporter, strain and soot etched on his face, and a man who stands beside him, dressed in mustard yellow, a divot around his mouth and nose, the marks of breathing apparatus left behind.

'We at CalFire, we will not rest until we know that the people of Destino are safe. I mean, I grew up here. A Destino boy born and bred. And I have been fighting fires in this area since I was nineteen years old. I gotta tell you, it is a privilege to be in the position to protect the ones I love.' Mack looking at the camera then, offering a winning smile, and the reporter clapping him on the back. 'A true hometown hero.'

And Mags and Bonnie and Zeke, they are all standing now, gazes hooked upwards on the television. As one, letting out a snort. As one, all eyes turning to her.

'Just ignore him, Scar,' Zeke saying.

Scarlett shakes her head, vision clearing, leans in closer to the mirror, her breath fogging up the glass. A toilet flushes and a stall door swings open, an elderly woman walking awkwardly towards the basins, glancing at her and then quickly away.

She concentrates, pulling out memories from Scarlett's life.

Of the house with the sunroom, with the plants that crawl all over it, the effect one of a living house. Of toys scattered across throw rugs, of artwork hung haphazard from twisting vines. Of her father, a memory now of him coming into the room, filling it up with his presence, the smell of smoke hanging off him, his face scuffed up with ash, a smile wide enough to light up the room. A memory of a shriek that seems too delighted to ever have belonged to her, of shoving luminous artwork aside and flinging herself across the room into arms that engulfed her.

Then another memory, of legs curled up beneath her, the long dangling vines that brush up against her face. Of pretending that they are fingers brushing away the tears. Of the sound of shouting. The words are lost to her, filtered the way they are through the closed bedroom door and down the corridor and through the family room. But the tone of them, that is unmistakable. It is fury and disgust and despair. The tone of her world changing. Then the bedroom door flinging open, bouncing off its hinges. The words 'After everything I have put up with from you, all the times I forgave you. How could you do this to us?' sallying forth, weaving themselves through the leaves and the petals. And her father, striding with long steps, his face grey, jaw set. Calling out to him, 'Where are you going? What's happening?' And then, the one that threw him off stride, if only for a moment, 'What did you do?'

She never did get an answer.

Another memory now. Of a mustard uniform that hangs heavy on her. The weight of breathing apparatus that presses deep into her flesh. The smell of smoke, the heat, and the sense it brings with it, of having come home. Her arms rising up and over, swinging the pickaxe. Knowing she was who she was always meant to be.

How long had it lasted? Scarlett looks into the mirror, concentrates. Five, six years maybe. Enough that they had talked about her potential. Enough that the words had been bandied about, like 'promotion', 'CalFire's rising star'. But there had been other words too, hadn't there, 'It's just a shame about her father.' Whispers of sweet-smelling, alcohol-tinged breath. Of tardiness and recklessness. Enough for gossip, but always falling just that little bit short of action. The warning signs of worse to come.

The feeling as though the father she had always known was a mirage that propinquity had shattered.

And then . . .

Scarlett's breath catches in her throat. A noise coming out that sounds a lot like a growl. The elderly woman at the next sink looks at her with a start.

The memory then of a late-season fire, a consequence of an ill-advised barbecue that catches against dry brush. Breathlessly hot, her back aching, smoke catching at her throat. The whisper of flames as they edge closer. The sound of traffic down below, people evacuating their homes and lives. The pickaxe swinging up and over and down.

The fateful words, 'Hey, anyone seen Mack?'

Had she known then? It seems, in retrospect, that the truth should have been obvious to her. Had she let herself see it, of course. She could not have known, because if she *had* known, things would not have spilled out the way they did.

'We have to start a search. He could be injured.'

'He's not injured.'

'You don't know that.'

Every part of her body screaming with the urgency of it, that they have to search, that they have to find him, because who knows how long her father might have left if they do not. The sense of shouting underwater, of making sounds but no one hearing them. The glances the team exchange, like they are part of some secret she does not know, a group she has been excluded from.

Her Captain taking her by the arm, moving her away from the fire line, their words vanishing into the crackle of flame. 'Scarlett, look, I know he's your dad, but you gotta be honest with yourself here. This has been a long time coming. Billy saw him walking from the camp. He isn't missing. He isn't injured. He *left*. I know this is shitty and you don't wanna think that of your father, but the only place we're gonna be searching are the local bars.'

There is no memory of what came next. Only a feeling, of hot, red rage. And then her hands are up, on her Captain's chest, shoving him backwards. Then . . .

The sense of inevitability that follows. That everything she has ever dreamed of is lost.

'Shit, ' Scarlett mutters again.

The elderly woman spins on her heels, hurrying from the bathroom.

Then follow those few precious hours. Of righteous fury. The loss of all she had ever wanted mitigated by the sense of defending her father. They lasted right up until she found him, propped up against the counter in a dive bar a couple of miles from the fire camp.

He had been allowed to resign, a sympathetic hearing because, after all, wasn't it the stress of the job that drove him to drink in the first place? If you get that under control, if you get the help you need, maybe there will be a place for you here, sometime in the future.

She had received no such mercy.

The memories are coming in thick and fast now. The official termination that arrives through the mail. The sense that the entirety of her life has come to a crashing halt. That first bottle of Jim Beam – can't even remember where she got it from now, just remembers the soft edged relief it brought. Then a kaleidoscope of images, wild abandon, liquid escape. Of meeting Zeke in the same dive bar her father had run to – the irony bright and clear. Zeke seeking an escape of his own. And so they flee together. Straight to the bottom of a bottle.

Calm. Think.

But it isn't thought now. Now it is pure feeling. Hurt and grief and anger and relief and . . . She stares into Scarlett's eyes, focusing on the grey of them.

Say the many-worlds theory is right. Assume this is not actually a dream, but rather another world, lying right alongside her own. Say she has sidestepped into a different version of herself, one where that dream of a family united was true. She studies the sunken cheeks and the chapped lips, the dark circles beneath her eyes. And she begins to laugh. The consequences of getting precisely what you ask for!

Scarlett rubs her hands over her face, turns on the spot, begins to pace. Had to calm down. Had to focus. Had to pay attention to what mattered. That Mack was dead.

Scarlett stops in the middle of the bathroom floor, runs her fingers through the air. A sensation now like gasping for air. Because it was too much. All of it. And there was that ticket, tucked inside her backpack. To Oxnard.

Then a sound, a bing-bong from the tannoy, an announcement on its way.

'The bus to Oxnard is now ready to depart. Would all remaining passengers please make their way to stand E.'

A feeling of pure relief and Scarlett's body moves. There is no thought, just a swift avalanche of motion. She slams open the bathroom door, hard enough that it rebounds with a crash. She strides, running in everything but name. Can see the bus, the driver sitting at the wheel, expression one of boredom. The door stands open, passengers already aboard. The sign flashes 'Final call'.

Scarlett moves without thought, the unavoidable knowledge settling on her that she is running, that she is always running, has done this so many times that her body knows the score.

No.

She stops dead.

The voice in her head, in Scarlett's head, it is Robyn's.

It feels that her feet have been concreted to the floor. *You cannot leave.* Thoughts and body have slipped out of sync. Legs strain, fighting to move. A sudden awareness settling over her.

That she does not know her dad in this world or in that. That she has been built by the choices he has made. In this world and in that.

That she needs to know the truth of it, who he is. Of his life and his death.

That she has to stay. Because Harper is here. Because Zeke is here. If you stay for nothing else, you have to stay for them.

'This is the last and final call for all passengers departing to Oxnard. Your bus is ready to depart.'

Scarlett's heart is racing, sweat beading across her forehead. The muscles in her neck, thighs, straining to run, to get away.

You have to stay.

She stands there, in the middle of the wide-open bus station floor. Voices ricochet around her, rebounding off the high ceiling. The sneakers have emerged from beneath the chairs now, are attached to a girl, perhaps six or so, who is crying, her arms folded, face crumpled up into useless fury. Her mother has turned her back to her, is gathering up her remaining children. Tears roll down her own cheeks. An engine honks. A crash as someone drops a soda can on the floor, the flurry of activity as people dive out of the way of the spreading liquid. She stands there, and she stands there, and her body strains and her chest aches, and yet her mind is calm, unyielding. *No. Stay.*

She stands there, her gaze on stand E, on the bus to Oxnard, its bored driver. She stands there as the driver bursts into action, as his hand moves across, the door sliding into place. She stands there as the beeping begins, the bus beginning its reverse. She stands there and she watches it go.

Chapter Thirty-Seven

Robyn Sandoval – 25th September, 11.07 a.m.

'Are you OK?'

'Huh?'

'You . . . you just kind of zoned out there for a minute.'

Robyn blinks in the bright daylight, smoke catching at her throat. 'Sorry.'

'No, it's fine.' Zeke is studying her, expression one of concern. 'It's just . . .'

'It's petit mal,' says Robyn, quickly. 'Kind of like seizures. You know, from the stress.'

Zeke nods, slowly. 'Oh sure, sure. Well, I mean, you've had quite the day.' He glances towards the car. 'Should we?'

Robyn nods, trying to look casual, and moves around the car, climbing into the driver's side.

'You, ah,' Zeke climbs in beside her, looks her up and down, 'you . . . OK to drive?'

Is she?

Robyn smiles, going for confident. 'Oh, sure. I'm fine.' She turns the key in the ignition, optimism resolutely winning out against good sense, and rolls the car forward. Her gaze tracks across the trailers, each one shut up now, the cars lined up ahead of them, evacuation well and truly underway. The clouds have crept closer, hang lower, and Robyn sits up taller in her seat, looking beyond the tree line.

'Can you see it yet?' Asks Zeke. 'The fire?'

A distant glow, far enough away that she can kid herself it is her imagination. 'I can smell it.'

It fills the air, the promise of trouble coming, coats her throat, pricks her eyes until they water.

They follow the trail of cars, rolling slowly forward out through the gate, turning left onto the narrow road that leads down the hill. As the road tilts downwards, past the part buried sign for the trailer park, there is a break in the trees, one that gives out towards the brittle green of the valley. There, at the opposite peak, there sits the glow of fire, undeniable now.

'Oh no,' murmurs Robyn.

Zeke lets out a low moan. 'Perhaps it won't come any further,' he says, not believing it.

They sit, stuck, gazes locked on the fire. *Stay there. Stay there.* And perhaps in one version of this day and this place, that is precisely what it does. But that is not this day and this place. Because as they sit there, they see it, a whoosh too far away to hear, a glow that carries, climbs. Spreading.

'Oh God,' mutters Zeke.

The car rolls forward.

They have made it a couple of hundred yards, maybe a little more. A hurry-up-and-wait evacuation, the line of cars before them stretching off into the vanishing distance. They snake down the hill, winding their way through the tunnel of trees, another stop, the road before them filling up with brake lights.

Robyn leans forwards, drumming fingernails against the steering wheel. A feeling suddenly, of claustrophobia. There is movement further down the hill, and she sits up straighter, waiting for the brake lights ahead to blink out. But then it dawns on her: the movement is not coming from their line of traffic, but rather is spilling out from a gap in the overhanging trees.

'We're being held up by the traffic that's coming from Destino Heights,' Zeke says, a statement and a question both.

'Yeah.'

Unavoidable that her thoughts dart to Harper, of her words, what the presence of Destino Heights would do to any evacuation.

Then a gap opens up before her and she releases the handbrake, a triumphant journey of a few feet.

'So,' says Zeke, conversationally, 'what do you do?'

She laughs, the sound alien. 'Um . . .'

'Was that a tough question?'

Robyn considers. 'Well, up until an hour or so ago, I was all set to join my family's company. However, recent events . . .'

'You mean, your dad . . .?'

She pulls in a deep breath, bracing. 'OK, so, it's a little complicated. I'm adopted. My parents, my adoptive parents . . . they are the Sandovals.'

He pulls back, studies her. 'Oh.'

'Uh huh.'

'Wow. You're basically Destino royalty.'

Robyn snorts. 'I wouldn't go that far.'

'So, your dad . . .'

'Mack. My biological father.'

'OK . . .' He hesitates, choosing his words carefully. 'So, why aren't you all set to join the Sandoval Company now?' He leans in, voice dropping to a faux whisper, 'I hear they're pretty successful. You know, just as an FYI.'

'They are. I'm just . . . I'm just not sure if, y'know, that's who I want to be.'

Zeke nods. 'Fair enough.'

A moment, then, 'Also, I'm a little bit concerned my adoptive mother may have murdered my biological father.'

A densely packed silence.

'Oh.'

'Yes.'

'Well.'

'Quite.'

Zeke shakes his head. 'You really do like to pack everything into your mornings, don't you?' A moment, then, 'OK, so we'll put joining your family's uber-successful company in the maybe column.' He considers. 'You're pretty good at evacuating strangers from trailer parks if that helps.'

Robyn finds herself smiling, a flush that clambers up her cheeks. 'Well, I will definitely be adding that to my CV.'

A sound breaks through the rumble of idling engines, wailing sirens. The fire trucks are distant flashes between the trees, drawing closer and closer

'Here comes the cavalry,' mutters Zeke. 'Thank God. That park is a dump, but it's got people's entire lives in it.'

Uneasiness bubbles up in Robyn's stomach.

And then it happens, with a painful inevitability. The fire engines slow, slow, almost stop. Then they turn, inexorably, into Destino Heights. Her insides sink.

'Why are they – the fire, it's going to hit the trailer park first, right?'

Robyn nods.

'So, why . . .?'

'Money,' Robyn says, grimly.

Zeke sits back, his shoulders slumping, chews on her words for a time. 'Great,' he says, finally.

The brake lights blink out on the car in front and she releases the handbrake. A slow roll downhill, but some momentum now. Not much, but enough. Main Street is down below, the traffic of it standing bumper to bumper now, the entire town pouring forth, forced into a bottleneck of inaction.

Robyn flips the indicator on. 'I'll let you out up ahead. There's hundreds of cars heading out, if you can flag someone down . . .'

Zeke nods, seriously. 'Sure. Sure. Or,' he says, brightly, 'I could just come with you. You know, provide backup while you investigate the crime scene.'

Robyn looks at him, startled. 'What?'

'Well, I mean, I figure what with you going full Sherlock Holmes, you could probably use a Dr Watson.'

'But the evacuation . . .'

'Ah, it'll be fine. I'll help you. Y'know, bring my forensic expertise to bear.'

'Do you have any forensic expertise?'

'I watched CSI once.'

'Oh. Excellent.'

Robyn eases the car into the junction of Oak and Main, and hesitates. 'Zeke, are you sure . . .?'

He nods, firmly, gaze locked on the congested road ahead. 'Yup. I'm sure. Let's go, Holmes.'

She studies him for a moment, then nods slowly. 'OK,' she murmurs. And she feels her shoulders sink, relief flooding her, her lips forming into an almost smile in spite of . . . all this. She shakes her head, focusing on the road, and puts her foot down, forcing her way into the steady stream of traffic heading out of town. She pulls across it, heading in the opposite direction, and they wind their way around oncoming traffic, pulling off the road towards the set-back diner. It is locked up now, windows dark. Robyn snaps the engine off, pushes at the driver's door, clambering out and slamming it behind her.

'It's this way.' She turns onto the narrow footpath leading up past the diner towards her father's house where the police tape twists in the wind.

'Woah,' mutters Zeke.

'What?'

'Well, I mean, I knew it was a crime scene. I mean, you know, the logic of it and all that, but I'm just realising that we are actually going to crash a crime scene.'

She studies him. 'Yes,' she agrees, cautiously.

He nods. 'OK then. Just as long as we're all on the same page.'

Robyn ducks under the tape, feels the trailing edge of it pull at her hair, tries not to linger, to process precisely what the crime tape means. She walks quickly down the path. The door is closed now, the light turned off. She pulls the key from her pocket, suddenly aware that her hand is shaking as she lines it up with the lock.

'Hey. You OK?'

She nods, lying. 'Fine.' Pushes the door open.

There is a smell here. Not of death, not quite. But of musk and smoke and of dishes that have sat too long in the sink. It catches at her throat, pricks tears in her eyes. Robyn shakes her head, walking slowly into the kitchen. Little has been done here. Little preserved. It waits, a scene in stasis for the technicians to come.

'What do you want me to do?' Zeke murmurs, a church kind of voice.

'Take pictures,' she says. 'Of everything you can think of.'

She walks through the kitchen, into the lounge. The Jim Beam is still there. The two glasses. Did Eve drink from one? A moment, then she turns, retracing her steps to the front porch, her father's backpack hanging from a hook above his hiking boots.

'What are you doing?' asks Zeke, voice still little more than a whisper.

'I'm bagging the evidence,' she says, quietly.

'Sure,' he agrees. 'CSI.'

She grabs a roll of kitchen paper, unspools it. The glasses get wrapped up, slid into the bag, then the bottle. She sets the backpack carefully on the ground. Then steps around it towards the cabinet tucked in the far corner of the lounge. Has been here as long as Mack has. Has been opened once, twice in her recollection.

Memory of a windblown autumn night, not long after he had arrived. Of dinner from takeout cartons, cans of Budweiser open on the table. 'I know.' Her father jumping up. 'Let me show you the photo albums. Of your mom, me, when we were first married. You when you were a baby.' Of him ducking around the sofa, slipping the latch on the cabinet, the photo albums stacked on one shelf, box files on another. 'Keep all my most precious stuff in here,' he had said.

Robyn lifts the latch.

It is all as it should be, the photo albums sitting right there. A sudden flash of grief that he had not been looking at them when he died.

But why would he?

She is being ridiculous.

She pulls out the photo albums, stacking them to one side. Not evidence, these. Just for her. An envelope, unsealed, with baby photos inside. She peers in, flicks through. There amongst them, a glint of gold.

Robyn frowns, pulls out a narrow gold chain, locket hanging from it.

'That's weird.'

'What?'

She reaches inside her top, pulls out the locket that hangs from her neck. 'He gave me this one six years ago.' She shakes her head. 'Why would he buy two?'

Zeke reaches over, takes the locket into his own fingers, flips it open. 'It's empty.' He shrugs. 'Maybe it was a mistake? Ordered two instead of one and just never returned the spare?'

'I guess.'

Robyn watches as he slides the locket back into the envelope, adding it to the stack of albums.

Then she pulls out the box files, kneels on the carpet beside them. The top one is house stuff, deeds and escrow information.

Some bills, certificates for utilities. She sets it to one side, opens the next.

'Are you looking for anything specific down there?' Zeke asks, phone in hand.

Robyn nods. 'Yup. Just don't know what yet. Hoping I'll know it when I see it.'

She shuffles through CalFire stuff. Mack's training and schedule, certifications. And then, the letter. There is a sense of inevitability to this, that she has been here before. And in all honesty, she has.

CalFire hereby terminates the employment of Mackenzie Morgan.

'It was such a shame,' he'd said. 'My back gave out. My career was going so great, then bam, back is gone, medical retirement.'

It had been sent a little over five years ago. Must have been shortly before he returned to Destino, right before he knocked on her door, her long-lost father.

Robyn closes her eyes, a moment of grief. Why didn't he tell her? Why did he lie?

Then she pulls in a deep breath, shakes her head, closes the file, setting it aside.

She had wanted the truth.

She flips open another file. This one, the documents are older. Printed for the most part, but the pages have grown yellow with age. Robyn slows, carefully flipping through the pages.

And then she sees it.

The words Destino Heights.

Robyn lets out a soft gasp, pulling the paper from its sheaf.

'What?'

She ignores him, studying the words.

It has been concluded that the Sandoval Company has not proven that they can provide sufficient community facilities for the proposed new subdivision (Destino Heights). A study of the area has found that the facilities within the town of Destino itself will be insufficient to support the additional population likely to be generated by such a development. Particular note was made of roadways, in terms of ingress and egress, particularly in emergency situations.

Consideration was also given to the report submitted by Mrs Harper Morgan, re the wildfire risk associated with the positioning of Destino Heights at the Wildland Urban Interface. Following a full evaluation of this report and the responding advice provided by the Sandoval Company, it has been determined that the development of Destino Heights cannot be supported at this time.

*Yours Sincerely
Mr John James Averill*

'Who's John James Averill?'

Robyn starts, looks over her shoulder at Zeke, squinting at the letter in her hand. 'I don't . . .' A flash then, of Harper, her words, worked out pretty well for Averill. 'I mean, I've heard . . . no, wait . . . Yes, I do. I know him. He . . .'

Another memory, of Robyn's now, down in the big house this time. A Christmas party, the Christmas tree set up in the front hall, strung with lights. Of the room, set aside for the children, with Christmas carols playing on the stereo. Of uneven dancing, a kiss beneath the mistletoe with some kid named Tim. Of slipping out, along the corridor, into the kitchen, thinking to sneak a look at the living room and the adults with their shimmering dresses and penguin suits. Hearing voices. 'You best remember, John, that you and me, we are draped right over the same barrel.' Seeing her father, toe to toe with a man, shorter than him, the lights reflecting off his bald head. 'You want those constituents of yours asking how you pay for that nice big house you got yourself? Maybe they'll start asking, Is John James Averill really the man we want representing us to congress?'

'What?' says Zeke

Robyn bites her lip. 'I think he's a congressman now. But he used to be Mayor of Destino. When I was a kid.'

'Cool. Cool. Robyn?'

'Yeah?'

'What the hell are we doing here? For real this time.'

She looks up at him, considers. Then, reluctantly, 'My mom. She was paying Mack. Was giving him money every month. And I don't know why.'

He nods slowly. 'You think he was blackmailing her.'

She doesn't answer. She flips, onto the next page. A newspaper article now, the headline stark. **Destino Heights Approved**.

Zeke squats down beside her, gives a low whistle. 'Now, how the hell did that happen?'

'Look at the dates,' says Robyn. 'Just two weeks apart. Whatever happened. It happened fast.'

She scans the text of the article. 'In a surprise announcement today, Mayor Averill informed reporters that the controversial Destino Heights development has been given the go ahead. This comes despite fierce opposition from environmentalists and community groups, who feel that the positioning of the development creates a significant wildfire risk.'

'Well,' mutters Zeke, 'Mayor Averill, what have you done?'

'I'm guessing,' says Robyn, 'that what he has done is sell his soul.'

'To who?'

'My parents,' she says grimly.

She hands him the paper, flipping forward to the next sheet.

'Oh my God!'

'What?'

'Look at this.' She holds out a printout: financial statements for the Sandoval Company. 'Check out the date. Two days before the acceptance of the Destino Heights subdivision.'

Her gaze hooks on the number $500,000 paid to Hacienda Co. Then to the next sheet. Registered owner of Hacienda Co. John James Averill.'

'Well,' Mutters Zeke, 'now isn't that interesting? The Sandoval Company pays half a million and suddenly Destino Heights gets built.' He hesitates. 'You think this is it? You think Mack, your dad, he was blackmailing your mother over this?'

She doesn't want to think that, really doesn't want to think that. Yet she finds herself nodding anyway. 'Yes,' she murmurs. 'Yes, I do.' She drums her fingernails on the lid of a box file. 'He emailed me before he died, told me he had something to tell me. Maybe this was it. Maybe he was going to come clean, tell me what the Sandoval Company had done.'

'But . . .' Zeke takes the paper from her hands, studying it, 'why does it matter? I mean, yeah, sure, bribing public officials isn't great. But it was thirty years ago.'

Robyn briefly closes her eyes, pulls in a breath. 'I was about to become CEO. I guess he thinks – thought – I should know.'

'OK,' says Zeke. 'But . . . I mean, you really think your mother could have done this? Really? You really think your mom has it in her to kill him? And over old news?'

'The Sandoval Company is going to be going public in the next couple of years. It's a delicate time. Something like this could bring the whole thing crashing down.'

'So you think she could . . .'

'I don't know.' Robyn stares at him. 'I just don't know anymore.'

Then, just like that, the darkness comes.

Chapter Thirty-Eight

Scarlett Morgan – 25th September, 11.15 a.m.

The Uber driver is young, worryingly so. He drives lazily, one hand on the wheel, the other resting on the rim of the open window. He smells of weed, strong enough that Scarlett considers asking him to share.

Scarlett.

Robyn.

She leans her head back against the headrest, looks out into the bright day. Beyond that, the cloud of smoke, hovering over the landscape.

'You said Motel 6, right.'

She struggles to focus on the driver's words.

'The Surfside,' she agrees. The words are clipped. Do not invite conversation.

The driver swings a left, taking the corner hard enough that she slides in her seat.

'Hey!' Scarlett says.

The driver waves it away, sliding into a flow of traffic that has built up as far as the eye can see.

Scarlett sits up taller in her seat. Can just about make out the distant sign of the motel. 'Hey,' she says again. 'I'll walk from here. Thanks.' She doesn't wait for an answer, pushes open the door, clambers out into the hot day. She throws Zeke's backpack over her shoulder, hops up onto the sidewalk, walks with long strides. With a purpose. That purpose remains fuzzy for the moment, the cloudiness of the shift from one world to another making memory sparse, loose about the edges. But she remembers the name John James Averill and the payment of half a million dollars.

She picks up pace, the memories spilling back as she walks.

I need to find Harper.

Up ahead, the lights of the motel, the sound of teenagers laughing, skateboard wheels on a hard ramp, beneath the blinking No Vacancies sign. Scarlett ducks between an SUV and a Chevvy, sweat already rolling down between her shoulder blades. The parking lot is full, sound spilling from the rooms beyond, ricocheting off the cars. She squeezes through the lot, onto the walkway that wraps its way around the rooms. The sounds of televisions, different shows overlapping, waft out from open doors. She passes an elderly couple, sitting out on the front stoop, her on a wooden chair, him on an upturned icebox. They pass a box of cookies back and forth between them. No conversation, just the sound of chewing. She passes them by, and the room beyond that, the opening chords of the *Big Bang Theory* tumbling out at her.

At the lobby building, the line is out the door now, harassed parents, crying kids. Scarlett pulls her backpack higher up on her shoulder, squeezing her way past a middle-aged man, shirt pulled out from waistband, circles of stain ringing his armpits. He doesn't look up, is scrolling manically through his phone. Scarlett angles her way into the lobby proper, can just about make out the clerk behind the desk, phone jammed to her ear. She looks ready to cry too.

Through the still-open set of doors, the conference room. Scarlett puts her head down, striding forward. It has filled in a little now. The trestle tables laid out with supplies, clothing and toiletries, anything that a person might need when they have left their whole world behind.

Harper is sitting, her head resting back against the wall, staring at the television screen mounted high up on the wall. The aerial shots of fire, of Destino down below.

'Hey,' says Scarlett tentatively. 'I . . .' Scarlett chokes on it, so Robyn pushes it through 'I'm sorry, I overreacted.'

Harper turns to her, gaze distant. 'Yeah, well, we all got reason to overreact right about now.' She smiles, sadly. 'I'm sorry too, for what it's worth.' She studies her. 'You're not going to the job interview?'

Scarlett shrugs. 'Thought about it a bit more. Figured it's not really the direction I want my life to be heading in right now.'

Her mother nods, poker-faced. 'Fair enough. Zeke'll be pleased you're back.'

Scarlett shrugs. 'Yeah. I'm saving that surprise for a bit.' She looks around. 'Can I do anything?'

Harper shakes her head, weary. 'No. It's all done. Just waiting.' She waves towards the lobby. 'Once those people out there get their accommodation needs sorted, they're pretty soon going to start thinking about all the other needs they left behind.' She opens her arms out, indicating the spread. 'Then we'll be here.' She nods towards the television. 'You seen this?'

Scarlett shakes her head, takes a seat beside her mother. Their upper arms touch briefly and an electric current races through her. She pulls in a breath, steadying herself. 'What are they saying?'

'The fire is heading to Destino. But slowly. The reporter was up there talking about the Wildfire Preparedness group, how we're a great example of community engagement, how our hard work has stripped the forest of excess fuel.'

'That's good.'

Harper nods firmly, gives her daughter a swift smile. 'It *is* good. We did good, kid.'

Scarlett smiles back, but tears prick at the back of her eyes. She must remember this. The way her mother's lips curl, the sparkle as the light hits her eyes. She must remember this once she is lost again. She pulls in a deep breath, fighting back the tears that threaten.

'Can I ask you something?'

'Sure.'

'Tell me about Destino Heights.'

Harper sits up straighter then, brow furrowed. 'What?'

Scarlett shrugs. 'I'm guessing you know far more about it than you have ever let on. You said it passed suddenly, unexpectedly. Tell me? Please?'

Harper's eyes narrow, the faintest of smiles. 'What do you know, Scarlett?'

'Well,' Scarlett slides into the seat beside her, 'I know that Destino Heights didn't pass on its merits. And I know you know all about that.'

Harper doesn't answer, just smiles. What was that expression? Pride almost. 'OK?'

'OK. So. Tell me about it.'

Now a Cheshire Cat kind of smile, and she stretches her arms out above her head. 'Scarlett, this is some old stuff . . . why are we—'

'Please? Just humour me.'

Harper grins. 'It's just like when you were little. Please, Mommy. Just one more story. Fine . . . OK, so, you know that I was . . . how to say it? . . . a thorn in the side of the Sandovals during their mission to build Destino Heights. So the plan they had was to embed it within the forest, surrounded by trees. Of course, what that means is that you're carving a giant chunk right out of that forest to make that happen. Sadly, no one cared. Believe me,' she says with an eye-roll, 'I tried with the inherent value of trees angle. No dice. However, the other thing it means is a high wildfire risk. That, people were more concerned about. No one likes the idea of buying a nice piece of property up in the mountains only to have it swallowed up by the next fire that sweeps through. And, I thought I'd done it. I thought I'd won.'

A flash of memory, of the letter.

It has been determined that the development of Destino Heights cannot be supported at this time.

'Sure,' murmurs Scarlett.

'So imagine, then, my surprise when suddenly Destino Heights is approved.' Harper balls her hands up into fists, bumps them onto her knees. 'I knew it was bad. I just damn well knew it. But I couldn't prove it. Then one day, I found it. The financials. Evidence that a bribe had been paid.'

Scarlett bites her lips. Thinks of the Sandoval monument, far more elaborate than Harper's own. 'So,' she says, slowly, 'what happened? No one here . . . no one knows, do they? In Destino, I mean?'

Harper sighs, plucks at a loose thread at her knee. 'So, I found the information, the evidence of the payment going out from the Sandovals, into the accounts of Averill's shell company. Only I found it on the day the Sandovals died.'

Scarlett stares at her, brain freezing here, selves slipping between worlds. 'The day of the crash?'

Her mother nods. 'I was out in the library in Cambria when I found it. Of course, I wanted to head back and rain thunder down on the Sandovals. My God, I was so angry. So, I'm rushing, obviously. And then . . .'

'And then?'

Harper shrugs. 'I almost tripped, on my way out the door. Came within a hairs breadth of dropping my papers all over the floor.' She looks down at her hands, lost in thought for a moment. Then, 'I often wonder, what would have happened, if I had actually dropped those papers. Could so easily have been me in that crash.'

The world hangs in stasis. Long moments.

Then Harper shakes her head. 'I'll never forget the look on Viv's face when I saw her the next morning. It was . . . She was too young. To see something like that.'

'Vivienne was there?'

Harper nods. 'She was in the car behind the Sandovals. Her and Luis. Happened upon the crash just moments after it happened. Of course,' she says, 'entire town was in shock. The Sandovals, they were . . . important people.' She leans forward, elbows on her knees. 'Seemed like there was no point in destroying their reputation, especially given that was all they had left.'

'So you just . . . let it go?'

Harper looks at her daughter, gives her a wicked grin. 'Not exactly. Turns out, Alex Sandoval, he was the last of his clan. The last Sandoval there was. So the company, it wound up landing in the lap of some cousin out East. He had little to no interest in a little town in the California mountains. His plan, such as it was, was to carry out the Destino Heights plan, sell up, get the most he could for all of the Sandoval properties, make bank and retire early.'

'But . . .'

'But then I show up. Arrange a sit-down appointment with him. Seemed like a nice enough kind of guy. Had the decency to at least pretend to be horrified when I laid out the bribe, pointed out the Sandoval Company had been party to a crime. Of course, that kind of history . . . it can affect the sale price. Can affect it significantly.'

'Mom.' The word tastes sweetly strange. 'What did you do?'

Harper's grin widens. 'I blackmailed him.'

'What?'

She waves away her daughter's disbelief. 'OK, blackmail is a tad . . . hyperbolic. I merely pointed out the value of keeping such shady history sub rosa. I told him that I would bury it, would forget everything I knew, if he did something for me.'

'Drop the development of Destino Heights.'

Harper grinned widely. 'Yup. But that wasn't all. He had to cut us a deal. The town, I mean. The Sandoval Company, it owned properties up and down. Homes and businesses. I told him that I would bury what I knew if he allowed the tenants to buy their properties at, um, significantly reduced prices.' She shrugged. 'He agreed. I heard after that he sold the company, did pretty well out of the whole thing too. Bought a retirement place in Miami. Meanwhile, Destino, we got to own our own town. Made a difference, a big one, especially to the properties up and down Main Street, not having those rents to contend with.'

Scarlett leans back in her chair, nodding slowly. 'Wow . . .' she says slowly. 'I . . . just wow.'

'Yeah,' says Harper, 'my most profound bad-girl moment. To be honest, I'm quite proud.'

'You should be,' she says, quietly. Thinks of the shape of this world, how it compares to the other. The hole left by the loss of the Sandovals, of her parents, not really a hole at all.

'Mom . . .' that word again, 'can I ask you something? Something else, I mean.'

'Sure.'

'Do you think it's better?'

'What?'

'That they died. That Alex and Eve Sandoval died. Better for Destino, I mean?' Scarlett's voice cracks on that last.

Harper hesitates, studying her daughter. 'I . . . I mean, who can ever say, right? We all like to think of ourselves as indispensable. That the world just wouldn't work as well without us.' She sighs. 'I didn't know them well. I mean, obviously, they weren't my biggest fans. But, life, it does different things to all of us. I guess they were just on their path, didn't have anything to send them down a different one. Who knows who they could have been if they had. Who knows what they could have achieved, for themselves, the town. No. I don't think the world was better off without them. It was, I think, just very different.'

Scarlett sits there, rests her head back against the wall, suddenly so weary. Then a whoosh of dizziness, the shot across the bow, the change approaching.

'Look,' says Harper.

She points at the television, the camera zoomed in close now on the fire. It has reached the trailer park, has begun its steady sweep through the lives contained within. A figure on the fire line, hazy and indistinct, but Scarlett does not need more detail to recognise her father.

'He's going to love this,' mutters Harper. 'Going to be dining out on it for months.'

'Months?' Bonnie sweeps into the room, dwarfed by the large box in her hands. 'Try years!' She sets it down on the nearest table and turns towards Scarlett, offers a sympathetic smile. 'You OK, sweetie? I knew you'd be back, I told your mom.' She looks towards Harper, back to Scarlett. 'Try not to let him get to you so much. You're worth so much more than that.'

Scarlett opens her mouth, the question, right there on her lips. Who the hell are you? How did you get from that Bonnie to this?

She is going to say it. But it is too late, because her heart is thumping and her vision is narrowing and the darkness is sweeping in.

Chapter Thirty-Nine

Robyn Sandoval – 25th September, 11.21 a.m.

Robyn blinks. Is sitting on the floor of her father's house, her legs crossed, papers settled in her lap.

'OK . . .' Zeke lowers himself to the floor beside her, 'Let's say the money your mother was paying to Mack was of the hush variety. These payments go back years. Why snap now? Why kill him now? Why not when he first brought this to her?'

'I don't know.'

Zeke is quiet for a moment. Then he leans forward, elbows on his knees, his position mirroring her own. 'Let's look at this logically. Let's think about what we know about last night.' He holds up a hand, counting as he goes. 'We know Mack had been drinking, enough that he had to be brought home. But when he came home, he was still sober enough to email you.'

Robyn nods. 'At 11.45 p.m.'

'Right. So we know he was still alive then. We also know that Luis was somewhere else by then, so he didn't kill him and leave.' He gazes past her to the backpack slumped on the floor. 'We have the bourbon, two glasses. So at some point, someone came here and drank with him. Unless he was a glass in each hand kind of guy, which seems . . . unlikely. What else do we know about last night?'

'The front door was left open,' Robyn offers. 'The lights were left on.'

'Could he have left the front door open?'

She shrugs. 'I guess. But if Luis brought him in and let himself back out again, I can't see *him* doing that.'

'No, fair enough.' Zeke shakes his head. 'But he was killed in bed. So someone came in, when he was asleep, held a pillow over his face.'

Robyn winces, the movement involuntary.

'Sorry.'

'No . . . it's important.' She stares past him to the backpack, the Jim Beam, the two glasses hidden within it. 'So, the question is, how did they get in?'

He studies her. 'You have a key?'

She glances back at him. 'I didn't kill him.'

Zeke smiles sadly. 'That would have been quite the twist. But that wasn't actually what I was suggesting.'

'You're saying my mom could have used it.'

Zeke looks at her, pulls a face. 'Honestly, I don't know what I'm saying. I mean, sure. Your mom could have used your key, let herself in, killed him. Put the key back where it was. But my question still remains, why now? Why does your mom, a respectable business woman, all of a sudden decide that killing your father is the only possible solution?'

Robyn shakes her head, pushing back the sudden urge to cry. 'I don't know.' She turns her gaze from him, directing it instead out of the kitchen window. Can see only sky from here. The town below is invisible to her but that sky, it is thick with portent. Vivid blue has given way to thick grey. She breathes in and can taste the smoke. 'We should go' she says. 'It's getting worse.'

'Yeah,' Zeke says. He unfolds long legs, pushes himself up. 'You wanna take these?' He gestures to the stack of photo albums, the envelope with the locket in it on top.

'Please.' Robyn stands, movements awkward. 'I'm gonna go get his laptop.'

She leaves Zeke loading up a bag and hurries to the bedroom. She does not look at the bed. Will not allow herself to see the memory of her father's dead body, the indent that has been left behind on the mattress. Instead she forces her vision to narrow down to a tunnel, forces a focus on the dresser, on the laptop closed up on the top of it. She picks it up, tucks it into the backpack. Tells herself that she will return, once all of this is done.

'Robyn?' Zeke stands in the doorway, albums cradled in his arms. 'You ready?'

She nods, turns on her heel. Will not allow the thought that this will be the last time. Follows him out into the dense air. And then . . . Her gaze locks on it, the distant ridge. It is not grey now. Rather red. The glow of fire hangs, marking out the shape of the valley, a red line on a term paper. She stands, stares at it. Is dimly aware of the sound, over the steady drone of car engines, the distant whirr of helicopters. The distant roar of fire.

The fire has crossed the ridge.

'Oh no!'

'Robyn, we need to go,' says Zeke, his voice tight, urgent. 'Now.' He ushers her before him, pulling shut the front door behind them, and then they take off running, down the steep incline of the footpath. The smoke catches at her throat and she coughs, the pull of it encircling her chest.

Robyn pops open the trunk, setting the evidence down carefully, then hurries around to the driver's side. The thud of the trunk closing, Zeke's footsteps fast behind her. She clambers in behind the wheel, jams the key into the ignition, waits while Zeke climbs into the seat beside her.

'I think it is officially time for us to leave,' he says, pulling the belt across him.

'Agreed.' Robyn tugs the gearshift into reverse, pulls out onto Main Street, forcing the car into the dense line of traffic. 'Holy shit,' she mutters.

'Yeah,' agrees Zeke. 'This is . . . wow!' He leans forward, looks up towards the ridge.

There is no denying it now. It is not smoke, or headlights or the glow of a belated dawn. It is fire. And it is here.

Robyn can feel her heart beating harder.

Zeke gestures to the traffic ahead of them, to the line of traffic to their immediate left that bisects Main Street, oozing its way down the mountain, along Oak Street. 'These people . . . they're not all going to get out.'

It's what happens. It is the inevitable consequence of Destino Heights, of Harper's loss. Robyn opens her mouth. Later she will wonder just what it is she was about to say, whether she was about to let loose, spill it all.

But she never gets the chance.

Because, up on Oak, a Ford Galaxy snaps, pulling free from the line of unmoving traffic, into the lane for oncoming cars. It plunges down the mountain, the sudden sense of freedom and fear combining to force the accelerator to the floor. And so, by the time it reaches the junction with Main Street, it is going far faster than it should. Certainly too fast to stop.

For Robyn and for Zeke, it happens in an instant.

For Robyn and for Zeke, it is a flash of movement, an intake of breath, and then the Galaxy is on them, its hood driving into the driver's side door in a scream of crumpled metal.

The entire world folding in upon itself.

Chapter Forty

They are moving now. The flurry of activity, in house after house. The course set. Evidence clear. The evacuation under way. They think they have a plan, think they know what they will do. Because they are capable and responsible and haven't they lived in Destino long enough to know the way out?

Of course, it's different, isn't it, once the fire crosses the ridge? Once the smoke descends, rolling down the mountainside until it fills up the streets, making everything that was once so well known, opaque and ill-defined. Once the fear takes hold.

They begin to flee. In car after car, family after family. They pile out into packed streets, each of them trailing one behind the other.

Can you feel it? The tension in the air?

After all, all animals know to run from fire.

Don't they?

They pour along Oak and along Vine. The Randolphs from number 98, Maya Higgins and her three German Shepherds from number 7. These people who have lived beside one another for year on year. The faces as familiar as the sign that hangs from Destino Vino, a part of the place they call home. Only now, it is different. Now the Randolphs are in the way, are clogging up the road with their beat-up old sedan that never did manage to get above thirty miles an hour. Now Maya Higgins and her damn dogs, and where the hell did she learn to drive? Is she kidding with that move, she's slowing everyone down. Don't they see there's a fire?

For those people, the ones who flee, it is obvious. What else would one do? Isn't it built into the very DNA of us? And so the Randolphs at number 98 and Maya Higgins from number 7, they are not neighbours. Now they are obstacles.

Then there are others. The ones who run, not away from the fire, but rather towards it. The ones who were not at home when the alert went out, who were in work or in school or visiting family over in Paso Robles. For these people, it is not about flight, at least, not yet. For these people it is about something else – family. And so they travel, salmon swimming upstream, a deep instinct calling them home. Back into Destino, back towards their husbands and their wives and their children and their cockapoo named Dave. Heading straight for trouble. But that is it, isn't it? That is what makes us human. When danger comes, sometimes we do not flee. Sometimes we flock.

After all, we are social animals, tied together with furious bonds. Evacuation only happening if the people we care most about are beside us. These people, they know that these choices are not simple. And that when the smart choice involves leaving behind the people you love, most of us will find ourselves to be dumb.

Look at it now. Look at Main Street.

It is lined, the traffic a solid chain that snakes about the inconvenient roadworks, abandoned by workers who now urgently have somewhere else to be. It trails past The Artist's Way and Destino Vino, past Bar 53. A solid mass of brake lights, of honking horns and frayed tempers.

There will be others, too. Destino residents who are less finely tuned to danger, who have not rehearsed the inevitability of disaster within their own imaginations. These people, they will wait. Will not flee at the first sign of trouble. Perhaps they will scoff at those who do. Perhaps they will roll their eyes, call them snowflakes. And so these people, they stand in their driveways and they look to the ridge, the one that, for long decades has protected Destino from the fires that rip through this part of the world. And they wait, for the evidence to come.

Us humans, we are not comfortable with uncertainty. It makes our brains itch. And so we seek the information, something that will bridge that gap, make the uncertain certain. We look to our officials, to our community, to the information that comes from our own senses. And so we are influenced by what our neighbour does, by how much the world around us reacts to the danger that is coming. We look for reassurance that we are doing the right thing. We push back our evacuation until the danger is inevitable.

And then when it is, we are afraid. We hurry to our cars. We forget to lock the front door or turn off the gas. We find ourselves clumsy, thick fingers that suddenly will not do our bidding. We leave the go-bag on the drive. And we drive faster than we should, pulling out from a line of stationary traffic on Oak and heading downhill at speed. Whipping out onto Main Street and straight into the driver's side of an idling vehicle.

There is a link between the two – car accidents and disasters – one that would seem to indicate a particular churlishness in Nature's personality. One would think that a single catastrophe would be sufficient. And yet as the world turns upside down – from earthquake or wildfire or any of the other myriad ways life can attempt to kill us – the number of car accidents increases. Because of anxiety or sleep deprivation or our brain's ancient mammalian system focusing on the imminent threat of death rather than the positioning of a stop sign. Nature's way of pointing out to us that a frightened brain is not a careful brain. That surviving the immediate threat does not guarantee future survival.

And back in Destino, there will be yet another group. Those who do not flee and do not fight. The Destino residents who will remain. Who will trust to history, of fires that have veered away at the last moment, of evacuations that proved to be an exercise in futility. Those who believe that the past predicts the future.

For many of those, by the time they realise they are wrong, it will be too late.

Chapter Forty-One

Scarlett Morgan – 25th September, 11.28 a.m.

'I don't know. I mean, what goes through people's minds? Look. Look at this. Mittens. Who donates mittens. It's 100 degrees outside.'

Scarlett reaches out, clutches onto the edge of a plastic bin, tattoos catching the light. Nausea washes over her, a burst of a headache that just as rapidly recedes.

'I mean, I ask you,' Bonnie is muttering, is rifling through the tub of fabric on the table in front of her. 'Look! A sock. A single sock.' She sniffs. 'If I was being unchristian, I would be inclined to say this was less about the good people of San Luis Obispo county helping out, than it was a way of them getting rid of their trash.' She stops, peers at Scarlett. 'You OK, honey? You've gone awful pale.'

Scarlett is staring at the tattoos on her arms and, for a moment, she simply cannot remember who she is, what brought her here.

'I . . .'

She stares at Bonnie and suddenly, the image of her shimmers and, for just a moment, she sees her looking older, thinner. Scarlett blinks and then it is gone again. But it is enough.

'Robyn . . .' Scarlett murmurs. Her legs feel unsteady beneath her and she sways.

'Woah, now, honey.' Bonnie is at her side, guiding her to a chair. 'You look awful. Likely the heat.' She pushes her down, firm. 'You sit there, I'll run, get you some water.'

Scarlett's fingers clutch the hard edge of the seat. Barely hears her. Her head filled with the sound of metal impacting metal. Of the shattering of glass. And it settles over her, inevitable. The suddenness of the dark, the switch that came from the blue, from Scarlett to Robyn.

Robyn is gone.

She can feel it, something strange happening, the clearing out of thoughts in her head. Of life in the big house, of being a Sandoval. And now, she can't remember what she was wearing when she was Robyn, who she was talking to. The memories, they vanish, one after the other, ice melting beneath flame, until in the end, there is nothing left.

Now she is Scarlett alone.

She sits, flopping down onto the hard plastic chair. Is becoming aware now of her leg dancing up and down. Of how much she needs a cigarette. Looks down at her hands, shaking like they do not belong to her. And now she can't quite remember what it is she is doing here. She has that interview down in Oxnard to get to.

She sits, in the bright-lit room. Can hear the tumble of conversation in the room beyond. Can feel it all sliding back into place, the memories of her life, of Scarlett's life. And Scarlett's life alone.

And, as it slips away from her, she thinks that this must be how it ends. Two worlds that collapse back down into one.

Scarlett looks about the room, lit by a blue-tinged strip-light glow. A sudden urge to call for her mother, the memory of her words, . . . OK, I'm going to speak to the manager, see if I can get us another room to use, be back soon. So she pushes it down. That she is good at. She looks about, the conference room, trestle tables pushed up against the walls. Beside her, tubs of clothing.

She stands, carefully, head still swimming. With the memory comes the image of her father on television, the hometown hero. Then the anger, and, along with it, the urge to escape. She looks down at her shorts. She shouldn't wear shorts to an interview. Even to a dive bar in Oxnard. Reaches out, picks up a flannel shirt that is splayed across the top, buttery soft to the touch. She pulls it on. Sifts through the pile until she finds rough denim jeans that are too big, but that she pulls on nonetheless, tugging them over her shorts. Glances around the room.

She stoops back down to pull her sneakers on and the motion brings with it a fresh wave of nausea and . . . something else. She sits up, can feel her breath coming in short, sharp bursts. Raises her hand to her cheek and it comes away wet. Scarlett frowns at the teardrop that catches the light on her fingertip. She rarely cries.

No, says a voice in her head. But Robyn does.

And then, it is odd, it is as if her body is reacting to something her mind is oblivious to, because out comes what is undeniably a sob. Her body folds itself in half, resting her elbows on her knees, head in her hands. Tears drip down the sleeves of her new flannel shirt.

Robyn is gone. If you were to ask her, right now, why it was she wept, Scarlett would be hard-pressed to tell you. But she weeps anyway. A sense that crowds in on her of something significant being lost. And as she cries, there is an overhanging sense of disbelief. Because Scarlett does not cry. And as for what is lost – Scarlett does not care. Has spent a lifetime learning not to care. And still she weeps. The thought rising unbidden, *I am not enough. Not alone. Not without . . .*

The door opens then and Scarlett shifts, an electric shock start that rearranges her limbs, hands whipping across her cheeks to dry the tears.

'Oh, sweetie.' Bonnie bustles towards her, sets a plastic cup of water on the table beside her. Scarlett shakes her head. Is ready to protest. That really, no, she is fine. Only the words will not come and suddenly she is folded into the older woman's arms and her senses are filled up with the smell of vanilla, the soft brush of jersey on her cheek.

'It's going to be . . . OK, honey,' murmurs Bonnie. 'We're going to get through this. We just have to keep putting one foot in front of the other, keep walking until we see daylight.'

From somewhere behind them comes the sound of a door opening, of footsteps. 'Hey!' Zeke's voice, heavy with concern. 'Everyone OK in here?'

Bonnie pulls back, studies Scarlett. 'Well,' she says, gently, 'I think someone here could do with some looking after.' She steps aside, steering Scarlett into Zeke's arms. 'Why don't you guys head on out and grab some lunch? Get away from all of this for a bit.'

Zeke slides his arm around her shoulder, pulling her in tight to him. 'Sounds like a plan.'

And then, they are out, are into the lobby. There are too many people. They knot together in packs, filling up the lobby. The soft thrum of conversation, like a flock of geese flying overhead. It stays her feet, the sound of them all, a thousand conversations she has no business being a part of. For a moment, her stomach enters free fall, hands clammy, throat dry.

'Come on,' murmurs Zeke. 'Let's get out of here.'

She feels the weight of his arm on her back, can smell his cologne. And then her mouth is opening and the words are tumbling out. 'Zeke,' she hears herself saying, 'there's something I have to tell you . . .'

Chapter Forty-Two

Scarlett Morgan — 25th September, 11.36 a.m.

Zeke sits on the queen-sized bed, his feet on the floor, elbows resting on his knees. He doesn't look at her, but down at the ground. His knee twitches.

'Zeke?' Scarlett says, tentative.

'I'm . . . yeah . . . just, just give me a minute.'

'Uh huh.' Scarlett lowers herself to the bucket chair that has been pushed up against the window. Shouldn't have said it, shouldn't have said it.

'So . . . OK, so, quick question, you been doing any mushrooms today?' He glances up. 'Any colourful toadstools made their way into your diet?'

Scarlett smiles in spite of herself. 'No.'

'OK.' He hesitates. 'Is it possible that you were dreaming? Or . . .'

'I've been through every option, Zeke. Everything I can think of. And none of it fits. Apart from what you said.'

He frowns. 'What did I say?'

'You know, the theory that there are multiple worlds, all lined up alongside one another? That each time you make a choice, a new world is formed,' Scarlett recites, hoping she is right.

Zeke shakes his head, slowly. 'Sure. I mean, the many-worlds theory. I mean, it's a neat theory. Elegant, you know. And . . . yeah, sure. I'd like to think there's a Zeke out there who's living in a fancy-ass house and teaching at Caltech.' He considers, then says, 'And you're sure you haven't accidentally taken . . .? No, OK, fine. So, I mean, what you're saying . . . I mean, yeah, it's theoretically supported in quantum physics. But in terms of it actually happening . . .'

'It *is* actually happening.'

'Well, yeah, sure, but like, on the atomic level . . .'

'No. On *all* levels. I know it sounds crazy. I know you would have to be crazy to believe me. But it's happening. To me.'

Zeke falls silent, long moments. He stares at her, eyes darting back, forth, like he is trying to make sense of her insanity.

'I know it's . . . nuts,' Robyn says quietly.

Zeke opens his mouth, closes it again. Then leans over, rubs his face, and blows out a heavy sigh. 'OK,' he says, 'OK, we can do this. OK, let's consider this scientifically. Tell me exactly what is happening to you.'

And so she tells him. This morning, finding her father, the world bifurcating into two versions of her, one moment Scarlett, the next Robyn. And then the car crashing into Robyn and then . . . nothing. When the words finally tail off, she sits, waiting. A knot lying low in her stomach.

Zeke lets out a low whistle. 'OK. OK. So . . . OK.' A low whistle on the out breath. 'Let's assume, just for a moment, that you are not actually insane.'

'Thanks.'

'You're welcome,' he says. 'So, what the many-worlds theory says is that, when we are in a position in which multiple options are available to us, all of these options come to pass.'

'Um . . . what?'

He grins. 'Right, so there is this cat . . .'

'And I'm the one who is insane?'

'No, bear with me. So this physicist, Schrodinger, he

proposed a thought experiment. There's a cat in a box.'

'Well, of course there is.'

'Yeah, based on some of Schrodinger's shenanigans, we should just thank our lucky stars it was only a cat . . . anyway, so, there's a cat in a box. The box is sealed, and inside the box is a small amount of radioactive substance. Over the course of an hour, there is an equal probability of some of that radioactive substance decaying as there is of it not decaying. Decay means dead cat. No decay means not-dead cat. With me so far?'

'I have a headache.'

His head snaps towards her. 'Does that mean you're going?'

'No, it means that you're talking to me about quantum physics and zombie cats.'

Zeke pulls a face, lets out a soft laugh. 'Stay with me. What Schrodinger proposed, in essence, is that until we open the box, the cat is in effect both living and dead. It's what physicists call a superposition of states. Because the survival of the cat depends on an event that we cannot see, that has a 50/50 chance of occurring, we can think of it as being both dead and alive. Both things happen at the same time. The cat lives. The cat dies. We turn both left and right. According to the many-worlds theory, every different option will actually happen. But, because we are mere piddly humans, we don't have the perceptual abilities to see them. We only see the decoherence. Essentially, the opening of the box. Once the quantum state interacts with the environment, once the observer opens the box, that is when the wave function collapses.'

'The . . .?'

He waves her away. 'Doesn't matter. The important thing is that, because of our human limitations, we can only see one outcome. The others all happen. We just can't see them. Some theorists think that things remain in a state of superposition – the cat remains both alive and dead – until we look at it. That it's our perception that causes decoherence, causes the world to collapse into one option or the other.'

Scarlett rubs her hands over her face. 'I think my brain is broken.'

'It's quantum physics,' Zeke says, brightly. 'Your brain is supposed to be broken.' He grins at her. 'Look, basically, what I'm saying – in a very roundabout way – is that, if what you are saying is true, if you aren't actually a raging lunatic . . . and I'm not saying I've ruled that one out, then it's possible that what happened to the other version of you today, the shock of finding your father the way that you did, it changed your perceptual abilities. It made you able to *see* the superposition. You may be both Robyn and Scarlett, but the truth is, you always have been. It's just that now you can see it.' He stops, considers. 'If I believed you, that is – which I'm not saying I do. Obviously.'

'Obviously,' murmurs Scarlett.

Zeke looks up at her. 'This . . . this other version of me. He's . . . I . . . I'm doing good?'

Scarlett considers him for a moment, a sudden bloom of sympathy. 'Yes,' she says gently 'You are. You're working on your master's.'

He looks down, folds his hands neatly into his lap, nods slowly to himself.

'You believe me?' asks Scarlett.

He doesn't look at her for a moment, is studying his hands. When he does look up, his eyes are red. 'Y'know, it's probably crazy. And you're probably full of shit and are going to wind up using my affinity for quantum physics to run some kind of really elaborate long con on me. But, honestly, I want to believe you.' He smiles sadly. 'It's nice to think of a version of myself out there who has gotten his shit together.'

Scarlett nods slowly. 'Thank you.'

He shrugs. 'Don't thank me. Just remember, when the scam

does kick into gear, that I live in a trailer and own two pairs of shoes.'

Scarlett smiles. She studies him, his wide-open, unprepossessing gaze, the concave cheeks, forehead pulled up in to a crease of concern. And she tries to compare him to the other him. Only the memory has become opaque, the wispy edges of it petering out. 'I think she is dead, Zeke . . .' she says, quietly.

Zeke reaches out, encloses her hand in his. 'OK. You think. But, I mean, do you actually *know* she's dead.'

'When the car hit, I was just pulled out. It was like that world just vanished. And I feel . . . different. Like I'm just Scarlett now. And Robyn's memories, they're slipping. It feels like I can't keep hold of them.'

Zeke frowns, considers. 'OK, I mean, sure. That could mean she's gone. But it could also mean . . . something else.'

'Like what?'

'OK, bear with me here. Because, let's be honest. We have no real clue how any of this works. At the moment, it's all just untested hypotheses.'

Scarlett grins in spite of herself.

'What?'

'Nothing. You just sound exactly like the other Zeke.'

'Oh, well, isn't he lucky,' he says, primly. 'Right so, let's work this through. Look, I mean, we've been together for a little while now. And, while you are delightful, obviously . . .'

Scarlett snorts.

'Well, sort of delightful. But it's like . . . don't hit me . . . it always felt like you were not really here.'

Scarlett frowns. 'What do you mean?'

'It's like, you know those movie sets, where they build like, the front of the house, but then you open the door and there's nothing behind it?'

She stares at him. 'Yes. I know. I'm insulted but I know.'

Zeke waves his hand, placating. 'No, I mean, you were just like, all front. Like you had this facade which was the bit of yourself you presented to the world. But whatever was behind it, that was locked down tight. I just . . . it was like there was no getting through to the real you.'

'OK . . .'

'Only, now, I don't know, you're different.'

Scarlett looks down. 'You mean I'm different when I'm Robyn. Or, when she is me, rather.'

Zeke smiles. 'I don't, actually. It's weird. I've noticed you holding yourself differently. Now, I'm wondering if that's when it happens, when she's here. Or at least, that was how it was in the beginning. But you're changing. Even when she's not here. Even when it's just you. It's like you've started to let the world into what's behind the facade.'

'But, what's that got to do with—'

He waves, grinning. 'I'm getting there, sheesh. No, so, my theory is that perhaps, in the beginning, it was easy for Robyn to simply step in and take over your body and your brain, because the part of you that's you was locked down so tight, there was nothing there to compete with her.'

Scarlett chews her fingernails. 'And now?'

He shrugs. 'Now you have a you. Perhaps her memories are fading because you don't need them anymore. Because you're filling up the space yourself.'

Scarlett rubs her chin against the rough denim on her knees. A feeling bubbling up, warmth and light, tears pricking at the back of her eyes.

'What if she *is* dead?' Scarlett asks quietly. 'What if it is just me?'

He shrugs. 'What if it is just you? I don't know how you feel, but from my perspective, just you, it's enough.'

A tear spills over, hot on her cheek.

Chapter Forty-Three

Scarlett Morgan – 25th September, 11.45 a.m.

They chatter like starlings. The children sit, cross-legged on the floor. A meeting room this, another one hijacked by Harper and Bonnie. But instead of tables there is wide-open space, cushions scattered here and there, a projector screen pulled down from the ceiling, **Moana** written in bold across it, the pause making the word shimmy and shudder.

Scarlett – for there is no doubt now, that it is her and her alone – leans against the doorjamb, watching the children. It is transformative, this. The tumbled cushions, the bowls of popcorn set out at spaced intervals. They come through the door, their eyes wide, faces locked-up tight, fingers clutching onto whichever adult happens to belong to them. And then they see it, the movie, the fun. And the day becomes about something else. About being a child and sprawling across the floor, eating popcorn by the fistful.

A shout of laughter reverberates across the room and Harper looks up at her, winks.

Scarlett smiles, shakes her head. Her mother, it seems, is very good at this.

And then another thought, this one dousing cold water down her back. Of a Destino where Harper has been lost. Where the children do not have anyone to turn their day about.

What did they have in her place? They had the Sandovals. That image darts through her mind again, of Eve, a pillow held taut in her hands, pressed down over Mack's face. She feels nausea rise and shakes her head to shoo it away.

Scarlett watches as Harper moves through the clustered children, teasing and checking. Bonnie tails her, a duckling trailing its mother, handing out candy. She smiles and comforts, and once again Scarlett is flung backwards to that other Destino. Has she ever seen Bonnie smile there? What happened here to make this Bonnie so very different?

She watches as the two women pause together, Harper leaning in, whispering something that makes Bonnie laugh out loud. And she wonders if this too is a change that begins with Harper. Perhaps it is merely the relentlessness of her mother's presence and persistence, the determination of her friendship, that has turned Bonnie into someone else.

We are, after all, merely the sum of the parts of the people who love us.

She looks to Zeke. He hovers over the laptop, waiting for the go signal. But his gaze, that is on Scarlett herself. He gives her a grin, a swift wink. It is important, isn't it? That feeling that we are not alone? That in whatever lunacy life throws our way, there is another who stands at our back.

Robyn never had that.

Her hand moves to her neck, unbidden, and she feels about. It is bare, and that feeling of nothingness settles on her, wrong suddenly. It comes to her then in a flash, the locket. She does not wear the locket that Robyn wears, the one that her father deemed important enough that he bought two. She runs her hand about the back of her neck again, as though it will suddenly appear. But then, likely the locket simply was not necessary here. Because here she was never given away.

A figure appears in the doorway. Vivienne holds on tight to

her daughters' hands. Her gaze darts across the room, face pale.

'They can just come on in,' offers Scarlett.

Vivienne looks at her with a start. Her eyes are red-rimmed, looks as if she's been crying. But she forces a smile nonetheless.

'Hi.' She leans down to the children, resting a hand on each of their backs and gently shoos them into the room. She watches as they weave their way through the sea of children, then glances across at Scarlett, a sudden look of wariness. 'You . . .' She selects her words carefully. 'You . . . OK? I mean, the police station . . .?' Her shoulders have tensed.

Scarlett holds up her hands, an 'I come in peace' gesture. 'Yeah, sorry . . .'

Vivienne forces a smile. 'It's . . . OK. Been stressful for everyone.'

Scarlett hesitates. 'You . . . OK?'

The smile falters, just a little. 'Yes, I . . .' Her breath catches, and her gaze darts. 'It's just Luis. He's still up there. In Destino.' Her eyes fill then and she looks away. 'Running the evacuation. I'm hoping he'll be getting out soon.'

'He'll be OK,' Scarlett lies. Would he? Or when the world split itself in two again, would Vivienne find herself on the branch she fears most. She forces her face into a sympathetic expression. 'I'm sure he will be.' Or perhaps it wasn't a lie. Because when the decoherence came, there would be a world in which Luis was perfectly fine. The question is, is that this world?

Vivienne nods, a glance back to her children.

'So,' says Scarlett, casually, 'how long you guys been together now?'

Vivienne gives her a wan smile. 'A long time. I mean, obviously, we both grew up here . . . not here, Destino . . . so we've known one another our entire lives. But it was one of those things, never really looked at him that way. I often tell him, he was just part of the furniture.'

Scarlett thinks of the other them, the version who grew up together, who passed the time of day, the ones who never made the leap. 'What changed?'

'I guess . . .' Vivienne pulls a face, gaze distant, 'it was the crash.'

The world freezes, locking in place.

'The crash?'

A burst of laughter comes from the gathered children and Vivienne smiles, glances back at her. 'Oh, you would be too young to remember, of course. It was a long time ago now. Back in the 90s. The one that killed the Sandovals?'

There is something here. Scarlett struggles to keep her face still. 'My mom,' she says, carefully, 'she said you were first on the scene.'

Vivienne doesn't answer, merely looks at her, long enough that Scarlett can feel it, the urge to run. Her fists knot themselves up, tight enough that her nails dig half-moon circles into her palms.

'I was,' Vivienne says, finally. 'Well. We were.'

'How old were you?'

Vivienne stares at her, then sighs, comes and stands next to Scarlett, her gaze on her children. 'Just a kid. Nineteen. The scene was . . .' a breath, 'it was bad. I'd been visiting friends, out in Haven. Horrible night. A big storm with rain like you wouldn't believe. Horizontal. So, I was up on the highway, struggling to see the road in front of me. Then my tyre blows, and I'm sliding right across the road.' She shakes her head. 'I thought for sure I was going over the edge into the ravine.'

Just like Harper did. Was it that close? Were the divergences so finely separated? One wrong move leading to an entirely different world. What then would that have looked like?

'So, I'm sitting there, wondering how the hell you go about changing a tyre, when Luis pulls in behind me. He still refers to it as his white knight moment. He deposits me into his car, says we'll come back the next day to rescue mine, and we head back into Destino.' She hesitates, then, 'I often wonder what would have happened, if the tyre had never blown, if the crash hadn't happened.'

'And then?' prompts Scarlett.

Vivienne shakes her head. 'It's . . . I just remember it in a series of flashes. Driving rain and a headlight coming towards us. Then . . . it had already happened by the time we got there. The Sandovals' car was all folded up into the cliff face. I . . . that night, it changed everything. We get out of the car, try to do something to help. Anything. Of course, there was nothing to be done. The Sandovals, they were already gone.' She goes quiet, slowly shakes her head. 'It was just awful. They were so young. Had so much life in front of them. I've always wondered, what could they have done had they lived?'

Scarlett shifts, uncomfortable now.

'Anyway, I guess it was the trauma. At first, anyway. We were so young. We'd never seen anything like that. It was too much to cope with. So we turned to each other. And it just kind of grew from there.'

The lights in the room blink off. *Moana* begins to play.

A figure moves around the edge of the darkened room, pressing herself up against the walls to keep the children's view clear. Harper reaches them, ducks in close. 'I'm going to take a quick shower while they're occupied,' she murmurs. 'I won't be long.' She squeezes Scarlett's arm, and then is gone.

Scarlett stares at the screen, thoughts scattered. But then they coalesce. 'Wait . . . what headlight?'

'Huh?'

'You said there was a headlight? Coming towards you. I thought the Sandovals were on their way into Destino too? So you wouldn't have seen their headlights because they were ahead of you, especially with the way that highway winds.'

Vivienne frowns. 'You know an awful lot about a thirty-year-old car crash.'

Scarlett flounders, briefly. Then, 'I'm interested in local history,' she says, limply.

'Uh huh.' Vivienne studies her, then her gaze shifts, considers. 'I . . . I don't know. I'd never thought about it. I mean, obviously, the crash kind of grabbed my attention.' She shrugs, frowning. 'I don't know. I guess there was another car on the highway. Heading out of town.'

Scarlett considers, remembering now a conversation with Harper. About how she had hydroplaned up onto Main Street. *Maybe I was dazzled by the headlights coming towards me.*

'How close was this? The headlights, I mean. How close were they to the site of the crash?'

Music is playing now, 'Where You Are'. Off-key childish voices sing along.

Vivienne frowns, calculating. 'I guess . . . You know, this is so weird. I haven't thought about this bit for a long time. The before, I mean. Whenever I think of that night, it's the Sandovals I think of. But before . . . Luis and I, we were talking . . . he's telling me about how he wants to be a cop. And then . . . there was a car coming towards us. Well, I say a car . . . at first, I thought it was a motorbike.'

'Why?'

'Because one of the headlights was out.'

Scarlett's breath catches in her throat. Harper had spoken of headlights. Plural. So on Main Street, there had been a car, heading out of town. Headlights. Plural. But by the time it gets to Vivienne, one of the headlights is out.

'You OK?'

Scarlett makes a noncommittal noise. Because it is settling on her, this sudden realisation that the crash that split the worlds in two, it did not happen in a vacuum. There was someone else involved.

Chapter Forty-Four

Scarlett Morgan – 25th September, 11.47 a.m.

Scarlett walks quickly, weaving her way through the lobby. It is crowded with parents now, made redundant by the *Moana* viewing. They stand clustered in small groups, fingers working like they now do not know what to do without small hands gripping theirs. She skirts around them, keeping her head down. Snatches of conversation and, from more than one location, the sound of crying. Squeezes out through the lobby door, into the dense, hot day.

Harper opens her door on the second knock. A loose fit T-shirt over jean shorts, her hair wrapped up tight in a towel on her head. And she smiles when she sees Scarlett, the kind of smile that makes her stomach knot, that turns her into a little girl again.

'Hi, Mom,' she says. That word, it is easier now. Perhaps because it is only her here, perhaps because Robyn is gone. Her stomach knots tighter now, panic rising, but she pushes it back.

'Hey, baby. Come on in.' She steps aside, holding the door open. The room is neat, a plate of sandwiches on the dresser, a can of soda, beads of sweat clinging to the sides. 'You want a sandwich?'

'No.' But then her stomach growls in disagreement and it

occurs to her suddenly that she has no idea when she last ate. Or who she was when she did so. How would that work? If you ate a feast as Robyn would you still be hungry as Scarlett? 'Actually . . .' she says carefully, 'yes. If that's . . . OK.'

Her mother picks up a sandwich, takes a bite and nods, waving her towards the chair pushed up against the window. Scarlett eases into it, watching as her mother slides a plate before her, ham and cheese, a side of pickles.

'Soda?'

Scarlett nods, taking a large bite of the sandwich. It tastes good, unreasonably so for chewy packaged bread and processed meats. Must have been a while since her last meal.

Harper slides into the seat across from her, takes a pull from her own soda. 'So,' she says, with a smile, 'you OK, sweetie?'

She hesitates. In truth, there is no easy answer. Then she nods, betting that, in some reality, that answer is the truth.

'Your dad, he called from Destino. Says they've got a good line set up around the town. Reckons that the fire's moving more slowly now, has lost a lot of its ferocity.' Harper sighs, sets the can down on the table with a clink. 'Hopefully they'll be able to keep it contained.' She studies her daughter. 'Scar, I'm so sorry about this.'

Scarlett chews slowly, thankful for the momentary reprieve, casts back into Scarlett's memory searching for the appropriate response. But all that is there is the image of headlights, two becoming one. She swallows, yields. 'Sorry about what?'

Harper picks up her sandwich, turns it around in her hands, making no move to eat. 'I know this is tough for you. Especially with the fire coming to Destino. I know being able to protect your own town was all you ever wanted.' She takes a small bite, chews thoughtfully. 'It just . . . it seems so unfair. With your dad and all.'

A cascade of memories flood her. Of childhood dress up, a plastic oxygen tanks strapped to her back, the helmet that slipped down over her eyes, blinding her. Of watching her father hurrying out the door, uniform crinkling with the movement. Of his smoke-stained skin, red-rimmed eyes. The words, 'I want to be just like my daddy when I grow up.' Of a tank that is strapped to her back, the weight of it pressing down on her shoulders, a helmet that fits. The smell of smoke that lingers for days after. Of an axe that swings, up and around, making her muscles ache. And then that feeling that builds up from her stomach, of sinking, inescapable despair.

'Scarlett?'

The crackle of fire, the hot red glow of it that arcs across a mountain. That feeling of having stepped out from her body, of time becoming meaningless, of all of her poured into this moment and these flames. The moment when it is done. When red turns to black and disaster is averted, and the feeling filling her up that this is what she was put on this earth to do.

'Honey, what's wrong?'

Her father working beside her, the swing and the thud of his axe synchronising with her own.

And then . . .

Collapse.

'It's OK to be sad, baby,' says Harper, quietly. 'I know you lost a lot.' She looks down. 'Not just CalFire. I know you lost your ability to pretend, to see your dad as the hero you needed him to be.'

Scarlett opens her mouth, but the words will not come.

'Sweetheart, every child needs their parents to be heroes. And, in truth, your dad, he was. He really was. Back in the day, he was Destino's golden boy. The entire town worshipped that man. Then you get faced with this painful truth, that your hero has some really serious flaws. And I think, ever since, that has been all you have been able to see, the bad side. I think – I hope – that eventually you will come to see him as the rest of the world does, as a whole person, with a good side and a bad side.'

Her eyes are burning. The lies in the other world, the betrayal in this. Did she ever truly know her father? Her heart begins to beat faster and, for a moment, Scarlett puts it down to the revelation — because if Mack truly was this, then likely there was more than one person who wanted him dead.

'Is that why you guys broke up?' Scarlett asks. 'You started to see more of the bad than the good?'

Harper looks down. Shakes her head sadly. 'I guess I had my own moment of epiphany, just like you did. My own event where I just couldn't pretend anymore.'

Scarlett's heart beats, faster, faster. Then it comes, the sides of her vision darkening, and her stomach drops as she realises what this means. That she is going.

Harper squeezes Scarlett's hand tight, her voice coming to her from a long way away. 'I guess,' she says, 'it's just impossible to keep pretending when you find out your husband has a secret child.'

A wave of dizziness and Scarlett is gone.

Chapter Forty-Five

Mags Reyes – 25th September, 11.47 a.m.

'Hello, ma'am?'

Mags presses the cell phone tighter against her ear. 'I'm here.' She turns on her heel, begins to pace, back and forth across the diner floor. 'Do you have something?' Has walked a thousand miles, backwards and forwards, phone pressed against her ear. Waiting as hold music plays, searching for an ambulance that can come rescue her father.

The line crackles. Then, 'Well, OK, so I've spoken with our transport manager. He says they're going to do their best to get up there to your father. But I gotta warn you, ma'am, we're stretched pretty thin here. We got ambulances up in Seven Hills, and with all the traffic evacuating from Destino, we're going to have one hell of a time getting someone to you. Y'all sure there's no way you can get your father out yourselves?'

Mags kicks a chair, hard enough that the legs scrape across the floor. 'Ma'am, my father is receiving end-of-life care. He is far too weak to be moved at all, let alone in the back of a Camry.'

Her words reverberate around the empty diner.

A pause, the line falling silent for a moment, then, 'OK,

so . . . suggest you guys hang tight and we'll get up to you just as soon as we can.'

Then the call disconnects and Mags doesn't know if the line has dropped out, or if she has been hung up on. She slams the phone down on the counter, lets out a sob. She taps the screen of her cell, lighting it up, her hand unconnected from her, an alien phantom limb. Her thumb presses the phone app, scrolls to *Mom*, and she listens as it rings and rings. Finally, an answerphone picks up, an automated message telling her to wait for the tone. She hangs up.

The screen is bright, shows her missed calls. Twelve to her parents' house so far. Each one unanswered. Her heart rate climbing higher with each 'wait for the tone'.

Mags rubs her face, fingers pulling at her hair, and turns on the spot. As if the answers will lie somewhere within the empty diner. Then there is a sound, cutting through the air, and she grabs for the phone.

'Hello?'

'Mags? It's Viv.'

Mags stomach clenches. 'Are you all OK?'

'We're . . . OK. I just wanted to let you know that we arrived. We're all tucked up cosy in the shelter. We got our cots and everything, and the kids are watching *Encanto* on my iPad.'

Mags lets out a breath she hadn't known she was holding. 'Thank you.'

'You on your way?'

'Not yet,' Mags says. 'I'm still trying to get transport out to my dad. It's a nightmare.'

There is a long pause, and then Vivienne's distant voice says, 'Mags, are you watching TV?'

'No.' She reaches out for the remote, snaps on the television. And for a moment, she cannot make sense of it. Because what had been a distant glow is now a fearsome inferno. It bounces and rages, seems to rip through the forest. She stares at the screen, trying to superimpose the Destino that she knows on what she sees. 'Is that—'

'It's taken out the trailer park, Mags. It's at the edge of Destino Heights now.' Vivienne's voice drops. 'Mags, this is bad. And once it gets through Destino Heights, it won't be long until it hits the highway. You need to get out.'

'I . . .' Mags shakes her head, struggling to focus. 'I'm coming. I'm going after my parents now. Please, just take care of my babies, . . . OK?'

And then—

Does the line go dead or does she hang up? She does not know. She will make them leave. Whatever her mother says, her arguments so much smoke now anyway. She will carry her father to the car if she has to. Her mother will not stay long without him.

Is outside of the diner before she is aware of moving. Freezes. Because what was bumper to bumper traffic is now carnage. The traffic has given up all pretence, no one concerning themselves with the rules of the road. The cars are packed, filling up both lanes of traffic as far as she can see. And down at the intersection of Oak and Main, two cars have collided, smoke rising from the folded up hood of one.

Mags freezes. A moment then of dislocation, a feeling of being frozen in space. What now?

OK . . . OK. *Think.*

Mags turns on her heel, runs back along the path and up the front steps of the diner, tugs at the front door, leaving it hanging open behind her. The lights have gone out, the television going black. Power finally giving out. She darts past empty tables, dodging around the coffee machine. She takes the stairs two at a time.

The backpack is in the hall closet.

She drags it out, throws in a flashlight, spare batteries, the wind-up radio that she keeps for emergencies. She fills up a water bottle, all the way up to the brim. She pushes off her sneakers, tugging on pants that cover her legs, a long sleeve tee to protect her arms. She drags hiking boots from the back of the closet, too heavy, too hot, but she pulls them on anyway. She tucks her riotous curls beneath a baseball cap, soaks a scarf with water and ties it around her neck. The sodden fabric sends a shiver down her spine.

She hesitates, tries her mother's cell one more time, listens as it rings out.

Then she hurries down the stairs, out through the back door, into the alleyway that runs behind the house, and heads off up the mountain.

Chapter Forty-Six

Bonnie Aubrey – 25th September, 11.47 a.m.

Bonnie wakes with a start. Her cheek rests on the arm of the sofa, the seam of it pressing hard into her skin. Her mouth is dry, neck cricked at an unfortunate angle. It takes a moment for her to notice that it is too quiet. She pushes herself up, back aching, a spasm of pain shooting up her arm, making her wince. She blinks, struggling to focus. The television had been on, had been tuned to *Dr Phil* when her eyes had begun to feel heavy. When did she turn it off?

She sits up straighter, is aware of a heaviness, almost like she has been crying. But Bonnie does not cry. There was a dream, one that she can only just grasp the tail of, a room full of children, a screen showing some Disney movie or other, a sense of disaster averted. Bonnie shakes her head, looking around the room. The ceiling fan is still now, has given up on its sluggish movement, the one that did nothing to cool the stagnant air. She reaches out, feeling for the switch on the lamp beside her and flicks it to on. Nothing.

The power is out.

That does it; the irritation surges back up again. And she welcomes it, the way it shoves away the tail end of that dream, pushing back the uneasy sense of having woken up in the wrong life. 'Damn power company,' she mutters. She clambers to her feet, movements awkward. 'They best be giving refunds on this.'

Bonnie stuffs her bare feet into her slippers, shuffles out into the front hall. Perhaps it was the circuit breaker again, AC tripping it out. Damn contractor should have rewired it last summer when he did the kitchen refit. It is dark, enough so that she flings out her hands, lets her fingers trace their way along the walls, suddenly unsure of her steps. She feels her way to the dresser, tugs open a drawer and finds the flashlight, offering up a brief prayer that the batteries still have life in them. A sudden memory of Mags, warning her that the batteries needed checking, and she scowls, shaking her head to dislodge the image. She toggles the switch, a narrow beam of white light. 'Well,' she mutters, 'that's something.'

She stands there for a moment, watching the angled beam of light, and it is only then that she realises that it is not yet noon, that it should not be as dark as this at this time of day. The realisation comes in hard, and suddenly the drifting shapes within the beam of light take form and function – curling wisps of smoke.

Her stomach has knotted up, her shoulders tightening as though part of her knows exactly what it is that's coming. She moves towards the front door, movements slow, careful. Feels for the latch and pulls the door open.

First comes the smell of smoke. It sweeps in on the breeze and catches in her throat, making her cough. She steps out onto the front porch.

'Oh no . . .' she murmurs. Because the distant ridge is awash with fire.

It is not real. If she stands here long enough, she will wake, will find herself alone in her bedroom. Like all those times she dreamt of Kelvin, hale and healthy, as he was before, waking to find that Kelvin resolutely gone.

Bonnie stands on her front porch, a hot wind whipping at her loose-fit shirt, and she blinks at the fierce patch of brightness that pocks the smokey haze. Her eyes prickle. She shakes her head, dashes the back of her hand across her eyes. Her feet have sunk down through the floorboards, are welded in place, her mind has shuddered to a halt.

How many times has she stood here, looking out over Destino? How many moments have there been? She traces the arc of the ridge, the fire marked out red across it. That – that was where the trailer park once stood. And there – there is Destino Heights. She watches the swathe of red as it moves across the subdivision, and it feels like she is falling. Beyond Destino Heights is the ravine, and beside the ravine is the highway. And once the highway is gone . . .

Bonnie stands on her front porch. She closes her eyes, tilts her chin upwards, so that the smoke and the wind that carries it buffer up against it. And it settles over her that this is to be her last day. Tears snake their way down her cheeks.

And she wishes, with all that she has in her, that she had been strong enough to live her life differently.

She opens her eyes. The station wagon sits, parked up flush against the garage. And it occurs to her that she could use it. That she could drag Kelvin from his bed, could take them down the mountain and along Main Street and out into clean air.

She turns on her heel, walks slowly back into the house, pulling the door tight shut behind her. Her fingers run along the walls, tracing the divot where generations of children have flung open that door, where it has rebounded against the wall. Gazes on the scuffed-up floorboards, the weight of so many different lives marking up the woodgrain, so that in the end it is a story book of what has been.

Bonnie suddenly becomes aware that she is still holding the torch. She studies it, carefully flicking the switch to off, sets it down on top of the dresser, right beside the wedding photo that has always stood there, its silver frame tarnished with age. For a brief moment she allows herself the luxury of regret. Of sorrow for who she might have been.

But a moment is all there is. And so she turns away, walking carefully along the hallway towards the closed door of Kelvin's room. She should perhaps be rehearsing what will come next. How she will tell him where her choices have led them. But it seems that she does not have the energy for that, her mind finally coming to rest on the creak of her footsteps on old wooden boards, on the distant, dim sound of her husband's breath. She pushes open the door, stands there on the threshold, and watches the uneasy rise and fall of his chest. The gasp on the in-breath that was not there before.

'Oh, Kelvin,' she murmurs, 'I'm so very sorry.'

Chapter Forty-Seven

Robyn Sandoval – 25th September, 11.47 a.m.

It is a rude awakening. One of those moments where easy sleep warps into a fall from height. She snaps awake, an inhalation of breath, as if she has freshly broken the surface of the water after a deep dive. Her fingers quest for something to hold onto and they find fingers and so she clings to them.

'Robyn. Robyn, are you . . . OK?'

Robyn. Is that who she is now? She blinks, brake lights dazzling ahead. She struggles, parsing through her thoughts to find the Robyn in there.

'Robyn?' It is cautious this time, doubtful.

Her vision widening out now, the tunnel broadening. She can see Zeke. Or *a* Zeke at least. She stares at him, trying to separate one Zeke from the other. But this one is fuller of face, does not have that painful sunkenness about him, nor the dark circles beneath his eyes. She shifts her gaze, looks about her. Can see the gleam of sunlight that bounces off car exteriors. Can smell smoke.

'Robyn?' Zeke says again.

'Wait!' she snaps, unthinking. That single word, not Robyn's voice, but Scarlett's. Was she . . . had something shifted, a solid base given way? She looks to the dull red glow of fire that hovers above the town, dizzy. Unable to be either one, Robyn nor Scarlett. What was the word? Superposition. She was both now, a superposition of Robyn and of Scarlett.

Then there is a sound, of metal unravelling itself from metal, the scream of an engine as a car pulls backwards, the hood tearing away from where it had sat, embedded into the driver's door of another car.

She looks down at her arms. No tattoos.

And just like that, decoherence.

She is Robyn.

'Zeke,' she says, and this time the voice is her own.

There are patches of memories. The screech of metal meeting metal, of horns sounding, someone calling her name. She blinks. A headache wraps its way around her skull, her hands shake. The sense of waking and falling, waking and falling, unable to parse out what is dream from what is reality.

'You OK?' Zeke is close to her, breath warm against her cheek. 'You whacked your head pretty good back there.' He studies her, gentle fingers taking her chin into his hands, tilting it towards him. He peers into her eyes. 'You might have a concussion. You were kind of out of it for a while.'

Robyn lets her cheek rest against the palm of his hand. 'Yes,' she agrees, quietly. 'But I'm back now.'

She looks up, struggling to piece it together. There is the sound of car engines, idling, of voices calling, and an argument, barely contained. She shifts her gaze towards it. Can see Luis, the sweat patches staining his uniform dark. Is talking to the driver of the Galaxy, words clipped, expression hard. The traffic has knotted up now, locked around the crash site.

She is sitting on the sidewalk, her back resting against the wall of the police station. How long has she been here? Then she looks up, following the curve of the mountain, and all becomes still. The fire is here now. What once was a distant glow, an impressionistic arc of fire, is now undeniably flame.

It bounces, dances, leaping from tree to tree, clambering inexorably downwards. Is eating its way through the trailer park, hovering over Destino Heights.

'Is it . . .'

'Yes,' says Zeke, grimly. 'The trailer park is almost gone.' He is crouched beside her, her hands still wrapped up in his. 'There are fire crews up in Destino Heights, trying to protect it, but . . .' He shakes his head. 'It's not looking good.'

The sound of footsteps approaching, and Robyn looks up. Luis looks worn down, exhausted. A sudden recollection that his day began yesterday morning, that the world had gone badly wrong for him a long time before the arrival of the fire. He looks down at her, shaking his head.

'Should never have let you borrow my car,' he mutters.

'Sorry.'

He smiles, rolls his eyes. 'Whatever. I'm going to get this mess cleared away. You wanna take her inside, get her some water?' This last to Zeke. 'I don't like the way you lost consciousness. I'm going to get this dealt with and then, I'm putting you in a car out of town. Understood?' Luis reaches down, helps her to stand, and swings a backpack from his shoulder. 'This is yours, I believe.'

Robyn watches as Zeke accepts it, slinging it over his shoulder, one arm sliding about her waist. 'Come on,' he murmurs.

She lets him lead her into the police station, deafeningly quiet. It is dark, the air stale and hot. He guides her into a chair, lowers the backpack to the floor beside her. 'You wait here, OK? I'm going to get you a drink and then figure out how we're getting out.'

Robyn nods, lets her head fall back against the wall behind her. Where was she? When she was Scarlett? What has she left behind?

And then it hits her, a jolt equal to the impact of the Galaxy.

Another child. Her father had another child. A wave of dizziness washes over her, but she pushes it away, straining to focus on the thought. That there was someone else who had been left behind. A sudden thought bubbles up and she pulls the backpack closer, fingers questing for the envelope of photographs. She drags it out, resting it on her lap. There inside are the baby pictures, the ones she has already seen without ever really looking. She looks at them now, bringing them closer to her face in the dim light. And now she sees it. The shape of the nose, the shape of the cheekbones. That child is not her. She studies the photograph, the differences obvious now that she knows to look for them. The eyes, they were the same though, looked just like hers. Just like Mack's.

Robyn lets the picture fall back into her lap. What did it mean? Had Eve somehow found out about it, him, her, this mystery sibling? Perhaps then, it was a rage directed in a different direction, not about money at all, but rather about her own daughter's pain. Of course, Eve would have known, for almost as long as Mack had been around, that he was not the hero her daughter believed him to be. Blackmail tends to strip away any rose-coloured illusions quite effectively. But had she learned something else, uncovered one more of Mack's myriad secrets? Had that been enough to tip her over the edge?

Beyond the closed door of the police station there is the sound of engines shifting, of cars beginning to move.

She reaches down, pulls out Mack's laptop and flips it open. Types in the password – her birthday. Can hear the distant sound of a faucet running, of water hitting glass. There is another child. Perhaps Mack has been communicating with them. Perhaps they hold some pieces of the puzzle. She powers up the computer, moves to the email folder. Is dimly aware that she should feel something here, betrayal perhaps, heartbreak. But it seems to her now that she has spent all the grief she has, has frittered it away as each layer of her father peeled itself back.

She opens the inbox and scans it quickly. Nothing jumps out at her, no conveniently titled 'from your long lost child' communication.

The faucet squeals, the water stopping. The sound of footsteps approach.

She moves the cursor quickly towards the sent folder.

There, at the very top, is her own email address. *There's something I have to tell you.*

What? What did you have to tell me? About the Sandoval Company bribes? About the blackmail? About you being fired or the fact that I have a sibling? Which one of your secrets were you planning on sharing?

And then, immediately below, another email address, one she recognises.

Eve Sandoval, sent yesterday, at 2.00 p.m.

Her heart begins to beat faster and she clicks on it.

Eve,
I'm sorry. I should never have done what I did. I've put the
money you gave me into a separate account. It will go to Robyn.
I'm going to destroy the documents. I'm sorry. Please forgive me.
   Mack

'Robyn?'

Her heartbeat surges and the dizziness takes her and the world fades to dark.

Chapter Forty-Eight

Scarlett Morgan – 25th September, 11.55 a.m.

'Scarlett? Hey, you . . . OK?'

'I . . . Zeke?'

He must have heard it, recognised the difference, the shift in tone. Because he is standing in front of her, staring, his gaze tracking across her face. 'You went, didn't you? It happened, didn't it?'

She nods.

'Shit! Holy shit. I mean, I gotta be honest, I couldn't help but think you were crazy. But this, I mean, I was talking to you and then you were just . . . gone. Just for a few moments, but it was like you were just out of it. Jesus,' he says, 'this . . . this is wild.'

They stand outside the hotel lobby, hot sun beating down on the tarmac. The parking lot is full, so many hunks of metal radiating heat from the day. Can hear music, drum and bass from a nearby bar, the sound of traffic, a steady rolling thrum. It is hot enough that beads of sweat prickle at her upper lip, and yet still she feels fingertip chills run down her spine.

She reaches out, clasps hold of Zeke's hand. An attempt to ground herself, to find a solid place to stand in this reality.

It wasn't Eve. Eve did not kill him. Because why would she?

After all those years of blackmail, why would she kill him when he had relinquished his control of her? When he had promised to return the money to the family pot, to destroy the evidence of her misdeeds.

'You OK?' he says again.

And she looks at him, shaking her head slowly, because what did you say? I was convinced that my mother was a murderer. I was so convinced that my belief in it rewrote everything I knew of her, wiping clean the years of morning kisses and bedtime stories, cool fever cloths, that quiet belief, unquestionable, that her daughter could do anything she damn well pleased. I was convinced enough that I wondered, was the world simply better off without her.

Scarlett shakes her head. 'I feel like I'm going insane.'

Zeke pulls her in, her cheek pressing against his chest, the smell of cedar and cinnamon, and she clings to him, tight. There are no answers. Every corner turned bringing only more questions. Who killed her father morphing into something else: who was her father?

'I feel like I don't know anyone,' Scarlett murmurs, voice muffled by his shirt. 'Not really.'

Zeke doesn't answer for long moments, then hugs her tighter. 'You know me.' He pulls back, tilts her chin upwards with his fingers. 'Whatever this is, whatever is happening here . . . it's going to be OK.' He leans in, kisses her. 'We'll be OK.'

For a moment, the world stills, Robyn and Scarlett sliding into one. Two halves becoming a whole.

'Would you put that man down?'

It crashes in on them, that voice, and they pull apart, turning to see Harper, her grin wide. 'You two, you're like a pair of teenagers.' She winks at her daughter. 'I was going to ask you to help me wrap up the movie screening but I can see you have your hands full.'

Scarlett flushes. 'I'm coming, I'm coming.'

She steps back, giving Zeke an apologetic look, and slips into her mother's wake.

The lobby is quiet now. The young woman behind the desk stands, staring into space, eyes damp. The movie screening room is still dark, tumbling musical notes filtering from beneath the door. Harper hesitates, then turns away, heading through towards the conference room, pushing at the closed door. It gives easily, slamming open, pushed by a sudden gust of wind, the smell of smoke. Conversations stop, heads turn, gazelles scenting a lion, people moving closer together, each seeking the comfort of kin. At the other end of the room, Bonnie stands, frozen before the trestle table, a tray of cloth-covered sandwiches in her hands. She closes her eyes for a moment, the line that runs down the centre of her forehead deepening, the downturns at the corners of her mouth. She is searching for it, the scent of her burning house on the wind. And then she gives her head the smallest of shakes, forcing an unconvincing smile at Harper and Scarlett.

'Oh good, you guys are here. You can give me a hand with the coffee urn.' She gestures towards the kitchen, sets the tray down with a flourish, and turns, heading out of the conference room. Scarlett and Harper follow along in her wake, in through the swinging kitchen door.

It is bright in here. Mags stands, her back to them, rolling soft cookie dough into balls. A television sits on a metal trolley. It is tuned to the news, inevitably, the sound echoing off the metal surfaces. A rolling banner lines the base of the screen. **CalFire says the fire has slowed in its progress towards Destino.** Scarlett stops, studies the footage, a helicopter camera that circles above vivid flames. Then it ducks down, zooming in on the ridgeline that surrounds Destino, on the line of figures in CalFire uniforms. Then it descends further, the figures taking shape. And there he is. One among many, but she knows the shape of him, the way he moves his arms, the way he stands.

'Mack.' She says it quiet enough that it could vanish, disappearing into the chatter from the room beyond. But Harper and Bonnie and Mags, they turn to her nonetheless.

'He'll be OK, Scar,' says Mags, gently.

'She's right,' agrees Bonnie. 'Try not to worry too much. That man, he's got more lives than a cat.' Her voice fades away and she stands for a moment, staring at the bowl of chips. Then she looks up, shakes her head. 'He's been in worse situations than this, come out of them smiling. My Kelvin, he always said that man could fall in manure and come up smelling of roses.' She glances up, a sudden spasm across her face. 'I'm sorry, sweets, I didn't mean . . .'

Scarlett shakes her head, waving it away. The memory coming in hard now, of the fireline, of her fist pulled back, the captain falling beneath the weight of her fury. Of Mack slumped against the bar in O'Callaghan's. *I didn't ask you to punch anyone. Not my fault you blew it.*

Rage, red hot, rises up through her and she forces herself to breathe.

'Scarlett,' says Harper, 'it's OK to be angry at him. It's OK to be scared for him. The two can exist in the same space.'

Bonnie empties potato chips into a bowl, doesn't look up. 'Love, it's complicated. Look at me and Kelvin. He loved me, never once did I doubt that. But my God, did he hate me, for a long time.' She glances up then, her eyes damp. 'That was OK though. *I* hated me too. But it was the truth that saved me, my marriage. Without that, I don't like to think where we would have ended up.' She looks down, her voice cracking. 'Three years I have lived without that man. And that has been hard enough. But if I hadn't been able to tell him the truth of me, to show him all that I was, the good and the bad, I'd have had to live without him a whole hell of a lot longer. It's hard to love someone who will not accept reality, of themselves or of the world around them.' She dashes her hand across her eyes, pushes the bowl to one side, reaching for another. 'We all make mistakes, Scarlett. We all get things wrong. Sooner or later though, you're going to have to forgive yourself.'

Scarlett is aware now, that they are looking at her, Harper and Bonnie and Mags, that they are waiting for it, some kind of epiphany. The memories cascade. Of nights where she can no longer tell up from down, falling asleep in the bathroom, a bottle of tequila curled in the crook of her arm. Of anger, a roaring fury that sweeps across the landscape, unadulterated, uncontrollable. Of that ever-present sense of falling, that the ground she has been standing on is not solid at all.

Of a hand holding hers.

Zeke.

Harper.

Bonnie.

Mags.

Come back. Come back to us. This fury will destroy you. Let it go.

And then, another memory, of standing on the plateau, watching the sun rise. The hint of smoke already in the air. Had that really only been this morning? Looking down across the valley, across Destino's Main Street, all the way down to the highway beyond. The distant trailer park, metal glinting in sunlight. Feeling fury ebb and despair flow, and the thought that comes with it – help me. Help me. Looking down at the tattoos that wrap themselves around her arms and seeing only the thorns, not the flowers, and feeling the vines clambering up her, choking her with the sudden knowledge that if something does not give, then she will not survive what she has become. Looking out over Destino, this place that she has walked each day of her life, and . . . was it a prayer? To her knowledge, Scarlett has never prayed before. And yet, whatever it was, the words had spilled out, loud enough to startle a sparrow from a nearby tree. It burst into the air, taking to flight. Her words following it. Please help me.

And then the world shimmering, the edges of it becoming indistinct and then . . . Robyn.

Was that it? Was that what had caused this? A death for Robyn and, for Scarlett, a prayer. Two versions of herself finding themselves tumbling at precisely the same moment.

'Scarlett?'

She comes back into the room with a crash. A sense of dislocation. Her gaze settles on the television again, on the distant form of her father. The camera has pulled out now, and so he is nothing but an indistinct patch of motion. Just one more hero.

Movement then, Mags pulling open the oven, a wave of heat and the clatter of a baking tray hitting metal. 'I think,' she says, sliding the door closed, 'that we could all use some coffee.' She glances back at Scarlett, a swift wink.

Then a blast of sound, foghorns blowing, and Mags jumps, reaching into her pocket. 'Oh, that's Jack. Mom, I'm going to go take this. My husband isn't coping well with having his wife and children in the path of an inferno.' She grins, mimicking her mother's voice. '"Come to Destino for a visit, Mags. It'll be relaxing, Mags." You guys really do offer the best holiday destinations.'

Bonnie shakes her head, grinning, as Mags raises the phone to her ear. 'Hi, babe, no we're fine . . .'

She hurries past Scarlett, pausing briefly to squeeze her arm, offer her a smile, and then she is gone. And Scarlett stares after her, her attention captured by the gold locket Mags wears around her neck.

Chapter Forty-Nine

Scarlett Morgan – 25th September, 12.03 p.m.

Scarlett stands in the lobby, frozen. Beyond the glassed-in doors, she can see Mags, walking backwards and forwards, phone pressed against her ear. And if she squints, if she focuses really hard, then she can see it, the way the sunlight glints from the gold locket around her neck.

It can't be the same. It's a locket. Who is to say that it is the same locket as the one she found? The twin of Robyn's own. It can't be the same.

Scarlett pushes open the lobby door. The heat rolls in at her, smoke catching at her throat.

Mags stands at the kerb, her back to her now.

It is a storm in a teacup, a something and a nothing. A gold chain that has transposed itself in her imagination, coming to mean more than it should.

Scarlett walks slowly, one step, then the next, seems like the whole world has slowed down, pouring molasses. Her heart, though, that has begun to beat faster. Scarlett shakes her head. No. I cannot go now.

A burst of laughter from Mags. It rolls over her.

Her sister's laugh? Was that what she was hearing now?

She stops, watching Mags, the way she tilts her head, the

way she smiles. Was this it? Was that what Mack was going to tell her? She thinks of the Jim Beam, the two glasses, and then another thought comes rolling on in. Was that you? Did you drink with him before he died? Then, inevitably, did you kill him?

She watches her. The toss of her curls. Her laugh, raindrops on a pond. The way she stands, her shoulders back, her head held high. So different from the other version of her, from the Mags she barely knows. What made the difference? What caused the branching for Mags, turning her from that into this?

Now she is moving again, one foot before the next, is pulled onwards. There isn't a plan, just instinct. Robyn's. Scarlett's. Who can tell?

'OK . . .' Mags brushes back a curl from her eyes, 'No, I'm going to stay and help Mom. Oh, you know how she is, like a damn general leading an army. I know. No, I know. Let's be honest, her and Harper have been preparing for this for most of their lives. Yes . . .' She glances back, spotting Scarlett, gives her a wave. 'No . . . OK. I'll talk to you later. Love you too.'

Is it you? Are you my sister?

Was it you? Did you kill him?

The phone slides from Mags' ear and she grins, shakes her head. 'Well, he's about three feet from a nervous breakdown.' She studies Scarlett. 'You OK? That was a lot, back there.'

'I . . .'

But there is nothing else. No more words will come. Because how the hell did you say it? How did you put it into words.

She pulls in a deep breath. Then, 'Mags, this is going to sound weird. But will you tell me something?'

'OK . . .'

'Will you tell me about the day that you found out?' The words hang there, waiting. 'That we are sisters.'

It is a plunge into an icy lake, a cold blast against her skin.

For a moment the world freezes in place.

Mags stares at her, and she cannot tell what she is thinking. Then she tilts her head, and there is something about the play of light, the way it falls on her eyes, and she sees it, grey. Just like Mack's. Just like hers.

'That was a long time ago,' she says, reluctant, and for a moment it seems that she will not answer. But then, 'I haven't thought about that in a long while. . .' She studies her, then, a deep breath. 'I was eight years old,' she says quietly. 'I came home from school, and my dad, he says he's going to take the boys, that they're going to run some errands. He says that my mom, she has something she needs to talk to me about.' She hesitates, pulls in a breath. 'And he kisses me, right here on my forehead.' Mags eyes fill, her voice threatening to give. 'And says, "You, young lady, are my special girl. Now and always. Don't you ever forget that."' A tear spills and she pauses, wiping it away with the back of her hand. 'My mom . . . see, you wouldn't remember this. You were still so little. God, she was a pill. She used to be just so . . . edgy. Like she was always angry, always waiting for me to do something wrong.' She hesitates. 'To be honest,' she lowers her voice, 'I just didn't like her very much. Not back then.' Her voice trails away, then, 'Scar, you know this, why are you asking me?'

It is as the colouring-in of a picture, Mags' words bringing depth and colour to sketched-out lines. Memories beginning to take form.

'Please?'

Mags studies her, then nods, her face softening. 'Well,' she says, gently, 'that was when she said it. She was . . . so unlike herself. I was so used to her being prickly and hard. But that day . . . She'd been crying. I could tell. And she just looked like this little kid who'd been caught stealing cookies. And she just said it, that my dad, he wasn't my birth dad. That I was half made up of someone else.'

'Mack,' says Scarlett, quietly.

'Mack,' Mags agrees. 'She told me that she'd made a mistake, early on in their marriage. That they had been going through a hard time, my dad working long hours. That she'd been lonely. And she'd spent time with someone she shouldn't have.' Mags shakes her head. 'You want to turn an eight year old's world upside down, that's a great way to do it.' She sighs. 'On the plus side, I got to have a second mom in Harper. And I got you.' She smiles sadly. 'I'd always wanted a sister.'

Scarlett feels a hot tear drift down her cheek and she dashes it away, a sense that the Scarlett who never cries has done little but cry today.

'Hey!' And then Mags' arms are around her, pulling her in tight, her cheek pressed up against her sister's. 'What's going on?'

The bass of her voice reverberates through Scarlett's chest, the beat of it joining with the thrum of her breath.

'I feel like I don't know anything, anymore.' Scarlett's voice cracks. 'I thought I understood what my world looked like. And now I'm realising that nothing is what I thought it was, no one is who I thought they were. Just layers of possibility, like if the world works one way they become this person, if it works that way, they become someone entirely different. There are no clear answers anymore. Nothing to hang onto. I believed that Mack was a hero, that he was a good man. And I was wrong.' She looks down. 'I thought *I* was good. And look at all the ways in which I've failed.'

Mags pulls back, studying her. 'But, my love, that is the way of it, isn't it?' she says gently. 'Nothing is definitive. People can change. People react to their environment, changing according to their circumstances. I see it with my clients. I had one woman who came to see me after a suicide attempt. She tells me that she is just flawed . . . just a bad person who doesn't deserve to live. It took weeks, weeks and weeks, for me to peel back that layer of self-hatred, to see what was going on behind it. Turned out she was stuck in this shitty marriage, that her husband is drip-feeding her this narrative of how useless she is. Her problems, who she had become, it was just a reaction to the environment she was in. Nothing is definitive. None of us are good or bad. We are just . . . potential.' Mags smiles, her voice serious. 'Scarlett, you are perhaps the strongest person I have ever met. Yes, life has been tough for a while, and you've had things thrown at you that you wouldn't choose. But those layers of possibility you talked about? You have those within you as well. Which means, whatever life throws at you, you have everything you need to handle it. And you can go off the rails for a while, fall into a bottle, let the anger take over. But that doesn't mean that is who you are. There is a never-ending range of possibilities. Which means that who you are, my dear sister, is for *you* to decide.'

The tears are flowing freely now, the sense of a dam breaking. And then, just like that, she becomes aware of it, her heart thudding, the pressure building in her head. She is going.

'Mags,' Scarlett says, urgently, 'I have to . . . Mack . . . Dad . . . have you ever been angry with him? I mean, angry enough to . . . do something about it?'

Mags is fading now, the image of her becoming looser around the edges. Her voice comes from far away. 'Of course not.'

The world goes dark.

Chapter Fifty

Robyn Sandoval – 25th September, 12.03 p.m.

Someone is holding her hand. She looks down to see the laptop on her knees, one of Zeke's hands clasping hers, a glass of water in the other.

Robyn blinks.

'Robyn, you need to drink this.'

She feels the glass forced into her fingers, cold against her skin, the laptop being pulled from her lap. Her hand moves obediently, raising the glass to parched dry lips. She sips, cold water spilling into her mouth.

'We need to get you to a hospital,' says Zeke, his words all sharp edges. 'You seemed really out of it then.'

'I'm . . . OK,' Robyn says, distant.

The switches, they are coming faster now. She raises her hand to her head, can still trace the lines of the headache. It was the stress, the building up of danger here, of pressure there. They are speeding up the transitions, so that she is flipping faster and faster.

Robyn lets out a slow breath, closes her eyes. Tries to calm her racing heart.

Think.

I have a sister.

Did Mags know? Here, in this world? Had anyone told her? In that world, Bonnie had told the truth, had confessed her affair to her husband, to her daughter. Mags had said that she was a different person back then, hard, just like Bonnie here. Was that where the two worlds branched? That moment of truth? And the hardness in this Bonnie, had that come from so many years of living a lie?

'Come on,' says Zeke. He pulls the backpack to him, sliding the laptop in. 'We have to get out of here.' He swings the backpack over his shoulder. 'Drink some water. I'm going to go hitch us a ride out of town.' He turns on his heel, walks towards the police station door with long strides, and then is gone, the door slamming shut behind him.

Robyn raises her hand to her cheek, can still feel the warmth of her sister's skin pressed against her own. Then a sound, the ringing of a phone. Her fingers move without thought, reaching into her pocket to pull out her cell phone.

Mom.

It wells up in her then, a rush of guilt. For what she had believed. For what she had forgotten.

She thumbs answer. 'Mom?'

There is a crackle and then a sound like an intake of breath. 'Robyn. Where are you? Are you out?'

What has she done?

'No. I'm still in Destino.'

The breath becomes a sob now, the edges of it shrill and desperate. 'Robyn, you have to get out! You have to get out. Please. It's all over the news, the fire is coming, Robyn. Please. I can't lose you too.'

Robyn opens her mouth, closes it again. Her mother who loves her, is afraid for her. Her mother who lied to her, who cheated the town. What was there to say? Her mother, both good and bad. A superposition of states. But then, who wasn't?

'It's . . . OK, Mom,' she says, softly, 'I'm just getting a ride out now.' She pushes herself up to standing, a wave of dizziness washing over her. 'Where are you?'

'I'm at the shelter.' It comes out as a sob. 'Only they won't let me bring the dog in, and the hotels are all full, so I'm just standing outside and Vivienne has tried to talk to them, to get them to let me bring him in so we have somewhere to rest out of the sun, only they won't. And she couldn't stay with me to help, because she has Mags' children, so—'

'Wait.' Robyn clutches onto the back of the chair, tight enough that her fingernails fold over on themselves. 'What do you mean, Vivienne has Mags' children? Where is Mags?'

The line crackles, falls silent. Then, '. . . gone up the mountain. To get her parents.' Another break, then, 'love y . . .' Then nothing.

Robyn pulls the phone from her ear, stares at it. No signal. And then she is moving, is running along the corridor. She tugs open the door to the police station, hot air and the sound of car engines spilling in. The air is dense now, smoke hanging low enough over the town that the surrounding hillside is lost. It scratches at her throat, makes her eyes tear. She looks right, along the line of traffic that has picked up speed, a universal agreement that death is imminent without some kind of momentum. The knot about the church has eased, the occasional flash of tarmac visible between evacuating cars. She hesitates, tracks her gaze up the mountain. There are few lights now. No cars coming down from Bonnie's. Strains, can see Mags' car, still parked in front of the diner, and, off in the distance, the faint shape of Bonnie's sedan, still outside their home.

They're still up there!

It is not a decision. There is no thought that goes into it, merely action. She is running.

Zeke stands at the corner, backpack slung over his shoulder. He turns as he sees her coming. 'Come on. We gotta go.'

Robyn pulls up sharp in front of him, the smoke making her cough. 'I can't.'

'*What?*'

'Mags . . . from the diner. She went up the mountain. She hasn't come back down.'

Zeke hesitates, looks about him. 'We should tell that cop . . . I don't know where he went.'

Robyn reaches out, touches his arm. 'There's no time, Zeke. If they don't get out soon, they won't get out at all.'

He stares at her, then runs his hand through his hair. 'You really are a trouble magnet, aren't you?' He turns towards her, folds his arms across his chest. 'You are aware that we managed to write off the last car we borrowed? How do you propose we get up there?'

We.

She smiles in spite of herself, turns on the spot, considering. Then, 'By any chance, have you ever stolen a car?'

Chapter Fifty-One

Mags Reyes – 25th September, 12.05 p.m.

Mags cannot breathe. The smoke, it claws at her throat, raking all the way down into her lungs. She ducks, bending so that she climbs at a right angle almost, her fingers brushing against the hard-packed dirt of the hiking trail. Little difference between this and crawling. Her fingers dig into the dirt and she pushes off, forcing her body on.

She can't look back. Keeps her head down, her gaze locked on the path beneath her feet. Just one step, then another. Because if she looks back she will see it. Will see the fire that rings the mountain side, the thunderous clouds that hang over the top of it, the thick, toothsome smoke. She can't look back. Because if she looks back she will see it – the imminent outline of disaster.

Another step.

It is falling away now. Miniature disasters swallowed up in the face of catastrophe. The diner and the divorce, the bone-aching loneliness, the sense of a life barely worth living. Strange, how looming death could change those calculations.

She pushes onwards, half staggering, half crawling, until the roughshod hiking trail gives way to a dirt plateau. She clambers onto it, pushing herself up to standing. This is the place where everyone comes to get the best view down over Destino. And so she has no choice but to look. At the dark thunderclouds that loom overhead, at Main Street, the false smoke-filled twilight pocked with brake lights, the traffic rolling now, steady and determined to get out, get away. She can see the diner, set back from the road, sleeping and silent. How she has cursed that place. How she has longed to give up, give in, unable to look up, her only concern survival for just one more day. Strange then, how alive she feels, now that her survival truly is in doubt. She looks beyond the diner, her gaze running along the length of Main Street to the distant valley wall. And there to the fire. Destino Heights, carved from the forest, is now ablaze. Red flame creeps across the subdivision, a steady march, pushing ever onwards through the million-dollar homes. On the highway below, the cars pour outwards, a steady stream of flight.

Mags shakes her head, allows herself a moment for a coughing fit, one that does little to shift the smoke that has built up in her lungs. And then she turns, pushing onwards. Cannot think about it. About the fire, or the highway, about her children waiting for her to escape, about Jack. Cannot think about her father. She can only push on, one step in front of the other.

She slips, her boots losing their grip on the hard-packed dirt beneath her feet, lands heavily, one arm flinging out to break her fall. A sob then, one that wells up in spite of her.

No.

This will not be it. This will not be how it ends. On a uneven hiking trail perched on the mountainside, surrounded by fire.

She plants her palms on the ground, pushing hard, forcing herself up, forward. Up and up, and then the break in the trail, the one that snakes its way across the mountain, narrower this one, the brush cutting up against her arms.

She can see it now, up ahead. The distant dark shape of her parents' house.

She begins to run.

A sudden dark thought, that they are already gone, have left without her, that she will be stranded, up here on the mountain. The forgotten daughter, again. Mags foot slips on the incline, but she keeps her balance. No. Don't think about Mom and feeling invisible and all of the other shit you think about. Because none of that matters now. She pushes on harder.

Then brush gives way to wide-open driveway and she rounds the corner and the car is still there, all as she left it so short a time before. She runs towards the house, footsteps thudding heavy on the front steps. A sudden sinking feeling, that she has forgotten her key, that all of this will have been for nothing. But her hand snakes out and she twists the door handle and it yields beneath the pressure of her touch.

'Mom?'

The house is still, silent, smelling of sweet sugar and smoke.

'Mom? Dad?'

The weight of the air presses down on her, pushing her down through the floor, as if the house itself is trying to keep her down, push her back out of the door. Mags' footsteps reverberate, echoing through the silent house.

'Mom?' Quieter this time, a sudden feeling of shouting in a crypt.

She slows, coming to a stop outside her father's bedroom door. It is closed tight. It is never closed tight, is always left just a little ajar so that her mother can hear him if he calls, if he needs something. She reaches out her hand, takes hold of the handle, shoulders raised, defensive against what is to come. Then she twists. For a moment, there is nothing. But then, finally, the door yields to the weight of her, opening with a low groan onto a dark bedroom, drapes still closed against the smoke-dimmed day beyond.

Silent.

Mags steps inside, cautiously. Her breath has stilled in her chest. She is blind, the dark of the room shading out the shapes of it. But then, as her eyes slowly adjust, she sees the shape of her father, laying prone in his bed. Then the figure sitting in the chair beside him.

She steps closer, floorboards creaking beneath her.

'Mom?' She whispers it.

'It's too late,' her mother says, quietly. 'He is gone.'

Chapter Fifty-Two

Robyn Sandoval – 25th September, 12.15 p.m.

It appears as fog. The smoke sits low ahead of them, funnelled by the built-up walls of brush on either side into a dense mist. Didn't they say that, in fires, most people die from smoke inhalation? The headlights cut a swathe of light. It presses down upon Robyn, snatching away her breath. Her fingers grip tight to the seat's edge.

Zeke guides the car, taking the tight curves of the mountain road slowly, empty but for them. 'You think Mags will mind that I jimmied her car door open?' He glances across at Robyn. 'I scratched the paintwork up a bit.'

Robyn stares at him. 'Seeing as we're going up the mountain to rescue her from a raging inferno I feel like she'll be OK with it.'

Zeke nods slowly. 'Fair enough.' Then, 'You didn't ask me.'

'Ask you what?'

'How I know how to hot-wire a car.'

Robyn looks away, over the curve of mountain. 'No,' she agrees, 'I didn't.'

Silence, then, 'See, I had a bit of a . . . a wild period. Went off the rails a bit.'

'Uh huh.'

'I'm much better now,' he adds. 'An almost entirely respectable citizen. If you forget about the fact I just hot-wired a car, of course.' He glances across at her. 'Don't want you to think that I'm a bad guy.'

She finds herself smiling, looks back at Zeke. He is watching her, waiting for some kind of verdict. 'Everyone makes mistakes, does bad things from time to time. Doesn't make them bad. I guess it's about what they choose to do next.' She looks him up and down. 'You decided to accompany a crazy lady you just met on, not one wild goose chase, but on two. In my book, that clearly makes you a good guy.' She grins. 'Not, like, a particularly sensible one, but good nonetheless.'

Zeke nods slowly. 'OK. Good to know.'

Robyn considers for a moment. Then, 'Why did you agree to come with me?' She studies him. 'I don't mean to judge, but it does suggest you're a bit . . .'

'Heroic?'

'Insane.'

Zeke looks across at her, the moment lasting long enough that she feels herself begin to flush. 'I don't know,' he says, finally. 'I guess I like you.' His attention shifting back to the road ahead. 'Besides, it was this or hanging out on a camp bed in a high school gymnasium with all of the other Destino evacuees.' He slows, steering around the switchback. 'This is much more . . .'

'Insane?'

'I was going to say heroic.' He grins. 'You know what, I think we are going to be friends.'

A gust of wind sweeps down the mountain. The brush dances, smoke rolling, the car sways.

'Oh!' Robyn clutches tighter to her safetybelt, fingers claws.

Zeke sits up straighter, holding tighter to the wheel.

She forces herself to breathe. 'You do?'

'I do. There was something very endearing about the way

you marched into my trailer like you had lived in it for years. You're kind of like a stray cat, in that way.'

'Excellent,' says Robyn, doubtfully.

'I mean stray cat in a good way,' offers Zeke.

'No, sure, sure. It sounded like a compliment.' Robyn reaches into her pocket, pulls out her cell phone. 'Signal is still out.'

'I gotta ask,' says Zeke, 'are you OK?'

'You mean after the car accident? I'm fine. Just a bit of a headache.'

'No, I mean . . . your dad. It's gotta be . . . tough.'

Robyn looks out over the brush, snorts. 'You have no idea.'

'I'm serious. This should have been a day for you to grieve. Instead you're running around rescuing people. Again, you're very good at the rescuing . . . just feels like it couldn't have happened on a worse day for you.'

Robyn lets her gaze move across to the passenger side mirror. To the smoke clouds, the red glow of fire. Was it closer now, or was that merely her imagination?

'Everyone has different layers to them,' she says, distantly, 'different people who they can become depending on their environment.' She looks back at Zeke, smiles sadly. 'I'll be the grieving daughter tomorrow.'

Zeke nods, slowly. 'That's quite brilliant, you know.'

Robyn nods. 'It is. My sister told me that.'

'Oh, so you have a sister? Cool. Have a couple of them myself. What's yours like?'

'Depends on her environment,' Robyn mutters. 'Hey,' she sits up taller in her seat, 'you see that?'

'What?'

Robyn leans towards Zeke, peering out of his window, up the mountainside. 'I thought I saw . . .'

The car rounds a hairpin bend and there before them is fire. It creeps through the treeline, fingers of it reaching out towards them. Angular trees go up, so many torches littered across the mountain.

'Holy shit!' Zeke slams on the brakes, twisting in his seat. 'But, it's . . . how? How is it here? I thought it hadn't crossed the highway yet.'

Robyn feels herself going cold. 'It's followed the curve of the ridge. It's surrounded us.' She lets out a low moan. 'Oh my God, it's everywhere.'

And then there comes a flicker of light, a sound that comes from somewhere ahead. Zeke sitting up straighter, lifting his foot off the gas, speed dropping fast enough that the momentum pushes Robyn forward against her seatbelt.

'What . . .?' Robyn begins. But then it happens, the car that speeds around the corner, too fast for this road. Oncoming headlights fill their vision and for a moment it seems inevitable that the car will careen straight off the mountain road, plunging down the side. Then comes a high-pitched sound, Zeke's hand pressed hard against the horn, and the oncoming car reacts. Suddenly the headlights are full on them, there is a scream of brakes and then the light flickers, is yanked away. And now life has slowed down, is moving at a crawl. The oncoming car is skidding, has pirouetted to be side on to them, their own headlights lighting up the mismatched panels.

The car in centre stage as it skids, as it slams headfirst into the overhanging tree.

Chapter Fifty-Three

Mags Reyes – 25th September, 12.22 p.m.

Mags' fingers grip the steering wheel. She leans forward, close enough that it presses against her sternum.

He is gone.

There are no tears.

There should be tears, shouldn't there?

When you say goodbye to your father for the final time, there should be tears.

Instead there is a sense of disembodiment. Of her feet dragging her forward, of her hands helping her mother into her shoes, guiding her into the car. It was as if they were going shopping. As if she was packing the car up, all ready for a trip to Publix. As if they would sweep down the mountain and through the town, would buy the groceries, would sweep right back up and walk back in and carry on where they left off.

He is gone.

The words, they roll around and around in her head. She is almost tempted to put music to them. Can't seem to punch through, to get to the meaning buried within them. Because it is not real, is just a story someone has told her and soon the story will stop and she will turn the car around and go back to her parents' house and he will be there.

He is gone.

'I'm going to stay with him.' Her mother's voice seemed to reverberate around the darkened room. 'You should go, Maggie. You should get to the children.'

To Mags it had seemed that she was frozen in place, held there by the still form of her father. Not sleeping. Not dying. Dead. And for the wildest of moments, it made sense – she too could sit herself down beside him, sink into the silence and simply wait for the world to end.

'No,' Mags says. 'No. You are coming with me. The children need their grandmother.' A moment, then, 'I need my mother.'

Movement then, that seemed to come from outside her, she a mere marionette, and she skirted the bed with swift steps, hooking her hands beneath her mother's elbows, and then somehow they were both standing, both moving, out of the mausoleum of a bedroom, out into the smoke-filled hall. Her mother, feather-light beneath the force of her will. Was this, she wondered, the first time? That she had not had to fight for each inch of land gained?

Then she was guiding her mother into the seat that waited by the front door, was easing her feet out from her slippers, stuffing them into an old pair of worn sneakers. A wince, waiting for the complaint, that she only wears these sneakers for gardening, Maggie, what if someone sees? Only there is nothing, just her mother's foot, a dead weight in her hand. Somehow the silence was worse.

She grabbed the keys to her mother's sedan from the dresser, pushed open the front door, smoke billowing in on a stiff breeze that has sprung up. Denser than before. Mags' eyes tear up, and it feels like there is a pillow, held before her face, like someone is pushing down on it.

And then . . .

It is at the front porch. That is where it all ends. Her mother planting her feet, firm as a thousand-year-old tree. 'No. I can't.'

She sounded different, not like the Bonnie Mags knows at all. She studies her, long moments that they do not have, as if somehow she has been switched, her mother snatched away, another set there in her place.

Her mother looks at her, and it feels to her like it is for the first time. Scans her face, searching for . . . what?

'Mom. We have to go.'

'I'm so sorry, Maggie. I should have told you the truth. I should have told *him* the truth.'

'It's OK, Mom. You meant it for the best. Let's go.'

'But you don't understand . . .'

And she doesn't, does she? How can she? Because her senses are singing, skin prickling with the pressing-down danger. The smoke that fills up her lungs, the distant glow of flame. And a sound, something that shouldn't be there. The crackle of fire. Could she think, it would occur to her to wonder, why can I hear that? The fire is too far away. But she is far beyond thinking now, is all instinct. And so it is the instinct that grabs her mother by the arm, that drags her, rough enough that she stumbles, down the front steps towards the sedan. Somehow she gets her in the car. Somehow they are moving, sliding out of the driveway, downhill.

'Maggie.' Bonnie's voice is low, quiet enough that for a moment she mistakes it for the rut of the tyres against tarmac.

Mags clutches tight to the steering wheel, guiding them round a hairpin bend. 'It's OK, Mom. We're going to be OK.'

The brush stands high by the side of the road, is pocked with boulders and rocky outcroppings, barely visible through the thick haze of smoke.

'There's something I have to tell you.'

They are rolling downhill, faster than they should. And Mags experiments with it, with lifting her foot from the gas. But it will not stick and she flattens her foot to the floor, dark brush whipping past them. It is primitive now, a moment of pure flight. They whip round a corner, car swinging wide. Down beneath them, the dim shape of Destino, and she sits up taller, straining to see the line of brake lights through the canopy of smoke.

'Mags...'

It breaks through. That one solitary word. Her mother has never called her that before, and the shock of it yanks Mags' gaze over towards the passenger seat, her foot lifting, ever so slightly, from the gas.

Then she sees it.

Beyond her mother's expectant gaze, beyond the window and the smoke. A patch of light. For a moment she thinks that they are headlights. But then, that is pure mountainside. Where would they be coming from? And then the pieces slide together and she realises. It is fire.

It has topped the ridge, sneaking up on Destino from its rear. Has begun to race downhill, through dried-out brush and tinder-crisp trees. Embers fly on the air, whipping at the car window, spot fires breaking out where they land.

She presses the gas pedal, all the way to the floor, taking the corner wide.

Then there is a glare of lights, and a squeal of brakes, the blare of a horn, and her hands spin the wheel, hard enough that her back spasms. And then seconds become minutes and the tree looms at them, bigger and bigger and bigger. Then all is dark.

Chapter Fifty-Four

Scarlett Morgan – 25th September, 12.22 p.m.

It comes with a crash, a sudden slide into Scarlett's body. Her fingers dig into her thighs, rough denim grazing against the pads of her fingers. She is sitting on hard floor, rough carpet beneath her, her legs pulled up to her chest. Can hear the distant chatter of children from the screening room, the distant strains of *Moana*, the movement of figures beyond the adjacent conference room doors. The lobby is quiet, the clerk gone.

'You OK?' Zeke leans over, rubs her back.

The smell of coffee, and she glances down at the to-go cup that sits beside her.

'Did you . . .' Zeke leans closer, angling his head for a better view of her face. 'You went again, didn't you?' He stares, grins widely. 'This is wild!' He leans back, lets out a laugh. 'Wow. I mean, just, wow! This is *wild*. I mean, I can see the decoherence happen. I mean, I can see it. Just . . . poof. And the light changes in your eyes. Jesus . . . you know, there's gotta be a way to explain this. I gotta take a look at the academic literature. I mean, maybe experimental physics—'

'Zeke?'

'Yeah?'

'I'm getting a headache again.'

He grins, apologetically. 'Sorry. Just nerded out there for a minute.'

Scarlett smiles, shifting her gaze as the conference room doors swing open. At the people who gather together in bunches, the children who weave their way around them. At the television. It shows a distant view of Destino, from a helicopter that hovers above the fire.

'Where is it?' she asks, quietly. She nods towards the television. 'The fire.'

Zeke follows her gaze. 'TV says it's trying to do an end run around the fire crews. It's followed the ridgeline, up and around Destino. Lucky they spotted it – town would have been lost otherwise.'

A flash of memory, of fire where it shouldn't be.

'They're saying that CalFire have managed to put a defensive ring around Destino. Let's just hope it holds.' He looks back at Scarlett. 'So? Where are we? In the other Destino, I mean?' He says the final words tentatively, as if saying them aloud will snatch it all away.

Scarlett shakes her head. 'I don't know. It's so different there, Zeke. The people. Bonnie, Mags. Even me. I thought that it was just Harper, that she was the key difference. But her being there, it has spilled out, has affected everything.' She glances at him. 'Apart from you, that is.' A wan smile. 'You're the same.'

He grimaces. 'Apart from that me having his shit together, you mean?'

She leans her head back against the wall. 'That's just window dressing. The core of you, who you are, that's the same.' Her head slides across the wall, coming to rest on Zeke's shoulder. 'I'm so tired . . .'

He slides his arm behind her back, pulling her closer. 'It's been a lot,' he says, quietly. 'You're grieving.'

She let that settle over her. 'How can I ever know what happened, Zeke? Someone killed him. I have to know, I have to understand what happened, else, how can I ever feel safe again? But the truth is, I didn't know him. How can I ever know who would want to kill him if I didn't even know who he was?'

'So, find out.'

'What?'

'Well, I mean, you have this quite insane opportunity, here, in this world. He exists. He lives. You are surrounded by people who know him. I mean, obviously, it would be easier if he was here, not back in Destino, but even so . . . this is an opportunity, Scar.'

She looks at him, considers. Then the screening-room door swings open. Together they watch as the children begin to swarm through the open doors, chattering starlings that fill the lobby. They ebb and flow and, for a moment, Scarlett and Zeke are buried within the crowd. Then they filter in through the bottleneck of the conference room doors, two at a time. The adults turn, fixing on their faces bright and expectant looks.

'Zeke?' A voice that is new and deeply familiar both. Harper's head appearing around the door to the screening room. 'Would you help me stack up these chairs?'

He nods, plants a swift kiss on Scarlett's cheek and is gone.

She pushes herself up, grabbing her coffee cup, and makes her way into the kitchen. The sound of water running, of dishes hitting soapsuds. Bonnie, alone.

'Hi.' The older woman glances over her shoulder. 'You wanna dry for me?'

Scarlett nods, sets down her cup and picks up a tea towel. She selects a glass from the drainer. 'Bonnie . . . I needed to ask you something.'

'Shoot.'

'It's kind of personal.'

Bonnie gives her a smile. 'I think we know one another well enough by now.'

'You and my dad . . .'

Bonnie nods, douses a cup into the hot water, doesn't answer for long moments. 'It was a long time ago.' The words sound like a defence, but the tone, that suggests the beginning of a story. 'I was . . . stupid. And young. Young enough that the hours Kelvin was working, they seemed like a personal slight, not the actions of a good man, trying to provide for his family.' She glances at Scarlett. 'It's not an excuse, just . . .'

'The environment?'

Bonnie smiles, sets the cup down on the drainer. 'Precisely.' She falls silent, then, finally, says, 'I'd known your dad my whole life, had come up through school together. So, I mean, I knew what he was like, town hero, kind of a playboy. This was before he met your mom, back when he would wander through town, different woman on his arm every night. Seemed like he never had a shortage of them. And then, one night . . . Kelvin was working late again. I mean, I should have been grateful. Him helping my mom and dad out with the diner. But we were living over in Haven, in this little house, and so I was all on my own over there. And truth was, I was lonely. And angry at what I perceived to be his neglect of me. So I took myself off to Bar 53. And there's your dad, same as he ever was, funny and charming and full of tales of heroism. And I guess I just . . . I just let myself fall for it. I got drunk. Again, not an excuse. I think I already knew then which path I had chosen. I think the alcohol was, I don't know, maybe a way to grease the wheels, to let myself forget that what I was doing was wrong. And that was it. One time. It was enough, though. Next thing I know, I'm pregnant and in a whole world of trouble.'

'You didn't tell Kelvin?'

'Not then. Couldn't bring myself to say it. So I just squashed it down, pretended like it never happened at all. Of course, your dad, he wasn't happy. Knew damn well that the baby was his, started making this whole song and dance about how he has a right to be a father to his child.' She shakes her head.

'Seemed to me like the whole damn world was against me. Like everywhere I turned there was something else to be afraid of. It made me . . . different.'

'Different how?'

'Edgy. I was snapping all the time. I think, deep down, I was angry at myself. 'Bout what I had done, about the lies I was telling. But it's always easier to be angry with the world than with yourself.'

Scarlett picks up a plate, slowly rubs the teacloth across it. 'So . . . what changed?'

Bonnie shakes her head. 'Your mom, that's what. I guess Mags would have been . . . seven, eight maybe. Now I had barely ever spoken to your mom, couldn't bring myself to, what with everything. Guess I couldn't face her. Found it difficult to face anyone back then. I was in the diner, alone. Looking back, I think I had already begun to annoy people sufficiently that they stopped coming in. Seemed like I just couldn't control my temper. Can't blame them for not wanting to spend money to be shouted at over coffee and cake. Then the door opens and Harper walks in and I just knew.' She wipes her hands on her apron, wipes away a tear. 'Damn woman just marches in, tells me to take a seat. Says that her and Mack, they've broken up. That she'd caught him out in yet another affair. He'd taken to drinking, not long after you were born – of course, you know that. You've had your own price to pay for his tendency to dive into the bottle. I don't know what happened, whether it was just growing older that did for him. But it just seemed like his life had slipped out of control. I mean, you know who your mom is, how lucky he was to have her. But I guess he had too many demons to recognise what he had while he had it. Anyway, so while he was confessing this latest set of sins, he'd also decided to come clean about his history. He'd told her about Mags.' She sighs heavily. 'It was like a gut punch, like this thing that I had kept buried for so long had finally risen up to swallow me whole. But, your mom, she got the bit between her teeth. There was no arguing, no condemnation. Just a plan. That the truth needed to come out. For Mags' sake, for yours. For mine too. The way she did it, laying it out like that, seemed like she was predicting a future that was already all set. Nothing to do then but go along with it.'

'How did Kelvin take it?' asks Scarlett, quietly.

Bonnie shakes her head, wipes away another tear. 'I told him that night. That man, he just looks at me, nods once and says, yes, I knew that. Turns out he suspected that something had happened that night, that he'd come home earlier than I was expecting and I wasn't there. That he noticed the change in me afterwards. And then, when Mags was born . . . well, she had her father's eyes.' She turns, leans back against the sink, sighing heavily. 'I don't know why he didn't leave me. Especially the way I was back then. But he didn't, just went along with it, God bless him.'

Scarlett sets down the plate, folds the tea cloth in her hands, over and over again. Picking out the words with care. 'Were you angry with him?'

'Who? Kelvin?'

Scarlett shakes her head. 'My dad.'

Bonnie looks at her, considering. 'Once, I was. But that was a long time ago. Now, I just mostly feel sorry for him.'

The words reverberate through Scarlett's head as the world goes dark.

Chapter Fifty-Five

Robyn Sandoval – 25th September, 12.22 p.m.

For a moment, Robyn's life hangs still. The silence in the empty aftermath of screaming brakes, metal hitting wood. But there is no time for that, no translation from this world to that. And she is moving, pawing at the door handle, fingers thick and unwieldy.

Then she is out. Into the dense air. Is running, boots sticking to tarmac.

The car has folded up, its hood concertinaed into the leaning tree. All is still, silent, apart from that roar.

Robyn runs. Time stretches out, so that no matter how fast she moves, she does not get any closer. Glass lies shattered, flecks of it sparkling across the ground. A bumper sticker, **My grandchild is an honour student**. And beyond the car, fire. It clambers down the mountainside, the flames leaping, eating through the brush.

There is little time.

Robyn reaches the driver's side, pulls at the door handle. She struggles to look beyond the tinted glass. The sense of a crossroads having been reached. Beyond this door, life or death, and, while the door remains closed, both.

Then the handle yields, and the door swings open.

Her sister sits, slumped forward, her head resting on the steering wheel, a line of blood seeping from a wound to her forehead.

'Mags!' It comes out as a cry.

Then hands are gripping her, moving her aside, and Zeke is reaching into the car, his hands gentle. 'OK, Mags, come on.'

A moment of superposition, then there is movement and slowly, ever so slowly, Mags raises her head, blinking, a hand moving to her forehead, to the pooled blood. She looks at the tips of her fingers, the dark stain there, looks up, her gaze locking on Robyn's. 'Rob—'

'I've got her,' says Zeke, quickly. He glances up at the fire, creeping ever closer. 'You get the mother.'

Robyn hurries around the car. Bonnie is visible here, her head resting up against the window, eyes closed. Robyn tugs at the handle, the door unyielding, metal warped with the impact. A movement, and Zeke has joined her, is pulling with her.

'Wait,' says Robyn.

She turns, pulling open the rear door, clambering awkwardly inside. The crackle of fire louder now. Can smell hot steel, blood. Can't focus on that now. Instead, she snakes a narrow arm between the seats, fingers questing for the door handle.

'It's OK, Bonnie,' she says, speaking not to this Bonnie, but to the other one, with her bright smile, sparkling eyes. 'It's OK.'

She struggles with the handle, fingers awkward. Pulls and then finally it yields. Zeke's fingers wind their way through the narrow gap, pulling as Robyn pushes. And then a groan of metal, and the door swings open, squealing on its hinges.

'Bonnie,' says Zeke. 'Bonnie, can you hear me?'

Nothing but silence.

Robyn's breath comes tight in her chest, her body concertinaed up to fit into the narrow space. She reaches across towards Bonnie and tries not to panic. The older woman's head has rebounded off the window, the glass of it fractured in a spider-web pattern. She looks to be sleeping, eyes closed, lips slack.

'Bonnie?' Zeke's fingers feel their way towards the older woman's pulse. 'Bonnie?'

There is an extended silence, one that stretches out long enough that Robyn's stomach knots. Then Bonnie raises her head from the shattered glass, lets out a soft moan.

Robyn releases a breath she had not known she was holding. She steps back as Zeke eases the older woman from the car. A glance behind her at the fire, the heat from it scalding her neck. 'We have to go,' she murmurs. 'Hurry.'

Then they are moving, limping in an uneasy convoy towards the other car.

Mags hesitates. 'Is that . . . is that my car?'

'Uh huh.' Robyn moves around her, opening the rear door, guiding her in. 'We stole it. Hope that's OK.' She folds her inside. Movement from the other side as Zeke deposits Bonnie beside her.

'Why?'

'Wrote off our other one.' Offers Zeke. 'Nothing like a car crash to rearrange your plans.'

'You came to get us?' asks Mags, voice distant.

'Yup.' Robyn nods. The light from the fire plays across Mags' grey eyes. It is like looking in a mirror. 'I wanted to make sure you were safe.' She squeezes her hand, then a realisation. 'Where's your dad?'

Chapter Fifty-Six

Scarlett Morgan – 25th September, 12.26 p.m.

'Scarlett? You OK?'

They stand in the kitchen, the tea cloth still wrapped tight around her hands. Bonnie stares at her, brow furrowed.

Scarlett twists the cloth between her fingers, can feel the heat of fire on her skin, smoke in her lungs. An almost-memory that plays at the back of her mind. What was it?

Then Zeke's voice. *Nothing like a car crash to rearrange your plans.*

Because that was it, wasn't it? Everyone had told her that Mack had changed. That he had once been the golden child, the home-town hero. But that something had happened along the way, sending him spiralling down a different path. Not the hero now, but head first into the bottle. And she had assumed that it was Harper's death, that he had fallen apart because he had lost his wife. Only . . . he hadn't lost her, had he. Not here. And still he had fallen apart, become someone different.

'Bonnie . . .' she says, slowly, 'you said Mack changed. The drinking and all that. When was that?'

The older woman studies her, considering. 'I . . . I don't know. I mean, you have to remember, I was staying pretty well clear of him, especially back in those early days.'

'But,' says Scarlett, thinking, 'do you think it was because of Mags? Because he had a daughter whose life he wasn't a part of?'

Bonnie recoils and for a moment Scarlett thinks she has gone too far. But then she shakes her head. 'I mean, who's to say? I guess only he could answer that. But the drinking, that didn't start until . . . I guess some time after you were born.'

Scarlett nods, firmly. A sense of pieces beginning to slot together. 'I gotta go find my mom.' She turns on her heel, hurries out of the kitchen, through the lobby. The screening-room doors have been propped open now, the chairs stacked neatly. Her mother leans over a desk in the corner, fingers dancing over the laptop.

She glances up. 'Hey.'

'Mom.' Scarlett pulls up sharp in front of her. 'I need to ask you something.'

Harper frowns. 'OK . . .'

'When did Dad start drinking?'

Harper hesitates, then shakes her head. 'Honey, I think maybe you need to . . .'

'No, it's OK. This is not about me, and CalFire. This is . . . look, it's just too hard to explain, but do you remember? When he started getting out of control?'

She studies her, then, 'I guess it was a year or two into our marriage.'

'When I was a baby, right?'

'I guess so.'

Scarlett pulls in a deep breath. 'Mom, you know the night of the Sandoval crash?'

Harper is staring at her now, expression one of foreboding. 'Yes . . .'

'Where was Dad?'

'He . . .' She hesitates, considering. 'He was at home with . . .' Then she stops.

'What? He was at home with me, is that what you were going to say?'

'I . . . yes . . . I mean, he was supposed to be. He was supposed to be at home taking care of you. I was in Cambria, and then I was going straight to the town council meeting. Only . . .'

'What?'

Harper doesn't answer immediately, her gaze locked off on the middle distance, calculating. 'Only, a couple of days later, our neighbour, the woman who used to sit for you sometimes, she comes over to me and she says that you left your pacifier at her house. That it was that night. And I . . . I wasn't paying attention, not really. Your dad, he hadn't come home and so I was worried, and I just wasn't focusing on what she was saying. Turned out he'd gone to the bar and was drinking himself unconscious. Later, when I asked him about it, he shrugged it off, said she must have gotten her days mixed up. I just put it down to her being confused.'

Scarlett breathes deeply, walks closer, takes hold of her mother's hand. 'Mom. After that night. . . Dad's car, was one of his front lights out?'

Harper stares at her daughter. 'He said someone reversed into him. In a parking lot. Scarlett, how did you know that?'

Chapter Fifty-Seven

Robyn Sandoval – 25th September, 12.30pm

There is music playing. Has it always been there? It weaves itself in through the rough tread of the mountain road, an offbeat harmony against the roar of the fire. It is close now, eating at the brush to the left of them and to the right, as they plunge downhill towards Main Street. Robyn can feel the heat of it, can feel the beads of sweat pricking at her forehead, between her breasts. The car bounces, tyres sticking to fire-softened tarmac, and she grips on tight to the seat.

'You OK?' asks Zeke.

Robyn cannot answer. There are no words.

It was Mack. Her father had caused the crash. That night, the night that split the world in two, that killed her mother. *He* caused it. Robyn cannot breathe. Cannot think. He did this. In this world. In that. He did this.

She cannot breathe.

She keeps her eyes forward, relentlessly on the road ahead, searching for the lights of Destino. But there is nothing, only fire, night black darkness.

And the thought, inexorable, of thirty years ago, the stretch of highway, the rain pounding down, a flash of headlights. A car that pulls to the right, tumbling down into the ravine below. A car that pulls to the left, folding itself up into the cliff face. The memorials, to Harper, to Alex and Eve. Thinks of Robyn. Of Scarlett. One person, spliced in two by the events of that night.

By Mack.

'This is bad,' murmurs Mags from the back seat. 'This is so bad.'

For a moment Robyn is inclined to agree with her sister. But then the realisation comes that Mags knows none of this. That she is speaking of something else. And so she pulls herself free, up and out of the eddies of what ifs and if onlys. To the fire.

It is closer now, no longer a burning red glow off in the distance. It surrounds them, lining both sides of the mountain road, eating up the dried brush that edges the road, the half-dead trees. The flames lap at the outside of the car. Testing, tasting. Heat radiates through the windows. Embers fly, caught with the fire-generated wind. They spiral up into the air, dancing, so many fireflies. Where they land, spot fires break out, patches of light that litter the waiting brush on the road's western flank.

A gust of wind and the fire leans into them, sweeping across the hood, and for a moment it seems that all is lost. Bonnie lets out a sob, Mags a quiet gasp. Zeke presses down hard on the gas and they plunge downhill, towards Main Street. The windshield glows, hot with the weight of the flames.

'Come on,' Robyn mutters. She leans forward, as if that will make some kind of difference.

But then there is light, a flash of day beyond the flame. And then they are through and out. And the fire recedes and the road ahead shifts from incline to flat, and the church is to one side and Main Street is up ahead, all of Destino beyond that.

'Hell, yes!' mutters Robyn.

Then they round the corner, taking a right onto Main Street and Zeke's foot lifts from the gas.

A movement in the back, Mags leaning forward, her body protruding through to the front seat. 'My God,' she breathes.

The eastern flank of Main Street – Destino Vino and the art gallery and Bar 53 – they look to be sleeping. Dark, closed up. But behind them, up on the arc of the mountain, the glow of fire. It highlights them, casting the shape of them into shadow, leering and dancing in the background. Robyn twists in her seat, can see all the way down the end of Vine. The houses there have begun to burn, embers twisting and spiralling up into the air, sweeping the fire onto the adjacent lawns.

The roads have emptied out now. The bumper-to-bumper traffic is gone. Up ahead there are a couple of brake lights, a few solitary stragglers heading out of town. A fire truck stands outside Bar 53, its occupants lost somewhere in the dense clouds of smoke.

A sound from the back seat, Bonnie pulling in a gasp of air. 'Maggie!' It comes out as a sob. 'It's . . .'

'I know, Mom,' Mags says quietly. 'I know.'

'We need to get out,' says Robyn. 'Zeke . . .'

'You're right,' says Zeke. 'We need to go.' He pushes his foot down on the gas, steering carefully around the spot fires that have broken out on Main Street. Keeps his gaze on the horizon, on the road's end.

And Robyn looks to what remains of her home town. To this version of it. To the right of them, set back from the street, the diner. And above, all but lost to the haze of smoke, Mack's house. Mere hours since she stood there last. Lifetimes ago.

You did this.

Harper.

Alex and Eve Sandoval.

You did this.

Robyn.

Scarlett.

Mags.

Bonnie.

All of the lives rewritten in that moment. All of the futures recast. And beyond that, the ripples spreading further still. To Vivienne and to Luis, to Harry in Bar 53, Logan in Destino Vino, Faith in The Artist's Way. How many destinies had he changed on that one night?

Robyn twists in her seat, looking back towards the fire truck. There is no defensive line in this Destino. No uniformed Cal-Fire army protecting their homes. No cordon to keep the town safe. That, too, was lost on that night out on the highway.

And so, this Destino will burn.

They drive along Main Street towards Destino's end.

To the right, the big house. Her home.

Robyn allows herself a moment to say goodbye.

Then the road dips down again, into the tunnel of rock. A moment, and then they break through the other side.

They are out of Destino, on the highway beyond.

And Robyn allows herself to let out the smallest of breaths.

She should have waited.

Chapter Fifty-Eight

It was easy to forget that fire and forest have lived on this earth, far, far longer than us. That this dance of theirs was one they knew very well indeed. The fire, it lingered now, taking its time as the brush burned right up against the waterfall. Up above, on the highway, the odd flash of headlights. Most of the town had gone, pouring out along that two-lane road. Those left behind, they all have good reasons for it, justifications for the delay. The cat that would not come when it was called, the station wagon that wouldn't start. The justifications will count for little, though. Fire does not care for your reasons.

Perhaps, had the flow of the waterfall been stronger, had there been more snow across the winter, had the subsequent spring melt not been so woefully inadequate, perhaps then there would have been more moisture. More water plunging over the rocks towards the river below, but also the kind of moisture that hung in the air, infusing itself into the plants that grew from the rocky gully wall. Perhaps then the fire would have struggled more, would have found it harder to take hold. Ifs and buts. None of it really mattered.

Because that was another world, not this one.

In this one, the brush was bone dry, parched. And the fire had already taken out the trailer park, was now furiously working its way through the grandeur of Destino Heights. It had clambered its way down the wall of the gully, past the waterfall, mindless of the highway that sat right above the opposing bank. Because in spite of what some may think, fire is not malicious. Fire does not set out to kill. Fire simply is. And so it does what it has always done. It eats, moving fast, metre by metre.

The fire worked its way, lower and lower. Reaching down until the flames lapped at the narrow ribbon of water. Not a river. Now barely a stream.

Perhaps, had things been different, the water would have presented a barrier of some kind, a boundary to the fire.

But that was not this world.

For, in this world, the fire burned through the brush, the heat radiating from it, spreading out, touching the opposite wall of the gully. Up above, stood a fire crew, a small group of people working to keep the flames from the highway.

But by the time they recognised the danger they were in, it was already too late.

It was a single spark. An ember, swept on the fire charged wind. It spiralled, up into the air, dancing, dancing. Then, landing. It sank down into the brush that stood proud from the dried-out sides of the riverbed. The brush quickly catching alight.

And then . . .

A thing you should know about gullies. They can act as wind tunnels. They can take the air, can funnel it, just like a chimney.

There came an awful silence, the inhalation before the scream.

Then the fire exploded.

If you could slow the world down, you would see it happen, would see the fire, turbocharged now. Would see it roll across the fire crew, charging up the steep incline of the gully, picking up fuel as it went. It climbed, faster, faster until it reached the gully's edge.

It would not stop there.

The fire swept upwards, up and across the dried-out grass bank, rolling over the town sign. That going up fast, forty years old and dry as tinder.

The fire would barely notice. Instead, roaring across the grass and over the sign, building up, until, by the time it reached the highway, it had worked itself up into a wall of fury.

The drivers left on the only road out of town, they would not have time.

Because in the blinking of an eye, the fire was on them, over them. The entire world, burning.

Chapter Fifty-Nine

Robyn Sandoval – 25th September, 12.40 p.m.

Zeke slams on the brakes, the car weaving and skidding. A moment when it seems that history, or *a* history at least, will repeat, that they will ricochet straight into the cliff face. But then time unsticks and the car screeches to a halt.

Then Robyn is out and running along the flame-flecked highway. Can hear only the blood pounding in her ears, her breath rasping in her chest. It seems that the entire world is burning beyond. The town sign is on fire. She registers it, the way flames eat through the name of Destino, without ever slowing. Then to the road. It is a scene of catastrophe. Cars burn, a wall of fire that cuts off the town from the world beyond.

There are shapes within the flames, of cars, of figures folding up beneath the fire. And she moves, as if to run in, but the fire, it pushes her back, the heat of it shoving her away. Tears stream down her face, the heat turning them from liquid to gas, drying instantly. There is no way in. There is no way through.

Then movement to her right, a woman emerging from the furthest car, clutching an infant to her chest, both wailing.

'Get away from the cars!' Robyn bellows.

She feels a hand on her elbow, Zeke, his expression urgent.

'That car.' He points to a silver Pontiac, the front already on fire. 'There's someone still in it.'

And then Robyn is moving, weaving between spot fires, then her hands are on the car. It is white hot, she can feel it burning her fingertips, but she does not let go. She tugs and tugs on the driver's side door handle. The fire laps at her, blisteringly hot. She pulls, but the door will not give. Then a figure beside her, pushes her aside, arms raised, a rock in his hand. He smashes the window. The explosion of glass showers her. Zeke reaches through the open window, fingers searching for the latch. Then the door is open, and Robyn is clambering in, across the inert figure, is releasing the safetybelt, pulling the figure towards her.

The woman makes a sound, a groan, a protest, but Robyn ignores it, digs her fingers in tighter to the rough wool sweater.

'That's it. You've got her!' shouts Zeke. And then she is out, and they are moving, half carrying, half dragging the elderly woman. Further and further back, past the burning sign, to where a knot of people has gathered, watching their cars burn.

Robyn slides her arm from around the elderly woman, lowering her carefully to the ground. She is conscious, softly weeping, and Zeke sinks to the floor beside her, wrapping his arm around her, so that her head rests on his shoulder.

He looks up at Robyn. 'We're trapped.'

Chapter Sixty

Scarlett Morgan – 25th September, 12.50 p.m.

Scarlett's pumps flap against the tarmac, breath tight in her chest. Something sharp held tight between her fingers, car keys that dig into the palm of her hand. The dislocation, the sudden jolt of Robyn's reappearance, startles her, and she slips, one foot sliding out of the pump. She stumbles, arms outflung to catch herself, only it is too late. She is falling, a slower process than one would believe to be possible. Her hands hit first, the key sailing out of her fingers, the sound of it harsh as it hits a car door. Her arm folds, capitulating beneath her weight. Then her left knee, smacking hard enough into the ground that, for a moment, she wonders if it is broken. And then she is down proper, is lying prostrate on the cooling ground, can see the dark undersides of vehicles, the silver lightning strike where the key has hit a yellow Nissan.

It is, she is willing to concede, a ridiculous position to be in.

Her heart is thudding in her chest. The tips of her fingers white hot. She raises them, looks for blisters, and then the realisation, that the scalding hot door handle, that was in the other world, not this. They are trapped, Robyn and Zeke. They are trapped as Destino burns.

She lets out a low moan, pulling herself up to sitting, her

head resting back against the sun-warmed metal of the Nissan.

How has it come to this?

She looks down at the ground, at where the car keys have fallen beside her. Where was she going? It doesn't take long. She is good at the transitions now, the fall notwithstanding. The night of the crash, the night her father was not where he was supposed to be, headlights where there should be none, a damaged car in the aftermath – she was going to Destino.

Her knee pulses, sharp shards of pain that shoot along her thigh, and she looks at the keys again. An absurd decision, all things considered. And yet, nonetheless, she was heading home, to the town that, in one world at least, would soon be lost. And she would stand before him, this father of hers. How long had she fallen into it, this trap of believing that the world rotated around the axis of him? And now comes the realisation, it did. But not in the way she had thought.

She leans her head back against the Nissan, looks up towards the mountains, the hanging clouds of smoke, the distant glow of flame.

She had begun this seeking to understand what happened, why her father died. The question now, what price his life? His actions spilling out, severing realities. A death here. A death there. Building a Robyn and a Scarlett, and a Mags who is lost and a Mags who is found. A tear rolls down her cheek. A moment of grief for the man she had wanted her father to be, lost now.

Scarlett thinks of a memory, one from Robyn. Of Mack folded up over a photograph of Harper, crying. Of Logan's words, 'He's been getting worse . . . made it his mission to drink me dry . . .' And the pieces slide into place. Mack's growing struggle as the anniversary of Harper's death approached. The drinking, the tears. They were not only about the death of his wife, not grief alone, but rather grief that has been flecked with guilt. He killed her. Scarlett thinks of Mack's house, back in the other Destino, thinks of the framed photograph of himself in CalFire uniform. It always did matter to him that he see himself as a hero. Imagine what this would have done, the knowledge of his actions a slow-drip poison releasing across the decades. He would have tried to deny it, would have forced himself to forget, look the other way. But it would never have been enough, would have come at him in the middle of the night. The knowledge that his heroism was tainted with villainy.

Could this be what killed him? Could this be why he died? The anniversary of the day he killed Harper. But there was nobody left, in Robyn's Destino, for whom Harper mattered. There was nobody left who would have been angry enough about the crash to have killed him.

Apart from me. Scarlett rubs her hands over her face. I . . . Robyn . . . she was the only one left now with a motive to kill him. So if it wasn't her . . .

She blows out a slow breath, tries to bring her mind to focus. Because the truth of it is that in doing what he has done, the only other person Mack has hurt is himself. He has caused the loss of his wife, which led to the loss of his daughter. And in that interim period . . . what did he have? In their years apart, when Mack was just a name on a Christmas card to his only child, he had CalFire. She thinks of the letter, the one terminating his employment. It had been dated five years ago, shortly before he had returned to her life. And then a thought, one that twists her stomach. Was that why? Was that what made him return? Could no longer be the hero firefighter, so returned to the daughter he had left behind so long ago. Now the hero father.

'Scarlett? Why the hell are you sitting on the ground?'

Scarlett starts, twists, a sudden shooting pain, from her palm, her knee. Harper stands beside an Xterra, frowns down at her.

'Mom.'

'God, Scarlett.' Harper crouches down, examining her daughter's palms, the grazes that criss-cross them. 'What did you do?'

'I slipped,' she says, redundantly.

'You've been crying,' Harper says.

'Yes.'

Harper considers her daughter for a moment, then slides to the ground beside her, takes her damaged hands into her own. 'You wanna talk about it?'

Scarlett studies her hands for long moments.

'You know I used to dream about you? All the time when I was a kid. I used to dream about you coming back for me, and you would appear and I would just know it was you.'

Harper studies her, frowning. 'Scarlett . . . What?'

She shakes her head, smiles. 'Nothing. I . . . I'm just being silly.'

It had felt like a crime. To Robyn, that is. When she would wake, the early morning light dancing shapes across her bedroom. The bedroom that her parents had given her, with the doll's house and the rocking horse and everything that any self-respecting child could ever want. And she would wake up in it, and, when sleep was still heavy on her, had thought she felt Harper's hands, holding on to her own the way they were right now. It was all a mistake, she would say. The accident. Reports of my death greatly exaggerated. And she would help Robyn up out of bed and she would take her downstairs and then she and Eve would hug like they were old friends, and then they would make pancakes together, passing the batter between them like it is a dance they have done a thousand times before.

'Sweetheart, are you OK? You seem . . . different.'

Scarlett smiles sadly. 'I think different is actually a pretty good thing.'

Harper studies her, considering. 'You've always been

different, my love. Have always stood your own solid ground, been undeniably yourself. Even when it drove me to absolute distraction. And I think that's a very good thing.'

Scarlett looks at her. 'Even with all this, even with the mess I've made of everything?'

Harper snorts. 'We all make a mess. It's the one thing that connects each and every one of us. None of us know what the hell we're doing. We just make it up as we go along, and when we stumble try to pick ourselves up again. You know,' she says, conversationally, 'it seems to me that you're under the impression that you're fatally flawed. That in the good versus bad test, you somehow land on the side of bad.' She shrugs. 'Truth is, none of us fit into either side, not truly. We react. We build ourselves depending on the demands of the world around us. Sometimes that means we do things that, from the outside, look kind of shitty. Doesn't mean that we're shitty people, just that the world around us had led us down a path.' She squeezes Scarlett's hand. 'But the good news? We can always choose a new path.'

'Can we?' Scarlett studies her, genuinely curious. 'If we're built by the world around us . . .?'

Harper grins. 'Yeah, sometimes you just need to flip the bird to the world. And I think that sometimes an event will come along, something that will hold a mirror up to your life, that makes you question: is this what I want? And that's the moment, the point at which you choose, left or right? Guess that's the beauty of it, we can always change direction.'

Scarlett looks away, beyond the metal hulks of cars that surround them, towards the mountains. Destino. 'Mom,' she says, slowly, 'I have to go somewhere.'

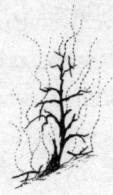

Chapter Sixty-One

Bonnie Aubrey – 25th September, 1.00 p.m.

There is a pulsing in Bonnie's head. A wraparound pain that throbs, rhythm matching the patter of her heartbeats. She blinks, tries to focus. But the world around her feels opaque, like it is hovering on the cusp of something. Someone is talking to her. A face that is close to hers, an arm around her waist. Her daughter smells of lavender. Her hair sweeps against Bonnie's face. She closes her eyes, pretends that it is long grass. That she is young, or younger at least. Is walking the mountain ridge that backs onto her house. That Kelvin is near.

'Mom?'

Bonnie starts, forces her gaze to focus on her daughter.

'It's OK,' murmurs Mags.

Bonnie looks around her, the sudden recognition of crying, the low murmur of voices, the distant roar of fire. She looks about her and it takes long moments to understand just what it is that she sees.

That the fire has swept across the highway.

That they are trapped.

There should be something there, despair perhaps. But there is only the weary sense of déjà vu, an inevitable end approaching.

There is movement. Not fire. But rather, people. A mother, small child on her hip. A man, tall and lean, his arm tucked around the waist of an elderly woman. Bonnie wonders, has she seen him before? Robyn Sandoval.

'We have to go back,' Robyn says, expression grim. 'There's no way through.'

A moment, then Mags pulls in a deep breath.

'We'll go to the diner,' she says, voice firm. Alien. 'We'll be safe at the diner.'

And then . . .

They are there, standing on the path, Main Street at their back. The diner, her diner, is right before her. How did she get here? Bonnie lets out a breath that comes out as a sob. Her diner. The place where she took her first wavering steps. The place with Kelvin, still here, embedded within every tile, every chair.

Maggie is ahead. She releases Bonnie's hand and pushes open the diner door, slipping inside. And Bonnie wonders, why does she not turn on the lights? It is dark, inside and out, a false night brought by smoke. The only light that which spills from the fire at their backs. Bonnie opens her mouth, the words waiting there to point out her daughter's thoughtlessness.

'Come on, Mom,' says Mags softly. 'Step careful up here. It's dark without the power.'

The power. Bonnie nods slowly, climbs the front steps. She had forgotten about the power.

Mags holds open the door for her and Bonnie steps into the darkened diner. Now she is eight years old, has sneaked down the rear stairs while her parents slept. Light on bare feet as she inches her way towards the freezer, her goal the tub of pecan ice cream on the bottom shelf.

Maggie ducks under the counter, stands, candles in hand. A flash of light, the sharp smell of smoke sending shivers down her spine. The low glow from the candle.

'Here,' says Mags. 'Why don't you sit?' She pulls out a chair, legs scraping against floor.

And now Bonnie is thirty-two and Kelvin's hand rests on the nape of her neck.

That sound again, of chair legs against linoleum. And she remembers the people. They move past her in the dim-lit room. Robyn Sandoval. The tall man, still vaguely familiar, where does she know him from. He half supports, half carries an older woman. A young woman, a small baby. And her daughter.

She watches as Maggie bustles, table to table, filling glasses with cold water. She smiles, reassuring, as though it is any other day.

Bonnie feels tears fill her eyes, feels them spill over.

'Hey,' murmurs Robyn Sandoval, suddenly at her elbow, 'it's . . . OK.'

Bonnie doesn't look at her, gaze still on her daughter, on the tight lines at her jaw, the tension in her eyes. But still Maggie smiles. And her voice, when she speaks, is light and comforting.

'Bonnie. It's going to be OK,' Robyn says again.

Bonnie doesn't look at the younger woman, but she shakes her head. 'I made a mistake,' she says.

Robyn hesitates. Then, 'It's OK. We all make mistakes.'

Chapter Sixty-Two

Mags Reyes – 25th September, 1.10 p.m.

The diner is dark, dim puddles of light spilling from candles that line the counter. It would be comforting, pleasant even, if it weren't for the glow of fire beyond the window. Mags sets a glass of water on the table, leaves behind a smile for the young mother, the baby asleep on her breast. The woman is tear-stained, rocks to and fro, to comfort herself or her child. More likely, both.

'We'll be OK,' Mags says, her voice steady, calm. No clues there that she is lying.

She turns her back and ducks into the kitchen. It is darker here, stiflingly hot. Leans back against the counter, lets out a sob. She clamps her mouth shut, closes it down quick. Glances towards the door. She shifts, locks her gaze on the floor at her feet, the lines where the tiles vanish beneath her sneakers, tracks her gaze along the lines, forces herself to breathe.

Jack would be there by now. Would have reached the kids in Morro Bay. They would be OK. Their father would look after them.

And her?

There is a glorious irony to it, this diner as her last place of refuge.

Mags looks up. There is a high shelf, just within her line of sight, rows of plates stacked upon it. On her worst days, she has dreamed of smashing those plates. Of taking a baseball bat, of bringing it down, again and again and again, until the floral design is shattered, daisies pockmarking the floor.

And here she is, this diner her only place of safety, waiting to see which way the world would spin.

Triumph or tragedy. Who could tell?

The distant tinkle of the doorbell, and Mags pulls in a breath, forces the thoughts away. She wipes her hands over her face, fixes on a half-smile, goes to open the kitchen door. Only she does not get the chance. It swings in to meet her, Robyn standing in the half-light.

She doesn't say anything, not for long moments, is studying her. Then Robyn reaches out her hands, takes Mags' tight in her own. 'Your mom,' she says, quietly, 'it's not that she doesn't love you.' Robyn squeezes her fingers. 'We'll be OK, Mags. We have each other.'

Chapter Sixty-Three

Scarlett Morgan – 25th September, 1.20 p.m.

Scarlett wakes to the purr of a car engine. To the putt, putt, putt of tyres against a roughened-up road. There is no time now. No easy waking. Scarlett sits up, straight, straining against the safetybelt, looks at the driver. Zeke leans close to the steering wheel, knuckles bleached white with the force of his grip. His jaw is tight, lips pursed.

'How far out are we?' asks Scarlett. No need to ask where they are going.

Zeke doesn't answer, nods to the sign as it flashes past. Destino, 5 miles.

Journey's End.

The place of beginning. The place of ending.

He is there, somewhere up ahead. The man who has already died once today, whose death triggered something in her, the horror of it somehow bringing it all to light, making the superposition visible, so that she becomes Scarlett and Robyn both. Whole worlds spooling out before her in the wake of his demise. Whole worlds coming into being because of one night on a rain-buffeted road.

Because of a decision that he made.

'You are aware,' Zeke says, tightly, 'that this is a terrible idea?'

'I am aware,' Scarlett says.

But he is the beginning of it. He is the end. The road snakes, curling around the mountain, the smoke pressing down heavy on them. Up ahead, the glow of fire. It has ringed the town, here too, kept back from the homes and the businesses by the ring put around Destino by CalFire.

'This is crazy,' mutters Zeke. 'Do we even know that the road is still open?'

Destino, two miles.

'Why did you come?' Scarlett turns to face him. His back tight, hands gripping the wheel tight. 'Why didn't you just let me come alone?'

He glances across at her, a frown flitting across his face, like he is questioning her sanity. 'Because I love you, dumbass.'

The road curves ahead and the car swings wider than it should around the bend, the road arcing out precipitously over the river beneath.

And then they see it. Destino up ahead. The mountains glow, moving and shifting, alive with flame. Black thunderheads above, a firestorm just waiting to be unleashed. And then dark smoke, enough that the road vanishes at the hood's end. Zeke stamps on the brake, and they screech to a halt, rock walls giving way to mountain on one side, brush to the other. All of it burns.

Scarlett lifts her fingertips to the window, mesmerised. Pulls back sharp as the heat of it blisters her skin. The flames, they are not content with what they have got. They reach out to the car, teasing, lunging. Tendrils of them arc across the windshield, dance back.

'Damn,' mutters Zeke.

'We shouldn't have come. I shouldn't have . . .' says Scarlett. 'Can you reverse?'

Zeke turns in his seat, looks back towards the rear window, face pale.

Scarlett sits up tall, struggles to see through the smoke. Can just about make out the gully, a basin of flame. Looks up ahead, struggling to pick out features, get a bearing. But all she can see is smoke rolling in at them.

'Zeke . . .'

'This is tight, Scar.'

She squints up towards the town itself. A gust of wind and the smoke moves and she can see it, the ravine below. Cold fingers trace their way down her back. She has seen this before.

'Zeke, we have to get out of here! We have to get out of here *now*.'

And somewhere, the devil laughs.

A gust of wind that rolls down the opposite mountainside and the fire roars, leaps. A bang, fracture lines lacing the windshield and the car swerves, the rear fishtailing, Zeke struggling to pull it back, away from the ravine's edge.

The car slows, almost stops. An oak tree leers over the road ahead of them, aflame now.

The engine roars, tyres fighting against hot tarmac. And then it comes, a crack, the sound like the breaking open of the bowels of the earth. The oak tree shudders, sways, the tops of it flaming torches. Then it gives into the whims of gravity, the trunk cleaving in two along the jagged crack, and then it is falling.

Time pools.

Scarlett feels it yet again. That the world has split.

For a moment, the roof of the car is heaving and the sides are buckling and her body is folded beneath the weight of the oak tree, a tangle of metal and dying limbs.

And then she blinks – and the car is leaping forward, the tree is falling, the branches fingernails across the rear. But it has missed them, its girth thumping down onto tarmac behind, its weight making the car bounce and shimmy. And they look behind, each of them taking a moment to consider what could have been. The flames eat their way along the horizontal tree trunk until they reach the brush on the other side and the two fires meet in a whoosh of flame.

'Scar,' says Zeke quietly, 'I think the road is closed now.'

Chapter Sixty-Four

Robyn Sandoval – 25th September, 1.30 p.m.

Luis stands in front of the counter, a strained kind of calm on his ash-streaked face. The smoke is thicker now, is beginning to seep its way in beneath doors, through window frames.

'So,' says Luis gravely, 'the highway is cut off. Which, obviously, is not what we would hope for. We've been on to county and we're hoping they're gonna get a plane out to us to do a water drop, try and get that road open again.'

'Will they be able to fly?' Robyn asks. 'In all this wind?'

Luis glances at her, gives a wistful smile. 'I don't know. We had hoped to get a rescue helicopter in, get you folks out. Wind put paid to that.'

A soft, despairing sigh echoes through the diner.

Luis raises his hands, placating. 'I know, guys, but look, we've got firefighters holding the fire back behind the church. We lost some good men,' his voice breaks, 'over on the highway. So we're short, but the guys we have are fighting hard. If we can get a retardant drop . . .' His words tail off. 'We'll be OK,' he says.

Robyn watches him, his head sinking, weighed down with the knowledge that he is lying. A feeling of grief washes over her. For Luis, the life he never got to live. Is there something in him that knows? That recognises it when Vivienne passes him in the street, the road not taken?

She watches him as he accepts a glass of water from Mags, the grateful smile. Does he know that the entirety of his life changed on that night?

'You OK?' Zeke is watching her.

'This morning I thought that he might have killed my father,' she says, softly, nodding towards Luis. Her voice trails away and she glances up at Zeke, smiles. 'He didn't. But . . . funny isn't it, how everything you know about the world can change in so short a space of time.'

He reaches out his arm, loops it about her waist, the move feeling like habit, even though it is brand new. 'I've said it before, I'll say it again,' he says, shaking his head. 'It's been a hell of a day for you.'

Robyn smiles. *You do not know the half of it.*

'I'm sorry,' she says. 'If it wasn't for me, you wouldn't be here. You would be out in Morro Bay, reading about dark matter or something equally lowbrow.'

Zeke smiles, shrugs. 'Well, I can do that any time.' He considers for a moment, then, 'I'm here because I want to be here.' A glance towards the window, the fire. 'Besides, that's the problem with physics. So much of it is theoretical. One thing you can say about fire, it really makes you focus on reality.'

Perhaps, thinks Robyn, this is it. The end of all things. Perhaps this was always what it was about, arriving back at the beginning and knowing it for the first time.

There is movement now, behind the counter, and she looks to Mags. She stands, her cell phone cradled in her hands, gaze off into the middle distance. And Robyn glances up at Zeke, a silent communication, and releases her grip on him, moving away. Towards her sister.

'Are you OK?'

It seems at first that Mags has not heard her, but then she

reacts, pulling her gaze back, forcing a smile. Her eyes are damp.

'I just . . . I thought I'd see if I could reach them. Jack. The kids. See if I could get through one last . . .' Her voice catches, and her eyes fill. Then she forces herself to calm. A breath in, out. 'Lines are still down.'

'We will be . . .OK, Mags,' Robyn says, quietly. And she can no longer tell if she is lying.

Mags nods, smiles sadly. 'I made my decision. I could have gone with them. Gotten out. I decided to stay.' She shakes her head slowly. 'You know, all these years, I've been so angry. With my mom, even my dad . . .' her voice cracks 'for how my life has turned out. Thing is, I've been forgetting. I *chose* this. I chose to walk away from Jack. I chose to come back to Destino, to do this. I *chose* what my life became.'

Robyn nods. 'Yes. And once this is over, you can choose to do something else.'

Mags smiles. 'Never took you for the glass half-full type.'

Robyn shrugs. 'I decided that was what I wanted to be.' She glances over her shoulder at the gathered people. They have grouped together now, chairs pulled towards one another, the presence of strangers easing their fears. Apart from Bonnie. She sits beside the window, her chair angled to peer out, across the empty lot, down towards Main Street and the fire that burns right behind it.

'Is your mom OK?' asks Robyn.

'I think she's in shock,' says Mags. 'I should get her a glass of water.' She reaches beneath the counter, pulling a glass out. 'Course, I'm willing to bet she'd prefer a Jim Beam.'

And just like that decoherence.

'Jim Beam?' Robyn's voice comes to her from far away.

'She doesn't drink much, not anymore. But when she does, it's always Jim Beam.'

Chapter Sixty-Five

Bonnie Aubrey – 25th September, 1.32 p.m.

Bonnie sits at the table, the one nearest the window. Her hands folded neatly in her lap. They do not feel like they are her own.

Kelvin.

It is a dream. A horrendous dream from which she will soon wake.

She looks at her hands.

Not hers.

Kelvin.

She blinks, the world arcing into and out of focus. It could have been different. It could all have been so different.

And then there is a sound, one which comes to her from far away. The scraping of chair legs across linoleum. A figure moves into her vision, Robyn Sandoval sitting before her. Waiting.

'It was you,' she says.

It is not a question and so does not require a response. But Bonnie nods, nonetheless.

'Yes,' she agrees. 'It was me.'

But it was not her, was it? Or rather, it was her hands and her body, but seems to her now as if they belonged to someone else. Another her.

She had been carrying pies. Such a mundane way for the end of the world to begin. Had pulled the car up into the spaces before the diner, nose in. Had looked up at the windows, searching for movement behind them, for some sign of life. It was, after all, breakfast time, by rights should have been the morning rush. Only there was nothing. Just those damn windows with the smudges where people do insist upon setting greasy fingers against glass.

Perhaps, if she was honest with herself, there was a moment there of recognition. That the rush had not rushed for long years now. That she has scared off the customers, with her eye-rolls, her warnings about fingers on windows.

She unclipped her seatbelt and pushed open the door. Noting the flowers that had begun to die in the tub by the door. That the paint on the porch has begun to peel. Moves around to the trunk and pops it open, reaching in, hefting two pies. One banana cream, one cherry. Closing the boot with her hip.

'Bonnie.'

He had been waiting for her, was the only explanation for it. Had been lingering at the point where the footpath meets the flat, where the bushes have built up so that a person, even one measuring in at six and a bit feet, could linger should they not want to be seen.

She felt a burst of something. Could call it irritation, but in truth, it was so much more than that. Rather the tipping place of a lifetime of weight, all of it pressing down, crushing the her out of her.

'What?' She had shifted the pies, uneasy. A wild moment where she had considered just pulling her arm back and swinging, watching the pies arc through the air, imagining the satisfying thud as they landed, square in the centre of Mack's face. 'What? What do you want?'

He doesn't answer. Not immediately. Just studies her. And she can see it in him, can read the thoughts plain in his face.

That he is weighing it up, comparing the her of today with the one she used to be.

Anger sparks, running along her shoulders, down along her arms, out through the tips of her fingers.

She could scream. Just flat-out bellow.

But then, of course, someone would come running. Likely Maggie. She looks to the diner, can see her daughter's figure moving about beyond the windows.

And then it would all crumble, wouldn't it? All of her secrets spilling on out.

'Why are you here, Mack?'

He looks at her sadly. He has gotten old. The lines in his face chisel-carved now, his eyes reddened, jowls hanging. It will be the alcohol that will have done for him. Or perhaps rather just his secrets, the weight of them carving themselves across his face.

'I'm sorry, Bonnie.'

Her stomach drops away beneath her. 'No.'

'I have to.' He sighs, rubs his face. 'I can't live with it anymore. I can't see Mags every day and have her not know who I am to her. She thinks I'm just some neighbour, some sad old man. I can see it in her eyes, Bon. She has to know who I am. I need to be a father to her.'

It feels to Bonnie like the ground is opening up beneath her. She stares at him. 'Are you . . .'

'I have to.'

'You can't. Kelvin . . . he can't . . . I can't let him find out. Not now. Not here at the end of it all. Mack . . . he is *dying*.' The word is stark, luminous. And she feels herself buckle beneath the weight of it, this word she has not even allowed herself to think until now. But now it is out there and the truth of it hits her.

He will die.

'Please.' Her voice is different now. Decades of anger stripped away, leaving it brittle. 'Please, just wait.'

Mack looks down, he shuffles his feet. 'Bonnie . . . Robyn has the right to know she has a sister. And Mags, she has the right to have me in her life, to know her father. And . . . thing is, I see her. Mags is sad, all of the time. Always this look, like she has the weight of the world on top of her. I can help her, Bonnie. I can . . . support her, be a dad.'

Bonnie blinks. 'Mack . . . you can't . . . please, don't do this to me. Not now. Just . . . please wait.'

And for a moment it feels that it has worked, that he has listened, and she watches his eyes flit back and forth, calculating. But then he stands up straighter and his shoulders drop and his chin raises, and he shakes his head. 'No. I'm sorry, Bonnie. I am telling our daughter the truth. It is the right thing to do.'

It is a door slamming shut.

'I'm sorry, Bon. I'm going to speak to Robyn tomorrow. And then, I'm going to tell Mags.'

She stands, frozen in place. Watches as he turns. Trudges back up the path.

She cannot feel her body.

What came next . . . well . . . looking back on it, it would seem to be a day like any other. Her body moving through the motions of her life. She remembers little of the day. Just this pulsing pressure in her head, as if the world is cleaving itself in two. There are flashes, of Kelvin's face, his breathing shallow and pained. Of her fingers, holding a cup of English breakfast tea up to his lips. Of the effort that a single sip takes him. Of the look he gives her, of grateful affection.

And she imagines then how that look will morph, once he knows the truth.

And Maggie.

Only, seemed like she couldn't go there, couldn't reach out to it, that future. Her daughter learning of all the lies she has told.

It is close to midnight when the moment comes. Not a

decision. Rather her body shifting her from its inertia. And then, somehow, she is dressed and moving. Is walking, picking her way along the dark, winding path, the one that snakes its way around the mountain, dropping down above the sleeping diner. It is dark, the night lit up by the fullness of the moon, and she picks her way carefully. But after all she knows this place well. Her feet have walked this path for sixty-five long years.

The knock, when it comes, is loud. Seems as though it reverberates across Destino. Then, only silence, long enough that she begins to wonder if her efforts have been in vain.

For a moment, she considers leaving.

Afterwards, she will wonder what that world would have looked like, the one in which she turned away. But that world is not this world.

The door opens.

Mack, he has been drinking. That much is clear. The sweet smell of stale alcohol oozes from his pores and he struggles to hook his roving gaze on her. 'Bon.'

She walks past him, not waiting for an invitation. The house is still, overheated and smelling of stale food.

'Drink?' He has closed the door behind her, magicked up a bottle of Jim Beam, two glasses. 'This still your tipple of choice?' His words are loose, unwieldy. He pours, one glass, two. Knocks back his. 'Not going to change my mind.'

Bonnie sits, silent for a moment. Then, 'We had fun once, didn't we, Mack?'

He grins, eyes sliding closed, open, closed. 'We had fun,' he agrees.

'Please, Mack. Please don't do this to me. To Kelvin. Please, just wait. It will only be . . .' Her voice breaks. 'He won't last long now.'

And for the briefest of times it seems that he will agree. For a moment, it seems that all can still be well.

But then he shakes his head. 'I'm sorry, Bon. I've waited long enough. I've been doing some re-evaluating, having a think about who I am, how I'm living in this world. Done some things I'm not proud of and I'm going to pay my penance on that. And one of those things is to let my daughter live her life not knowing who she is. I owe her the truth. I owe both of my daughters the truth.' He rubs his hand across his face. 'Look, I'm wasted. I gotta go to bed. I'll see you out.'

Bonnie sits, her head bowed, elbows upon her knees. A sense that the future is already set.

'You go on,' she says. A tear sliding down her cheek. 'I'll see myself out.'

In another world he would be wiser.

In another world, he would be more aware, would insist upon it.

That world is not this one.

In this world, he merely nods, stumbles, feeling his way along the wall, inching his way back to his bedroom. In this world, she waits, her head bowed. The tears roll now, one after the other, down her cheeks.

It takes moments, scant few, for the snoring to begin. In this world, Bonnie picks up her glass, swallows the bourbon. In this world, Bonnie stands.

There is no question now, no space remaining for debate. Only her body, following steps that have already been laid out for her. Around the table that still bears the bottle of Jim Beam, the two glasses. Into the hallway. Into the bedroom.

He lies on his back, eyes closed, gentle, sputtering snores. A pillow has fallen from the bed, has landed on the floor.

Bonnie picks it up.

In one world, she studies his sleeping form. In one world, she remembers it, a time when that face had made her smile.

This, however, is not that world.

'You killed him,' Robyn says, quietly.

'Yes,' says Bonnie. 'I killed him.'

Chapter Sixty-Six

Scarlett Morgan – 25th September, 1.36 p.m.

Scarlett locks eyes with Zeke. Tears burn at the back of her eyes, threatening, her hands shaking against the safetybelt.

Zeke reaches out, squeezes her fingers. 'It's OK,' he says. 'We made it through.'

She opens her mouth to tell him that the tears are not for the fallen down tree, the flames that block the highway behind them. That they are for the father that she thought she had. For Bonnie and who she could have been. But the words won't come. She pulls in a breath, wipes her eyes with the back of her hand. Then they are at the town sign, burning now, then they are through the tunnel of stone, and Destino spreads out before them, a sea of flame.

Zeke lets out a low whistle.

Destino, this Destino, still stands. A picture-postcard place, a stage set of what a California town should be. But behind that stage set stands a wall of flame. The fire has run the length of the ridge, encircling the town. But beneath that ridge, carved into the mountainside, a clear-cut swathe of ground, gouged out of brush and trees, ringing the homes that make up Destino proper.

Scarlett looks up Main Street, can see movement at the end of it. CalFire. A flash of memory. Of heat and smoke and weight and knowing that she was doing entirely what she had been born to do. But she shakes it off. CalFire man the perimeter, the one carved out on a hot spring day, with handpicks and elbow grease, all of Destino spilling out onto the hillside. A battalion of figures that move in a coordinated defence, keeping the fire back behind the line.

And amongst them, Mack.

Things unfold fast then. Because, before she knows what is happening, Scarlett is out of the car, is running. A fleeting figure closing the distance between them in long, loping strides.

Zeke's footsteps heavy behind her.

The sound of it. It moves through her, the roar building up and up, up through her feet, reverberating through her chest. Burning sparks land on her skin, the heat settling over her, filling up her lungs.

And then she is on him.

A branch point here. In some worlds, likely that she hauls back, her fist arcing, the entire shape of her body twisting with the throw of it. Then a whoomp of sound as bone meets bone, a crack as Mack roars, blood spurting from his nose. A punch landed for all the pain that has marked out her life, in this world and the others.

That is not this world.

In this world, her father sees her coming, and his face pales, the blood leaching from his skin and he drops his axe and grabs hold of her arms.

'What the fuck are you doing here, Scarlett?'

'You killed the Sandovals!'

'Scarlett? What the . . .'

'Thirty years ago. Thirty years ago today. You caused the crash, out on the highway. You killed the Sandovals!'

Scarlett studies him. Ash-streaked, wild-eyed. The

cheekbones that are hers. The eyes that are hers. And then, the world shifts and the image alters, to one of pale skin, unmoving, dead upon a bed. He does not answer, does not move. His gaze locked on hers. Afraid.

She steps closer, is dimly aware of Zeke at her elbow, his breaths coming short and sharp. 'You have no idea what it is you have done. You have no idea what you have caused, the consequences of your actions.'

Her father pulls in a breath, and, for a moment, she thinks that he will deny it. Then, 'Scar . . . look, it was an accident. I didn't mean for it to happen . . . I was upset that night. I was driving and I wasn't concentrating. See, once I had you . . . it just meant so much to me, to be a father. But all I could think of was that there was another little girl out there, another one who should know I was her daddy, who should be a sister to you. And I just couldn't bear it anymore. Was going to go on out to Haven and deal with it, head on, tell Kelvin the truth. I was trying to do the right thing, Scarlett. I was trying to do what should be done. Only, it was a bad night, and I wasn't paying attention and—'

'You hit the car head on.'

'I hit the car head on. I should have stopped. I know I should have stopped. I was going to stop, only then, somehow, I didn't, and I was driving, and then I see a car coming the other way, and I figure they will help them. I'll just get in the way, so I just kept on and—'

'Left them to die!'

'Sweetheart, they . . . yes, it's awful, but they were not good people. You don't know. You were too young. But they were greedy and they had this town in their pocket. If they had lived . . .'

'Yes, you're right. If they had lived, they would have done bad things. But they would also have done good things.' Destino Heights and sky-high rents. Bedtime stories and a small hand tucked into a larger one. 'You took this world from them. You took them from this world.'

'It was an accident.'

'It was *you*. It was you not being able to tell yourself the truth, of who you are, what you do. You are so determined to see yourself as the hero that you can't see the costs of your actions. To Mom, me. The Sandovals. To Bonnie.'

'Bonnie?'

Scarlett shakes her head. 'Why couldn't you have just waited? Why, just once, didn't you look beyond what *you* wanted, how you wanted the world to see you? If only you could have understood, been patient, recognised that there are other people and that they have troubles of their own . . . If you could have seen the pressure that other people are under . . . all of this, all that has happened here . . . it has happened because of you.'

He stares at her for long moments, forehead creased in confusion, opens his mouth to ask only he never gets the chance.

Because there is a gust of wind, and the flames leap. Shouts of 'get back!'. Zeke wrapping his arm around her waist, pulling her backwards. And Scarlett looks about. Destino is an island now, a dark oasis in a desert of flame. The fire has wrapped its way around the town. It leers and leaps, bright against the dark. As she watches, a fleck of bright light spirals up into the sky, twisting and dancing in the wind. It sails down, landing on the roof of the church. A moment, then the single ember has become a flame. There is movement, CalFire turning en masse towards its new target. Another gust of wind, and embers rise up into the air and rain down on them.

Mack turns back towards her, his ash-dark face tear-stained now. 'I'm sorry. I'm so sorry. I know . . . I know I've hurt you. I know the things I've done, they've ruined your life. I never meant . . .'

A whoosh and the church roof is fully ablaze.

Mack steps closer, pulling her to him. 'You have to get out, Scarlett.'

She studies him, gives him a sad smile. 'It's too late for that, Dad.'

He looks from her to Zeke, back again. Then, taking her hand within his. 'Come with me.'

And she is moving, half dragged, half running, Zeke following along behind.

Towards the parked fire truck, and then Mack is diving into the bowels of it, is emerging with a stack of something, pushing them into her arms.

'If the fire breaks through the line, you take these blankets, and you run. I want you to—'

'Go to the empty lot,' interrupts Scarlett, her gaze locked on her father. 'Cover ourselves, head to toe with these blankets. Lie on the ground. And pray.'

Mack catches himself, looks to his daughter. 'I forget,' he says, quietly, 'that you know this as well as I do.'

'Yes.'

'Oh God, Scarlett, I am so sorry. For everything that I've done.'

A distant shout, and he glances towards the fire, back to his daughter. 'You get through this, OK? This world needs you in it.'

Chapter Sixty-Seven

Robyn Sandoval – 25th September, 1.45 p.m.

She blinks, stumbles. Feels an arm around her waist, righting her. Looks up. Zeke.

She is Robyn.

'We have to move!' a voice bellows and she turns in place, the feel of rough gravel beneath her feet, already knows what it is she will see.

The diner is alight now, the eastern edge of its roof burning up fast. Luis brings up the rear, pushing them away from the burning building.

'It's going to be OK,' she hears herself saying.

It has kicked in proper now, fear coursing through the group, leaping from person to person faster than the flames. Her heart races and for a second it seems that she will simply go again, that such is her destiny, ping-ponging back and forth between lives until the inevitable comes and there is no life to ping-pong back to. The baby wails, its cry piercing, and its mother bounces on the balls of her feet, face white with fear. 'Where do we go? What are we going to do?'

Robyn turns, Mags close behind her, expression one of forced calm. She holds tight to her mother's hand, Bonnie's gaze distant, on the diner as it burns. On what was Mack's home above. Her lips move, *Hail Mary, full of grace . . .*

'What shall we do?' Mags says it quietly, desperation barely concealed.

'The empty lot.' The words come from Robyn's mouth, but it is Scarlett that speaks. 'It's all we have left.'

'What?' Luis shouts to make himself heard above the roar of fire.

Robyn swivels to face him. 'We have to get everyone to the empty lot!' she shouts. 'Get them to the centre of it and make sure there is nothing flammable around them.'

Luis hesitates, then nods. 'Where are you going?'

'Just go!' she shouts. 'I need to get something.'

She takes off at a run, dimly aware of Mags calling her name. The fire . . . it is the whole of her world now, is everywhere she looks. The air is dense, smoke filling up her lungs, nostrils, pricking at her eyes. The roar is that of a hurricane, flames hot enough now that they create their own winds, that howl and leap. She rounds the corner onto Main Street. Hard to get her bearings, to find her path in this town she has known for the entirety of her life. The mountain before her burns, out of control now. Smoke forming thunderclouds, arcs of lightning that rip from the sky, crashing into the burning hillside with a deafening crack. A hand on her arm and Robyn spins in place.

Zeke, breathing hard, eyes streaming from the smoke. 'What are we doing?'

'There are fire blankets!' she shouts. 'In the back of the fire truck. I just have to find them.'

Zeke nods, spins. Then, 'There.' He points towards the truck. As they watch, the windscreen pops, shattering beneath the force of the heat.

'Come on!' shouts Robyn.

They take off running, legs heavy, breath burning, poisonous. They dart between spot fires, ducking as embers pirouette through the sky, landing burning behind them. Then to the truck. It is ripe. Ready to burst. The paint crawls across the hood, bubbling, boiling. Zeke reaches for the door handle.

'No!' yells Robyn. She turns, gaze scouring the ground, eyes finding a half brick. She grabs it, pushes Zeke aside. 'The handle will be too hot.' She pulls back her arm and throws, all the force of Scarlett and Robyn combined. The window caves in on itself and she reaches in, sleeve over her hand, yanks open the door. They are there. Just as Scarlett had seen, fire blankets stacked neatly. She grabs an armful, shoving them into Zeke's waiting grasp. Grabs another armful.

'Now!' she shouts, taking off in a loping run. Is dimly aware of an explosion behind them, the gas tank finally giving way to the heat. But she doesn't look back, no time for that now. Darts about the fallen timber and along Main Street and then . . .

They have done as she has asked. The straggled survivors knotted together. The tears are gone now. Now they simply stand, meek as lambs. Have moved to a place beyond fear, waiting to see what comes, death or life.

'Here.' Robyn forces a blanket into Luis' hands. 'Take this.' One for Mags and one for the mother and baby and one for the elderly woman whose name she still does not know. One for Bonnie.

The older woman looks down at the blanket, hands unmoving.

'You have to take it, Bonnie,' Robyn says.

For a moment it looks as though she will argue, but then her shoulders sink and her hand reaches out and the blanket is hers.

One left.

'We'll share,' says Zeke, firmly, the gaze lasting long moments.

Her insides flip, and Robyn allows herself a moment to wonder, *what if?*

Then she shakes her head, forces a smile. What if? will happen somewhere.

'OK.' She directs her attention to the group, shouting loudly. 'I want you to lie down, right here in the centre of this lot. You're going to cover yourselves with a blanket, and you're going to make sure you are entirely covered . . . OK?'

'Is that it?' asks Mags. 'Is that all we can do?'

'It will work,' says Robyn, firmly. She doesn't add that there is no other choice. 'Come on, now. Down to the ground. I'm going to check you're all tucked in.'

And so they fold, one by one by one, curling up on the concrete slab, fire blanket coatings leaving specks of silver in the dark.

A crash in the distance and Robyn knows that the church has fallen. But she doesn't look up, walks calmly from figure to figure, tucking in the edges. 'You too, Bonnie.'

Bonnie watches as her daughter lies on the ground, pulling the blanket over herself, her hands shaking. 'I'm just making sure that Mags is safe.' Her voice oddly calm. 'I'm going to tuck her in, just like I used to when she was little.'

There is a crash, a gust of wind, and the fire leaps, sending hot embers ricocheting at their skin. A tree at the edge of the lot breaks into flame.

'Robyn, we gotta go.' Zeke is waiting for her, has already spread the blanket spread out across the ground, a corner of it lifted, waiting.

'Bonnie . . .'

She leans over, makes good on her word, carefully tucking the blanket around the edge of her daughter's prone figure. She stands up, steps back.

'Bonnie, now.'

'When this is done,' says Bonnie quietly, 'just make sure she knows the truth.'

'What? I . . .'

Robyn reaches out her hand to the older woman, but then there is a gust of hot wind and a whoosh of flame and here it comes. Hands grab her around the waist and Zeke is bodily carrying her, is pushing her to the ground, and the blanket is over her, and his weight is on her, and the sound of fire shrieks.

Zeke pulls her close, his body shielding hers.

'So,' he says, conversationally, shouting against the roar of fire, 'what do you think? Are we going to make it?'

'No,' shouts Robyn. 'And *yes*.'

A breathless moment and then it comes.

It fills Robyn's eardrums, pressing down on her chest. The fire is on them. It claws and rips at the blanket, tugging at it, howling and moaning. She can hear Zeke whispering softly to her, to himself, 'We'll be OK, we'll be OK.'

And Robyn presses herself closer into him and closes her eyes and waits for the box to open.

Alive and dead.

Epilogue

Two weeks later

There is a woman. She stands before the tumbledown remains of a town sign. It is a skeleton now, little more, two solitary upright struts left behind as an indicator of what once was. A stiff breeze tugs at the woman's hair, rain misting against her face from the low-hanging clouds that sit cradled within the ravine. She brushes the hair aside, stooping down, sifting through the burnt-out debris with her fingertips, looking for anything that would remind her of what this sign once showed. But there is nothing.

A hand touches her shoulder and she glances back, forcing a smile. He looks different now, seems to have aged precipitously in the weeks that have passed. But then, she considers, haven't they all? She takes hold of his hand and follows his lead, picking their way between burnt-out hulks of cars that have been pulled to the side of the highway. They slot into place, bringing up the rear, as the group trudges its way slowly along the highway, as it turns left into the carved-through tunnel of rock, up into Destino.

Destino.

The home of gold rush prospectors and those who ride their coat tails. Of the straight-through Main Street that points the people all the way up to the aged church. Of Destino Vino and Bar 53 and a thousand histories all locked between the steep flanks of the mountain.

The group bring themselves to a unanimous halt, feet stilled by the destruction before them. For it is swept clean. Nothing remains here now, but the stacked-up remnant of once were homes. There is no Main Street, no Destino Vino, no Bar 53. No Elsie's Diner.

Perhaps in another world. But not in this one.

'You OK?' he says it quietly, his breath warm on the nape of her neck.

And Robyn nods, a tear spilling nonetheless. She reaches down and takes hold of Zeke's hand, squeezing it tight enough that her muscles begin to ache. In a silent agreement, they begin to move again, footsteps squelching through the rain-soaked debris. And her gaze tracks up and to the left, to where the big house once stood, now nothing but empty space. The pit bull at her side lets out a soft whine.

They trudge on towards Main Street where piles of rubble mark the boundary of the road. Beyond it, the fallen-down remains of the homes that once spilled outwards. They walk slowly, a funeral procession, but you can hear it, the thoughts that fill the air. That there stood the police station, there the bench where that kid from up on Vine stripped naked and danced atop it until his mother threatened to burn his comic book collection. And soon enough, the thoughts mutate, becoming words. Remember that time when Henry locked himself out of the bar and he was convinced he'd left a pan on the stove, and so he breaks back in through the window, only he overestimates the window's size and underestimates his own girth, and so he gets stuck like Winnie the Pooh in his hole? A roll of laughter that reverberates across the empty space where the town should be, grief and joy, two sides of the same coin.

They drift to a halt at the empty lot, the group of them spreading out so that together they encircle it.

'If this lot hadn't been here . . .' Eve Sandoval wears jeans, a T-shirt that is too big for her, her face scrubbed raw from crying.

'If Robyn hadn't known to get those fire blankets . . .' says Vivienne. Her husband stands at her shoulder, close enough to her that he can snatch her up, should she threaten to disappear again. Their daughters left with the other children, Henry from Bar 53 and Logan from Destino Vino roped in as ad hoc babysitters out in Morro Bay. They set up a screening room. They are watching *Moana*. 'You know,' says Vivienne, her gaze hooked on Robyn, 'if it hadn't been for you, Rob . . .'

Robyn smiles, but her attention, that is elsewhere. It is on the racing of her heart and the pulsing in her head, and for a moment she thinks that this is it, that it will come again. And yet the world remains as it is, with the rain clouds hanging low over them, the mist of it soaking through layers of clothes to skin beneath. It does not go dark. She pulls back the sleeve of her jacket, studying the arm beneath. There are no vines there. Robyn blinks back tears.

She has not been back. In two long weeks she has not been Scarlett, has not seen Harper. Has not seen Mack.

Destino, they say, is a special place. A place that has stamped itself upon the landscape, the end of a journey. It is a place people come to settle, a place of origin and of return. Perhaps then, Robyn ponders, with its destruction has come the closing of a door.

Decoherence.

She is Robyn Sandoval.

Zeke's hand squeezes hers, and she looks up, smiles, that feeling of waiting, of pressure, giving way to something else. Something lighter, filled with promise.

A figure separates itself out from the group, lingering only long enough to speak quietly with the man beside her. Jack brushes the hair back from her face. 'Take all the time you need,' he says, softly. Mags nods, closing her eyes briefly, then turns, pausing to set her hand on Robyn's arm, before she moves off, walks slowly towards the diner.

And Robyn watches, thinking of that moment, with the roar and the fire and the flame, of Bonnie's hands, tucking her daughter in . . .

It was days before the body was found, crushed beneath the roof of the fallen-down diner. It was days before Mags would understand why, before Robyn was able to disentangle her from the children that hung from her like limpets, the husband, disbelieving of his good fortune in gaining a precious second chance. Before Mags would hear the story, would know the truth of all that had passed.

Robyn watches as her sister stoops down, setting a small bunch of chrysanthemums before the diner's ruin.

And then, silence. The small group each pondering, what has been lost, what comes next.

'Have you thought,' says Zeke finally, 'what you will do now?'

Robyn doesn't answer for long moments, and he glances at her, a look about him that seems to question if she has gone somewhere else entirely. But then she looks up at him, smiles.

'This place,' she says, slowly, 'this town. It needed something it didn't have.'

'What's that?'

'Harper,' she says. 'Destino, it needed my mom.' She glances across at Eve crouched outside the rubble remains of the church, her head bowed. 'My other mom. I'm not her. But I can still do the things she would have done. And,' she shrugs, 'as Sandoval Company CEO, I think I could do it pretty well.'

Zeke nods. 'It's nice, you wanting to honour your first mom, even though you never got the chance to know her.'

There is a moment there, a branching point where the world could go left or right.

And then Robyn smiles. 'Yeah. So. About that . . . There is something I need to tell you.'

Acknowledgements

I don't know where to begin. That is always true when writing acknowledgements. It's only as an author that you truly realise just how many people are involved in making a book what it needs to be. But this book, this one was different.

This book began in February 2020, when my dear editor, Fran Pathak, sat me down and asked me a question - what would you write if you could write anything at all? It took a minute. Not least because she asked the question while we were eating the biggest bowl of melted cheese I've ever seen and I was distracted because . . . well, come on. It's cheese. I am not someone who works well within boundaries. There is a reason I have been self employed my entire adult life. Does not play well with others. And so, when Fran asked me that question, I thought about the books that I love. The ones that made me want to be a writer in the first place. The ones that make me want to be a better writer now. And those books always have one thing in common - they nudge at the boundaries, making what was once solid opaque and ephemeral. They play with the limits of genre. And I thought of another thing - what if.

My life has forever been a what if kind of game. I was adopted at three months old. I grew up here in Wales, while the rest of my birth family lived their lives in the States. How much different would my life have been had different decisions been made? Who would I have been then?

And so, this book was born. Or, the notion of it was, anyway. Because three weeks after our cheese lunch, Covid slammed into our shores and, more specifically, into my house. We were luckier than many. My children's brush with it was fleeting, my husband's relatively brief. Mine was not. The gift Covid left for me was a lingering weakness, Long Covid. And suddenly the question of who I might be were my life different became crashingly real. Because now my life was different. Now my body was no longer mine to control. It was unpredictable, prone to chronic pain, devastating fatigue, weakness where once there was strength. A butterfly had flapped its wings in the Amazon and I was now someone entirely different. I didn't write. Not for a long time. I couldn't write. I couldn't read. Words would not stay, vanishing somehow between the page and my brain. I couldn't think, certainly could not do the mental heavy lifting that is involved in creating an entirely new world. I could only curl up on the sofa, and mourn the me I once was.

I don't remember when I finally came back to this book. Don't remember the first day of putting pen to paper. There was an easing, gradual and sporadic, a lifting of the fog, so that some days my brain would sputter into action and I would have to quickly dash words down before the weather changed. But somewhere in amongst this mess that my life had become, Robyn/Scarlett had come to life for me. And, somehow, their story began to unfold.

Because of this, I have leaned more on the people in these acknowledgements than I have ever had to before.

In editorial terms, it was rather a behemoth. Perhaps because of my illness, or perhaps because when you shove quantum theory into a book, you are going to make it complicated! So, my thanks, first and foremost to my lovely Fran Pathak. When I was recently asked what has been my best experience in publishing, I talked about you, and that question - 'What would you write if you could write anything at all?' This. I would write this. I miss you, and I will always be grateful that you gave me this opportunity.

To Sarah Benton, who inherited me and my wildly complicated manuscript after Fran's departure to pastures new. It is fair to say that you made this book what it is, by looking through the chaos and seeing what it could be. Without your editorial input, I would never have seen this world as clearly or understood the story I was trying to tell as well. To Bethan Jones, for stepping in when everything changed again.

To Sam Eades, for recognising when I was struggling and for your determination to make my life better. I am so grateful. To Snigdha Koirala for ensuring everything runs as it is supposed to.

To my wonderful friend and agent, Camilla Bolton at Darley Anderson Agency. For once again proving that I would be lost without you. You are all kinds of awesomeness and I am so lucky to have you in my life.

And now, to the people beyond the world of publishing. You always need back-up as an author. This is a tough industry. But, for this book, it is fair to say that it would not exist without the people who helped me make it through the worst days of my Long Covid. To my dear friends, Sarah, Nina (podcast queen), Lisa and my sister in law, Debs. I love you all. To my author friends who let me cry on them - knowing you are always there is the biggest relief. To the women who run the Hyperbaric Oxygen Treatment facility that turned my Long Covid around and allowed me to function again, and specifically to Rhian and Kelly - thank you will never be enough. To the people I have met in treatment, each with their own burdens but each so generous with their support of others. You are all lovely.

To my mum and dad - you have ever been unfailing in your belief in me. For your constant support, even when you have had your own troubles to endure, I will always be grateful.

To my husband Matthew, my children, Daniel and Joseph. Whichever turn my life took that brought me to you, I will never not be grateful. I love you.

And finally to my dogs. Dobby, get down. No, down. Yes, I love you. Stop it. Dobby! Luna – who's a good girl . . .